Emily Sarah Holt

The White Rose of Langley

English Life in the Olden Time.

THE ATTENTION OF ALL LOVERS OF GOOD LITERATURE IS INVITED TO THE

CHEAP RE-ISSUE OF THE WELL-KNOWN STORIES OF

EMILY S. HOLT,

Which are so admirably adapted for all Home, School, and Parish Libraries, combining, as they pre eminently do,

Correct History, Interesting Narrative, & Christian Teaching.

IN LARGE CROWN 8vo,

Price THREE SHILLINGS and SIXPENCE each,
in uniform binding.

THE FOLLOWING VOLUMES ARE NOW READY:

IMOGEN.   A Tale of the Early British Church.

THE WHITE ROSE OF LANGLEY.   A Story of the Olden Time.

MARGERY'S SON.   A Story of the Fifteenth Century.

ISOULT BARRY OF WYNSCOTE.   A Tale of Tudor Times.

LETTICE EDEN.   A Tale of the Last Days of King Henry VIII.

ROBIN TREMAYNE.   A Tale of the Marian Persecution.

CLARE AVERY.   A Story of the Spanish Armada.

SISTER ROSE; or, The Eve of St. Bartholomew.

JOYCE MORRELL'S HARVEST.   A Story of the Reign of Elizabeth.

ASHCLIFFE HALL.   A Tale of the Last Century.

"Miss Holt's Tales of English Life in the Olden Time form a very valuable course of reading. We do not know one of her stories which does not deserve high commendation on account of its own intrinsic merit, and also because of the sound principles by which it is animated."—*Record.*

LONDON: JOHN F. SHAW & Co., 48, PATERNOSTER ROW, E.C.

THE

White Rose of Langley :

A STORY OF

*THE COURT OF ENGLAND IN THE
OLDEN TIME.*

BY

EMILY SARAH HOLT,

AUTHOR OF "MISTRESS MARGERY," "SISTER ROSE," "A TANGLED WEB,"
ETC.

"The days will grow to weeks, the weeks to months,
 The months will add themselves and make the years,
 The years will roll into the centuries,
 And mine will ever be a name of scorn. . . . .
 Let the world be: that is but of the world." TENNYSON.

New Edition.

LONDON:

JOHN F. SHAW AND CO.,

48, PATERNOSTER ROW, E.C.

Emily Sarah Holt

The White Rose of Langley

ISBN/EAN: 9783337077341

Printed in Europe, USA, Canada, Australia, Japan

Cover: Foto ©Andreas Hilbeck / pixelio.de

More available books at **www.hansebooks.com**

PREFACE.

THE question may be asked by some who take up this book,—"Is it a martyr's story?"

In the conventional sense, No.

If martyrdom mean only resisting unto blood—only the dungeon, and the torture-chamber, and the death of fire then this is no tale of martyrdom.

But if it be held, as of old, to signify *witness-bearing*— if it include not death only, but what is harder to bear than death—no introduction to an earthly torture-chamber, but the breathing of a perpetual atmosphere of moral torture—no ignominious scaffold set up before the crowd, but the dreadful knowledge, through life and death, that

> "The years would roll into the centuries,
> And hers would ever be a name of scorn"—

if sufferings such as these go to make martyrdom, then it may be that the White Rose of Langley was a martyr. Not that she was a brilliant example of saintship, nor that she would form at all an attractive subject for modern biography. A good many of God's jewels look but pebbles to human eyes; and much of man's jewellery is mere spar. A bruised reed—a brand plucked from the burning—she was that, and no more.

Through all the ages which have lain between her day and ours, for five hundred years her name has been a name of scorn, and the world has never known that it was most likely for Christ's sake. If that were so, the Day shall declare it; and she will be abundantly compensated for the worldly anguish of her sullied name, when that name upon which the centuries cast such contempt shall be

> "Heard where lips are free from guile,
> Read from the Book of Life by Christ,
> And consecrated by His smile."

CONTENTS.

The King laid the document on the table . . . . she knelt down to sign, holding
the pen a moment idle in her fingers

WHITE ROSE OF LANGLEY.

CHAPTER I.

NOBODY'S CHILD.

"Oh, how full of briars is this working day world!"—SHAKSPERE.

"IT is so cold, Mother!"

The woman addressed languidly roused herself from the half-sheltered nook of the forest in which she and her child had taken refuge. She was leaning with her back supported by a giant oak, and the child was in her arms. The age of the child was about eight. The mother, though still young in years, was old before her time, with hard work and exposure, and it might be also with sorrow. She sat up, and looked wearily over the winter scene before her. There was nothing of the querulous, complaining tone of the little girl's voice in hers; only the dull, sullen apathy of hopeless endurance.

"Cold, child!" she said. "'Tis like to be colder yet when the night cometh."

"O Mother! and all snow now!"

"There be chiller gear than snow, maid," replied the mother bitterly.

"But it had been warmer in London, Mother ?—if we had not lost our road."

"May-be," was the answer, in a tone which seemed to imply that it did not signify.

The child did not reply; and the woman continued to sit upright, and look forward, with an absent expression in her face, indicating that the mind was not where the eyes were.

"Only snow and frost!" she muttered—not speaking to the child. "Nought beyond, nor here ne there. Nay, snow is better than snowed up hearts. Had it been warmer in London? May-be the hearts there had been as frosty as at Pleshy. Well! it will be warm in the grave, and we shall soon win yonder."

"Be there fires yonder, Mother?" asked the child innocently.

The woman laughed—a bitter, harsh laugh, in which there was no mirth.

"The devil keepeth," she said. "At least so say the priests. But what wit they? They never went thither to see. They will, belike, some day."

The little girl was silent again, and the mother, after a moment's pause, resumed her interrupted soliloquy.

"If there were nought beyond, only!" she murmured; and her look and tone of dull misery sharpened into vivid pain. "If a man might die, and have done with it all! But to meet God! And 'tis no sweven,[1] ne fallacy, this dread undeadliness[2]—it is real. O all ye blessed saints and martyrs in Heaven! how shall I meet God?"

"Is that holy Mary's Son, Mother?"

"Aye."

[1] Dream.   [2] Immortality.

"Holy Mary will plead for us," suggested the child. "She can alway peace her Son. But methought *He* was good to folks, Mother. Sister Christian was wont to say so."

"To saints and good women like Sister Christian, may-be."

"Art thou not good, Mother?"

The question was put in all innocence. But it struck the heart of the miserable mother like a poisoned arrow.

"Good!" she cried, again in that tone of intense pain. "*I* good? No, Maude!—I am bad, bad, bad! From the crown of mine head to the sole of my foot, there is nothing in me beside evil; such evil as thou, unwemmed[1] dove as thou art, canst not even conceive! God is good to saints—not to sinners. Sister Christian—and thou, yet!—be amongst the saints. I am of the sinners."

"But why art thou not a saint, Mother?" demanded the child, as innocently as before.

"I was on the road once," said the woman, with a heavy sigh. "I was to have been an holy sister of St. Clare. I knew no more of ill than thou whiteling in mine arms. If I had died then, when my soul was fair!"

Suddenly her mood changed. She clasped the child close to her breast, and showered kisses on the little wan face.

"My babe Maude, my bird Maude!" she said. "My dove that God sped down from Heaven unto me, thinking me not too ill ne wicked to have thee! The angels may love thee, my bird in bower! for thou art white and unwemmed. The robes of thy chrism[2] are not yet soiled;

---

[1] Undefiled, innocent.

[2] The anointing at baptism, when a white cloth was always placed on the head.

but, O sinner that I am! how am I to meet God? And I must meet Him—and soon."

"Did not God die on the rood, Mother?"

The woman assented, the old listless tone returning to her voice.

"Wherefore, Mother?"

"God wot, child."

"Sister Christian told me He had no need for Himself, but that He loved us; yet why that should cause Him to die I wis not."

The mother made no answer. Her thoughts had drifted away, back through her weary past, to a little village church where a fresco painting stood on the wall, sketched in days long before, of a company of guests at a feast, clad in Saxon robes ; and of One, behind whom knelt a woman weeping and kissing His feet, while her flowing hair almost hid them from sight. And back to her memory, along with the scene, came a line from a popular ballad [1] which referred to it. She repeated it aloud—

"'Christ suffered a sinful to kisse His fete.'

"Suffered her, for that she was a saint?" she asked of herself, in the dreamy languor which the intense cold had brought over her. "Nay, for she was 'a sinful.' Suffered her, then, for that she sinned? Were not that to impeach His holiness? Or was He so holy and high that no sin of hers could soil the feet she touched? What good did it her to touch them? Made it her holy? —fit to meet God in the Doom,[2] when she had thus met Him here in His lowliness? How wis I? And could it make me fit to meet Him? But I can never kiss His

[1] "The Ploughman's Complaint."   [2] Judgment.

feet.   Nor lack they the ournment[1] of any kiss of mine. Yet methinks it were she, not He, which lacked it then. And He let her kiss His feet. O Christ Jesu! if in very deed it were in love for us that Thou barest death on the bitter rood, hast Thou no love left to welcome the dying sinner? Thou who didst pity her at yonder feast, hast Thou no mercy for Eleanor Gerard too?"

The words were spoken only half aloud, but they were heard by the child cradled in her arms.

"Mother, why christened you me not Eleanor?" she asked dreamily.

"Hush, child, and go to sleep!" answered the mother, startled out of her reverie.

Maude was silent, and Eleanor wrapped her closer in the old cloak which enfolded both of them. But before the woman yielded herself up to the stupor which was benumbing her faculties, she passed her hand into her bosom, and drew out a little flat parcel, folded in linen, which she secreted in the breast of the child's dress.

"Keep this, Maude," she said gravely.

"What is it, Mother?" was Maude's sleepy answer.

"It is what thou shalt find it hereafter," was the mysterious rejoinder. "But let none take it away, neither beguile thee thereof. 'Tis all I have to give thee."

Maude seemed too nearly asleep for her curiosity to be roused; and Eleanor, leaning back against the tree, resigned herself to slumber also.

Not long afterwards, a goatherd passing that way in search of a strayed kid, came on the unconscious pair, wrapped in each other's arms. He ran for help to his hut, and had them conveyed to a convent at a little dis-

---

[1] Adornment.

tance, which the wanderers had failed to find. The rescue was just in time to bring the life back to the numbed limbs of the child. But for the mother there was no waking in this world. Eleanor Gerard had met God.

Four years after that winter evening, in the guest-chamber of the Convent of Sopwell sat a nun of middle age and cheerful look, in conversation with a woman in ordinary costume, but to whom the same description would very nearly apply.

"Then what were the manner of maid you seek, good Ursula?" inquired the nun.

"By St. Luke's face, holy Sister, but I would not have her too cunning.[1] I count (though I say it that need not) I am none ill one to learn her her work; and me loveth not to be checked ne taunted of mine under-lings."

The nun, who had known Ursula Drew for some time, was quite aware that superfluity of meekness did not rank among that worthy woman's failings.

"I would fain have a small maid of some twelve or thirteen years. An' ye have them elder, they will needs count they know as much as you, and can return a sharp answer betimes. I love not masterful childre."

"But would you not she were something learned?"

"Nay! So she wit not a pig's head from a crustade Almayne,[2] 'tis all one to me, an' she will do my bidding."

"Then methinks I could right well fit you. We have here at this instant moment a small maid of twelve years, that my Lady the Prioress were well fain to put with such as you be, and she bade me give heed to the same.

---

[1] Clever.   [2] A kind of pie of custard or batter, with currants.

'Tis a waif that Anthony, our goatherd, found in the forest, with her mother, that was frozen to death in an hard winter; but the child abode, and was saved. Truly, for cunning there is little in her; but for meekness and readiness to do your will, the maid is as good as any. But ye shall see her I think on."

Sister Oliva stepped to the door, and spoke in a low tone to some person outside. She came back and re-seated herself, and a minute afterwards there was a low, timid tap at the door.

"Come in, child," said the nun.

And Maude came in.

She was small and slight for her twelve years, and preternaturally grave. A quantity of long dark hair hung round her head in a condition of seemingly hope-less tanglement, and the dark eyes, proportionately larger than the rest of the features, wore an expression of mingled apathy and suspicion, alike strange and pain-ful to see in the eyes of a child.

"Come forward, Maude, and speak with Mistress Drew. Mercy on us, child! how hast moiled thine hair like a fowl his pennes!"[1]

Maude made no reply. She came a few steps nearer, dropped a rustic courtesy, and stood to be questioned.

"What is thy name?" inquired Mistress Ursula, as though she were beginning the catechism.

"Maude," said the child under her breath.

"And what years hast—twelve?"

"Twelve, the last Saint Margaret."

"And where wert born? Dost know?"

Maude knew, though for some reason with which she

[1] Feathers.

herself was best acquainted, she had been much more chary of her information to my Lady the Prioress than she now chose to be.

"At Pleshy, in Essex."

"And what work did thy father?"

Maude looked up with a troubled air, as if the idea of that relative's possible existence had never suggested itself to her.

"I never had any father!" she said, in a pained tone. "Cousin Hawise had a father, and he wrought iron on the anvil. But I had none—never! I had a mother— that was all."

"And what called men thy mother?"

"Eleanor Gerard."

"Then thy name is Maude Gerard," said Oliva, sharply.

Maude's silence appeared to indicate that she declined to commit herself either affirmatively or negatively.

"And what canst do, maid?" inquired Ursula, changing the subject to one of more practical purport.

Perhaps the topic was too large for reply, for Maude's only response was a nervous twisting of her fingers. Sister Oliva answered for her.

"Marry, she can pluck a chick, and roll pastry, and use a bedstaff, and scour a floor, and sew, and the like. She hath not been idle, I warrant you."

"Couldst cleanse out a pan an' thou wert set about it?"

"Aye," said Maude, under her breath.

"And couldst run of a message?"

"Aye."

"And couldst do as folk bid thee?"

"Aye."

But each time the child's voice grew fainter.

"Sister Oliva, I will essay the little maid, by your leave."

"And with my very good will, friend Ursula."

"Me counteth I shall make the best cook of her in all Herts. What sayest, maid?—wilt of thy good will be a cook?"

Maude looked up, looked down, and said nothing. But nature had not made her a cook, and the utmost Ursula Drew could do in that direction was to spoil a good milliner.

So little Maude went with Ursula—into a very different sphere of life from any which she could hitherto remember. The first home which she recollected was her grandfather's cottage, with the great elms on one side of it and the forge on the other, at which the old man had wrought so long as his strength permitted, and had then handed over, as the family inheritance, to his son. Since the world began for Maude, that cottage and the forge had always stood there, and its inhabitants had always been Grandfather, and Uncle David, and Aunt Elizabeth, and Cousin Hawise, and Cousin Jack, and Mother.

At some unknown time in the remote past there had been a grandmother, for Maude had heard of her; but with that exception, there had never been anybody else, and her father was to her an utterly mythic individual. She had never heard such a person named until Ursula Drew inquired his calling. And then, one awful winter night, something dreadful had happened. What it was Maude never precisely knew. She only knew that there was a great noise in the night, and strange voices in the cottage, and cries for mercy; and that when morning broke Uncle David was gone, and was seen afterwards no more.   So then they tried to keep on the old forge a little longer; but Grandfather was past work, and Cousin Jack was young and inexperienced, and customers would not come as they had done to brawny-armed Uncle David, to whose ringing blows on the anvil Maude had loved to listen.   And one day she heard Aunt Elizabeth say to Grandfather that the forge brought in nothing, and they must go up to the castle and ask the great Lord there, whose vassals they were, to find them food until Jack was able to work: but the old man rose up from the settle and answered, his voice trembling with passion, that he would starve to death ere he would take food from the cruel hand which had deprived him of his boy. So then, Cousin Jack used to go roaming in the forest and bring home roots and wild fruits, and sometimes the neighbours would give them alms in kind or in money, and so for a while they tried to live.   But Grandfather grew weaker, and Mother and Aunt Elizabeth very thin and worn, and the bloom faded from Cousin Hawise's cheeks, and the gloss died away from her shining hair. And at last Grandfather died.   And then Aunt Elizabeth went to a neighbouring franklin's farm, to serve the franklin's dame; and Cousin Jack went away to sea; and Maude could not recollect how they lived for a time.   And then came another mournful day, when strange people came to the cottage and roughly ordered the three who were left to go away.   They took Cousin Hawise with them, for they said she would be comely if she were well fed, and the Lady had seen her, and she must go and serve the Lady.   And Maude never knew what became of her.   But Mother wept bitterly, and seemed to think that Hawise's lot was a very unhappy one. So then they set out, Mother and Maude, for London. The reasons for going to London were very dim and vague to Maude's apprehension. They were going to look for somebody; so much she knew: and she thought it was some relation of Grandmother's, who might perchance give them a home again. London was a very grand place, only a little less than the world: but it could not fill quite all the world, because there was room left for Pleshy and one or two other places. The King lived in London, who never did any thing all day long but sit on a golden throne, with a crown on his head, and eat bread and marmalade, and drink Gascon wine; and the Queen, who of course sat on another golden throne, and shared the good things, and wore minever dresses and velvet robes which trailed all across the room. Perhaps the houses were not all built of gold; some of them might be silver; but at any rate the streets were paved with one or other of the precious metals. And of course, nobody in London was at all poor, and everybody had as much as he could possibly eat, and was quite warm and comfortable, and life was all music, and flowers, and sunshine. Poor little Maude! was her illusion much more extravagant than some of ours?

But, as we have seen, the hapless travellers never reached their bourne. And now even Mother was gone, and Maude was left alone in all the world. The nuns had not been particularly unkind to her; they had taught her many things, though they had not made her work beyond her strength; yet not one of them had given her what she missed most sympathy. The result was that the child had been unhappy in the convent, and yet she could not have said why, had she been asked. But nobody ever asked that of little Maude. She was alone in all the world—the great, bare, hard, practical world.

For this was the side of the world presented to Maude.

The world is many sided, and it presents various sides and corners to various people. The side which Maude saw was hard and bare. Hard bed, hard fare, hard work, hard words sometimes. Had she any opportunity of thinking the world a soft, comfortable, cushioned place, as some of her sisters find it?

This had been the child's life up to the moment when Ursula Drew made her appearance on the scene. But now a new element was introduced; for Maude's third home was a stately palace, filled with beautiful carvings, and delicate tracery, and exquisite colours, all which, lowest of the low as she was, she enjoyed with an intensity till then unknown to herself, and certainly not shared by any other in her sphere. That sense of the beautiful, which, trained in different directions, makes men poets, painters, and architects, was very strong in little Maude. She could not have explained in the least *how* it was that the curves in the stonework, or the rich colours in the windows of the great hall, gave her a mysterious sensation of pleasure, which she could not avoid detecting that they never gave to any of her kitchen associates; and she obtained many a scolding for her habit of what my Lady the Prioress had called "idle dreaming," and Mistress Drew was pleased to term "lither laziness;" when, instead of cleaning pans, Maude was thinking poetry. Alas for little Maude!

her vocation was not to think poetry; and it was to scour pans.

The Palace of Langley, which had become the scene of Maude's pan-cleaning, was built in a large irregular pile. The kitchen and its attendant offices were at one end, and over them reigned Ursula Drew, who, though supreme in her government of Maude, was in reality only a vice-queen. Over Ursula ruled a man-cook, by name Warine de la Misericorde, concerning whom his subordinate's standing joke was that "Misericorde was rarely[1] merciless." But this potentate in his turn owed submission to the master of the household, a very great gentleman with gold embroidery on his coat, concerning whom Maude's only definite notion was that he must be courtesied to very low indeed.

Master and mistress were mere names to Maude. The child was near-sighted, and though, like every other servant in the Palace, she ate daily in the great hall, her eyes were not sufficiently clear, from her low place at the extreme end, to make out anything on the distant daïs beyond a number of grey shapeless shadows. She knew when the royal, and in her eyes semi celestial persons in question were, or were not, at home; she had a dim idea that they bore the titles of Earl and Countess of Cambridge, and that they were nearly related to majesty itself; she now and then heard Ursula informed that my Lord was pleased to command a certain dish, or that my Lady had condescended to approve a particular sauce. She had noticed, moreover, that two of the grey shadows at the very top of the hall, and therefore among the most

---

[1] Extremely.

distinguished persons, were smaller than the rest; she inferred that these ineffable superiors had at least two children, and she often longed to inspect them within comfortable seeing distance. But no such good fortune had as yet befallen her. Their apartments were inaccessible fairy-land, and themselves beings scarcely to be gazed on with undazzled eyes.

Very monotonous was Maude's new life :—cleaning pans, washing jars, sorting herbs, scouring pails, running numberless infinitesimal errands, doing everything that nobody else liked, hard-worked from morning to night, and called up from her hard pallet to recommence her toil before she had realized that she was asleep. Ursula's temper, too, did not improve with time; and Parnel, the associate and contemporary of Maude, was by no means to be mistaken for an angel.

Parnel was three years older than Maude, and much better acquainted with her work. She could accomplish a marvellous quantity within a given time, when it pleased her; and it generally did please her to rush to the end of her task, and to spend the remaining time in teasing Maude. She had no positive unkind feeling towards the child, but she was extremely mischievous, and Maude being extremely teasable, the temptation of amusing her leisure by worrying the nervous and inexperienced child was too strong to be resisted. The occupations of her present life disgusted Maude beyond measure. The scullery-work, of which Ursula gave her the most unpleasant parts, was unspeakably revolting to her quick sense of artistic beauty, and to a certain delicacy and refinement of nature which she had inherited, not acquired; and which Ursula, if she could have comprehended it, would have despised with the intense contempt of the coarse mind for the fine. The child was one morning engaged in cleaning a very greasy saucepan, close to the open window, when, to her surprise, she was accosted by a strange voice in the base court, or back yard of the palace.

"Is that pleasant work—frotting[1] yonder thing ?"

Maude looked up into a pair of bright, kindly eyes, which belonged to a boy attired as a page, some three or four years older than herself. Something in the lad's good-natured face won her confidence.

"No," she answered honestly, "'tis right displeasant to have ado with such feune !"[2]

"So me counted," replied the boy. "What name hast thou, little maid ?"

"Maude."

"I have not seen thee here aforetime," resumed the page.

"Nor I you," said Maude. "I have bidden hither no long time. Whereabout sit you in hall ?"

"Nigh the high end," said he. "But we are only this day come from Clarendon with the Lord Edward, whom I and my fellows serve. Fare thee well, little maid !"

The bright eyes smiled at her, and the head nodded kindly, and passed on. But insignificant as the remarks were, Maude felt as if she had found a friend in the great wilderness of Langley Palace.

The next time the page's head paused at her window, Maude summoned courage to ask him his name.

"Bertram Lyngern," said he smilingly. "I have a longer name than thou."[3]

---

[1] Rubbing.   [2] Dirt.

[3] Bertram, Ursula, Parnel, Warine, and Maude and her family, are all fictitious persons.

"And a father and mother?" asked Maude.

"A father," said the boy. "He is one of my Lord's knights; but for my mother,—the women say she died the day I was born."

"I have ne father ne mother," responded Maude, sorrowfully, "ne none to care for me in all the wide world."

"Careth Mistress Drew nought for thee?"

Maude's laugh was bitterly negative.

"Ne Parnel, thy fellow?"

"She striveth alway to abash[1] and trouble me," sighed Maude.

"Poor Maude!" said Bertram, looking concerned. "Wouldst have me care for thee? May be I could render thy life somewhat lighter. If I talked with Parnel——"

"It were to no good," said Maude, brushing away to get her sink clean. "There is nothing but sharp words and snybbyngs[2] all day long; and if I give her word back, then will she challenge[3] me to Mistress, and soothly I am aweary of life."

Weary of life at twelve years old! It was a new idea to Bertram, and he had found no answer, when the sharp voice of Ursula Drew summoned Maude away.

"Haste, child!" cried Ursula. "Thou art as long of coming as Advent Sunday at Christmas. Now, by the time I be back, lay thou out for me on the table four bundles of herbs from the dry herb closet an handful of knot grass, and the like of shepherd's pouch, and of bramble-seeds, and of plantain. Now, mark thou, the top leaves of the plantain only! Leave me not find thee

---

[1] Frighten.   [2] Scoldings.   [3] Accuse.

idling ; but have yonder row of pans as bright as a new tester when I come, and the herbs ready."[1]

Ursula bustled off, and Maude set to work at the pans. When they were sufficiently scrubbed, she pulled off the dirty apron in which she had been working, and went towards the dry herb closet. But she had not reached it, when her wrist was caught and held in a grasp like that of a vice.

"Whither goest, Mistress Maude?" demanded an unwelcome voice.

"Stay me not, I pray thee, Parnel!" said the child entreatingly. "Mistress Drew hath bidden me lay out divers herbs against she cometh."

"What herbs be they?" inquired Parnel demurely, with an assumption of gravity and superior knowledge which Maude knew, from sad experience, to mask some project of mischief. But knowing also that peril lay in silence, no less than in compliance, she reluctantly gave the information.

" There is no shepherd's pouch in the closet," responded Parnel

"Then whither must I seek it?" asked Maude.

"In the fields," said Parnel.

"Aye me!" exclaimed the child.

"And 'tis not in leaf, let be flower," added her tormentor.

"What can I do?" cried Maude in dismay.

Still keeping tight hold of her wrist, Parnel answered the query by the execution of a war-dance around Maude.

---

[1] The herbs were to be boiled and the liquid drunk, for a sprain, bruise, or broken bone.

"Parnel, do leave go!" supplicated the prisoner.

"Mistress Maude is bidden lay out herbs!" sang the gaoler in amateur recitative. "Mistress Maude hath no shepherd's pouch! Mistress Maude is loth to go and pluck it!"

"Parnel, *do* leave me go!"

"Mistress Maude doth not her mistress' bidding! Mistr——"

Suddenly breaking off, Parnel, who could be as quick as a lizard when she chose, quitted her hold, and vanished out of sight in some incomprehensible manner, as Ursula Drew marched into the kitchen.

"Now, then, where be those herbs?" demanded that authority, in a tone indicative of a whipping.

"Mistress, I could not help it!" sobbed the worried child.

"By'r Lady, but thou canst help it if thou wilt!" returned Ursula. "Reach me down the rod; thy laziness shall be well apaid for once."

Maude sobbed helplessly, but made no effort to obey.

"Where be thine ears? Reach the rod!" reiterated Ursula.

"Whom chastise you, Mistress Drew?" inquired Bertram's voice through the door; "she that demeriteth the same, or she that no doth?"

"This lazy maid demeriteth fifty rods!" was the pleasing answer.

"I cry you mercy, but I think not so," said Bertram judicially. "An' you whipped the demeritous party, it should be Parnel. I saw all that chanced, by the lattice, but the maids saw not me."

Parnel was not whipped, for her quickness made her a

favourite; but neither was Maude, for Bertram's intercession rescued her.

"The saints bless you, Master Bertram!" said Maude, at the next opportunity. "And the saints help me, for verily I have an hard life. I am all of a bire,[1] and sore strangled,[2] from morn to night"

"Poor little Maude!" answered Bertram pityingly. "Would I might shape thy matters better-good. Do the saints help, thinkest? Hugh Calverley saith no."

"Talk you with such like evil fawtors,[3] Master Bertram?" asked Maude in a shocked voice.

"Evil fawtors, forsooth! Hugh is no evil fawtor. How can I help but rede[4] his sayings? He is one of my fellows. And 'tis but what he hath from his father. Master Calverley is a squire of the Queen's Grace, and one of Sir John de Wycliffe's following."

"Who is Sir John de Wycliffe?" said Maude.

"One of the Lord Pope his Cardinals," laughed Bertram. "Get thee to thine herbs and pans, little Maude; and burden not thy head with Sir John de Wycliffe nor John de Northampton neither. Fare thee well, my maid. I must after my master for the hawking."

But before Bertram turned away, Maude seized the opportunity to ask a question which had been troubling her for many a month.

"If you be not in heavy bire Master Bertram——"

"Go to! What maketh a minute more nor less?"

"Would it like you of your goodness to tell me, an' you wit, who dwelleth in the Castle of Pleshy?"

"'An' I wit'! Well wis I. 'Tis my gracious Lord of Buckingham, brother unto our Lord of Cambridge."

[1] Ifuiry, confusion. [2] Tired. [3] Factor, doer. [4] Attend to.

"Were you ever at Pleshy, Master Bertram ?"

"Truly, but a year gone, for the christening of the young Lord Humphrey."

"And liked it you to tell me if you wot at all of one Hawise Gerard among the Lady's maidens ?"

Maude awaited the answer in no little suppressed eagerness. She had loved Cousin Hawise ; and if she yet lived, though apart, she would not feel herself so utterly alone. Perhaps they might even meet again, some day. But Bertram shook his head.

"I heard never the name,' he said. "The Lady of Buckingham her maidens be Mistress Polegna and Mistress Sarah :¹ their further names I wis not. But no Mistress Hawise saw I never."

"I thank you much, Master Bertram, and will not stay you longer."

But another shadow fell upon Maude's life. Poor, pretty, gentle, timid Cousin Hawise ! What had become of her ? The next opportunity she had, Maude inquired from Bertram, "What like dame were my Lady of Buckingham's greathood ?"

Bertram shrugged his shoulders, as if the question took him out of his depth.

"Marry, she is a woman !" said he ; "and all women be alike. There is not one but will screech an' she see a spider."

"Mistress Drew and Mother be not alike," answered Maude, falling back on her own small experience. "Neither were Hawise and I alike. She would alway stay at holy Mary her image, to see if the lamp were alight ; but I—the saints forgive me !—I never cared thereabout. So good was Cousin Hawise."

---

¹ Fictitious persons.

"Maude," suggested Bertram in a low voice, as if he felt half afraid of his own idea, "Coun'est that blessed Mary looketh ever her own self to wit if the lamp be alight ?"

Maude was properly shocked.

"Save you All Hallows, Master Bertram ! How come you by such fantasies ?"

Bertram laughed and went away, chanting a stave of the "Ploughman's Complaint"[1]—

> "Christ hath twelvè apostles here ;
>> Now, say they, there may be but one,
> That may not errè in no manere
>> Who 'leveth[2] not this ben lost echone.[3]
>> Peter errèd   so did not Jhon ;
> Why is he clepèd the principall ?[4]
>> Christ cleped him Petèr, but Himself the Stone—
> All falsè faitours[5] foulè hem fall !"[6]

Late that evening a mounted messenger crossed the drawbridge, and stayed his weary horse in the snow-sprinkled base court. He was quickly recognised by the household as a royal letter bearer from London.

"And what news abroad, Master Matthew ?"

"Why, the King's Highness keepeth his Christmas at Eltham ; and certain of the Council would fain have the Queen's Bohemians sent forth, but I misdoubt if it shall be done. And Sir Nicholas Brembre is the new mayor. There is no news else. Oh, aye ! The parson of Lutterworth, Sir John de Wycliffe —"

---

[1] Wright's *Political Poems*, i. 304, *et seq*. The date of the poem given by Wright is anticipated by about nine years.

[2] Believeth.   [3] Each one.

[4] Why is Peter called the "Prince of the Apostles ?"

[5] Doers.   [6] Evil befall them.

"The lither heretic!" muttered Warine, for he was the questioner. "What misturnment[2] would he now?"

"He will never turn ne misturn more," said the messenger. "The morrow after Holy Innocents a second fit of the palsy took him as he stood at the altar at mass, and they bare him home to die. And the eve of the Circumcision,[8] two days thereafter, the good man was commanded to God."

"Good man, forsooth!" growled Warine.

"Master Warine," said Hugh Calverley's voice behind him, "the day may come when thou and I would be full fain to creep into Heaven at the heels of the Lutterworth parson."

[1] Perversion.   [2] December 31st, 1384.

CHAPTER II.

SOMEBODY'S CHILD.

> "'Now God, that is of mightès most,
>   Grant him grace of the Holy Ghost
>   His heritage to win :
>   And Mary moder of mercy fre
>   Save our King and his meynie
>   Fro' sorrow and shame and sin.'"

THE song was trilled in a pleasant voice by an old lady who sat spinning in an upper chamber of Langley Palace. She paused a moment in her work, and then took up again the latter half of the strain.

"'And Mary moder of mercy fre'—Called any yonder ?"

"May I come in, Dame Agnes ?" said a child's voice at the door.

The old lady rose hastily, laid down her distaff, and opening the door, courtesied low to the little girl of ten years old who stood outside.

"Enter freely, most gracious Lady ! Wherefore abide without ?"

It was a pretty vision which entered. Not that there was any special beauty in the child herself, for in that respect she was merely on the pretty side of ordinary.

She was tall for her age—as tall as Maude, though she was two years younger. Her complexion was very fair, her hair light with a golden tinge, and her eyes of a peculiar shade of blue, bright, yet deep the shade known as blue eyes in Spain, but rarely seen in England. But her costume was a study for a painter. Little girls dressed like women in the fourteenth century ; and this child wore a blue silk tunic embroidered with silver hare-bells, over a brown velvet skirt spangled with rings of gold. Her hair was put up in a net of golden tissue, ornamented with pearls. The dress was cut square at the neck ; she wore a pearl necklace, and a girdle of turquoise and pearls. Two rows of pearls and turquoise finished the sleeves at the wrist ; they were of brown velvet, like the skirt. This finery was evidently nothing new to the little wearer. She came into the room and flung herself carelessly down on a small stool, close to the chair where Dame Agnes had been sitting—to the unfeigned horror of that courtly person.

"Lady, Lady ! Not on a stool, for love of the blessed Mary !"

And drawing forward an immense old arm chair, Dame Agnes motioned the child to take it.

"Remember, pray you, that you be a Prince's daughter !"[1]

The child rose with some reluctance, and climbed into the enormous chair, in which she seemed almost lost.

"Prithee, Dame Agnes, is it because I be a Prince's daughter that I must needs be let from sitting whither I would ?"

[1] The child was Constance, only daughter of Edmund Duke of York (seventh son of Edward III.) and Isabel of Castilla.

"There is meetness in all things," said the old lady, picking up her distaff.

"And what meetness is in setting the like of me in a chair that would well hold Charlemagne and his twelve Peers?" demanded the little girl, laughing.

"The twelve Peers of Charlemagne, such saved as were Princes, were not the like of *you*, Lady Custance," said Dame Agnes, almost severely.

"Ah me!" and Constance gaped (or, as she would herself have said, "goxide.") "I would I were a woodman's daughter."

Dame Agnes de La Marche,[1] whose whole existence had been spent in the scented atmosphere of Court life, stared at the child in voiceless amazement.

"I would so, Dame. I might sit then of the rushes, let be the stools, or in a fieldy nook amid the wild flowers. And Doña Juana would not be ever laying siege to me—with 'Doña Constança, you will soil your robes!' or, 'Doña Constança, you will rend your lace!' —or, 'Doña Constança, you will dirty your fingers!' Where is the good of being rich and well-born, if I must needs sit under a cloth of estate[2] all the days of my life, and dare not so much as to lift a pin from the floor, lest I dirty my puissant and royal fingers? I would liefer have a blacksmith to my grandsire than a King."

"Lady Custance! With which of her Grace's scullion maidens have you demeaned yourself to talk?"

---

[1] Agnes de La Marche had been the nurse of two of Edward III.'s sons, Lionel and Edmund. She lived to old age, and was long in receipt of a pension from the Crown for her former service.

[2] Canopy.

"I will tell thee, when thou wilt answer when I was suffered to say so much as 'Good morrow' to any maid under the degree of a knight's daughter."

"Holy Mary, be our aid!" interjected the horrified old lady.

"I am aweary, Dame Agnes," said the child, laying herself down in the chair, as nearly at full length as its size would allow. "I have played the damosel[1] so long time, I would fain be a little maid a season. I looked forth from the lattice this morrow, and I saw far down in the base court a little maid the bigness of me, washing of pans at a window. Now, prithee, have yon little maid up hither, and set her under the cloth of estate in my velvets, and leave me run down to the base court and wash the pans. It were rare mirth for both of us."

Dame Agnes shook her head, as if words failed to express her feelings at so unparalleled a proposal.

"What sangst thou as I was a-coming in?" asked the child, dropping a subject on which she found no sympathy.

"'Twas but an old song, Lady, of your Grace's grandsire King Edward (whom God assoil![2]) and his war of France."

"That was ere I was born. Was it ere thou wert, Dame?"

"Truly no, Lady," said Agnes, smiling; "nor ere my Lord your father."

"What manner of lad was my Lord my father, when he was little?"

"Rare meek and gent, Lady,—for a lad, and his ire saved."[3]

---

[1] Person of rank —used of the younger nobility of both sexes.
[2] Pardon.　　　　[3] Except when he was angry.

Dame Agnes saved her conscience by the last clause, for gentle as Prince Edmund had generally been, he was as capable of going into a genuine Plantagenet passion as any of his more fiery brothers.

"But a maiden must be meeker and gentler?"

"Certes, Damosel," said Agnes, spinning away.

The child reclined in her chair for a time in silence. Perhaps it was the suddenness of the next question which made the old lady drop her distaff.

"Dame, who is Sir John de Wycliffe?"

The distaff had to be recovered before the question could be considered.

"Ask at Dame Joan, Lady," was the discreet reply.

"So I did; and she bade me ask at thee."

"A priest, methinks," said Agnes vaguely.

"Why, I knew that," answered the child. "But what did he, or held he?—for 'tis somewhat naughty, folk say."

"If it be somewhat naughty, Lady Custance, you should not seek to know it."

"But my Lady my mother wagged her head, though she spake not. So I want to know."

"Then your best way, Damosel," suggested the troubled Agnes, "were to ask at her Grace."

"I did ask at her."

"And what said she?"

"She said she would tell me another day. But I want to know now."

"Her Grace's answer might have served you, Lady."

"It did not serve Ned. He said he would know. And so will I."

"The Lord Edward is two years your elder, Lady."

"Truth," said the child shrewdly, "and you be sixty

years mine elder, so you should know more than he by thirty."

Agnes could not help smiling, but she was sadly perplexed how to dismiss the unwelcome topic.

"Let be. If thou wilt not tell me, I will blandish some that will. There be other beside thee in the university.[1]—What is yonder bruit[2]?"

It was little Maude, flying in frantic terror, with Parnel in hot pursuit, both too much absorbed to note in what direction they were running. The cause was not far to seek.

After Maude had recovered from the effects of her exposure in the forest, she lighted unexpectedly on the little flat parcel which her mother had charged her to keep. It was carefully sewn up in linen, and the sewing cost Maude some trouble to penetrate. She reached the core at last. It was something thin and flat, with curious black and red patterns all over it. This would have been the child's description. It was, in truth, a vellum leaf of a MS., elaborately written, but not illuminated, unless capitals in red ink can be termed illumination. Remembering her mother's charge, to let "none beguile her of it," Maude had striven to keep its possession a secret from every one, first from the nuns, and then from Ursula Drew. Strange to say, she had succeeded until that morning. It was to her a priceless treasure all the more inestimable because she could not read a word of it. But on that unlucky morning, Parnel had caught a glimpse of the precious parcel, always hidden in Maude's bosom, and had immediately endeavoured to snatch it from her. Contriving

<hr>

[1] World, universe.   [2] Noise.

to elude her grasp, yet fearful of its·repetition, Maude rushed out of the kitchen door, and finding that her tormentor followed, fled across the base court, took refuge in an open archway, dashed up a flight of steps, and sped along a wide corridor, neither knowing nor caring that her flying feet were bearing her straight in the direction of the royal apartments. Parnel was the first to see where they were going, and at the last corner she stayed her pursuit, daring to proceed no further. But Maude did not know that Parnel was no longer on her track, and she fled wildly on, till her foot tripped at an inequality in the stone passage, and she came down just opposite an open door.

For a minute the child was too much stunned by her fall to think of any thing. Then, as her recollection returned, she cast a terrified glance behind her, and saw that her pursuer had not yet appeared round the corner. And then, before she could rise, she heard a voice in front of her.

"What is this, my child?"

Maude looked up, past a gorgeous spread of blue and gold drapery, into a meek, quiet face—a face whose expression reassured and comforted her. A calm, pale, oval face, in which were set eyes of sapphire blue, framed by soft, light hair, and wearing a look of suffering, past or present. Maude answered the gentle voice which belonged to that face as she might have answered her mother.

"I pray you of pardon, Mistress! Parnel, my fellow, ran after me and affrighted me."

"Wherefore ran she after thee?"

"Because she would needs see what I bare in my

bosom, and I was loth she so should, lest she should do it hurt."

"What is that? I will do it no hurt."

Maude looked up again, and felt as if she could trust that face with any thing. So merely saying—"You will not give it Parnel, Mistress?" she drew forth her treasure and put it into the lady's hand.

"I will give it to none saving thine own self. Dost know what it is, little maid?"

"No, Mistress, in good sooth."

"How camest by it? 'Tis a part of a book."

"My mother, that is dead, charged me to keep it; for it was all she had for to give me. I know not, in very deed, whether it be Charlemagne or Arthur"—the only two books of which poor Maude had ever heard. "But an' I could meet with one that wist to read, and that were my true friend, I would fain cause her to tell me what I would know thereabout."

"And hast no true friend?" inquired the lady.

"Not one," said Maude sorrowfully.

"Well, little maid, I can read, and I would be thy true friend. What is it thou wouldst fain know?"

"Why," said Maude, in an interested tone, "whether the great knight, of whose mighty deeds this book doth tell, should win his 'trothed love at the last, or no."

For the novel-reader of the fourteenth century was not very different from the novel reader of the nineteenth. The lady smiled, but grew grave again directly. She sat down in one of the cushioned window-seats, keeping Maude's treasured leaf in her hand.

"List, little maid, and thou shalt hear—that the great Knight, of whose mighty prowess this book doth tell, shall win His 'trothed love at last."

And she began to read—very different words from any Maude expected. The child listened, entranced.

"And I saigh[1] newe heuene and newe erthe; for the firste heuene and the firste erthe wenten awei; and the see is not now. And I ioon[2] saigh the hooli citee ierusalim newe comynge doun fro heuene maad redi of god as a wyf ourned to hir husbonde. And I herde a greet voice fro the trone seiynge,[3] lo a tabernacle of god is with men, and he schal dwelle with hem, and thei schulen be his peple, and he, god with hem, schal be her[4] god. And god schal wipe awei ech teer fro the ighen[5] of hem, and deeth schal no more be, neithir mournyng neither criyng neither sorewe schal be ouer, whiche thing is firste[6] wenten awei. And he seide that sat in the trone, lo I make alle thingis newe. And he seide to me, write thou, for these wordis ben[7] moost feithful and trewe. And he seide to me, it is don, I am alpha and oo[8] the bigynnyng and ende, I schal ghyue[9] freli of the welle of quyk[10] water to him that thirstith. He that schal ouercome schal welde[11] these thingis, and I schal be god to him, and he schal be sone to me. But to ferdful men, and unbileueful, and cursid, and man- quelleris, and fornicatours, and to witchis and wor- schiperis of ydols and to alle lyeris the part of hem schal be in the pool brenynge with fyer and brymstoon, that is the secounde deeth. And oon[12] cam of the seuene aungelis hauynge violis ful of seuenè the laste ueniauncis,[13] and he spak with me and seide, come thou and I schal schewe to thee the spousesse[14] the wyf of the lombe.

---

[1] Saw. [2] John. [3] Saying. [4] Their. [5] Eyes.
[6] First things. [7] Are. [8] Omega. [9] Give.
[10] Quick- — living. [11] Possess. [12] One. [13] Vengeances – plagues.
[14] Bride.

And he took me up in spirit into a greet hill and high, and he schewide to me the hooli cite ierusalem comynge doun fro heuene of god, hauynge the cleerte[1] of god; and the light of it lyk a precious stoon as the stoon iaspis,[2] as cristal.   And it hadde a wall grect and high hauynge twelue ghatis,[3] and in the ghatis of it twelue aungelis and names writen yn that ben the names of twelue lynagis[4] of the sones of israel.   Fro the eest three ghatis, and fro the north three ghatis, and fro the south three ghatis, and fro the west three ghatis.   And the wall of the citee hadde twelue foundamentis, and in hem the twelue names of twelue apostlis and of the lombe.   And he that spak with me hadde a goldun mesure of a rehed[5] that he schulde mete the citee and the ghatis of it and the wall.   And the citee was sett in a square, and the lengthe of it is so mych as mych as is the brede,[6] and he mat[7] the citee with the rehed bi furlongis twelue thousyndis, and the highthe and the lengthe and breede of it ben euene.   And he maat[7] the wallis of it of an hundride and foure and fourti cubitis bi mesure of man, that is, of an aungel.   And the bilding of the wall thereoff was of the stoon iaspis and the citee it silff was cleen gold lyk cleen glas.   And the foundamentis of the wal of the cite weren ourned[8] with al precious stoon, the firste foundament iaspis, the secound saphirus, the thridde calsedonyus, the fourthe smaragdus,[9] the fifthe sardony,[10] the sixte sardyus,[11] the seuenthe crisolitus, the eighthe berillus, the nynthe topasius, the tenthe crisopassus, the elleuenthe iacinctus,[12]

---

[1] Glory.   [2] Jasper.   [3] Gates.   [4] Lineages   tribes.
[5] Reed.   [6] Breadth.   [7] Meted — measured.   [8] Adorned.
[9] Emerald.   [10] Sardonyx.   [11] Ruby.   [12] Jacinth.

the tweluethe amatistus.[1] And twelue ghatis ben twelue margaritis[2] bi ech,[3] and ech ghate was of ech[3] margarite and the streetis of the citee weren cleen gold as of glas ful schinynge. And I saigh no temple in it, for the lord god almyghti and the lomb is temple of it, and the citee hath not nede of sunne neither moone that thei schine in it, for the cleerite of god schal lightne it, and the lombe is the lanterne of it, and the kyngis of erthe schulen bringe her glorie and onour into it. And the ghatis of it schulen not be closid bi dai, and nyght schal not be there, and thei schulen bringe the glorie and onour of folkis into it, neither ony man defouled and doynge abomynacioun and leesyng[4] schal entre into it, but thei that ben writun in the book of lyf and of the lombe."

When the soft, quiet voice ceased, it was like the sudden cessation of sweet music to the enchanted ears of little Maude. The child was very imaginative, and in her mental eyes the City had grown as she listened, till it now lay spread before her   the streets of gold, and the gates of pearl, and the foundations of precious stones. Of any thing typical or supernatural she had not the faintest idea. In her mind it was at once settled that the City was London, and yet was in some dreamy way Jerusalem ; for of any third city Maude knew nothing. The King, of course, had his Palace there ; and a strong desire sprang up in the child's mind to know whether the royal mistress, who was to her a kind of far off fairy queen, had a palace there also If so but no ! it was too good to be true that Maude would ever go to wash the golden pans and diamond dishes which must be used in that City.

[1] Amethyst.   [2] Pearls.   [3] Each.   [4] Lying

"Mistress!" said Maude to her new friend, after a short silence, during which both were thinking deeply.

The lady brought her eyes down to the child from the sky, where they had been fixed, and smiled a reply to the appeal.

"Would you tell me, of your grace, whether our Lady mistresshood's graciousness hath in yonder city a dwelling?"

Maude wondered exceedingly to see tears slowly gather in the sapphire eyes.

"God grant it, little maid!" was, to her, the incomprehensible answer.

"And if so were, Mistress, counteth your Madamship that our said puissant Lady should ever lack her pans cleansed yonder?"

"Wherefore, little maid?" asked the lady very gently.

"Because, an' I so might, I would fain dwell in yonder city," said Maude, with glittering eyes.

"And thy work is to cleanse pans?"

Little Maude sighed heavily. "Aye, yonder is my work."

"Which thou little lovest, as methinks."

"Should you love it, Mistress, think you?" demanded Maude.

"Truly, little maid, that should I not," answered the lady. "Now tell me freely, what wouldst liefer do?"

"Aught that were clean and fair and honest!"[1] said Maude confidentially, her eyes kindling again. "An' they lack any 'prentices in that City, I would fain be bound yonder. Verily, I would love to twine flowers, or to weave dovecotes,[2] or to guard brave gowns with goodly

---

[1] Pretty.   [2] The golden nets which confined ladies' hair.

`lace, and the like of that, an’ I could be learned. Save that, methinks, over there, I would be ever and alway a gazing from the lattice.”

“Wherefore ?”

“And yet I wis not,” added Maude, thinking aloud. “Where the streets be gold, and the gates margarites, what shall the gowns be ?”

“Pure, bright stones,[1] little maid,” said the lady. “But there be no ’prentices yonder.”

“What ! be they all masters ?” said the child.

“‘A kingdom and priests,’” she said. “But there be no ’prentices, seeing there is no work, save the King’s work.”

Little Maude wondered privately whether that were to sew stars upon sunbeams.

“But there shall not enter any defouled thing into that City,” pursued the lady seriously; “no leasing, neither no manner of wrongfulness.”

Little Maude’s face fell considerably.

“Then I could not go to cleanse the pans yonder !” she said sorrowfully. “I did tell a lie once to Mistress Drew.”

“Who is Mistress Drew ?” enquired the lady.

The child looked up in astonishment, wondering how it came to pass that any one living in Langley Palace should not know her who, to Maude’s apprehension, was monarch of all she surveyed—inside the kitchen.

“She is Mistress Ursula Drew, that is over me and Parnel.”

“Doth she cleanse pans ?” said the lady smilingly.

---

[1] Wycliffe’s rendering of Rev. xv. 6. In various places he follows what are now determined to be the best and most ancient authorities.

"Nay, verily!　She biddeth us."

"I see—she is queen of the kitchen.　And is there none over her?"

"Aye, Master Warine."

"And who is over Master Warine?"

A question beyond little Maude's power to answer.

"The King must be, of force," said she meditatively. "But who is else—saving his gracious mastership and our Lady her mistresshood   in good sooth I wis not."

The lady looked at her for a minute with a smile on her lips.　Then, a little to Maude's surprise, she clapped her hands.　A handsomely attired woman   to the child's eyes, the counterpart of the lady who had been talking with her—appeared in the doorway.

"Señora!" she said, with a reverence.

The two ladies thereupon began a conversation, in a language totally incomprehensible to little Maude.　They were both Spanish by birth, and they were speaking their own tongue.　They said:

"Doña Juana, is there any vacancy among my maids?"

"Señora, we live to fulfil your august pleasure."

"Do you think this child could be taught fine needle-work?"

"The Infanta has only to command."

"I wish it tried, Doña Juana."

"I lie at the Infanta's feet."

The lady turned back to Maude.

"Thy name, little maid?" she gently asked.

"Maude, and your servant, Mistress," responded the child.

"Then, little Maude, have here thy treasure"—and she held forth the leaf to her—"and thy wish.　Follow this dame, and she will see if thou canst guard gowns. If so be, and thou canst be willing and gent, another may cleanse the pans, for thou shalt turn again to the kitchen no more."

Little Maude clasped her hands in ecstasy.

"Our Lady Mary, and Peter and Paul, bless your Ladyship's mistresshood! Be you good enough for to ensure me of the same?"

"Thou shalt not win back, an' thou do well," repeated the lady, smiling. "Now follow this dame."

Doña Juana was not at all astonished. Similar sudden transformations were comparatively of frequent occurrence at that time; and to call in question any act of the King of Castilla's daughter would have been in her eyes the most impossible impropriety. She merely noted mentally the extremely dirty state of Maude's frock, calculated how long it would take to make her three new ones, wondered if she would be very troublesome to teach, and finally asked her if she had any better dress. Maude owned that she possessed a serge one for holidays, upon which Doña Juana, after a minute's hesitation, looked back into the room she had left, and said, "Alvena!" A lively-looking woman, past girlhood in age, but retaining much of the character, answered the call.

"Hie unto Mistress Ursula Drew, that is over the kitchen, and do her to wit that her Grace's pleasure is to advance Maude, the scullion, unto room[1] of tire-woman; bid her to give thee all that 'longeth unto the maid, and bear it hither."

Alvena departed on her errand, and Maude followed Doña Juana into fairy land. Gorgeous hangings covered

---

[1] Situation.

the walls; here and there a soft mossy carpet was spread over the stone floor—for it was not the time of year for rushes. The guide's own dress—crimson velvet, heavily embroidered—was a marvel of art, and the pretty articles strewn on the tables were wonders of the world. They had passed through four rooms ere Maude found her tongue.

"Might it like your Madamship," she asked timidly, her curiosity at last overcoming her reserve, though she felt less at home with Doña Juana than with the other lady, "to tell me the name of the fair mistress that did give me into your charge?"

"That is our Lady's Grace, maiden," said Juana rather stiffly, "the Lady Infanta Doña Isabel, Countess of Cambridge."

"What, she that doth bear rule over us all?" said Maude amazedly.

"She," replied Juana.

"Had I wist the same, as wot the saints, I had been sore afeard," responded Maude. "And what call men your Grace's Ladyship, an' I may know?"

Doña Juana condescended to smile at the child's simplicity.

"My name is Juana Fernandez," she said. "Thou canst call me Dame Joan."

At this point the hangings were suddenly lifted, and something which seemed to Maude the very Queen of the Fairies crept out and stood before them. Juana stopped and courtesied, an act which Maude was too fascinated to imitate.

"Whither go you, Doña Juana?" asked the vision. "In good sooth, this is the very little maid I saw a-washing the pans. Art come to sit under the cloth of estate in my stead?"

Little Maude gazed on her Fairy Queen, and was silent.

"What means your Grace, Doña Constança?" asked Juana.

"What is thy name, and wherefore camest hither?" resumed Constance, still addressing herself to Maude.

"Maude," said the child shyly.

"Maude! That is a pretty name," pronounced the little Princess.

"The Señora Infanta, your Grace's mother, will have me essay to learn the maid needlework," added Juana in explanation.

"Leave me learn her!" said Constance eagerly. "I can learn her all I know; and I am well assured I can be as patient as you, Doña Juana."

"At your Ladyship's feet," responded Juana quietly, using her customary formula. She felt the suggestion highly improper and exceedingly absurd, but she was far too great a courtier to say so.

"Come hither!" said Constance gleefully, beckoning to Maude. "Sue[1] thou me unto Dame Agnes de La Marche her chamber. I would fain talk with thee."

Maude glanced at Juana for permission.

"Sue thou the Señorita Doña Constança," was the reply. "Be thou ware not to gainsay her in any thing."

There was little need of the warning, for Maude was completely enthralled. She followed her Fairy Queen in silence into the room where Dame Agnes still sat spinning.

[1] Follow.

"Sit thou down on yonder stool," said Constance. " My gracious Ladyship will take this giant's chair. (I have learned my lesson, Dame Agnes.) Now—where is thy mother ? "

"A fathom underground."

"Poor Maude! hast no mother ?—And thy father ? "

"Never had I."

"And thy brethren and sustren[1] ? "

"Ne had I never none."

"Maiden!" interjected Dame Agnes, "wist not how to speak unto a damosel of high degree? Thou shalt say 'Lady' or 'Madam.'"

"'Lady' or 'Madam,'" repeated Maude obediently.

"How long hast washed yonder pans ?" asked Constance, leaning her head on the arm of the chair.

"'Lady' or 'Madam,'" answered Maude, remembering her lesson, "by the space of ten months."

"The sely[2] hilding[3]!" exclaimed Agnes ; while Constance flung herself into another attitude, and laughed with great enjoyment.

"Flyte[4] her not, Dame Agnes. I do foresee she and I shall be great friends."

"Lady Custance! The dirt under your feet is no meet friend ne fellow[5] for the like of you."

"Truly, no, saving to make pies thereof," laughed the little Princess. "Nathless, take my word for it, Maude and I shall be good friends."

Was there a recording angel hovering near to note the words ? For the two lives, which had that day come in contact, were to run thenceforth side by side so long as both should last in this world.

---

[1] Sisters [2] Simple, stupid.
[3] Young person—of either sex. [4] Scold. [5] Companion.

But the little Princess was soon tired of questioning her new acquaintance. She sauntered away ere long in search of some more novel amusement, and Dame Agnes desired Maude to change her dress, and then to return to the ante-chamber, there to await the orders of Dame Joan, as Doña Juana was termed by all but the Royal Family. Maude obeyed, and in the ante-chamber she found, not Juana, but Alvena,[1] and another younger woman, whom she subsequently heard addressed as Mistress Sybil.[1]

"So thou shalt be learned?"[2] said Alvena, as her welcome to Maude. "Come, look hither on this gown. What is it?"

"'Tis somewhat marvellous shene!"[3] said Maude, timidly stroking the glossy material.

Alvena only laughed, apparently enjoying the child's ignorance; but Sybil said gently, "'Tis satin, little maid."

"Is it for our Lady's Grace?" asked Maude.

"Aye, when 'tis purfiled," replied Alvena.

"Pray you, Mistress Alvena, what is 'purfiled?'"

"Why, maid! Where hast dwelt all thy life? 'Purfiled' signifieth guarded with peltry."

"But under your good allowance, Mistress Alvena, what is 'peltry'?"

"By my Lady St. Mary! heard one ever the like?"

"Peltry," quietly explained Sybil, "is the skin of beast with the dressed fur thereon—such like as minever, and gris,[4] and the like."

"Thurstan," said Alvena suddenly, turning to a little

----

[1] A fictitious person. [2] You have to be taught.
[3] Bright. [4] Marten.

errand boy[1] who sat on a stool in the window, and whose especial business it was to do the bidding of the Countess's waiting-women, " Hie thee down to Adam[1] the peltier,[2] and do him to wit that the Lady would have four ells of peltry of beasts ermines for the bordure of her gown of blue satin that is in making. The peltry shall be of the breadth of thine hand, and no lesser ; and say unto him that it shall be of the best sort, and none other. An' he send me up such evil gear as he did of gris for the cloak of velvet, he may look to see it back with a fardel[3] of flyting lapped[4] therein. Haste, lad ! and be back ere my scissors meet."

Thurstan disappeared, and Alvena threw herself down on the settle while she waited for her messenger.

"Aye me ! I am sore aweary of all this gear snipping, and sewing, and fitting. If I would not as lief as forty shillings have done with broidery and peltry, then the moon is made of green cheese. Is that strange unto thee, child ?"

"Verily, Mistress Alvena, methinks you be aweary of Fairy Land," said little Maude in surprise.

"Callest this Fairy Land ?" laughed Alvena. "If so be, child, I were fain to dwell a season on middle earth."

"In good sooth, so count I it," answered Maude, allowing her eyes to rove delightedly among all the marvels of the ante chamber, "and the Lady Custance the very Queen of Faery."

"The Lady Custance is made of flesh and blood, trust me. An' thou hadst had need to bear her to her bed,

---

[1] A fictitious person.
[2] Furrier. Ladies of high rank kept a private furrier in the household.
[3] Parcel.   [4] Wrapped.

kicking and striving all the way, when she was somewhat lesser than now, thou shouldst be little tempted to count her immortal."

"An' it like you, Mistress Alvena——"

"Marry, Master Thurstan, it liketh me right well to see thee back without the peltry wherefor I sent thee! Where hast loitered, thou knave?"

"Master Adam saith he is unfurnished at this time of the peltry you would have, Mistress, and without fox will serve your turn——"

"Fox me no fox, as thou set store by thy golden locks!" said Alvena, advancing towards the luckless Thurstan in a threatening attitude, with the scissors open in her hand. "I 'll fox him, and thee likewise. Go and bring me the four ells of peltry of beasts ermines, and that of the best, or thou shalt wake up to morrow to find thy poll as clean as the end of thine ugsome[1] nose."

Poor Thurstan, who was only a child of about ten years old, mistook Alvena's jesting for earnest, and began to sob.

"But what can I, Mistress?" urged the terrified urchin. "Master Adam saith he hath never a nail thereof, never name an ell."

"Alvena, trouble not the child," interposed Sybil.

But Sybil's gentle intercession would have availed little if it had not been seconded by the unexpected appearance of the only person whom Alvena feared.

"What is this?" inquired Doña Juana, in a tone of authority.

Thurstan, with a relieved air, subsided into his recess, and Alvena, with a rather abashed one, began to explain

----

[1] Ugly.

that no ermine could be had for the trimming of the blue satin dress.

"Then let it wait," decided the Mistress—for this was Juana's official title. "Alvena, set the child a-work, and watch that she goeth rightly thereabout. Sybil, sue thou me."

The departure of Juana and Sybil, for which Maude was privately rather sorry, set Alvena's tongue again at liberty. She set Maude at work, on a long hem, which was not particularly interesting ; and herself began to pin some trimming on a tunic of scarlet cloth.

"Pray you, Mistress Alvena," asked Maude at length —wedging her question in among a quantity of small-talk—"hath the Lady Custance brethren or sustren ?"

"Sustren, not one ; and trust me, child, an' thou knewest her as I do, thou shouldst say one of her were enough. But she hath brethren twain—the Lord Edward, which is her elder, and the Lord Richard, her younger. The little Lord Richard is a sweet child as may lightly be seen ; and dearly the Lady Custance loveth him. But as for the Lord Edward an' he can do an ill turn, trust him for it."

"And what like is my Lord our master ?" asked Maude.

Alvena laughed. "Sawest ever Ursula Drew bake bread, child ?"

"Oh aye !" sighed the ex scullerymaid.

"And hast marked how the dough, ere he be set in the oven, should take any pattern thou list to set him on ?"

"Aye."

"Then thou hast seen what the Lord Earl is like."

"But who setteth pattern on the Lord Earl?" inquired Maude, looking up in some surprise.

"All the world, saving my Lady his wife, and likewise in his wrath. Hast ever seen one of our Princes in a passion of ire?"

"Never had I luck yet to see one of their Graces," said Maude reverently.

"Then thou wist not what a man *can* be like when he is angered."

"But not, I ensure me, the Lady Custance!" objected Maude, loth to surrender her Fairy Queen.

"Wait awhile and see!" was the ominous answer.

"Methought she were sweet and fair as my Lady her mother," said Maude in a disappointed tone.

"'Sweet and fair'!—and soft, is my Lady Countess. Why, child, she should hardly say this kirtle were red, an' Dame Joan told her it were green. Thou mayest do aught with her, an' thou wist how to take her."

"How take you her?" demanded Maude gravely.

"By 'r Lady! have yonder fond[1] books of the Lutterworth parson at thy tongue's end, and make up a sad[2] face, and talk of faith and grace and forgiving of sins and the like, and mine head to yon shred of tinsel an' she give thee not a gown within the se'nnight."

"But, Mistress Alvena! that were to be an hypocrite, an' you felt it not."

"Hu-te-tu! We be all hypocrites. Some of us feign for one matter, and some for other. I wis somewhat thereabout, child; for ere I came hither was I maid unto the Lady Julian,[3] recluse of Tamworth Priory. By

---

[1] Foolish. [2] Grave. [3] A fictitious person.

our dear Lady her girdle! saw I nothing of hypocrisy there!"

"You never signify, Mistress, that the blessed recluse was an hypocrite?"

"The blessed recluse was mighty fond of sweetbreads," said Alvena, taking a pin out of her mouth, "and many an one smuggled I in to her under my cloak, when Father Luke thought she was a-fasting on bread and water. And one clereful[1] night had we, she and I, when one that I knew had shot me a brace of curlews, and coming over moorland by the church, he dropped them —all by chance, thou wist! by the door of the cell. And I, oping the door—to see if it rained, trow! found these birds a-lying there. Had we no supper that night! and 'twas a vigil even. The blessed martyr or apostle (for I mind me not what day it were) forgive us!"

"But how dressed you them?" said Maude.

Alvena stopped in her fitting and pinning to laugh.

"Thou sely maid! The sacristan was my mother's brother."

Maude looked up as if she did not see the inference.

"I roasted them in the sacristy, child. The priests were all gone home to bed; and so soon as the ground were clear, mine uncle rapped of the door; and the Lady Julian came after me to the sacristy, close lapped in my cloak——"

How long Alvena might have proceeded to shock Maude's susceptibilities and outrage her preconceived opinions, it is impossible to say; for at this moment

---

[1] Glorious.

Thurstan opened the door and announced in a rather consequential manner—

"The Lord Le Despenser, to visit the Lady Custance, and Dame Margaret his sister."

Maude lifted her eyes to the height of Alvena, and found that she had to lower them to her own. A young lady of about sixteen entered, dressed in a rose-coloured silk striped with gold, and a gold-coloured mantle lined with the palest blue. She led by the hand a very pretty little boy of ten or eleven years of age, attired in a velvet tunic of that light, bright shade of apple-green which our forefathers largely used. It was edged at the neck by a little white frill. He carried in his hand a black velvet cap, from which depended a long and very full red plume of ostrich feathers. His stockings were white silk, his boots red leather, fastened with white buttons. The brother and sister were alike, but the small, delicately-cut features of both were the more delicate in the boy, and on his dark brown hair was a golden gloss which was not visible on that of his sister.

"Give you good morrow, Mistress Alvena," said Dame Margaret pleasantly. "The Lady Custance—may one have speech of her?"

Before Alvena could reply, the curtain which shrouded the door leading to the Countess's rooms was drawn aside, and Constance came forward herself.

"Good morrow, Meg," said she, kissing the young lady. "Thou hast mistaken thy road, Tom."

"Wherefore so?" asked Dame Margaret; for her little brother was silent, except that he offered a kiss in his turn, and looked rather disconcerted when no notice was taken of it.

"Why, Ned is playing quoits below, and Tom should have bidden with him. Come hither, Meg; I have a pretty thing to show thee."

"But Tom came to see your Ladysl'p."

"Well, he has seen me!" said the little Princess impatiently. "I love not lads. They are fit for nought better than playing quoits. Let them go and do it."

"What, Dickon?" said Margaret, smiling.

"Oh, Dickon!" returned Constance in a changed tone. "But Tom is not Dickon. Neither is he an angel, I wis, for I heard him gainsay once his preceptor."

Tom looked very unhappy at this raking up of by-gone misdeeds.

"Methinks your Ladyship is in ill humour this morrow," said Margaret. "Be not so hard on the lad, for he loveth you."

"When I love him, I will do him to wit," said Constance cuttingly. "Come, Meg."

Dame Margaret obeyed the command, but she kept hold of the hand of her little brother. When they were gone, Alvena laid down her work and laughed.

"Thy Queen of Faery is passing gracious, Maude."

"She scarce seemed to matter the lad," was Maude's reply.

"Yet she hath sworn to do his bidding all the days of her life," said Alvena.

"Why," said Maude, looking up in surprise, "would you say the Lady Custance is troth-plight unto this imp[1]?"

"Nay, she is wedded wife. 'Tis five years or more sithence they were wed. My Lady Custance had yea's

---

[1] Little boy.

four, and my Lord Le Despenser five. They could but just syllable their vows. And I mind me, the Lady Custance stuck at 'obey,' and she had to be threatened with a fustigation[1] ere she would go on."

"But who dared threaten her?" inquired Maude.

"Marry, my Lord her father, which fell into a fit of ire to see her perversity.—There goeth the dinner bell; lap thy work, child. For me, I am well fain to hear it."

[1] Beating, whipping.

CHAPTER III.

STRANGE TALES.

" Oh stay me not, thou holy friar !
Oh stay me not, I pray !
No drizzling rain that falls on me
Can wash my fault away." BISHOP PERCY.

ON entering the banquet-hall of Langley Palace, Maude the tire-maiden found herself promoted to a very different position from that which had been filled by Maude the scullion. Her former place had been near the door, and far below that important salt-cellar which was then the table-indicator of rank. She was directed now to take her seat as the lowest of the Countess's maidens, on a form just opposite the salt cellar, which was more than half way up the hall. Maude had hardly sat down when her next neighbour below accosted her in a familiar voice.

"Why, little Maude ! I looked for thee in vain at yon board end, and I was but now marvelling what had befallen thee. How camest up hither ?"

· Maude smiled back at Bertram Lyngern.

"It pleased the Lady's Grace to make me of her especial following."

"Long life to the Lady !—Now will I cause thee to wit who be all my friends. This on my left hand is Master Hugh Calverley, Mistress Maude (for thou art now of good degree, and must be spoken unto belike) ; he is mine especial friend, and a very knight-errant in succour of all unceli[1] damsels."

"And who is he that is next unto the Lady Custance ?"

"On her right hand, the Lord Edward, and the Lord Richard at her left—her brethren both."

Lord Richard pleased Maude. He was a winning little fellow of eight years old. But Edward she disliked instinctively : a tall, handsome boy of twelve, but completely spoiled by the supercilious curl of his lip and the proud carriage of his head.

"And the Lord Earl ?" she whispered to Bertram, who pointed out his royal master.

He was very tall, and extremely slender ; not exactly ungraceful, but he gave the impression that his arms and legs were perpetually in his way. In fact, he was a nervous man, always self-conscious, and therefore never natural nor at ease. His hair was dark auburn ; and in his lower lip there was a tremulous fulness which denoted at once great good-nature and great indecision.

It is a singular fact that the four English Princes who have borne the name of Edmund have all shared this character, of mingled gentleness and weakness ; but in each the weakness was more and the amiability less, until the dual character terminated in this last of our royal Edmunds. He was the obedient servant of any person who chose to take the trouble to be his master. And there was one person who found it worth his while to take that trouble. This individual—the Earl's youngest brother—will come across our path presently.

The dinner to day was more elaborate than usual,

---

[1] Distressed, unhappy.

for there were several guests present. Since the host was a Prince, the birds presented were served whole ; had both he and his guests been commoners, they would have been "chopped on gobbets." More interesting than any fictitious delineation on my part will be a genuine *menu* of the period, "The purveyance made for King Richard, being with the Duke of Lancaster at the Bishop's Palace of Durham at London," of course accompanied by their suites. That the suites were of no small size we gather from the provision made. It consisted of "14 oxen lying in salt, 2 oxen fresh, 120 heads of sheep fresh, 120 carcases of sheep fresh, 12 boars, 14 calves, 140 pigs ; 300 marrow-bones, of lard and grease enough, 3 tons of salt venison, 3 does of fresh venison. The poultry :—50 swans, 210 geese, 50 capons of grease (fat capons), 8 dozen other capons, 60 dozen hens, 200 couple conies (rabbits), 4 pheasants, 5 herons and bitterns, 6 kids, 5 dozen pullets for jelly, 12 dozen to roast, 100 dozen peions (peacocks), 12 dozen partridges, 8 dozen rabbits, 10 dozen curlews, 12 dozen brewes (doubtful), 12 cranes, wild fowl enough : 120 gallons milk, 12 gallons cream, 40 gallons of curds, 3 bushels of apples, eleven thousand eggs."

This tremendous supply was served in the following manner :

"The first course :—Venison with furmety ; a potage called viaundbruse (broth made with pork and onions) ; heads of boars ; great flesh (probably roast joints) ; swans roasted, pigs roasted ; crustade lumbard (custard) in paste ; and a subtlety. (The subtlety was an ornamental dish, representing a castle, ship, human figures, &c.)

"The second course :—A potage called jelly (jellies of

meat or fish were served as entrées); a potage of blande
sore (a white soup); pigs roasted ; cranes roasted; pheasants roasted ; herons roasted ; chickens roasted; breme
(pork broth ?); tarts ; brokebrawn; conies roasted ; and
a subtlety.

"The third course :—Potage brewet of almonds (another white soup, made with almonds and rabbit or
chicken broth); sewde lumbarde (probably some kind
of stew); venison roasted; chickens roasted; ıabbits
roasted ; partridges roasted ; peions roasted ; quails
roasted ; larks roasted ; payne puff (a pudding) ; a dish
of jelly; long fruits (a sweetmeat); and a subtlety."[1]

It must not be inferred that no vegetables were used,
but simply that they were not thought worth mention.
Our forefathers ate, either in vegetable or salad, almost
every green thing that grew.

Before Maude had been many days in her new position, she made various discoveries—not all pleasant
ones, and some at complete variance with her own preconceived fancies. In the first place she discovered that
her Fairy Queen, Constance, was neither more nor less
than a spoiled child. While the young Princess's affec-
t'ons were very warm, she had been little accustomed to
defer to any wishes but her own or those of her two
brothers. . The pair of boys governed their sister, but
they swayed different sceptres. Edward ruled by fear,
Richard by love. "Ned" must be attended to, because
his wont was to make himself very disagreeable if he
were not; but "Dickon" must have every thing he
wanted, because Constance could not bear to deny her
darling any thing. Bertram told Maude, however, that

<hr>

[1] Harl. MS. 4016, ff. 1, 2.

nobody could be more fascinating than Edward when he liked : the unfortunate item being that the happy circumstance very rarely occurred.

But Bertram's information was not exhausted.

"Hast heard that the Lady of Buckingham cometh hither ?"

"When ?" Maude whispered back.

"To morrow, to sup and bide the night. So thou mayest search her following for thy Mistress Hawise."

"But shall all her following follow her ?" inquired Maude.

"Every one, for she goeth anon unto her place in London to tarry the winter, and shall be here on her way thither. And hark thou, Maude ! in her train as thou shalt see   is the fairest lady in all the world."

"And what name hath she ?' was Maude's answer.

"The fair Lady de Narbonne, widow of Sir Robert de Narbonne, a good knight and true, that fell in these late wars. She hath but some twenty years e'en now, and 'tis full three summers sithence his death."

"And what like is she ?"

"Like the angels in Paradise!" said Bertram enthusiastically. "I tell thee, there is none like her in all the world."

Maude awaited the following evening with two-fold interest. She might possibly see Hawise, and she should certainly see some one who was like the angels in Paradise. The evening came, and with it the guests. One look at the Countess of Buckingham was enough. She certainly did not resemble the angels, unless they looked very cross and discontented. Her good qualities were not apparent to Maude, for they consisted of two coronets and an enormous fortune. Her ladies were much more interesting to Maude than herself. The first who entered behind her was a stiff middle-aged woman with dark hair.

"That is Dame Edusa,"[1] whispered Bertram, "the Lady Mistress. Here is Mistress Polegna—yonder little damsel with the dark locks ; and the high upright dame is Mistress Sarah. She that cometh after is the Lady de Say."

Not one of these was the golden-haired Cousin *Hawise*, whose years barely numbered twenty. Maude's eyes had come back in disappointment, when Bertram touched her arm.

"Now, Maude look now ! Look, the beauteous Lady de Narbonne ![1] Sawest ever maiden meet to be her peer ?"

Maude looked, and saw a young girlish figure, splendidly attired,—a rich red and white complexion, beautiful blue eyes, and a sunny halo of shining fair hair. But she saw as well, a cold, hard curve of the delicate lips, a proud cynical expression in the handsome eyes, a bold, forward manner. Yes, Maude admitted, the Lady de Narbonne was beautiful ; yet she did not care to look at her. Bertram was disappointed. And so was Maude, for all hope of finding Hawise had disappeared.

When supper was over, the tables were lifted. The festive board was at this time literally a board or boards, which were simply set upon trestles to form a table. At the close of a meal, the tables were reduced to their primitive elements, and boards and trestles were either carried away, or heaped in one corner of the hall. The

[1] A fictitious person.

dining-room was thus virtually transmuted into the draw-ing-room, ceremony and precedence being discarded for the rest of the evening—state occasions of course excepted, and the royal persons present not being addressed unless they chose to commence a conversation.

Maude kept pretty strictly to her corner all that evening. She was generally shy of strangers, and none of these were sufficiently attractive to make her break through her usual habits. Least attractive of all, to her, was the lovely Lady de Narbonne. Her light, airy ways, which seemed to enchant the Earl's knights and squires, simply disgusted Maude. She was the perpetual centre of a group of frivolous idlers, who dangled round her in the hope of leading her to a seat, or picking up a dropped glove. She laughed and chatted freely with them all, distributing her smiles and frowns with entire impartiality—except in one instance. One member of the Earl's household never came within her circle, and he was the only one whom she seemed at all desirous to attract. This was Hugh Calverley. He held aloof from the bright lamp around which all the other moths were fluttering, and Maude fancied that he admired the queen of the evening as little as she did herself.

All at once, by no means to Maude's gratification, the lady chose to rise and walk across the room to her corner.

"And what name hast thou, little maid?" she asked, with a light swing of her golden pomander—the vinai-grette of the Middle Ages.

Maude had become very tired of being asked her name, the more so since it was the manner in which strangers usually opened negociations with her. She found it the less agreeable because she was conscious of no right to any surname, her mother's being the only one she knew. So she answered "Maude" rather shortly.

"Maude—only Maude?"

"Only Maude. Madam, might it like your Ladyship to tell me if you wit of one Hawise Gerard anything?"

If the Lady de Narbonne would talk to her, Maude resolved to utilise the occasion; though she felt there could be little indeed in common between her gentle, modest cousin, and this far from retiring young widow That they could not have been intimate friends Maude was sure; but acquaintances they might be—and must be, unless the Lady de Narbonne had been too short a time at Pleshy to know Hawise. As Maude in speaking lifted her eyes to the lady's face, she saw the smiling lips grow suddenly grave, and the cold bright light die out of the beaming eyes.

"Child," said the Lady de Narbonne seriously, "Hawise Gerard is dead."

"Woe is me! I feared so much," answered Maude sorrowfully. "And might it please you, Madam, to arede[1] me fully when she died, and how, and where?"

"She died to thee, little maid, when she went to the Castle of Pleshy," was the unsatisfactory answer.

"May I wit no more, Madam? Your Ladyship knew her, trow?"

"Once," said the lady, with a slight quiver of her lower lip, "— long, long ago!" And she suddenly turned her head, which had been for a moment averted from Maude, round towards her. "'When, and how, and where'?" she repeated. "Little maid, some dying is

[1] Tell.

E

slower than men may tell the hour, and there be graves that are not dug in earth. Thy cousin Hawise is dead and gone. Forget her."

"That can I never!" replied Maude tenderly, as the memory of her dead came fresh and warm upon her.

The Lady de Narbonne rose abruptly, and walked away, without another word, to the further end of the room. Half an hour later, Maude saw her in the midst of a gay group, laughing and jesting in the cheeriest manner. Of what sort of stuff could the woman be made?

The Countess of Buckingham did not leave Langley until after dinner the next day—that is to say, about eleven a.m. A little before dinner, as Maude, not being wanted at the moment, stood alone at the window of the hall, leaning her arms on the wide window-ledge, a voice asked behind her,—" Art yet thinking of Hawise Gerard?"

"I was so but this moment, Madam," replied Maude, turning round to meet the eyes of the Lady de Narbonne, now quiet and grave enough. "'Tis little marvel, for I loved her dear."

"And love lasteth with thee—how long time?"

"Till death, assuredly," said Maude. "What may lie beyond death I wis nothing."

"Till what manner of death? The resurrection, men say, shall give back the dead. But what shall give back a dead heart or a lost soul? Can thy love pass such death as this, Maude Gerard?"

"Madam, I said never unto your Ladyship that Hawise Gerard was kinswoman of mine. How wit you the same?"

A faint, soft smile, very unlike her usual one, so bright and cold, flickered for a moment on the lips of the Lady de Narbonne.

"Not too far gone for that, Cousin Maude," she said.

"'Cousin'—— Madam! You are ——"

"I am Avice de Narbonne, waiting dame unto my Lady of Buckingham's Grace. I was Hawise Gerard, David Gerard's daughter."

"Hawise! Thou toldest me she was dead!" cried Maude confusedly.

"That Hawise Gerard whom thou knewest is dead and gone, long ago. Thou wilt never see *her* again. Thy mother Eleanor is not more dead than she; but the one may return to thee on the resurrection morrow, and the other never can. Tell me now whether I could arede thee, as thou wouldst have had it, how, or where, or when, thy cousin Hawise died ?"

"Our dear Lady be thine aid, Hawise! What has changed thee so sore?" asked Maude, the tears running down her cheeks.

"Call me Avice, Maude. Hawise is old-fashioned," said the lady coolly.

Maude seized her cousin's hands, and looking into her eyes, spoke as girls of her age rarely speak, though they think frequently.

"Come back to me, Hawise Gerard!—from the dead, if thou wilt have it so. Cousin Hawise—fair, gent, shamefaced, loving, holy! come back to me, and speak with the olden voice, and give me to wit what terrible thing hath been, to take away thyself, and leave but this instead of thee!"

Maude's own earnestness was so intense, that she felt

as if her passionate words must have moved a granite mountain ; but they fell cold and powerless upon Avice de Narbonne.

"Look out into the dark this night, Maude, and call thy mother, and see whether she will answer. The dead *cannot* come back. I have no more power to call back to thee the maiden I was of old, than thou. Rest, maid ; and do what thou wilt and canst with that which is."

"What can I ?" said Maude bitterly. "At least thou canst tell me what hath wrought this fearful change in thee."

"Can I ?" replied Avice, seating herself on the window-seat, and motioning her cousin to do the same. "And what shall I say it were—call it light or darkness, love or hate ? For six months after I left home I was right woesome. (It is all gone, Maude—the old cottage, and the forge, and the elms they razed them all !) And then there came into my life a fair false face, and a voice that spake well, and an heart that was black as night. And I trusted him, for I loved him. Loved him aye, better than all the saints in Heaven ! I could have died to save a pang of pain to him, and smiled in doing it. But he was false, false, false ! And on the day that I knew it O that horrible day !—my love turned to black hate within me. I knelt and prayed that my wrong should be avenged—that some sorrow should befal him. But I never meant that. Holy Mary, Lady of Sorrows, thou knewest I never meant *that !* And that very night I knelt and prayed, he died on the field of battle far away. I knew not he was in danger till four days after. When I so did, I prayed as fervently for his safety. The old love came back upon me, and I could have rent the heavens if my weak hands had reached them, to undo that fearful prayer. But she heard me not—she, the Lady of Pity! She had heard me once too well. And fifteen days later, I knew that I was a widow that he had died that night, with none to pillow his head or wipe the death-dews from his brow —died unassoiled, unatoned with either God or me! And I had done it. Child, my heart was closed up that day as with a wall of stone. It will never open again. It is not my love that is dead—it is my heart."

"But, Hawise, hadst no masses sung for his soul?" asked Maude in loving pity.

"Too late," she said, dropping her face upon her hands. "Too late!"

"Too late for what?" softly inquired a third voice— so gently and compassionately that no annoyance could be felt.

Avice was silent, and Maude answered for her.

"For the winning of a soul from Purgatory that hath passed thither without housel ne chrism."

"Too late for the mercy of God?" replied Hugh Calverley gently. "For the housel and the chrism, they be mercies of man. But the mercies of God are infinite and unchangeable unto all such as grip hold on Jesu Christ."

"Unto them that die in mortal sin?" said Avice, not lifting her head.

"All sin is mortal," said Hugh in the same quiet manner; "but for His people, He hath made an end of sin, and hath 'distreiede[1] deeth, and lightnide[2] lyf.'"

"That is, for the saints?" said Maude sadly.

---

[1] Destroyed.   [2] Brought to light.

"Mistress, an' it had not been for the sinners, you and I must needs have fared ill. Who be saints saving they that were once sinners?"

"Soothly, Master Calverley, these be matters too high for me. I am no saint, God wot."

"Doth God wot that, Mistress Maude? Then of a surety I am sorry for you."

Maude was silent, though she thought it strange doctrine. But Avice said in a low voice, recurring to her former subject, "You believe, Master Calverley, that God can raise the dead; but think you that He can quicken again to life an heart that is dead, and cold, and hard as yonder stone? Is there any again rising for such?"

"Madam, if no, there had been never none for neither you nor me. We be all dead souls by nature."

"Aye, afore baptism, so wit I; but what of mortal sin done after baptism?"

"I speak but as I am learned, Madam," said Hugh modestly. "I am younger even than you, methinks, and far more witless. But I have heard them say that have been deep skilled, as methinks, in the ministeries[1] of God, that wherein it is said that 'He mai saue withouten ende,' it scarce signifieth only afore baptism."

"Ah!" said Maude, with a sigh, "to do away sin done after baptism is a mighty hard and grievous matter. Good sooth, at my first communion, this last summer, so abashed[2] was I, and in so painful bire,[3] that I let drop the holy wafer upon the ground; and for all I gat it again unbroke, and licked well with my tongue the stide[4] where it had fallen, Father Dominic[5] said I had

---

[1] Mysteries.   [2] Nervous.   [3] Confused haste.
[4] Spot.   [5] A fictitious person.

done dreadful sin, and he caused me to crawl upon my knees all around the church, and to say an hundred Ave Marys and ten Paternosters at every altar. And in very deed I was right sorrowful for mine ill mischance; nor could I help the same, for I saw not the matter rightly. But Father Dominic said our Lord should be right sore offenced with me, and mine only hope lay in moving the mercy of our dear-worthy Lady to plead with Him. If it be not wicked to say the same," added she timidly, "I would God were not angered with us for such like small gear. But I count our Lady heard me, sith Father Dominic was pleased to absolve me at last."

"Will you give me leave to say a thing, Mistress Maude?"

"I pray you so do, Master Calverley."

"Then if the same hap should chance unto you again, I counsel you to travail[1] yourself neither with Father Dominic nor our Lady, but to go straight to our Lord Himself. Maybe He were pleased to absolve you something sooner than Father Dominic. Look you, the priest died not to atone God for your sins, neither our Lady did not. And if it be, as men do say, that commonly the mother is more fond[2] unto the child than any other, by reason she hath known more travail and pain[3] with him, then surely in like manner He that hath borne death for our sins shall be more readier to assoil them than he that no did."

These were bold words to speak in the year of grace 1385. But the Queen's squire, John Calverley, was one of those advanced Lollards of whom there were very few, and his son had learned of him. Even Wycliffe

<hr>

[1] Trouble.   [2] Foolishly indulgent.   [3] Labour.

himself would scarcely have dared to venture so far as this, until the latter years of his life. It takes long to convince men that no lesser advocate is needed between them and the one Mediator with God. And where they are taught that "Mary is the human side of Jesus," the result generally is that they lose sight of the humanity of Jesus altogether.

It was not, therefore, unnatural that Maude's answer should have been,—"But, Master Calverley! so saying you should have no need of our Lady." She expected Hugh to reply by an indignant denial; and it astounded her no little to hear him quietly accept the unheard-of alternative.

"Do you as you list, Mistress Maude," he answered. "For me, I am content with our Lord."

"Well-a-day! methought all pity[1] lay in worship of our Lady!" said Maude, in that peculiar constrained tone which implies that the speaker feels himself the infinitely distant superior of his antagonist.

"Mistress," was Hugh's answer, "I never said that I was content without our Lord. I lack an advocate, to the full as well as any; but Saint Paul saith that 'oo[2] God and a mediatour is of God and of men, a man, Christ Jesu.' And methinks he should be a sorry mediator that lacked an advocate himself."

Avice had lifted her head, and had fixed her eyes intently on Hugh. She had said nothing more; she was learning.

"Likewise saith He," resumed Hugh, "that 'no man cometh to the Fadir but by me.' Again, 'no man may come to me but if the Fadir that hath sente me drawe

---

[1] Piety.   [2] One.

him :' yet 'all thing that the Fadir gyueth me schal come to me.'"

Avice spoke at last.

"'All thing given' and none other? Then without we be given, we may not come. And how shall a man wit so much?"

"Methinks, Madam," said Hugh, thoughtfully, "that if a man be willing to come, and to give himself, he hath therein witness that he was given of the Father."

"But to give himself wholly unto God," added Maude, "signifieth that he shall take no more pleasure in this life?"

"Try it," responded Hugh, "and see if it signifieth not rather that a man shall enter into joys he never knew aforetime. God's gifts to us prevent our gifts to Him."

"Lady Avice! Dame Edusa hath asked twice where you be," said Polegna, running into the hall. "The bell shall sound in an other minute, and our Lady maketh no tarrying after dinner."

So the trio were parted. There was no opportunity after dinner for anything beyond a farewell, and Maude, with her heart full of many thoughts, went back to her sewing in the antechamber.

About an hour after Maude had resumed her work, Constance strolled into the room in search of amusement. She looked at the crimson tunic and black velvet skirt which were in making for her own wear at the coming Easter festival; gazed out of the window for ten minutes; sat and watched Maude work for about five; and at last, a bright idea striking her, put it into action.

"Doña Juana! lacked you Maude a season?"

Half an hour previous, Juana had been urging on her workwomen with reminders that very little time was left before the dresses must be ready ; but Maude had learned now that in the eyes of the Mistress, Constance's will was law, and she therefore received with little surprise the order to "sue the Señorita." Resigning her work into the hands of Sybil, Maude followed her imperious little lady into the chamber of Dame Agnes de La Marche, who was busy arranging fresh flax for her spinning.

"Your fingers be busy, Dame Agnes," observed the little Princess. "Is your tongue at leisure ?"

"Both be alway at your service, Damosel," replied the courtly old lady.

"Then, I pray you, tell to me and Maude your fair story of the Lyonesse."

"With a very good will."

"Then, prithee, set about it,' said Constance, ensconcing herself in the big chair. "Sit thou on that stool, Maude."

The old lady took her distaff, now ready, and sat down, smiling at the impatience of the capricious child.

"Once upon a time," she began, "the ending of the realm of England was not that stide[1] which men now call the Land's End in Cornwall. Far beyond, even as far as the Isles of Scilly, stretched the fair green plains : a kingdom lay betwixt the two, and men called it La Lyonesse. And in the good olden days, when Arthur was king, the Lyonesse had her prince, and on her plains and hills were fair rich cities, and through her forests pricked good knights on the quest of the Holy Grail,[2] that none, save unsinning eyes, might ever see.

---

[1] Place.

[2] The "Holy Grail" was one of the most singular of Romish super-

For of all the four and twenty Knights of the Round
Table, none ever saw the Holy Grail save one, and that
was Sir Galahad, that was pure of heart and clean of
life. Howbeit, one night came a mighty tempest. The
sea raged and roared on the Cornish coast, and dashed
its waters far up the rocks, washing the very walls of
the Castle of Tintagel. And they that saw upon that
night told after, that there came one wild flash of lightning that lightened sky and earth; and men looked and
saw by its light, statelily standing, the rich cities and
green forests of the Lyonesse; and then came black
darkness, and a roar, and a crash, and a rending, as
though all the rocks and the mountains should be
torent;[1] and then another wild flash lightened sky and
earth, and men looked, and the rich ci..ies and green
forests of the Lyonesse were gone."

Maude was listening entranced, with parted lips; Constance carelessly, as if she knew all about it beforehand,
and were chiefly amusing herself by watching the rapt
face of her fellow-listener.

"Long years thereafter," resumed Dame Agnes, "aye,
and even now, men said and say, that at times ye may
yet hear the sound and see the sight of the drowned
cities of the Lyonesse. Ever sithence that tempestuous
night, the deep green sea lies heavy on the bosom of

stitions. A glass vessel, supported by a foot, was shown to the people as
the cup in which Christ gave the wine to His disciples at the Last Supper;
and they were taught, not only that Joseph of Arimathea had caught the
blood from His side in the same vessel, but that he and Mary Magdalene,
sailing on Joseph's shirt, had brought over the relic from Palestine to Glas-
tonbury. "The Quest of the Saint Graal" was the highest achievement
of the Knights of the Round Table.

[1] Violently torn asunder.

the lost land; and no man of unpure heart, nor of evil life, ne unbaptized, ne unshriven, may see nor hear. But if one of Christian blood, a christened man, pure of heart and clean in life, that is newly shriven, whether man or maid, will sail forth at midnight over the green sea, and when he cometh to the place where lieth the Lyonesse, will bend him down from the boat, and look and listen, then shall come up around his ears soft weird music from the church bells in the silver steeples of the doomed cities: yea, and there have been so pure, and our Lady hath shown them such grace, that they have seen the very self streets down at the bottom of the sea, where the dead walk and speak as they did of old— the knights and the ladies, as in the days gone by, when Arthur was King, a thousand years ago, when he held his court in the palaces of the lost land. And the Islands of Scilly, as men say, be the summits of the mountains, that towered once hoary and barren over the green forests and the rich cities."[1]

The story was being told to an uncritical and un-chronological audience, or Dame Agnes might have received a gentle intimation that she was antedating the reign of King Arthur by the short period of two hundred years.

The silence which followed—for both the little girls were meditating on the story, and Dame Agnes's flax was just then entangled in a troublesome knot—was broken, suddenly and very thoroughly, by the unex-pected entrance, quiet though it were, of the Countess herself. Dame Agnes gave no heed to her broken thread, but rose instantly, distaff in hand, with a low reverence;

---

[1] This story is a veritable legend of the Middle Ages.

Constance rubbed her sleepy eyes and slowly descended from her great chair; while Maude, recalled to the present, dropped her lowest courtesy and stood waiting.

There was a peculiar air about the Countess Isabel, which suggested to bystanders the idea of a tired, worn-out woman. It was not discontent, not irritability, not exactly even sadness; it was the tone of one who had never fitted rightly into the place assigned to her, and who never felt at home. Though it disappeared when she spoke, yet as soon as her features were at rest it came again. It was little wonder that her face wore such an expression, for she was the daughter of a murdered father and a slandered mother, and the wife of a man who valued her very highly as the Infanta of Castilla, but as Isabel his wife not at all. During her early years, she had sought rest and comfort in the world. She plunged wildly into every manner of dissipation and pleasure; like Solomon, she withheld not her heart from any good; and like Solomon's, her verdict at the close was "Vanity and vexation of spirit." And then—just when she had arrived at the conclusion that there was nothing upon earth worth living for—when she had "come to the end of everything, and cared for nothing," she met with an old priest of venerable aspect, a trusted servant of King Edward, whose first words touched the deepest chord in her heart, while his second brought the healing balm. His name was John de Wycliffe. Was it any wonder that she accepted him as a very angel of God?

For he showed her where rest was, not within, but without; not from beneath, nor from around, but from above. So the tired heart rested in Jesus here, looking forward to its perfected rest in the presence of Jesus hereafter.

For so far as the world was concerned, there was no rest any longer. It was fearfully up-hill work for Isabel to aim at such a walk as should please God. Her husband did not oppose her; he was as profoundly indifferent to her new opinions and practices as he had been to her old ones, as he was to herself. So far as her life was concerned, of the two he considered that she had altered for the better There had never been but one heart which had loved Isabel, and that heart she pierced as with a sword when she entered her new path on the narrow way.

To Constança of Castilla, the sister who had shared with her their "heritage of woe," this younger sister was inexpressibly dear. The two sisters had married two brothers, and they saw a good deal of each other until that time; but after Isabel cast in her lot with Wycliffe, very little. The Gospel parted these loving sisters as with a sword; the magnet was received by each at an opposite end. It attracted Isabel, and repelled Constança. The elder wanted nothing more than she had always had; the gorgeous ceremonies and absolving priests of the old Church satisfied her, and she demanded no further comfort. She was "a woman devout above all others" in the eyes of the monkish chroniclers. And that usually meant that in this world she never awoke to her soul's uttermost need, and she was therefore content with the meagre supply she found. So the difference between the sisters was that Constança slept peacefully while Isabel had awoke.

It was because Isabel had awoke, that she was unsatisfied with the round of ritual observances which were all in all to her sister. She could confess to man, and be absolved by man ; but how could she wrestle against the conviction that she rose from the confessional with a soul none the cleaner, with a heart just as disinclined to go and sin no more? The branches might be lopped; but what mattered that while the root of bitterness remained? It is only when we hear God say, "Thy sins are forgiven thee," that it is possible to go in peace And Isabel never heard it until she came to Him. Then, when she came empty-handed, He filled her hands with gifts ; He breathed into the harassed soul rest and hope.

This was what God gave her. But men gave her something very different. They had nothing better for this woman that had been a sinner, than the old comment of Simon the Pharisee. *They* were not ready to cast the remembrance of her iniquities into the depths of the sea—far from it. What they gave her was a scorned and slandered name, a character sketched in words that dwelt gloatingly on her early devotion to the world, the flesh, and the Devil, and left unwritten the story of her subsequent devotion to God. The later portion of her life is passed over in silence. We see something of its probable character in the supreme contempt of the monkish chroniclers ; in the heretical epithet of "pestilent" applied to her ; in the Lollard terms of her last will ; in her choice of eminent Lollards as executors ; in her bosom friendship with the Lollard Queen.

But at another Table from that of Simon the Pharisee, "many that are first shall be last, and the last first."

We have kept Maude standing for a long while, before her mistress, seated in the great chair in Dame Agnes de La Marche's chamber.

"And how lovest thy new fashion of life, my maid?" demanded the Countess, when she had taken her seat.

"Right well, an' it like your Grace."

"Thou art here welsomer[1] than in the kitchen?"

"Surely so, Madam."

"Dame Joan speaketh well of thy cunning."[2]

Maude smiled and courtesied. She was gradually learning Court manners.

"And hast thou yet thy book-leaf, the which I read unto thee?"

"Oh aye, Madam!"

"'Thy book-leaf!'" interjected Constance. "What book hast thou?"

"A part of God's Word, my daughter," replied her mother gravely; "touching His great City, the holy Jerusalem, which shall come down from God out of Heaven, and is lightened with His glory."

"When will it come?" said Constance, with unwonted gravity.

"God wot. To all seeming, not ere thou and I be either within the same, or without His gates for ever."

The Countess turned back to Maude.

"My maid, thou wouldst fain know at that time whether I had any dwelling in that city. Wist thou that an' thou wilt, there thou mayest dwell?"

"I, Madam! In very sooth, should it like your Grace to take me?" And Maude's eyes sparkled with delight.

"I cannot take thee, my child!" was the reply, spoken

_____
[1] More comfortable.   [2] Skill.

in a tone so grave that it was almost sad. "If thou wouldst go, it is Another must bear thee thither."

"The Lady Custance?" inquired Maude, glancing at her.

"The Lord Jesus Christ."

Agnes mechanically crossed herself. Maude's memory ran far back.

"Sister Christian, that was a nun at Pleshy," she observed, dreamily, "was wont to say, long time agone, unto Mother and me, that holy Mary's Son did love us and die for us; but I never wist nought beyond that. Would your Grace, of your goodness, tell me wherefore it were?"

"Wherefore He died? It was in the stead of thee, my maid, if thou wilt have it so: He died that thou mightest never die withouten end.—Or wherefore He loved, wouldst know? Truly, I can but bid thee ask that of Himself, for none wist that mystery save His own great heart. There was nought in us that He should love us; but there was every cause in Himself wherefore He should love."

Maude was silent; but the thought which she was revolving in her mind was whether any great saint had ever asked such a question of Him who to her was only "holy Mary's Son." Of course it would have to be asked through Mary. No one, not even the greatest saint, considered Maude, had ever spoken direct to Him, except in a vision. The next remark of the Countess rather startled her.

"My maid, dost ever pray?"

"An' it like your Grace, I do say every even the Hail Mary, and every morrow the Credo; and of Sundays and holy days likewise the Paternoster."

"And didst never feel no want ne lack, for the which thou findest not words in the Hail Mary ne in the Credo, if it be not an holy day?"

Aye, many a want, as Maude well knew: but what had Credo or Angelus to do with wants? Prayer, in her eyes, meant either long repetitions imposed as penances by the priest, or else the daily use of a charm, the omission of which might entail evil consequences. Of prayer as a real means of procuring something about which she cared, she had no more notion than Dame Agnes's squirrel, at that moment running round his cage, had of the distance and extent of Sherwood Forest. Maude looked up in the face of her mistress with an expression of deep perplexity.

"Child," said the Countess, "when Dame Joan would send word touching some matter unto Dame Agnes here, falleth she a-saying unto herself of Dan Chaucer's brave Romaunt of The Flower and the Leaf?"

"Surely, no, Madam."

"Then what doth she?"

"She cometh unto her," said Maude, immediately adding, in a matter-of-fact way, "without she should send Mistress Sybil or some other."

"Good. Then arede[1] me wherefore thou shouldst fall a-saying the Credo when thou wouldst send word of thy need unto God, any more than Dame Joan should fall a-saying the Romaunt?"

"But God heareth us, and conceiveth us, Madam," said Maude timidly, "and Dame Agnes no doth."

"Truth, my maid. Therein faileth my parable. But setting this aside, tell me,—how shall the Credo give to wit thy need?"

[1] Inform.

Maude cogitated for a minute in silence. Then she answered,

"No shall it, Madam."

"Then wherefore not speak thy lack straightway?"

Maude was silent, but not because she was stupid.

"My maid, what saith the Credo? When thus thou prayest, dost thou aught save look up to Heaven, and say, 'God, I believe in Thee'? So far as it goeth, good. But seest not that an' thou shouldst say to me, 'Madam, I crede and trust you,' thou shouldst have asked nought from me—have neither confessed need, ne presented petition? The Credo is matter said to men—not to God. Were it not better to say, 'Lord, I love Thee'? Or best of all, 'Lord, love Thou me'?"

"I wis, Madam, that our Lord loveth the saints," said Maude in a low voice.

She felt very much in the condition graphically described by John Bunyan as "tumbled up and down in one's mind."

"Ah, child!" was the Countess's answer, "they be lost sheep whom Christ seeketh. And whoso Christ setteth out to seek shall, sooner or later, find the way to Him."

CHAPTER IV.

IN THE SCRIPTORIUM.

"There are days of deepest sorrow
In the season of our life;
There are wild, despairing moments,
There are hours of mental strife;
There are times of stony anguish,
When the tears refuse to fall;
But the waiting time, my brothers,
Is the hardest time of all."—SARAH DOUDNEY.

BESIDE a Gothic window, and under a groined stone roof, that afternoon sat a monk at his work. The work was illumination. The room was bare of all kinds of furniture, with the exception of a wooden erection which was chair and desk in one. On the desk lay a large square piece of parchment, a future leaf of a book, in which the text was already written, but the illuminated border was not yet begun. There was a pen in the monk's hand, with which he was about to execute the outline; but the pen was dry, and the old man's eyes were fixed dreamily upon the landscape without.

"'In wisdom hast Thou made them all,'" he murmured half audibly. "O Lord, 'the earth is full of Thy riches!'"

It was early morning, for the illuminator was at work betimes. From a little cottage visible across the green, he saw a peasant go forth to his daily work, his wife watching him a moment from the door of the hut, and two little children calling to him lovingly to come back soon.

"And life also is full of Thy riches," whispered the solitary monk. "This poor hind hath none other riches than what Thine hand hath given him. Is he in truth the poorer for it? We live on Thy daily bounty even more than he; for like Thy lilies, we toil not, neither do we spin. Yet Thou hast given to him, as sweetening to his toil, solace denied by Thy holy will to us. Wherefore denied to us? Because we are set apart for Thee. So were Thy priests of old, in Thy Temple at Jerusalem: yet it was not denied to them. Why should we love Thee less for loving little children?"

The monk turned back abruptly to his work.

"Ah me! these be problems beyond mine art. And whatso be the solving of the general matter, I have no doubt as to Thy will *for me*. The joys of earth be not for me; but Thou art my portion, O Lord! And I am content—aye, satisfied abundantly. Maybe, on the golden hills of the *Urbs Beata*, we shall find joys far passing the sweetest here, kept for that undefouled company which shall sue the Lamb whithersoever He goeth. And could any joy pass that?"

The venerable head was bent over the parchment, upon which the grotesque outline of a griffin began to grow, twisted round a very conventional tree, with the stem issuing from its mouth, and its elongated tail executing marvellous spiral curves. The illuminator was taken by surprise the next instant, and the curve of the griffin's tail then pending was by no means round in consequence.

"Alway at work, Father Wilfred[1]?"

"Bertram Lyngern," said the monk calmly, "thou hast marred my griffin."

"What, have I made him a wyvern?"

"That had less mattered. A twist of his tail is square, thy sudden speech being the cause thereof."

"Let be, Father Wilfred. 'Tis a new pattern."

The monk smiled, but shook his head, and proceeded to erase the faulty strokes by means of a large piece of pumice stone. Bertram sat contemplating his friend's work, curled up in the wide stone window-ledge, to which he had climbed from the horse-block below it. The lattice was open, so there was no hindrance to conversation.

"I would I were a knight!' said Bertram suddenly, after a few minutes' silence on both sides.

"To wear gilded spurs?" inquired Wilfred calmly resuming his pen, and going on with the griffin.

"Thou countest me surely not such a loon, Father Wilfred? No,—I long to be great. I feel as though greatness stirred within me. But what can I do,—a squire? If I were a knight I could sign my shoulder with the holy cross, and go fight for our Lord's sepulchre. That were something worth. But to dangle at the heels of my Lord Edward all the day long, and fly an half-dozen hawks, and meditate on pretty sayings to the Lady's damsels, and eat venison, and dance—Father Wilfred, is this life meet for a man's living?"

---

[1] A fictitious person.

The illuminator laid his pen down, and looked up at the lad.

"Bertram," he said, "just fifty years gone, I was what thou art, and my thoughts then were thine."

"Thou wert, Father?" responded Bertram in an interested tone. "Well, and what was the end?"

"The end is not yet. But the next thing was, that I did as thou fain wouldst do: I signed me with the good red cross, and I went to the Holy Land."

"And thou camest back, great of name, and blessed in soul?"

"I came back, having won no name, and with no blessing, for I knew more of evil than when I set forth."

"But, Father, at our Lord's sepulchre!" urged Bertram.

"Youngling," said Wilfred, a rare, sweet smile flitting across his lips, "dost thou blunder as Mary did? Is the Lord yet in the sepulchre? 'He is not here; He is risen.' And why then should His sepulchre be holier than other graves, when He that made the holiness is there no longer?"

"But where then is our Lord?" asked Bertram, rather perplexed.

"He is where thou wouldst have Him," was the quiet answer. "If that be in thine heart, aye :—and if no, no."

Bertram meditated for a little while upon this reply.

"But seest thou any reason, Father, wherefore I should not become a great man?" he said, reverting to his original topic.

"I see no reason at all, Bertram Lyngern, wherefore thou shouldst not become a very great man."

Still Bertram was dissatisfied. He had an instinctive

suspicion that his great man and Wilfred's were not exactly the same person.

" But what meanest by a great man, Father?"

" What meanest thou?"

" I mean a warrior," said the lad, "dauntless in war, and faithful in love—brave, noble, and high-souled, alway and every whither."

" And so mean I."

" But I mean one that men shall talk of, and tell much of his noble deeds and mighty prowess."

" Were he less brave without?"

" He were less puissant, Father."

Wilfred did not reply for a minute, but devoted himself to hanging golden apples from the stiff boughs of his very medieval tree.

" The heroes of the world and those of the Church," he said at last, "be rarely the same men. A man cannot be an hero in all things. The warrior is not the statesman, nor is neither of them the bishop. Thou must choose thy calling, lad."

" Yet a true hero must be an hero all the world over, Father—in every calling."

" How much hast heard of one Master Vegelius?"

" Never afore this minute."

" I thought so much."

" Who was he?" inquired Bertram.

" The best and most cunning limner of this or any land."

" Oh! Only a scriptorius?"

" Only a scriptorius," said the monk quietly—not at all offended. "And it may be that he never heard of some of thy heroes."

"My heroes are Alexander and Charlemagne," said Bertram proudly. "He must have heard of them."

Wilfred dipped his pen in the ink with a rather amused smile.

"Now, Father Wilfred!"

"I was only thinking, lad, that when I set up my hero, he shall not be a man that met his death in a wine-butt."

"What?—Oh! Alexander. Well, we have all our failings," admitted Bertram, reluctant to give up his favourite.

"Thou sayest sooth, lad."

"Father Wilfred, who is thine hero?"

"Wist thou who is God's hero?" asked the illuminator, laying down his pen, and fixing his eyes on the boy. "God Himself once told men who was their greatest. And who was it, countest?"

"Was it Charlemagne?" eagerly responded the un-chronological Bertram.

"'Among men that are born of women, there hath not risen a greater than —— '"

"Whom?" interpolated the boy, when Wilfred paused.

"'John the Baptist.'"

Bertram's face fell with a most disappointed look.

"Why, what did he? How was he great?"

"He was great in four matters, methinks, in one whereof only thou or I may not have leave to follow him. In that he foreran our Lord, his deed is beyond our reach: but in three other concernments, in no wise. Firstly, he preached Christ."

"That the priests do," interjected Bertram.

"Do they so?" asked Wilfred rather drily. "Secondly,

he feared not, when need were, to gainsay a master in whose hand lay his life. And lastly, he knew how to deny himself."

"But, Father Wilfred! all those be easy enough."

"Be they so, lad? How many times hast tried them?"

"In good sooth, never tried I any of them," said Bertram honestly.

"Then wait ere thou say so much."

There was another pause; and then Bertram found another question.

"Father Wilfred, what thinkest of Sir John de Wycliffe?"

"I never brake bread with him, lad," said the monk, busy with the griffin.

"But what thinkest?"

"How should I know?"

Evidently the illuminator did not mean to commit himself.

"Is he a great man or a small?"

"God wot," said the monk.

"Hugh Calverley saith he is the greatest man that ever lived," said Bertram.

"Greater than St. John Baptist?"

"His work is of the like sort," pursued Bertram meditatively. "'Tis preaching and reproving men of their sins."

"God speed all His work!" said the monk.

"Father, what didst after thy turning back from Holy Land?"

"What all men do once a life. What thou wilt do."

"Marry, what so?"

"Why, I became a fool."

"Father Wilfred! I counted thee alway a wise man."

"A sorry blunder, lad," said Wilfred, putting in the griffin's teeth.

"Wouldst say a Court fool?"

"Nay—a worser fool than that."

"How so?"

"I trusted a woman," answered Wilfred,—bitterly, for him.

"Father! hadst thou ever a lady-love?"

Bertram's interest was intense at this juncture.

"Go to, Bertram Lyngern!" answered the monk, looking up with a smile. "Be thy thoughts on lady-loves already? Nay, lad; she that I trusted was a kinswoman—no love. Little love in very deed was there betwixt us. And yet—" his voice altered suddenly— "I knew what that was too—once."

"And she mocked thee, trow?" asked Bertram, who expected a small sensation novel to spring out of this avowal.

Wilfred worked in silence for a minute. Then he said in a low tone, "Forty years' violets have freshened and faded on her grave; nor one of all of them more fair ne sweet than she." But there was something in his manner which said, "Question me no further." And, curious as Bertram was, he obeyed the tacit request.

"And what stood next in thy life, Father?"

"This, lad," said the monk, touching his cowl.

Bertram did not consider this by any means satisfactory.

"Well! All said, Father Wilfred, we come back to the first matter. What wouldst thou do an' thou wert I?"

"Soothly, that wis I not," said the illuminator rather drily. "What thou shouldst do an' thou wert I, might be easier gear."

"Well—and that were?"

"To set claws unto this griffin."

"Now, Father Wilfred! My work is not to paint griffins."

"What thy work is, do," replied the monk sententiously.

"But 'tis sheer idlesse! 'Tis not work at all. It is but to wait till I am called to work."

"The waiting is harder than the work," replied Wilfred, again laying down his pen. 'If thou be well assured that waiting is thy work, wit thou that 'tis matter worthy of the wits of angels, for there is no work harder than to wait for God."

"But 'tis not *work*, Father!"

"If thou so think, thou art not yet master of that art."

"Of what art?"

"Waiting." Wilfred's pen pursued its journey for a moment before he added, "Lad, this that I am on is but play and revelry. But the lack thereof—the time passed in awaiting till the lad that enscribeth the text have fresh parchment ready—that is work."

Bertram frowned and pursed his lips as if he could not see it.

"For forty years, Bertram, all the wisdom of the wisest nation in the world was sometime taught unto a man named Moyses. His woik was to lead the chosei. folk of God into the land that God should give them. But at the end of that forty years, he was but half learned. So for other forty years, he was sent into a wilderness for to keep sheep."

"Why, he were past work then!"

"Nay, he was but then ready for it."

"And did he lead the folk after all?"

"He did so."

"And what gave him our Lord for guerdon, when his toil was done?

"Was the work no guerdon?" responded Wilfred thoughtfully. "Well, lad, He gave him—a grave in Moab, far away from home and friends and country, and from His land."

"Father, what mean you? That was no guerdon!"

"Then thou wist not that jewels be alway covered with stone-crust, ere the cutter polish them?"

"Soothly, Father, I can see the stone-crust yonder, but verily mine eyes be too weak to pierce to the gem."

"Ah! our eyes be rarely strong enough for that. It taketh God's eyes many times. They say," Wilfred went on dreamily, scanning the white clouds which floated across the blue—"they say, the old writers of the Jews, that this man Moyses died by the kiss of God. Methinks that were brave payment for the grave in Moab. And after all, every man of us must have his grave dug some whither. Is it of heavy moment, mewondereth, whether men delve it in the swamps of Somerset or in the Priory at Langley? God shall see the dust as clear in either; and shall know, moreover, to count it His treasure."

"Father Wilfred, where wouldst thou fain be buried?"

"What matter, lad?"

"I know where I would :—in the holy minster at Canterbury, nigh unto the tomb of Edward the Prince, that was so great an hero, and not far from the blessed shrine of Saint Thomas the martyr."

"Ah!" said the monk with a sigh, "there is a little

church among the hills of Cumberland, that I had chosen rather. But the days of my choosing are over. I would have God choose for me."

"But that might be the sea, Father Wilfred, or the traitors' elms[1] by London, or the plague dead-pit."

"Child! when the Lord cometh with all His saints, there will be no labels on the raised bodies, to note where the dust was found lying."

And Wilfred turned back to his desk, and took up his pen. Both were silent for a time; but it was the old monk who resumed the conversation.

"Thou wouldst fain attain greatness, Bertram," he said. "Shall I tell thee of two deeds done but this sennight past, that I saw through yonder lattice as I sat at my painting? Go to! I saw, firstly, a poor shepherd lad crossing the green one morrow, on his needful toil, clad in rough russet; and another lad lesser than he, clad in goodly velvets and brave broidery, bade him scornfully thence out of his sight, calling him rascal, fool, lither oaf, and the like noisome words—the shepherd lad having in nowise offended save by his presence. And I say, lad, that was a little deed—the deed of a little soul; a mean, base deed; and he that did it, except God touch his heart, will never be a great man."

"But, Father Wilfred! I saw it—it was the Lord Edward; and he is great even now, and like to be greater."

"Mark my words, lad,—he will never be a great man."

Bertram looked as if he thought the proposition incomprehensible.

"Well, the day thereafter," pursued Wilfred, "I was

[1] Tyburn.

aware, in the very same place, of other two lads bravely clad, though not so brave as he—bearing betwixt them a pail of water, for the easement of an halt and aged wife that might scarce lift it from the ground. And I heard the one say to the other, as they came by this lattice,—'How if some of our fellows see us now?'—with his answer returned,—'Be it so ; we do no wrong.' And I say, boy, that was a great deed, the deed of a great soul ; and I look for both those lads to be great men, though I verily think the greater to have been he that was in no wise shamed of his deed."

Bertram's face was crimson, for he very well knew that on this occasion the heroes of Wilfred's adventure were himself and his friend, Hugh Calverley. He remembered, moreover, that he had felt ashamed, and afraid to be seen, and had taken his share in the act, partly from his own kindness of heart, but partly from a wish to retain Hugh's good opinion.

"Shall I tell thee another tale, lad ?"

"Prithee, Father, so do."

"Touching greatness in a woman ?"

"By my Lady Saint Mary! can a woman be great ?"

"Methinks, Bertram, *she* was," said Wilfred quietly. "But it was not of Saint Mary, nor of any other saint, that I had intent to tell thee, but of one whom no Pope ever took the pain to canonise, and who yet, as methinks, was the greatest woman of whom ever I heard. It may perchance astound thee somewhat, to learn that I am not purely an English man. My mother came from far over seas,—from Dutchland,[1] in the dominions of the Duke's Grace of Austria. And when she was a

---

[1] Germany.

young maid, at home in her country, that befel of which I am about to tell thee. It happed that in the Court of the Emperor's Majesty,[1] which at that time was Albright[2] the First, was a young noble, by name Rudolph, Count von der Wart. My mother was handmaid unto my Lady Gertrude his wife, and she spake right well of her mistress. A young gentle lady, said she, meek and soft of speech, loving and obedient unto her lord, and in especial shamefaced, shrinking from any public note of herself or any deed she did. This lady had not been wed long time, when the Emperor Albright died. And he died by poison. Some among his following had given it; and his judges sat to try whom. God wot who it were, and assoil[3] him! But some men thought that his cousin, Sir Henry of Luxemburg, which was Emperor at after him, had been more in his place at the bar than on the bench. The sentence of the court was that divers men were cast for death. And one of them thus convinced[4] was the young Count von der Wart."

"But was he not innocent, Father?"

"He was innocent. But he was doomed to the awful death of the wheel, and he suffered it."

"Pity of his soul!" cried Bertram indignantly.

"And when the news was brought to the Lady Gertrude, she went white as death, and fell back in a swoon into the arms of my mother."

"And she was borne to her bed, and brake her heart, and so died!" interjected Bertram, who thought that this would be the proper poetical ending of the story.

---

[1] A title at this time restricted to the Emperor of Germany. The first English King to whom it was applied, was Richard II. It is often said that Henry VIII. was the first to assume it, but this is an error.

[2] Albert.　　[3] Forgive.　　[4] Convicted.

"Thou shalt hear. When the day of execution came, a great throng of men gathered in the market-place for to see the same. And when all was done,"—Wilfred evidently shrank from any lingering over the harrowing details—"when the dusk fell, and the prisoners had suffered their torments, such as yet overlived were left bound on the wheel to die there. Left, amid the jeers and mockings of the fool[1] throng, which dispersed not, but waited to behold their woe—left, with unbound wounds, to the chill night, and with no mercy to look for saving mercy of God. But no sooner were the executioners gone, than, lapped in a furred cloak, the Lady Gertrude left her house, and went out into the midst of the cruel, taunting crowd."

"But what did she?"

Wilfred's answer was in that low, tremulous voice, which would have hinted to a more experienced listener that his sympathies were deeply stirred by the story he was telling.

"She climbed up on the great wheel, lad, and sat upon the rim of it; and she did off her fur cloak, and laid it over her dying lord; and when that served not, so strong was the shivering which had seized him, she stripped off her gown, and spread that over him likewise. And when in his death-thirst he craved for water, she clomb down again, and drew from the well in her shoe, for she had nought else: and there sat she, all that woful night, giving him to drink, bathing his brows, covering his wounds, whispering holy and loving words. And when the morrow brake, there below were the throng, mocking her all they might, and calling her by every evil name their tongues might utter."

[1] Foolish.

"How could she hear it, and abide?"[1] broke forth Bertram.

"Did she hear it?" answered Wilfred in the same low voice. "Ah, child! love is stronger than death. So, when all was over—when Count Rudolph's eyes had looked their last upon her—when his voice had whispered the last loving word—'Gertrude, thou hast been faithful until death!'—and it was not till high noon, then she laid her hand upon his eyes, and clomb down from the wheel, and went back to her void and lonely home. Boy, I never heard of any woman greater than Gertrude von der Wart."[2]

"I marvel how she bare it!" said Bertram, under his breath.

"And to worsen her sorrow," added Wilfred, "when day brake, came the Duke's Grace of Austria, and his sister, Queen Agnes of Hungary, and all their following, to behold the scene men and women amongst whom she had dwelt, that had touched hand or lip with her many a time—all mocking and jibing. Methinks that were not the least bitter thing for her to see—if by that time she could see anything, save Rudolph in his agony, and God in His Heaven."

"And after that—she died, of force?" said Bertram, clinging still to the proper and conventional close of the tale.

"She was alive thirty years thereafter," replied Wilfred quietly, turning his attention to a bunch of leaves which ended a bough of his tree.

---

[1] Bear.

[2] It is surely not the least interesting association with the Castle of the Wartburg, whose best-known memories are connected with Luther, to remember that it was the home of Rudolph and Gertrude von der Wart.

Bertram privately thought this a lame and impotent conclusion. For a few minutes he sat thinking deeply, while Wilfred sketched in silence.

"Father Wilfred!" the boy broke forth at last, "why letteth God such things be?"

"If thou canst perceive the answer to that, lad, thou hast sharper sight than I. God knoweth. But what He doth, we know not now. Passing that word, none other response cometh unto us from Him unto whose eyes alone is present the eternal future."

"Must we then never know it?" asked Bertram drearily.

"Aye—'thou shalt know hereafter.' Yet this behest[1] is given alonely unto them that sue the Lamb whithersoever He goeth above; and they which begin not that suing through the mire of the base court, shall never end it in the golden banquet hall."

"But what is it to sue the Lamb?" replied Bertram almost impatiently.

Wilfred laid down his pen, and looked up into the boy's face, with one of his sweet smiles flitting across his lips. The sketch was finished at last.

"Dear lad!" he said lovingly, "Bertram Lyngern, ask the Lamb to show thee."

[1] Promise.

CHAPTER V.

CHANGES AND CHANCES OF THIS MORTAL LIFE.

"Now is done thy long day's work;
Fold thy palms across thy breast,
Fold thine arms, turn to thy rest,
    Let them rave "—TENNYSON.

THE Earl and Countess were away from home, during the whole spring of the next year; but Constance stayed at Langley, and so did Alvena and Maude. There was a grand gala day in the following August, when the Lord of Langley was raised from the dignity of Earl of Cambridge to the higher title of Duke of York: but three days later, the cloth of gold was changed for mourning serge. A royal courier, on his way from Reading to London, stayed a few hours at Langley; and he brought word that the mother of the King, "the Lady Princess," was lying dead at Wallingford.

The blow was in reality far heavier than it appeared on the surface, and to the infant Church of the Lollards the loss was irreparable. For the Princess was a Lollard; and being a woman of most able and energetic character, she had been until now the *de facto* Queen of England. She must have been possessed of consummate tact and prudence, for she contrived to live on excellent terms with half-a-dozen people of completely incompatible tempers. When the reins dropped from her dead hand a struggle ensued among these incompatible persons, who should pick them up. The struggle was sharp, but short. The elder brothers retired from the contest, and the reins were left in the Duke of Gloucester's hand. And woe to the infant Church of the Lollards, when Gloucester held the reins!

He began his reign—for henceforward he was virtually King—by buying over his brother of York. Edmund, already the passive servant of Gloucester, was bribed to active adherence by a grant of a thousand pounds. The Duke of Lancaster, who was not his brother's tool, was quietly disposed of for the moment, by making him so exceedingly uncomfortable, that with the miserable *laisser aller,* which was the bane of his fine character, he went home to enjoy himself as a country gentleman, leaving politics to take care of themselves.

But an incident happened which disconcerted for a moment the plans of the Regent. The young King, without consulting his powerful uncle, declared his second cousin, Roger Mortimer, Earl of March, heir presumptive of England, and—in obedience to a previous suggestion of the Princess—broke off March's engagement with a lady of the Arundel family, and married him to Richard's own niece, the Lady Alianora de Holand.

The annoyance to Gloucester consisted in two points: first, that it recognised female inheritance and representation, which put him a good deal further from the throne; and secondly, that Roger Mortimer, owing to the education received from his Montacute grandmother, had stepped out of his family ranks, and was the sole Lollard ever known in the House of March.

Gloucester carried his trouble to his confessor. The appointed heir to the throne a Lollard!—nor only that, but married to a grand-daughter of the Lollard Princess, a niece of the semi-Lollard King! What was to be done to save England to Catholicism?

Sir Thomas de Arundel laughed a low, quiet laugh in answer.

"What matters all that, my Lord? Is not Alianora *my* sister's daughter? The lad is young, yielding, lazy, and lusty.[1] Leave all to me."

Arundel saw further than the Princess had done.

And Gloucester was Arundel's slave. Item by item he worked the will of his master, and no one suspected for a moment whither those acts were tending. The obnoxious, politically-Lollard Duke of Lancaster was shunted out of the way, by being induced to undertake a voyage to Castilla for the recovery of the inheritance of his wife Constança and her sister Isabel; a statute was passed conferring plenipotentiary powers on "our dearest uncle of Gloucester;" all vacant offices under the Crown were filled with orthodox nominees of the Regent; the Lollard Earl of Suffolk was impeached; a secret meeting was held at Huntingdon, when Gloucester and four other nobles solemnly renounced their allegiance to the King, and declared themselves at liberty to do what was right in their own eyes. The other four (of whom we shall hear again) were Henry Earl of Derby, son of the Duke of Lancaster; Richard Earl of Arundel, brother of Gloucester's confessor; Thomas Earl of Nottingham

---

[1] Self indulgent, pleasure-loving.

his brother-in-law; and Thomas Earl of Warwick, a weak waverer, the least guilty of the evil five. The conspirators conferred upon themselves the grand title of "the Lords Appellants;" and to divert from themselves and their doings the public mind, they amused that innocent, unsuspecting creature by a splendid tournament in Smithfield.

Of one fact, as we follow their track, we must never lose sight:—that behind these visible five, securely hidden, stood the invisible one, Sir Thomas de Arundel, setting all these puppets in motion according to his pleasure, and for "the good of the Church;" working on the insufferable pride of Gloucester, the baffled ambition of Derby, the arrogant rashness of Arundel, the vain, time-serving nature of Nottingham, and the weak fears of Warwick. Did he think he was doing God service? Did he ever care to think of God at all?

The further career of the Lords Appellants must be told as shortly as possible, but without some account of it much of the remainder of my story will be unintelligible. They drew a cordon of forty thousand men round London, capturing the King like a bird taken in a net; granted to themselves, for their own purposes, twenty thousand pounds out of the royal revenues; met and utterly routed a little band raised by the Duke of Ireland with the object of rescuing the sovereign from their power; impeached those members of the Council who were loyalists and Lollards; plotted to murder the King and the whole Council, which included near blood relations of their own; prohibited the possession of any of Wycliffe's books under severe penalties; murdered three, and banished two, of the five faithful friends of the King left in the Council. The Church stood to them above all human ties; and Sir Thomas de Arundel was ready to say "*Absolvo te*" to every one of them.

This reign of terror is known as the session of the Merciless Parliament, and it closed with the cruel mockery of a renewal of the oath of allegiance to the hapless and helpless King. Then Gloucester proceeded to distribute his rewards. The archbishopric of York was conferred on Sir Thomas de Arundel, and Gloucester appropriated as his own share of the rich spoil, the vast estates of the banished Duke of Ireland.

And then the traitor, robber, and murderer, knelt down at the feet of Archbishop Arundel, and heard— from man's lips "Thy sins are forgiven thee"—but not "Go, and sin no more."

"Master Calverley, you? God have mercy! what aileth you?"

For Hugh Calverley stood at one of the hall windows of Langley Palace, on the brightest of May mornings, in the year 1388, his face hidden in his hands, and his whole mien and aspect bearing the traces of sudden and intense anguish.

"God had no mercy, Mistress Maude!" he wailed under his voice. "We had no friend save Him, and He was silent to us. He cared nought for us—He left us alone in the uttermost hour of our woe."

"Nay, sweet Hugh! it was men, not God!" said Bertram's voice soothingly behind them.

"He gave them leave," replied Hugh in an agonised tone.

It was the old reproachful cry, "Lord, carest thou not

that we perish ?" but Maude could not understand it at all. That cry, when it rises within the fold, is sometimes a triumph, and always a mystery, to those that are without. "You believe yourselves even now as safe as the angels, and shortly to be as happy, and you complain thus !" True ; but we are not angels yet. Poor weak, suffering humanity is always rebellious, without an accompanying unction from the Holy One. But it is not good for us to forget that such moods are rebellion, and that they often cause the enemies of the Lord to blaspheme.

Bertram quietly drew Maude aside into the next window.

"Let the poor fellow be !" he said compassionately. "Alack, 'tis no marvel. These traitor loons have hanged his father. And never, methinks, did son love father more."

"Master Calverley's father !—the Queen's squire ?"

"He. And look you, Maude, heard man ever the like ! the Queen's own Grace was on her knees three hours unto my Lord of Arundel, praying him to spare Master Calverley's life. Think of it, Maude ! Cæsar's daughter !"

"Mercy, Jesu !"—Maude could imagine nothing more frightful. It seemed to her equivalent to the whole world tumbling into chaos. What was to become of "slender folk," such as Bertram and herself, when men breathed who could hear unmoved the pleadings of "Cæsar's daughter ?" "But what said he ?"

"Who my Lord of Arundel ? The unpiteous, traitorous, hang dog lither oaf !" Bertram would apparently have chosen more opprobrious words if they would kindly have occurred to him. "Why, he said—'Pray for yourself and your lord, Lady, and let this be; it were the better for you.' The great Devil, to whom he 'longeth, be *his* aid in the like case!"

"Truly, he may be in the like case one day," said Maude.

"And that were at undern[1] this morrow, an' I were King!" cried Bertram wrathfully.

"But what had Master Calverley done?"

Bertram dared only whisper the name of the horrible crime of which alone poor Calverley stood accused.

"He was a Lollard—a Gospeller."

"Be they such ill fawtors?" asked Maude in a shocked tone.

"Judge for yourself what manner of men they be," said Bertram indignantly, "when the King's Highness and the Queen, and our own Lady's Grace, and the Lady Princess that was, and the Duke of Lancaster, be of them. Aye, and many another could I name beyond these."

"I will never crede any ill of our Lady's Grace!" said Maude warmly.

"Good morrow, Bertram, my son," said a voice behind them—a voice strange to Maude, but familiar to Bertram.

"Father Wilfred! Christ save you, right heartily! You be here in the nick of time. You are come——"

"I am come, by ordainment of the Lord Prior, to receive certain commands of my Lord Duke touching a book that he desireth to have written and ourned[2] with painting in the Priory," said Wilfred in his quiet

---

[1] Eleven o'clock a.m.   [2] Ornamented.

manner. "But what aileth yonder young master? for he seemeth me in trouble."

What ailed poor Hugh was soon told; and Wilfred, after a critical look at him, went up and spoke to him.

"So thou hast a quarrel with God, my son?"

"Nay! Who may quarrel with God?" answered Hugh drearily.

"Only men and devils," said Wilfred. "Such as be God's enemies be alway quarrelling with Him; but such as be His own dear children   should they so?"

"Dealeth He thus with His children?" was the bitter answer.

"Aye, oftentimes; so oft, that He aredeth[1] us, that they which be alway out of chastising be no sons of His."

Hugh could take no comfort. "You know not what it is!" he said, with the impatience of pain.

"Know I not?" said Wilfred, very tenderly, laying his hand upon Hugh's shoulder. "Youngling, my father fell in fight with the Saracens, and my mother—my blessed mother—was brent for Christ's sake at Cologne."

Hugh looked up at last. The words, the tone, the fellowship of suffering, touched the wrung heart through its own sorrow.

"You know, then!" he said, his voice softer and less bitter.

"'Bithenke ghe on him that suffride such aghenseiynge of synful men aghens himsilff, that ghe be not maad weri, failynge in ghoure soulis.' Bethink ye: the which signifieth, meditate on Him, arm ye with His patience. Look on Him, and look to Him."

[1] Tells.

Bertram stared in astonishment. The cautious scriptorius, who never broke bread with Wycliffe, and declined to decide upon his great or small position, was quoting his Bible word for word.

Hugh looked up in Wilfred's face, with the expression of one who had at last found somebody to understand him.

"Father," he said, "did you ever doubt of *every* thing?"

"Aye," said Wilfred, quietly.

"Even of God's love? yea, even of God?"

"Aye."

Bertram was horrified to hear such words. And from Hugh, of all people! But Wilfred, to his surprise, took them as quietly as if Hugh had been repeating the Creed.

"And what was your remedy?"

"I know but one remedy for all manner of doubt, and travail, and sorrow, Master; and that is to take them unto Christ."

"Yet how so," asked Hugh, heaving a deep sigh, "when we cannot see Christ to take them to Him?"

"I know not that your seeing matters, Master, so that He seeth. And when your doubts come in and vex you, do you but call upon Him with a true heart, desiring to find Him, and He will soon show you that He is. Ah!" and Wilfred's eyes lighted up, "the solving of all riddles touching Christ's being, is only to talk with Christ."

Bertram could not see that Wilfred had offered Hugh the faintest shadow of comfort; but in some manner inexplicable to him, Hugh seemed comforted thenceforward.

There was a great stir at Langley in the April of 1389; for the King and Queen stayed there a night on their way to Westminster. Maude was in the highest excitement: she had never seen a live King before, and she expected a formidable creature of the lion rampant type, who would order every body about in the most tyrannical manner, and command Master Warine to be instantly hanged if dinner were not punctual. She saw a very handsome young man of three and twenty years of age, dressed in a much quieter style than any of his suite; of the gentlest manners, a model of courtesy even to the meanest, delicately considerate of every one but himself, and especially and tenderly careful of that darling wife who was the only true friend he had left. Ever after that day, the faintest disparagement of her King would have met with no reception from Maude short of burning indignation.

King Richard recovered his power by a *coup d'état*, on the 3rd of May, 1389. He suddenly dissolved and reconstituted his Council, leaving out the traitor Lords Appellants. It was done at the first moment when he had the power to do it. But a year and a half later, Gloucester crept in again, a professedly reformed penitent; and from the hour that he did so, Richard was King no longer.

During all this struggle the Duke of York had kept extremely quiet. The King marked his sense of his uncle's allegiance by creating his son Edward Earl of Rutland. Perhaps, after all, Isabel had more power over her husband than he cared to allow; for when her gentle influence was removed, his conduct altered for the worse. But a stronger influence was at work on him; for his brother of Lancaster had come home; and though Gloucester moulded York at his will when Lancaster was absent, yet in his presence he was powerless. So peace reigned for a time.

And meanwhile, what was passing in the domestic circle at Langley?

In the first place, Maude had once more changed her position. From the lower place of tire-woman, or dresser, to the Duchess, she was now promoted to be bower-maiden to the Lady Constance. This meant that she was henceforth to be her young mistress's constant companion and habitual confidant. She was to sleep on a pallet in her room, to go wherever she went, to be entrusted with the care alike of her jewels and her secrets, and to do everything for her which required the highest responsibility and caution.

In the second place, both Constance and Maude were no longer children, but women. The Princess was now eighteen years of age, while her bower-maiden had reached twenty.

And in the third place, over the calm horizon of Langley had appeared a little cloud, as yet no more than "a man's hand," which was destined in its effects to change the whole current of life there. No one about her had in the least realized it as yet; but the Duchess Isabel was dying.

Very gently and slowly, at a rate which alarmed not even her physician, the Lollard Infanta descended to the portals of the grave. She knew herself whither she was going before any other eyes perceived it; and noiselessly she set her house in order. She executed her last will in terms which show that she died a Gospeller, as distinctly as if she had written it at the outset ; she left bequests to her friends—"a fret of pearls to her dear daughter, Constance Le Despenser ;" she named two of the most eminent Lollards living (Sir Lewis Clifford and Sir Richard Stury) as her executors ; she showed that she retained, like the majority of the Lollards, a belief in Purgatory, by one bequest for masses to be sung for her soul ; and lastly—a very Protestant item when considered with the rest—she desired to be interred, not by the shrine of any saint or martyr, but "whithersoever her Lord should appoint."

The priests said that she died "very penitent." But for what ? For her early follies and sins, no doubt she did. But of course they wished it to be understood that it was for her Wycliffite heresies.

It was about the beginning of February, 1393, that the Duchess died. Her husband never awoke fully to his irreparable loss until long after he had lost her. But he held her memory in honour at her burial, with a gentle respect which showed some faint sense of it. The cemetery which he selected for her resting-place was that nearest her home—the Priory Church of Langley. There the dust slept quietly ; and the soul which had never nestled down on earth, found its first and final home in Heaven.

It might not unreasonably have been expected that Constance, now left the only woman of her family, would have remembered that there was another family to which she also belonged, and a far-off individual who stood to her in the nominal relation of husband. But it did not please her Ladyship to remember any such thing. She liked queening it in her father's palace ; and she did not like the prospect of yielding precedence to her mother-in-law, which would have been a necessity of her married life. As to the Lord Le Despenser, she was absolutely indifferent to him. Her childish feeling of contempt had not been replaced by any kindlier one. It was not that she disliked him : she cared too little about him even to hate him. When the thought of going to Cardiff crossed her mind, which was not often, it was always associated with the old Lady Le Despenser, not at all with the young Lord.

Now and then the husband and wife met for a few minutes. The Lord Le Despenser had grown into a handsome and most graceful gentleman, of accomplished manners and noble bearing. When they thus met, they greeted each other with formal reverences; the Baron kissed the hand of the Princess; each hoped the other was well; they exchanged a few remarks on the prominent topics of the day, and then took leave with equal ceremony, and saw no more of one another for some months.

The Lady Le Despenser, it must be admitted, was not the woman calculated to attract such a nature as that of Constance. She was a Lollard, by birth no less than by marriage; but in her creed she was an ascetic of the sternest and most unbending type. In her judgment a laugh was indecorum, and smelling a rose was indulgence of the flesh. Her behaviour to her royal daughter-in-law was marked by the utmost outward deference, yet she never failed to leave the impression on Constance's mind that she regarded her as an outsider and a reprobate. Moreover, the Lady Le Despenser had some singular notions on the subject of love. Fortunately for her children, her heart was larger than her creed, and often overstepped the bounds assigned; but her theory was that human affections should be kept made up in labelled parcels, so much and no more to be allowed in each case. Favouritism was idolatry   affectionate words were foolish condescensions to the flesh; while loving caresses savoured altogether of the evil one.

Now Constance liked dearly both to pet and to be petted. She loved, as she hated, intensely. The calm, sedate personal regard, in consideration of the meritorious qualities of the individual in question, which the Lady Le Despenser termed love, was not love at all in the eyes of Constance. The Dowager, moreover, was cool and deliberate; she objected to impulses, and after her calm fashion disliked impulsive people, whom she thought were not to be trusted   And Constance was all impulse. The squeaking of a mouse would have called forth gestures and ejaculations from the one, which the other would have deemed too extreme to be appropriate to an earthquake.

The Lord Le Despenser was the last of his mother's three sons   the youngest-born, and the only survivor; and she loved him in reality far more than she would have been willing to allow, and to an extent which she would have deemed iniquitous idolatry in any other woman. In character he resembled her but slightly. The narrow-mindedness and obstinacy inherent in her family   for no Burghersh was ever known to see more than one side of any thing—was softened and modified in him into firmness and fidelity. His heart was large enough to hold a deep reservoir of love, but not so wide at its exit as to allow the stream to flow forth in all directions at once. If this be narrow-mindedness, then he was narrow-minded. But he was loyal to the heart's core, faithful unto death, true in every fibre of his being. "He loved one only, and he clave to her," and there was room in his heart for none other.

The Dowager had several times hinted to the Duke of York that she considered it high time that Constance should take up her residence at Cardiff, for she was a firm believer in "the eternal fitness of things," and while too much love was in her eyes deeply reprehensible, a proper quantity of matrimony, at a suitable age, was a highly respectable thing, and a state into which every man and woman ought to enter, with due prudence and decorum. And as a wife married in childhood was usually resigned to her husband at an age some years earlier than Constance had now attained, the Dowager was scandalised by her persistent absence. The Duke, who recognised in his daughter a more self-reliant character than his own, and was therefore afraid of her, had passed over the intimation, accompanied with a request that she would do as she liked about it. That Constance would do as she liked her father well knew; and she did it. She stayed at home, the Queen of Langley, where no oppressive pseudo-maternal atmosphere interfered with her perfect freedom.

But in the October following the death of her mother, a thunderbolt fell at Constance's feet, which eventually drove her to Cardiff.

The Duke was from home, and, as everybody supposed, at Court. He was really in mischief; for mischief it proved, to himself and all his family. Late one evening a courier reached Langley, where in her bower

Constance was disrobing for the night, and Maude was combing out her mistress's long light hair. A sudden application for admission, in itself an unusual event at that hour, brought Maude to the door, where Doña Juana, pale and excited, besought immediate audience of her Señorita.

The Princess, without looking back, desired her to come forward.

"Señorita, my Lord's courier, Rodrigo, is arrived hither from Brockenhurst, and he bringeth his Lord's bidding that we make ready his Grace's chamber for to-morrow."

"From Brockenhurst! Well, what further?"

"And likewise *her* Grace's chamber whom Jesu pardon!—for the Lady newly-espoused that cometh with my Lord."

"Mary Mother!" exclaimed Maude, dropping the silver comb in her sudden surprise.

Constance had sprung up from her seat with such quick abruptness that the chair, though no light one, fell to the ground behind her.

"Say that again!" she commanded, in a hard, steel-like voice ; and, in a more excited tone than ever, Doña Juana repeated her unwelcome tidings.

"So I must needs have a mistress over me! Who is she ?"

"From all that Rodrigo heard, Señorita, he counteth that it should be the Lady Joan de Holand, sister unto my Lord of Kent and my Lady of March. She is, saith he, of a rare beauty, and of most royal presence."

"Royal presence, quotha !—and a small child of ten years!" cried the indignant girl of nineteen. "Marry, I guess wherefore he told me not aforetime. He was afeard of me."

She pressed her lips together till they looked like a crimson thread, and a bright spot of anger burned on either cheek. But all at once her usual expression returned, and she resumed her seat quietly enough on the chair which Maude had mechanically restored to its place.

"Go, Doña Juana, and bid the chambers be prepared, as is meet. But no garnishing of the chambers of my heart shall be for this wedding. Make an end, Maude. 'A thing done cannot be undone.' I will abide and see this small damsel's conditions;[1] but my heart misgiveth me if it were not better dwelling with my Lord Le Despenser than with her."

Maude obeyed, feeling rather sorry for the Lord Le Despenser, whose loving spouse seemed to regard him as the less of two evils.

The new Duchess proved to be, like most of the Holands, very tall and extremely fair. No one would have supposed her to be only ten years old, and her proud, demure, unbashful bearing helped to make her look older than she was. The whole current of life at Langley changed with her coming. From morning to night every day was filled with feasts, junkets, hawking parties, picnics, joustings, and dances. The Duke was devoted to her, and fulfilled, if he did not anticipate, her every wish. Her youthful Grace was entirely devoid of shyness, and she made a point of letting Constance feel her inferiority by addressing her on every occasion as "Fair Daughter." She also ordered a much stricter observance of etiquette than had been usual

----

[1] Disposition.

during the life of the Infanta, whose rule, Spaniard though she was, had been rather lax in this particular. The stiff manners commonly expected from girls towards their mothers had only hitherto been exacted from Constance upon state occasions. But the new Duchess quickly let it be understood that she required them to the smallest detail. She was particular that her step-daughter's chair should not be set one inch further under the canopy than was precisely proper; her fur trimmings must be carefully regulated, so as not to equal those of the Duchess in breadth; instead of the old home name of "the Lady Custance," she must be styled "the Lady Le Despenser;" and the Duchess strongly objected to her using such vulgar nicknames as "Ned" and "Dickon," desiring that she would in future address her brothers properly as "my Lord." Angrily the royal lioness chafed against this tyranny. Many a time Maude noticed the flush of annoyance which rose to her lady's cheek, and the tremor of her lip, as if she could with difficulty restrain herself from wrathful words. It evidently vexed her to be given her married name; but the interference with the pet name of the pet brother was what she felt most bitterly of all. And Maude began to wonder how long it would last.

It was a calm, mild evening in January, 1394, and in the Princess's bower, or bedroom, stood Maude, re arranging a portion of her lady's wardrobe. The Duchess had been that day more than usually exacting and precise, much to the amusement of Bertram Lyngern, at present at Langley in the train of his master. The door of Constance's bower was suddenly opened and dashed to again, and the Princess herself entered, and began pacing up and down the room like a chafed lioness—a habit of all the Plantagenets when in a passion. She stopped a minute opposite Maude, and said in a determined voice:

"Make ready for Cardiff!"

And she resumed her angry march.

In this manner the Lady Le Despenser intimated her condescending intention of fulfilling her matrimonial duties at last. Maude knew her too well to reply by anything beyond a respectful indication of obedience. Constance only gave her one day to prepare. The next morning but one the whole train of the Lady Le Despenser set forth on their eventful journey.

CHAPTER VI.

TRUE GOLD AND FALSE.

"Woe be to fearful hearts and faint hands, and the sinner that
goeth two ways!"—ECCLUS. ii. 12.

WHATEVER may have been the feeling which
possessed the mind of Constance on her departure
from Langley, the incident was felt by Maude as a wrench
and an uprooting, surpassing any previous incident of her
life since leaving Pleshy. The old house itself had come
to feel like a mute friend; the people left behind were
acquaintances of many years; the ground was all familiar. She was going now once more into a new world,
to new acquaintances, new scenes, new incidents. The
journey over land was in itself very pleasant. But the
journey over sea from Bristol was so exceedingly unpleasant, that poor Maude found herself acquainted with
a degree of physical misery which until then she had
never imagined to exist. And when at last the great,
grim, square towers of the Castle of Cardiff, which was
to be her new home, rose before her eyes, she thought
them absolutely lovely—because they were *terra firma*.

It can only be ascribed to her unusual haste on the
one hand, or to her usual caprice on the other, that it

had not pleased the Lady of Cardiff to give any notice of her approach.   Of course nobody expected her; and when her trumpeter sounded his blast outside the moat, the warder looked forth in some surprise.   It was late in the evening for a guest to arrive.

"Who goeth yonder?"

"The Lady and her train."

"Saint Taffy and Saint Guenhyfar!" said the warder.

"Put forth the bridge!" roared the trumpeter.

"It had peen better to send word," calmly returned the warder.

"Send word to thy Lord, thou lither oaf!" cried the irate trumpeter, "and see whether it liketh him to keep the Lady awaiting hither on an even in January, while thou pratest in chopped English!"

Thereupon arose a passage of arms between the two affronted persons of diverse nationalities, which was terminated by Constance, with one of her sudden impulses, riding forward to the front, and taking the business on herself.

"Sir Warder," she said—with that exquisite grace and lofty courtesy which was natural to every Plantagenet, be the other features of his character what they might, —"I am your Lady, and I pray you to notify unto your Lord that I am come hither."

The warder was instantly mollified, and blew his horn to announce the arrival of a guest.   There was a minute's bustle among the minor officials about the gate, a little running to and fro, and then the drawbridge was thrown across, and the next moment the Lord Le Despenser knelt low to his royal spouse.   He could have had no idea of her coming five minutes before, but he did his best to show her that any omissions in her welcome were no fault on his part.

Thomas Le Despenser was just twenty years of age. He was only of moderate height for a man ; and Constance, who was a tall woman, nearly equalled him. His Norman blood showed itself in his dark glossy hair, his semi-bronzed complexion, and his dark liquid eyes, the expression of which was grave almost to sadness. An extremely short upper lip perhaps indicated blue blood, but it gave a haughty appearance to his features, which was not indicative of his character. He had a sweet low-toned voice, and an extremely winning smile.

The Princess suffered her husband to lift her from the pillion on which she rode behind Bertram Lyngern, who had been transferred to her service by her father's wish. At the door of the banquet-hall the Dowager Lady met them. Maude's impression of her was not exactly pleasant. She thought her a stiff, solemn-looking, elderly woman, in widow's garb. The Lady Elizabeth received her royal guest with the lowest of courtesies, and taking her hand, conducted her with great formality to a state chair on the daïs, the Lord Le Despenser standing, bare-headed, on the step below.

The ensuing ten minutes were painfully irksome to all parties. Everybody was shy of everybody else. A few common-place questions were asked and answered ; but when the Dowager suggested that "the Lady" must be tired with her journey, and would probably like to rest for an hour ere the rear-supper was served, it was a manifest relief to all.

A sudden incursion of so many persons into an unprepared house was less annoying in the fourteenth century than it would be in the nineteenth. There was then always superfluous provision for guests who might suddenly arrive; a castle was invariably victualled in advance of the consumption expected; and as to sleeping accommodation, a sack filled with chaff and a couple of blankets was all that any person anticipated who was not of "high degree." Maude slept the first night in a long gallery, with ten other women; for the future she would occupy the pallet in her lady's chamber. Bertram was provided for along with the other squires, in the banquet-hall, the chaff beds and blankets being carried out of the way in the morning; and as to draughts, our forefathers were never out of one inside their houses, and therefore did not trouble themselves on that score. The washing arrangements, likewise, were of the most primitive description. Princes and the higher class of peers washed in silver basins in their own rooms; but a squire or a knight's daughter would have been thought unwarrantably fastidious who was not fully satisfied with a tub and a towel. A comb was the only instrument used for dressing the hair, except where crisping-pins were required; and mirrors were always fixtures against the wall.

A long time elapsed before Maude felt at home at Cardiff; and she could not avoid seeing that a still longer period passed before Constance did so. The latter was restless and unsettled. She had escaped from the rule of her step-mother to that of her mother-in-law, and she disliked the one only a little less than the other; though "Daughter" fell very differently on the ear from the lips of a child of ten, and from those of a woman who was approaching sixty. But the worst point of Constance's new life was her utter indifference to her husband. She looked upon his gentle deference to her wishes as want of spirit, and upon his quiet, reserved, undemonstrative manner as want of brains. From loving him she was as far as she had been in those old days when she had so cruelly told his sister Margaret that "when she loved Tom, she would let him know."

That he loved her, and that very dearly, was patent to the most superficial observer. Maude, who was not very observant of others, used to notice how his eyes followed her wherever she went, brightened at the sound of her step, and kindled eagerly when she spoke. The Dowager saw it too, with considerable disapproval; and thought it desirable to turn her observations to profit by a grave admonition to her son upon the sin and folly of idolatry. She meant rightly enough, yet it sounded harsh and cruel, when she bluntly reminded him that Constance manifestly cared nothing for him.

Le Despenser's lip quivered with pain.

"Let be, fair Mother," he said gently. "It may be yet, one day, that my Lady's heart shall come home to God and me, and that she shall then say unto me, 'I love thee.'"

Did that day ever come? Aye, it did come; but not during his day. The time came when no music could have been comparable to the sound of his voice when she would have given all the world for one glimpse of his smile—when she felt, like Avice, as though she could have climbed and rent the heavens to have won him back to her. But the heavens had closed between

them before that day came.   While they journeyed side
by side in this mortal world, he never heard her say, "I
love thee."

The news received during the next few months was
not likely to make Constance feel more at home at
Cardiff than before.   It was one constant funeral wail.
On the 24th of March, 1394, her aunt Constança,
Duchess of Lancaster, died of the plague at Leicester;
in the close of May, of the same disease, the beloved
Lollard Queen; and on the first of July her cousin,
Mary Countess of Derby.   Constance grew so restless,
that when orders came for her husband to attend the
King at Haverford, where he was about to embark on
his journey to Ireland, she determined to go there also.

"I can breathe better any whither than at Cardiff!"
she said confidentially to Maude.

But in truth it was not Cardiff from which she fled,
but her own restless spirit.   The vine had been trans-
planted, and its tendrils refused to twine round the
strange boughs offered for its support.

The Princess found her father at Haverford, but the
pair were very shy of one another.   The Duke was
beginning to discover that he had made a blunder, that
his fair young wife's temper was not all sunshine, and
that his intended plaything was likely to prove his
eventual tyrant.   Constance, on her part, felt a twinge
of conscience for her pettish desertion of him in his old
age; for to her apprehension he was now an old man:
and she was privately conscious that she could not
honestly plead any preconsideration for her husband.
She had merely pleased herself, both in going and staying, and she knew it.   But she spent her whole life in

gathering apples of Sodom, and flinging away one after another in bitter disappointment. Yet the next which offered was always grasped as eagerly as any that had gone before it.

Perhaps it was due to some feeling of regret on the Duke's part that he invited his daughter and son-in law to return with him. Constance accepted the offer readily. The Duke was Regent all that winter, during the King's absence in Ireland; and, as was usual, he took up his residence in the royal Palace of Westminster. Constance liked her visit to Westminster; she was nearly as tired of Langley as of Cardiff, and this was something new. And a slight bond of union sprang up between herself and her husband; for she made him, as well as Maude, the confidant of all her complaints and vexations regarding her step-mother. Le Despenser was satisfied if she would make a friend of him about anything, and he was anxious to shield her from every annoyance in his power.

It appeared to Maude, who had grown into a quiet, meditative woman, that the feeling of the Duchess towards her step-daughter was not far from positive hatred. She seemed to seek occasions to mortify her, and to manufacture quarrels which it would have been no trouble to avoid. It was some time before Maude could discern the cause. But one day, in a quiet talk with Bertram Lyngern, still her chief friend, she asked him whether he had noticed it.

"Have I eyes, trow?" responded Bertram with a smile.

"But wherefore is it, count you?"

"Marry, the old tale, methinks. Two men seldom discern alike; and he that looketh on the blue side of a changeable sarcenet,[1] can never join hands with him that seeth nought save the red."

"You riddle, Master Lyngern."

"Why, look you, our Lady Custance was rocked in a Lollard cradle; but my Lady Duchess' Grace had a saint's bone for her rattle. And her mother is an Arundel."

"But so is my Lord's Grace of York[2] himself an Arundel."

"Aye as mecounteth you shall see, one day."

"Doth not the doctrine of Sir John de Wycliffe like him well?"

"Time will show," said Bertram, drily.

It was quite true that Archbishop Arundel had for some two years been throwing dust in Lollard eyes by plausible professions of conversion to some of the views of that party. At a time when I was less acquainted with his character and antecedents, I gave him credit for sincerity.[3] I know him better now. He was merely playing a very deep game, and this was one of his subtlest moves. His assumption of Lollardism, or of certain items of it, was only the assumption of a mask, to be worn as long as it proved serviceable, and then to be dropped and forgotten. The time for the mask to drop had come now. The death of Archbishop Courtenay, July 31, 1396, left open to Thomas de Arundel the sole seat of honour in which he was not already installed. Almost born in the purple,[4] he had

---

[1] Shot silk.   [2] The Archbishop.

[3] See "Mistress Margery," preface, p. vi.

[4] His mother, Alianora of Lancaster, was the daughter of Earl Henry, son of Prince Edmund, son of Henry III.

climbed up from ecclesiastical dignity to dignity, till at last there was only one further height left for him to scale. It could surprise no one to see the vacant mitre set on the astute head of Gloucester's confessor and prompter.

The Earl of Rutland presented himself at Westminster Palace before his sister left it, attended as usual by his squire, Hugh Calverley. Bertram and Maude at once wished to know all the news of Langley, from which place they had come. Hugh seemed acquainted with no news except one item, which was that Father Dominic, having obtained a canonry, had resigned his post of household confessor to the Palace; and a new confessor had been appointed in his stead.

"And who is the new priest?" asked Bertram.

"One Sir Marmaduke de Tyneworth."[1]

"And what manner of man is he?"

"A right honest man and a proper,[2] say they who have confessed unto him ; more kindly and courteous than Father Dominic."

"He hath then not yet confessed thee?"

"I never confess," said Hugh quietly.

The impression made upon Bertram's feelings by this statement was very much that which would be left on ours, if we heard a man with a high reputation for piety calmly remark that he never prayed.

"Never confess!" he repeated in astonished tones.

"Not to men. I confess unto God only."

"But how canst, other than by the priest?"

"What hardship, trow? Can I not speak save by the priest?"

---

[1] A fictitious person.   [2] A fitting, satisfactory man.

"But thou canst receive no absolving!"

"No can I?   Aye verily, friend, I can!"

"But——" Bertram stopped, with a puzzled look.

"Come, out with all thy *buts*," said Hugh, smilingly.

"Why, methinks—and holy Church saith it—that this is God's means whereby men shall approach unto Him : nor hath He given unto us other."

"Holy Church saith it?   Aye so.   But where saith God such a thing?"

Bertram was by no means ignorant of Wycliffe's Bible, and he searched his memory for authority or precedent.

"Well, thou wist that the man which had leprosy was bidden to show him unto the priest, the which was to declare *if* his malady were true leprosy or no."

"The priest being therein an emblem or mystery of Christ, which is true Healer of the malady of sin."

"Ah!" said Bertram triumphantly, "but lo' thou, when our Lord Himself did heal one that had leprosy, what quoth He?   'Show thyself to the priest,' saith He : not, 'I am the true Priest, and therefore thou mayest slack to show thee to yon other priest, which is but the emblem of Me.'"

"Because," replied Hugh, "He did fulfil the law, and made it honourable.   Therefore saith He, 'Show thyself to the priest.'   The law held good until He should have fulfilled the same."

"But mind thou," urged Bertram eagerly, "it was but the lither[1] Pharisees which did speak like unto thee. What said they save the very thing thou wouldst fain

---

[1] Wicked, abandoned.

utter — to wit, 'Who may forgyve synnes but God aloone?' And alway our Lord did snyb and rebuke these ill fawtors."

"Friend, countest thou that the Jew which had leprosy, and betook him unto the high priest, did meet with contakes because he went not likewise unto one of the lesser? Either this confession unto the priest is to be used with, or without, the confession unto God. If to be used without, what is this but saying the priest to be God? And if to be used with, what but saying that God is not sufficient, and the High Priest may not act without the lesser priest do aid Him?"

"But what sayest touching the Pharisees?" repeated Bertram, who was not able to answer Hugh's argument, and considered his own unanswerable.

"What say I?" was the calm answer. "Why, I say they spake very sooth, saving that they pushed not the matter to its full issue. Had they followed their reasoning on to the further end, then would they have said, and spoken truly, 'If this man can in very deed forgive sin, then is He God.' Mark, I pray thee, what did our Lord in this matter. He brought forth His letters of warrant. He healed the palsied man afore them—'that ye wite,' saith He, 'that mannes sone hath power in erthe to forgyve synnes.' As though He had said unto them, 'Ye say well; none may forgive sins but God alone: wherefore see, in My forgiving of sin, the plain proof that I am God's Son.' To show them that He had power to forgive sin, He did heal this man of his malady. And verily I ask no more of any priest that would confess me, but only that he bring forth his letters of warrant, as did his Master and mine. When I shall

see him to heal the sick with a word, then will I crede
that he can forgive sin in like manner. Lo' thou, if he
can forgive, he can heal: if he can heal by his word,
then can he forgive."

The waters were rather too deep for Bertram to wade
in. He tried another line of argument.

"Saint James also saith that men should confess their
sins."

"'Ech to othire' well: when it liketh Sir Marmaduke to knowledge his sins unto me, then will I mine
unto him, if we have done any wrong each to other.
But look thou into that matter of Saint James, and
thou shalt find it to touch not well men, but only sick;
which, knowledging their sins when their conscience is
troubled, and praying each for other, shall be healed of
their sickness."

"Moreover, Achan did confession unto Josue," said
Bertram, starting another hare.

"Ah! Josue was a priest, trow?"

"Nay, but if it be well to knowledge our sins each
to other, it shall not be worse because the man is a
priest."

"Nor better," said Hugh, in his quietest manner.

"Nay!" urged Bertram, who thought he had the
advantage here, "but an' it be well to confess at all, it
is good to confess unto any. and if to any, to a woman,
or if to a woman, to a man; or to a man, then to a
priest."

Hugh gave a soft little laugh.

"Good friend, I could prove any gear in the world
by that manner of reasoning. If it be good to confess
unto any, then unto anything that liveth; and if so, then

to a beast; and if to a beast, then to yonder cat. Come hither, Puss, and hear this my friend his confession!"

"Have done with thy mocking!" cried Bertram. "And mind thou, the Lord did charge the holy apostles with power to forgive sins."

"Granting that so be—what then?"

"What then? Why, that priests have now the like power."

"But what toucheth it the priests?"

"In that they be successors unto the apostles."

"In what manner?"

Hugh was evidently not disposed to take any links of the chain for granted.

"Man!" exclaimed Bertram, almost in a pet, "wist not that Paul did ordain Timothy Bishop of Ephesus, and bade him do the like to other,—and so from each to other was the blessed grace handed down, till it gat at the priests that now be?"

"Was it so?" said Hugh coolly. "But when and where bade Paul that Timothy should forgive sins?"

Bertram found it much harder to prove his assertion than to state it. He could only answer that he did not know.

"Nor I neither," returned Hugh. "Nor Timothy neither, without I much mistake."

"I must needs give thee up. Thou art the worst caitiff to reason withal, ever mortal man did see!"

Hugh laughed.

"Lo' you, friend, I ask but for one instance of authority. Show unto me any passage of authority in God's Word, whereby any priest shall forgive sins; or show unto me any priest that now liveth, which shall bring forth his letters of warrant by healing a man all suddenly of his sickness whatsoever, and I am at a point. Bring him forth, prithee; or else confess thou hast no such to bring."

"Hold thy peace, for love of Mary Mother!" said Bertram, passing his irrepressible opponent a plateful of smoking pasty, for the party were at supper; "and fill thy jaws herewith, the which is so hot thou shalt occupy it some time."

"My words being. somewhat too hot for thee, trow?" rejoined Hugh comically. "Good. I can hold my peace right well when I am wanted so to do."

When Constance returned home to Cardiff, she remained there for some little time without any further visit to Court. She alone of all the Princesses was absent from the Church of St. Nicholas at Calais, when the King was married there to the Princess Isabelle of France—a child of only eight years old. Something far more interesting to herself detained her at Cardiff; where, on the 30th of November, 1396, an heir was born to the House of Le Despenser.

That the will of "the Lady" stood paramount we see in the name given to the infant. He was christened after her favourite brother, Richard—a name unknown in his father's line, whose family names were always Hugh and Edward.

In their unfeigned admiration of this paragon of babies, its mother and grandmother sank all their previous differences. But when the difficult question of education arose, the differences reappeared as strongly as ever. The only notion which Constance had of bringing up a child was to give it everything it cried for;

while the Dowager was prepared to go a long way in the opposite direction, and give it nothing in respect to which it showed the slightest temper. The practical result was that the boy was committed to the care of Maude, whom both agreed in trusting, with the most contradictory orders concerning his training. Maude followed the dictates of her own common sense, and implicitly obeyed the commands of neither of the rival authorities; but as little Richard throve well under her care, she was never called to account by either.

The year 1397 brought a political earthquake, which ended in the destruction of three of the five grand traitors, the Lords Appellants. The commons had at last opened their eyes to the real state of affairs. The conspirators were meditating fresh projects of treachery, when by the advice of the Dukes of Lancaster and York, Gloucester was arrested and imprisoned at Calais, where he died on the 15th of September, either from apoplexy or by a private execution. Richard Earl of Arundel, the tool of his priestly brother, was beheaded six days later. The Earl of Warwick, who had been merely the blind dupe of the others, was banished to the Isle of Man. The remaining two the ambitious Derby, and the conceited Nottingham—contrived in the cleverest manner, not only to escape punishment, but to obtain substantial rewards for their loyalty! Derby presented a very humble petition on behalf of both, in which he owned, with so exquisite a show of penitence, to having *listened* to the suggestions of the deceased traitors, and been concerned in " several riotous disturbances "— professed himself and his friend to be so abjectly repentant, and so irrevocably faithful for ever henceforward—

that King Richard, as easily deceived as usual, hastened to pardon the repenting sinners. But there was one man in the world who was not deceived by Derby's plausible professions. Old Lancaster shook his white head when he heard that his son was not only pardoned, but restored to favour.

"'Tis hard matter for father thus to speak of son," he said to his royal nephew; "nathless, my gracious Lord, I do you to wit that you have done a fool deed this day. You shall never have peace while Hal is in this kingdom."

"Fair Uncle, I am sure he will repay me!" was the response of the warm-hearted Richard.

"Ha!" said John of Gaunt, and sipped his ipocras with a grim smile. "*Sans doute, Monseigneur, sans doute!*"

Westminster Hall beheld a grand and imposing ceremony on the Michaelmas Day of 1397. The King sat in state upon his throne at the further end, the little Queen beside him, and the various members of the royal line on either side—Princes on the right, Princesses on the left. The Duchess of Lancaster had the first place; then the Duchess of York, particularly complacent and resplendent; the Duchess of Gloucester, who should have sat third, was closely secluded (of her free will) in the Convent of Bermondsey. Next sat the Countess of March, the elder sister of the Duchess Joan, and wife of the Lollard heir of England. The daughters of the Princes followed her. Elizabeth, Countess of Huntingdon, daughter of the Duke of Lancaster, whom that day was to make a duchess, and who bore away the palm from the rest as "the best singer and the best dancer" of all the royal ladies, held her place, beaming with smiles, and radiant with rubies and crimson velvet. Next, arrayed in blue velvet, sat the only daughter of York, Constance Lady Le Despenser. Round the hall sat the nobles of England in their "Parliament robes," each of the married peers with his lady at his side; while below came the House of Commons, and lower yet, outside the railing, the people of England, in the shape of an eager, sight-seeing mob. There was to be a great creation of peers, and one by one the names were called. As each of the candidates heard his name, he rose from his seat, and was led up to the throne by two nobles of the order to which he was about to be raised.

"Sir Henry of Bolingbroke, Earl of Derby!"

The gentleman whose unswerving loyalty was about to be recompensed by the gift of a coronet (!) rose with his customary grace from his seat, third on the right hand of the King, and was led up by his father of Lancaster and his uncle of York. He knelt, bareheaded, before the throne. A sword was girt to his side, a ducal coronet set on his head by the royal hand, and he rose Duke of Hereford. As old Lancaster resumed his seat, he smiled grimly under his white beard, and muttered to himself—"*Sans doute!*"

"Sir Edward of Langley, Earl of Rutland!"

Constance's brother was similarly led up by his father and his cousin, the newly created Duke, and he resumed his princely seat, Duke of Aumerle, or Albemarle.

"Sir Thomas de Holand, Earl of Kent, Baron Wake!"

Hereford and Aumerle were the two to lead up the candidate. He was the son of the King's half-brother, and was reputed the handsomest of the nobles : a tall, finely-developed man, with the shining golden hair of his Plantagenet ancestors. He was created Duke of Surrey.

Hereford sat down, and Surrey and Aumerle conducted John Earl of Huntingdon to the throne. He was half-brother of the King, uncle of Surrey, and husband of the royal songstress who sat and smiled in crimson velvet. He had stepped out of the family ranks; for instead of being tall, fair, and good-looking, like the rest of his house, he was a little dark-haired man, whom no artist would have selected as a model of beauty. A strong anti-Lollard was this nobleman, a good hater, a prejudiced, violent, unprincipled man; possessed of two virtues only—honesty and loyalty. He had been cajoled for a time by Gloucester, but his brother knew him too well to doubt his sincerity or affection. He was made Duke of Exeter.

The next call was for—" Sir Thomas de Mowbray, Earl of Nottingham !" And up came the last of the " Lords Appellants," painfully conscious in his heart of hearts that while he might have been in his right place on the scaffold in Cheapside, he was very much out of it in Westminster Hall, kneeling to receive the coronet of Norfolk.

A coronet was now laid aside, for the recipient was not present. She was an old lady of royal blood, above seventy years of age, the second cousin of the King, and great-grandmother of Nottingham. Her style and titles were duly proclaimed as Duchess of Norfolk for life.

But when " Sir John de Beaufort, Earl of Somerset !"

was called for, the peer summoned rose and walked forward alone. He was to be created a marquis—a title of King Richard's own devising, and at that moment borne by no one else. The Earl came reluctantly, for he was very unwilling to be made unlike other people; and he dropped his new title, and returned to the old one, as soon as he conveniently could. He had a tall, fine figure, but not a pleasant face; and his religion, no less than his politics, he wore like a glove—well-fitting when on, but capable of being changed at pleasure. Just now, when Lollardism was "walking in silver slippers," my Lord Marquis of Dorset was a Lollard. Rome rarely persecutes men of this sort, for she makes them useful in preference.

And now the herald cried—"Sir Thomas Le Despenser, Baron of Cardiff!"

The Earls of Northumberland and Suffolk were the supporters of Le Despenser, who walked forward with a slow, graceful step, to receive from the King's hand an earl's coronet, accompanied by the ominous name of Gloucester a title stained by its last bearer beyond remedy. In truth, the royal dukedom had been an interpolation of the line, and the King was merely giving Le Despenser back his own—the coronet which had belonged to the grand old family of Clare, whose co-heiress was the great-grandmother of Thomas Le Despenser. The title had been kept as it were in suspense ever since the attainder of her husband, the ill fated Earl Hugh, though two persons had borne it in the interim without any genuine right.

Three other peers were created, but they do not concern the story. And then the King rose from his throne, the ceremony was over; and Constance Le Despenser left the hall among the Princesses by right of her birth, but wearing her new coronet as Countess of Gloucester.

Four months later, the Duke of Hereford knelt before the throne, and solemnly accused his late friend and colleague, the Duke of Norfolk, of treason. He averred that Norfolk had tempted him to join another secret conspiracy. Norfolk, when questioned, turned the tables by denying the accusation, and adding that it was Hereford who had tempted him. Since neither of these noble gentlemen was particularly worthy of credit, and they both swore very hard on this occasion, it is impossible to decide which (if either) was telling the truth. The decision finally arrived at was that both the accusers should settle their quarrel by wager of battle, for which purpose they were commanded to meet at Coventry in the following autumn.

Before the duel took place, an important event occurred in the death of Roger Mortimer, the Lollard Earl of March, whom the King had proclaimed heir presumptive of England. He was Viceroy of Ireland, and was killed in a skirmish by the "wild Irish." March, who was only 24 years of age, left four children, of whom we shall hear more anon, to be educated by their mother, Archbishop Arundel's niece, in her own Popish views. He is described by the monkish chroniclers as "very handsome and very courteous, most dissolute of life, and extremely remiss in all matters of religion." We can guess pretty well what that means. "Remiss in matters of religion," of course, refers to his Lollardism, while the accusation of "dissolute life" is notoriously Rome's pet charge against those who escape from her toils. Such was the sad and early end of the first and only Lollard of the House of Mortimer.

The duel between Hereford and Norfolk was appointed to take place on Gosford Green, near Coventry, on the 16th of September. The combatants met accordingly; but before a blow was struck, the King took the matter upon himself and forbade the engagement. On the 3rd of October, licence was granted to Hereford to travel abroad, this being honourable banishment; no penalty was inflicted upon Norfolk. But some event—perhaps never to be discovered—occurred, or came to light during the following ten days, which altered the whole aspect of affairs. Either the King found out some deed of treason, of which he had been previously ignorant, or else some further offence was committed by both Hereford and Norfolk. On the 13th both were banished—Hereford for ten years, Norfolk for life; the sentence in the former case being afterwards commuted to six years. Those who know the Brutus like character of John of Gaunt, and his real opinion of his son's proceedings, may accept, if they can, the representations of the monastic chroniclers that the commutation of Hereford's sentence was made at his intercession.

In the interim, between the duel and the sentence, Archbishop Arundel was formally adjudged a traitor, and the penalty of banishment was inflicted on him also.

Constance was too busy with her nursery to leave Cardiff, where this autumn little Richard was joined by a baby sister, who received the name of Elizabeth after the Dowager Lady. But the infant was not many weeks old, when, to use the beautiful phrase of the chroniclers, she "journeyed to the Lord." She was taken away from the evil to come.

It was appropriate enough that the last dread year of the fourteenth century should be ushered in by funeral knells. And he who died on the third of February in that year, though not a very sure stay, was the best and last support of the Gospel and the throne. It was with troubled faces and sad tones that the Lollards who met in the streets of London told one to another that "old John of Gaunt, time-honoured Lancaster," was lying dead in the Bishop of Ely's Palace.

But the storm was deferred for a few weeks longer. There were royal visits to Langley and Cardiff, on the way to Ireland, the Earl of Gloucester accompanying the King to that country. And then, when Richard had left the reins of government in the feeble hands of York, the tempest burst over England which had been lowering for so long.

The Lady Le Despenser and the Countess of Gloucester were seated at breakfast in Cardiff Castle, on a soft, bright morning in the middle of July. Breakfast consisted of fresh and salt fish, for it was a fast-day ; plain and fancy bread, different kinds of biscuits (but all made without eggs or butter) ; small beer, and claret. Little Richard was energetically teasing Maude, by whom he sat, for another piece of red herring, and the Dowager, deliberate in all her movements, was slowly helping herself to Gascon wine. The blast of a horn without the moat announced the arrival of a guest or a letter, and Bertram Lyngern went out to see what it was. Ten minutes later he returned to the hall, with letters in his hand, and his face white with some terrible news.

"Ill tidings, noble ladies!"

"Is it Dickon?" cried the Countess.

"Is it Tom?" said the Dowager.

"There be no news of my Lord, nor from Langley," said Bertram. "But my Lord's Grace of Hereford, and Sir Thomas de Arundel, sometime Archbishop, be landed at Ravenspur."

"Landed at Ravenspur! Banished men!"

The loyal soul of Elizabeth Le Despenser could imagine nothing more atrocious.

"Well, let them land!" she added in a minute. "The Duke's Grace of York shall wit how to deal with them. Be any gathered to them?"

"Hundreds and thousands," was the ominous answer.

"Aye me!" sighed the Dowager. "Well! 'the Lord reigneth.'"

Constance's only comment on the remarks was a quiet, incredulous shrug of her shoulders. She knew her father.

And she was right. Like many another, literally and figuratively, York went over to the enemy's ground to parley, and ended in staying there. One of the two was talked over but that one was not the rebel, but the Regent.

Poor York! Looking back on those days, out of the smoke of the battle, one sees him a man so wretchedly weak and incapable that it is hardly possible to be angry with him. It does not appear to have been conviction, nor cowardice, nor choice in any sense, which caused his desertion, but simply his miserable incapacity to stand alone, or to resist the influence of any stronger character on either side. *He* go to parley with the enemy! He might as well have sent his baby grandson to parley with a box of sugar-plums.

Fresh news   always bad news   now came into Cardiff nearly every day.

The King hurried back from Ireland to Conway, and there gathered his loyal peers around him. There were only sixteen of them. Dorset, always on the winning side, deserted the sinking ship at once. Aumerle more prudently waited to see which side would eventually prove the winner.

Exeter and Surrey were sent to parley with the traitors. They were both detained, Surrey as a prisoner, Exeter with a show of friendship. The latter was too fertile in resources, and too eloquent in speech, not to be a dangerous foe. He was therefore secured while the opportunity offered.

Then came the treacherous Northumberland as ambassador from Hereford, whom we must henceforth designate by his new title of Lancaster.

Northumberland's lips dropped honey, but war was in his heart. He offered the sweetest promises. What did they cost? They were made to be broken. So gentle, so affectionate were his solicitations to the royal hart to enter the leopard's den—so ready was he to pledge word and oath that Lancaster was irrevocably true and faithful that the King listened, and believed him. He set forth with his little guard, quitting the stronghold of Flint Castle, and in the gorge of Gwrych he was met by Northumberland and his army, seized, and carried a prisoner to Chester.

This was the testing moment for the hitherto loyal sixteen. Aumerle, who had satisfied himself now which way the game was going, went over to his cousin at once. Worcester broke his white wand of office, and retired from the contest. Some fled in terror. When all the faithless had either gone or joined Lancaster, there remained six, who loved their master better than themselves, and followed, voluntary prisoners, outwardly in the train of Henry of Lancaster, but really in that of Richard of Bordeaux.

These six loyal, faithful, honourable men our story follows. They were Thomas Le Despenser, Earl of Gloucester; John de Montacute, Earl of Salisbury; Thomas de Holand, Duke of Surrey; William Le Scrope, Earl of Wilts; Richard Maudeleyn, chaplain to the King; John Maudeleyn (probably his brother), varlet of the robes.

Slowly the conqueror marched Londonwards, with the royal captive in his train. Westminster was reached on the first of September. From that date the coercion exercised over the King was openly and shamelessly acknowledged. His decrees were declared to be issued "with the assent of our dearest cousin, Henry Duke of Lancaster." At last, on Michaelmas Day, the orders of that loving and beloved relative culminated in the abdication of the Sovereign.

The little group of loyalists had now grown to seven, by the addition of Exeter, who joined himself to them as soon as he was set at liberty. They remained in London during that terrible October, and most of them were present when, on the 13th of that month, Henry of Lancaster was crowned King of England.

There stood the vacant throne, draped in gold-spangled red; and by it, on either hand, the Lords

Spiritual and Temporal. The hierarchy were, on the right, Arundel at their head, having coolly repossessed himself of the see from which he had been ejected as a traitor; an expression of contemptuous amusement hovering about his lips, which might be easily translated into the famous (but rather apocryphal) speech of Queen Elizabeth to the men of Coventry—"Good lack! What fools ye be!" On the left hand of the throne stood Lancaster, his lofty stature conspicuous among his peers, waiting with mock humility for the farce of their acknow-ledgment of his right. Next him was his uncle of York, wearing a forced smile at that which his conscience dis-approved, but his will was impotent to reject. Aumerle came next, his face so plainly a mask to hide his thoughts that it is difficult to judge what they were. Then Surrey, with a half-astonished, half-puzzled air, as though he had never expected matters really to come to this pass. His uncle Exeter, who sat next him, looked sullen and discontented. The other peers came in turn, but their faces are not visible in the remarkable painting by an eye-witness from which those above are described, with the exception of the tellers, the traitor Northumberland, and the cheery round faced Westmoreland. These went round to take the votes of the peers. There were not likely to be many dissenting voices, where to vote No was death.

Henry stated his assumption of power to rest upon three points. First, he had conquered the kingdom; secondly, his cousin, King Richard, had voluntarily ab-dicated in his favour; and lastly, he was the true heir male of the crown.

"Ha!" said the little Earl of March, the dispossessed heir general, "*hæres malus*, is he?"

It was not a bad pun for seven years old.

If Henry of Bolingbroke may be credited, the majority of the loyal six, and Thomas Le Despenser among them, not only sat in his first Parliament, but pleaded compulsion as the cause of their petition against Gloucester, and consented to the deposition of King Richard, while some earnestly requested the usurper to put the Sovereign to death. While some of these allegations are true, the last certainly is false. One of those named as having joined in the last petition is Surrey; and his alleged participation is proved to be a lie. Knowing how lightly Henry of Bolingbroke could lie, it is hardly possible to believe otherwise of any member of the group, except indeed the time-serving Aumerle.

CHAPTER VII.

FAITHFUL UNTO DEATH.

> "Long since we parted !
> I to life's stormy wave—
> Thou to thy quiet grave,
> Leal and true-hearted !"

THE first regnal act of Henry IV. was to strip the loyal lords of the titles conferred upon them just two years before. Once more, Aumerle became Earl of Rutland ; Surrey, Earl of Kent Exeter, Earl of Huntingdon ; Wiltshire, Sir William Le Scrope ; and Gloucester, Lord Le Despenser.

Hitherto, King Richard had been imprisoned in the Tower, a lonely captive. But now, possessed by jealous fears of insurrection and restoration, the usurper hurried his royal prisoner from dungeon to dungeon : to Leeds Castle, Pickering, Knaresborough, and lastly, about the middle of December, to Pomfret, which he was never to leave alive.

The guilty fears of Henry were not unfounded ; but perhaps the judicial murder of Lord Wiltshire at Bristol quickened the action of the little band, now again reduced to six. They met quietly at Oxford in December, to concert measures for King Richard's release and restoration, resolving that in case of his death they would support the title of March. But there was a seventh person present, whom it is incomprehensible that any of the six should have been willing to trust. This was Aumerle, vexed with the loss of his title, and always as ready to join a conspiracy at the outset as he was to play the traitor at the close. The extraordinary manner in which this man was always trusted afresh by the friends whom he perpetually betrayed, is one of the mysteries of psychological history. His plausibility and powers of fascination must have been marvellous. An agreement was drawn up, signed by the six, and entrusted to Aumerle (who cleverly slipped out of the inconvenience of signing it himself), containing promises to raise among them a force estimated at 8,000 archers and 300 lancemen, to meet on the fourth of January at Kingston, and thence march to Colnbrook, where Aumerle was to join them.

On the day appointed for the meeting at Kingston, Aumerle, attired in a handsome furred gown, went to dine with his father. The Duchess appears to have been absent. Aumerle carried the perilous agreement in his bosom, and when he sat down to dinner, he pulled it forth, and ostentatiously placed it by the side of his silver plate. The six seals caught the old Duke's eye, as his son intended they should ; and his curiosity was not unnaturally aroused.

"What is that, fair son ?" inquired his father.

Aumerle ceremoniously took off his hat then always worn at dinner and bowed low.

"Monseigneur," said he obsequiously, "it is not for you."

Of course, after that, York was determined to see it.

"Show it me!" he said impatiently; "I will know what it is."

Aumerle must have laughed in his traitor heart, as with feigned reluctance he handed the document to his father. York read it through; and then rose from the table with one of his stormy bursts of anger.

"Saddle the horses!" he shouted forth to the grooms at the lower end of the hall.   And, turning to his son,— "Ha, thou thief! False traitor! thou wert false to King Richard; well might it be looked for that thou shouldst be false to thy cousin King Henry. And thou well knowest, rascal! that I am pledged for thee in Parliament, and have put my body and mine heritage to pawn for thy fidelity. I see thou wouldst fain have me hanged; but, by Saint George! I had liefer thou wert hanged than I!"

York strode out of the hall, calling to the grooms to hasten. Aumerle gave him time to mount the stairs to assume his riding-suit, and then himself went quietly to the stable, saddled a fleet barb, and rode for his life to Windsor.

"Who goes there?" rang the royal warder's challenge.

"The Lord of Rutland, to have instant speech of the King. Is my gracious Lord of York here?"

York had not arrived, and his son was safe. The warder had pushed to the great gates, and was leading the way to the court-yard, when to his astounded dismay, Aumerle's dagger was at his throat.

"How have I offended, my Lord?" faltered the poor man.

"No hast," was the response; "but if thou lock not up the gates incontinent, and give the keys to me ——"

The keys were in Aumerle's pocket the next minute. An hour later, when his story was told, and his pardon solemnly promised, York and his train came lumbering to the gate, to find his news forestalled. When Henry had read the agreement, which York brought with him, he set out immediately for London, while Aumerle calmly repaired to his tryst at Colnbrook. Here Exeter was the first to join him. Aumerle informed his friends that Henry was coming to meet them with a large army, but they determined nevertheless to advance. They passed Maidenhead Bridge in safety, but as soon as they crossed it, the vanguard of Henry's army was visible. To the amazement of his colleagues, Aumerle, on whom they had counted as staunch and loyal, doffed his bonnet with a laugh, and, spurring forward, was received by the enemy as an expected ally. There could be no doubt now that he had betrayed his too trusting friends. Yet even then, the little band held the bridge till midnight. But by midnight all hope was over. There was left only one alternative—flight or death. The loyal six set spurs to their horses; and Surrey's steed being fleetest, he soon outdistanced the others. All that night Surrey rode at a breathless gallop, and when morning broke he was dashing past Osney Abbey into the gates of Oxford. Exeter came up an hour or two later; the rest followed afterwards. But they did not mean to stop at Oxford for more than a few hours' rest. Then they spurred on to Cirencester. On reaching the city gate, Surrey, with his usual impulsive eagerness, shouted to the Constable, "Arm for King Richard!" The Constable, supposing that "the luck had turned," obeyed; but the next morning brought an archer from Henry, who must have discovered or guessed whither the fugitives had gone. Surrey received Henry's message and messenger with sovereign contempt; but the Constable, finding that Henry was still in power, immediately went over to the winning side, and there was a town riot. The peers had taken up their temporary abode in an inn, which was surrounded and besieged by the mob. Surrey, impetuous as usual, rushed to the window to address the mob. He was received with a shower of arrows. His friends sprang forward to rescue him; but time and the things of time were over for the young, dauntless, gallant Surrey. They could only lay him gently down on the rushes to breathe out his life. It was a sad end. Fairest and almost highest of the nobles of England, of royal blood, of un-blemished character, of great wealth, and only twenty-five—to die on the floor of an inn, in a mob riot!

But what was to become of the rest? Exeter's fertile brain suggested a way of escape.

"Quick   fire the rushes! And then ope the back windows, and drop down into the fosse."

It is manifest from the circumstances, that the back windows of the inn opened from the town wall upon the ditch which ran round it, and which in all probability was filled with water. John Maudeleyn gathered a handful of the rushes, with which he set fire to the room in two or three places. The five who remained   Exeter, Salisbury, Le Despenser, and the two Maudeleyns,— then dropped down from the window, swam across the fosse, and fled into the fields, where the scattered relics of their own army were advancing to join them. But Exeter's idea had been a shade too brilliant. He frightened by the fire not only his foes, but his friends.

His troops fancied that Henry had come up, and was burning Cirencester; and, panic-stricken, they dispersed in all directions. The five parted into three divisions, and fled themselves.

They fled to death.

Exeter set out alone. His destination was Pleshy, whence he meant to escape to France. But the angel of death met him there in the guise of a woman, Joan Countess of Hereford, mother-in-law of Henry, and sister of Archbishop Arundel. She had never forgiven Exeter for sitting in judgment on her brother the Earl of Arundel, and she rested not now till she saw him stretched before her, a headless corpse.

The two Maudeleyns went towards Scotland. Richard was apprehended, and executed. There is good reason to believe that John escaped, and that it was he who, in after years, personated King Richard at the Scottish Court.

The Lollard friends, Salisbury and Le Despenser, determined to attempt their escape together.

For a minute they waited, looking regretfully after Exeter : then Le Despenser said to his squire—

"Haste, Lyngern !—for Cardiff !"

They rode hard all that day—wearily all that night. Over hill and dale, fording rivers, pushing through dense forests, threading mountain passes, wading across track less swamps. Town after town was left behind ; river after river was followed or crossed ; till at last, as the sun was setting, they cantered along the banks of the broad Severn, with the towers of Berkeley Castle rising in the distance.

It was here that Salisbury drew bridle.

"''Tis no good!" he said. "I can no more. My Lord, mine heart misgiveth me that you be wending but to death. Had it been the pleasure of the Lord that we should escape our enemies, well: but if we be to meet death, let me meet it at home. Go you on to your home, an' it like you; but for me, I rest this night at Berkeley, and with the morrow I turn back to Bisham."

Le Despenser looked sadly in his face. It seemed as though his last friend were leaving him.

"Be it as you list, my Lord of Salisbury," he said. "Only God go with both of us!"

Who shall say that He did not, though the road lay through the dark river? For on the other side was Paradise.

So the Lollard friends parted: and so went Salisbury to his death. For he never reached Bisham; he only crept back to Cirencester, and there he was. recognised and taken, and beheaded by the mob.

A weary way lay still before Le Despenser and Bertram. They journeyed over land; and many a Welsh mountain had to be scaled, and many a brook forded, before—when men and horses were so exhausted that another day of such toil felt like a physical impossibility—spread before them lay the silver sea, and the sun shone on the grim square towers of Cardiff.

"Home!" whispered the noble fugitive, slackening his pace an instant, as the beloved panorama broke upon his sight. "Now forward, Lyngern home!"

Down they gallopped wearily to the gates, walked through the town—stopped every moment by demands for news—till at last the Castle was reached, and in the base court they alighted from their exhausted steeds. And then up stairs, to Constance's bower, occupied by herself, the Dowager, little Richard, and Maude. Bertram hurriedly preceded his master into the room. The ladies, who were quietly seated at work, and were evidently ignorant of any cause for excitement, looked up in surprise at his entrance.

"Please it the Lady,—the Lord!"

Constance rose quickly, with a more decided welcome than she usually vouchsafed to her husband.

"Why, my Lord! I thought you were in London."

"What ill hath happed, son?" was the more penetrating remark of the Dowager.

"Well nigh all such as could hap, Madam," said Le Despenser wearily. "I am escaped with life if I have so 'scaped!—but with nought else. And I come now, only to look on your beloved faces, and to bid farewell.—Maybe a last farewell, my Lady!"

He stood looking into her face with his dark, sad eyes, —looking as if he believed indeed that it would be a last farewell. Constance was startled; and his mother's theories broke down at once, and she sobbed out in an agony—

"O Tom, Tom! My lad, my last one!"

"You mean it, my Lord?" asked Constance, in a tone which showed that she was not wholly indifferent to the question.

"I mean it right sadly, my Lady."

"But you go not hence this moment?"

Le Despenser sank down on the settle like the exhausted man he was.

"This moment!" he repeated. "Nay, not so, even for

life. I am weary and worn beyond measure. And to part so soon! One night to rest; and then!——"

"My Lord, are you well assured of your peril?" suggested Constance. "This your castle is strong and good, and your serving men and retainers many, and the townsmen leal   "

She stopped, tacitly answered by her husband's sorrowful smile, which so plainly replied, "*Cui bono?*"

"My Lady!" he said quietly, "think ye there is this moment a tower, or a noble, or a rood of land, that the Duke of Lancaster will leave unto us? I cast no doubt that all our lands and goods be forfeit, some days ere now."

He judged truly enough. On the day of the fugitives' flight from Oxford to Cirencester, a writ of confiscation was issued in Parliament against every one of them. That was the 5th of January; and this was the evening of the 10th. There was a mournful rear-supper at Cardiff Castle that night; and no member of the household, except the wearied Bertram Lyngern, thought of sleep. Maude was busied in making up money and jewels into numberless small packages, under the orders of the Dowager, to be concealed on the persons of Le Despenser and his attendant squire. The intention of her master was to take passage on some boat bound for Ireland, and thence to escape into Scotland or France.

Le Despenser slept late into the morning—no wonder for a man who had scarcely been out of his saddle for six days and nights. The preparations for the continuation of his flight were nearly completed; but he had not yet been disturbed, when a strange horn was heard outside the fosse of the Castle. Constance, who had risen early, and was in an excited state of mind, hastily opened a lattice to hear who was the visitor.

"Who goes there?" demanded the warder's deep voice.

"Sir William Hankeford, Justice of the King's Bench, bearing his Highness' warrant. Open quickly!"

There could be no question as to his object—the arrest of Le Despenser. Constance breathlessly shut the window, bade Maude sweep the little packets of jewellery and coin into her pocket, dashed into her bower, and awoke her still slumbering husband.

"Rise, my Lord, this instant! Harry of Bolingbroke hath sent to take you. We must hide you some whither."

Le Despenser was almost too tired and depressed to care for apprehension.

"Whither, my Lady?" he asked hopelessly. "Better yield, maybe."

"*Niñerias!*"[1] cried Constance hastily, using a word of her mother's tongue, which she had frequently heard from the lips of Doña Juana. And springing to the wardrobe in the ante-chamber, she was back in a second, with a thick furred winter gown.

"Lo' you, my Lord! Lap you in this, and— "

And Constance glanced round the room for a safe hiding-place.

"And I—" said Le Despenser, smiling sadly, but doing as he was requested.

"Go up the chimney!" said Constance hurriedly. "They will never look there, and there is little warmth in yon ashes."

She caught up the shovel, and flung a quantity of cinders on the almost extinct fire. The idea was not a

---

[1] Nonsense! literally, *childishness.*

bad one. The chimney was as wide as a small closet; there were several rests for the sweep; and at one side was a little chamber hollowed out, specially intended for some such emergency as the present. With the help of the two ladies and Maude, Le Despenser climbed up into his hiding-place.

Ten minutes later, Sir William Hankeford was bowing low in the banquet-hall before the royal lady of the Castle, who gravely and very courteously assured him of her deep regret that her lord was not at home to receive him.

"An' it like you, Madam," returned the acute old judge, "I am bidden of the King's Grace to ensure me thereof."

"Oh, certes," said Constance accommodatingly. "Maude! call hither Master Giles, and bid him to lead my learned and worshipful Lord into every chamber of the Castle."

The judge, a little disarmed by her perfect coolness, instituted the search on which he was bound. He turned up beds, opened closets, shook gowns, pinched cushions, and looked behind tapestry. So determined was he to secure his intended prisoner, that he went through the whole process in person. But he was forced to confess at last that, so far as he could discover, Cardiff Castle was devoid of its master. The baffled judge and his subordinates took their departure, after putting a series of questions to various persons, which were answered without the slightest regard to truth, the replicants being ignorant of any penalty attached to lying beyond confession and penance; and considering, indeed, that in an instance like the present it was rather a virtue than a sin. When they were fairly out of sight, Constance went leisurely back to her bower, and called up the chimney.

"Now, my good Lord, you may descend in safety."

Le Despenser obeyed; but he came down looking so like a chimney-sweep that Constance, whose versatile moods changed with the rapidity of lightning, flung herself on the bed in fits of laughter. The interrupted preparations were quickly resumed and completed; and when all was ready, and the boatman waiting at the Castle pier, Le Despenser went into the hall to bid farewell to his mother. She was sitting on the settle with an anxious, care-worn look. Maude stood in the window; and at the lower end three or four servants were hurrying about, rather restlessly than necessarily.

The old lady rose when her son entered, and her often-repressed love flowed out in unwonted fervour, as she clasped him in her arms, knowing that it might be for the last time.

"Our Lord be thine aid, my lad, my lad! Be true to thy King; but whatso shall befall thee, be truest to thy God!"

"God helping me, so will I!" replied he solemnly.

"And Tom, dearest lad! is there aught I can do to pleasure thee?"

The tears sprang to his eyes at such words from her.

"Mother dear, have a care of my Lady!"

"I will, so!" answered the Dowager; but she added, with a pang of jealous love which she would have rebuked sorely in another—"I would she held thee more in regard."

"She may, one day," he said, mournfully, as if quietly

accepting the incontrovertible fact. " I told you once, and I yet trust, that the day may dawn wherein my Lady's heart shall come home to God and me."

Maude remembered those words five years later.

"And now, Mother, farewell! I trust to be other-whither ere Wednesday set in."

His mother kissed him, and blessed him, and let him go.

Le Despenser took his usual leave of the household, with a kind word, as was his wont, even to the meanest drudge ; and then he went back to his lady's bower for that last, and to him saddest farewell of all.

His grave, tender manner touched Constance's impressible heart. She took her leave of him more affectionately than usual.

"Farewell, my Lady!" he faltered, holding her to his breast. "We meet again where God will, and when."

"And that will be in France, ere long," said Constance, sanguinely. "You will send me speedy word of your landing, my Lord?"

"You will learn it, my Lady."

Why did he speak so vaguely? Had he some dim presentiment that his "other whither" might be Jerusalem the Golden?

No such hidden meaning occurred to Constance. She was almost startled by the sudden flood of pent-up, passionate feeling, which swept all the usual conventionalities out of his way, and made him whisper in accents of inexpressible love

"My darling! my darling! God keep and bless thee! Farewell once more Custance!"

They had never come so near to each other's hearts

as in that moment of parting.   And the moment after, he was gone.

In the court-yard little Richard was running and dancing about under Maude's supervision; and his father stayed an instant, to take the child again into his arms and bless him once more.   And then he left his Castle by the little postern gate which led down to the jetty.   There were barges passing up and down the Channel, and Le Despenser's intention was to row out to one of those bound for Ireland, and so prosecute his voyage.   He wore, we are told, a coat of furred damask; and carried with him a cloak of motley velvet.   The term "motley" was applied to any combination of colours, from the simplest black and white to the showiest red, blue, and yellow.   In the one portrait, occurring in Creton's life-like illuminations, which I am disposed to identify with that of Le Despenser, he wears a grey gown, relieved by very narrow stripes of red.   Perhaps it was that identical cloak or gown which hung upon the arm of Bertram Lyngern, just outside the postern gate.

"Nay, good friend!" objected Le Despenser, with his customary kindly consideration.   "I have wearied thee enough these six days.   Master Giles shall go with me now."

"My Lord," replied Bertram, deferentially, yet firmly, "your especial command except, we part not, by your leave."

Le Despenser acquiesced with a smile, and both entered the boat.   When Davy the ferryman returned, an hour later, he reported that his master had embarked safely on a barge bound for Ireland.

"Then all will be well," said Constance lightly.

"God allowing!" gravely interposed the old lady. "There be winds and waves atween Cardiff and Ireland, fair Daughter."

Did she think only of winds and waves?

No news reached them until the evening of the following Thursday. They had sat down to supper, about four o'clock, when the blast of a horn outside broke the stillness. The Lady Le Despenser, whom the basin of rose-water had just reached for the opening washing of hands, dropped the towel and grew white as death.

"Jesu have mercy! yonder is Master Lyngern's horn!"

"He is maybe returned with a message, Lady," suggested Father Ademar, the chaplain; but all eyes were fixed on the door of the hall until Bertram entered.

The worst apprehensions which each imagination could form took vivid shape in the minds of all, when they saw his face. So white and woe-begone he looked—so weary and unutterably sorrowful, that all anticipated the news of some heavy and irreparable calamity, from which he only had escaped alone to tell them.

"Where left you your Lord, Master Lyngern?"

It was the Dowager who was the first to break the spell of silence.

"Madam," said Bertram, in a husky, faltering voice, "I left him not at all—till he left me."

He evidently had some secret meaning, and he was afraid to tell the awful truth at once. Constance had risen, and stood nervously grasping the arm of her state chair, with a white, excited face; but she did not ask a question.

"Speak the worst, Bertram Lyngern!" cried the old lady. "Thy Lord — "

It seemed to Bertram as if the only words that would come to his lips in reply were two lines of an inscription set up in many a church, and as familiar to all present as any hackneyed proverb to us.

"' Pur ta pité, Jésu, regarde,
Et met cest alme en sauve garde.'"[1]

There was an instant's dead silence. It was broken by the mother's cry of anguish—

"Tom, Tom! My lad, my last lad!"

"Drowned, Master Lyngern?" asked a score of voices.

Bertram tacitly ignored the question. He walked languidly up the hall, and dropping on one knee before the Princess, presented to her a sapphire signet-ring— the last token sent by her dead husband. Constance took it mechanically; and Bertram, going back to his usual seat, filled a goblet with Gascon wine, and drank it like a man who was faint and exhausted.

"Sit, Master Lyngern, and rest you," pursued the Dowager; "but when you be refreshed, give us to wit the rest."

The tone of her voice seemed to say that the worst which could come, had come; and the dreadful fact known, the details mattered little.

Bertram attempted to eat, but almost immediately he pushed away his trencher, and regardless of etiquette, laid his forehead upon his arm on the table.

[1] "Jesu, in Thy dear love behold,
And set this soul in Thy safe fold."
These lines were spoken by the figure called "Pity," in the painting termed the "Five Wells" or wounds of Christ.

"I cannot eat! And how shall I speak what I must say? I would have died for him." Then, suddenly lifting his head, he spoke quickly, as if he wished to come at once to the end of his miserable task. "Noble ladies, my Lord of Salisbury is beheaden of the rabble at Cirencester, and my Lord of Exeter at Pleshy; and men say that Lord Richard the King licth dead at Pomfret, and that God wot how."

Constance spoke at last, but in a voice not like her own.

"God doom Henry of Bolingbroke!"

The words, if repeated, might have doomed her; but she feared no man.

That evening, Bertram told the details of that woful story.

The barge-master whom they had accosted was sailing westwards, and he readily agreed to take Le Despenser and his suite over to Ireland. Somewhat too readily, Bertram thought; and he feared treachery from the first. When the boat had pulled off to some distance, the barge-master asked to what port his passengers wished to go. He was told that any Irish port on the eastern coast would suit them; and he then altered his tone, and roughly refused to carry them anywhere but to Bristol. The man's evil intentions were manifest now; and Le Despenser, drawing his sword, sternly commanded him to continue his voyage to Ireland, if he valued his life. The barge master's only reply was a low signal-whistle, in answer to which twenty men, concealed in the hold, sprang on deck and overwhelmed the little band of fugitives. The barge then put about for Bristol, and on landing, the noble captive was delivered by the treacherous barge master into the custody of the Mayor. That officer put him in close prison, and despatched a fleet messenger to Henry to inquire what should be done with him. But before the answer arrived, the capture became known in Bristol, and a clamorous mob assembled before the Castle. The Mayor, to his credit, did his best to resist the rabble, and to save his prisoner; but the mob were stronger than authority. They carried the gates, rushed pell-mell into the Castle, and dragged the captive forth into the market-place. And then Bertram saw his master again a helpless prisoner, in the hands of a furious mob, among whom several priests were active. As he appeared, there was a great shout of "Traitor!" and a few cries, lower yet more terrible, of "Heretic!" They dragged him to the block erected in the midst of the market-place, by which stood the public executioner. Le Despenser saw unmistakably that his last hour had come; and he had not been so far from anticipating that closing scene, that he was unprepared for its coming.

"Sir," he said, turning to the executioner with his ordinary courtesy, "I pray you of your grace to grant me time for prayer, and strike not ere"—touching his handkerchief "I shall let this fall."

The executioner, a quiet, practical man, unpossessed by the fury of the mob, promised what was asked of him. Meantime Bertram Lyngern contrived to squeeze himself inch by inch through the crowd, until at last he stood beside his master.

"Ah, my trusty squire!" was the prisoner's greeting. "Look you have here my signet, which with Master Mayor's gentle allowing, you shall bear unto my Lady."

The Mayor nodded permission. He was vexed and ashamed.

"Farewell, good friend," resumed Le Despenser, with a parting grasp of his squire's hand. "Be sure to tell Madam my mother that I died true to God and the King—and say unto my Lady that my last thought was of her."

Then he knelt down to commune with God. But he asked for no priest ; and when they saw it, the cries of the mob became fiercer than ever.

"Traitor!" and "Heretic!" were roared from every part of the vast square.

Le Despenser rose, and faced his enemies.

"I am no traitor to my true King, and no heretic to the living God!" he cried earnestly. "I was ever a true man to God, and to the King, and to my Lady : touching which ye are not my judge, but God."

His voice was drowned by another roar of execration. Then he knelt again—and the handkerchief fell. But just as the executioner raised his arm

> "Just ere the falling axe did part
> The burning brain from the true heart "—

one word trembled on the dying lips "Custance!"

In another minute, lifting the severed head by its dark auburn hair, the executioner shouted to the sovereign mob "This is the head of a traitor!"

"Thou liest!" broke in a low fierce whisper from Bertram Lyngern.

"I wis that, Master!" returned the poor executioner.

He was not the first man, nor the last, who has been required to pronounce officially what his conscience individually refused to sanction.

The severed head was sent to London, a ghastly gift to the usurper. It was set up on London Bridge, beside that of Exeter. The body was carried into the Castle, saved by the Mayor from insult; and a few days afterwards they bore it by slow stages to Tewkesbury Abbey, and laid him in his father's grave.

Surrey and Exeter died for their King alone. But it was only half for King Richard that Salisbury and Le Despenser died; and the other half was for the word of God, and for the testimony of Jesus Christ. They were both hereditary Lollards and chiefs of the Lollard party; and they were both beheaded, not by Henry's authority, but by a priest-ridden mob. And at that Bar where the cup of cold water shall in no wise lose its reward, surely such semi-martyrdom as that day beheld at Bristol will not be forgotten before God.

CHAPTER VIII.

MOVES ON THE CHESSBOARD.

" O purblind race of miserable men,
How many among us at this very hour
Do forge a life-long trouble for themselves,
By taking true for false, or false for true !"
TENNYSON.

THREE months had rolled away since that thirteenth of January which had made Constance a widow Her versatile, volatile nature soon recovered the shock of her husband's violent death. The white garments of widowhood which draped her found little response either in the gravity of her demeanour or in the expression of her face. But on the Dowager Lady the effect was very different. She became an old, infirm woman all at once; but her manner was softer and gentler. She learned to make more allowance for temperaments which entirely differed from hers. There were no further efforts to repress her little grandson's noisy glee, no more cold responses to his occasionally troublesome demonstrations of affection. The alteration was quiet, but lasting.

It was an hour after dinner, and Maude sat alone at work in the banquet hall. She was almost unconsciously humming to herself the air of a troubadour chanson— an air as well known to ourselves as to her, though we have turned it into a hymn tune, and have christened it

Innocents, or Durham. A fresh stave was just begun, when the hall door opened, and a voice at the further end announced—

"A messenger from my Lord of Aumerle!"

Maude rose as the messenger approached her.

"Your servant, sir! If you bear any letter, I will carry the same unto my Lady."

"Here is the letter, Mistress Maude," replied the messenger with a smile. "Methinks I am more changed than you be."

Maude looked more narrowly at him.

"I know you now, Master Calverley," she said, a smile breaking over her lips. "But you ware not that beard the last time I did see you."

She took the letter to Constance, and when she returned, she found Hugh and his old friend Bertram in close conversation.

"Verily, sweet Hugh" Bertram was saying—"there is one thing in this world I can in no wise fathom! How thy Lord—"

"There be full many things in this world that I cannot," interposed Hugh.

"How thy Lord ordereth his dealings is beyond me," ended Bertram.

"In good sooth, I have enough ado to look to mine own dealings, though I should let other men's be," answered Hugh.

"Lo' you now, Mistress Maude! Here is my Lord of Aumerle   you wis somewhat of his deeds—high in favour with the King, and prevailing upon his Grace to grant all manner of delicates[1] unto our Lady. He hath

[1] Good things.

soothly-stirred[1] him unto the bestowal of every manor that was our late Lord's father s (whom God assoil!) and of all his jewels, and of the custody of the young Lord. And 'tis not four months gone since he sold our Lord to his death! What signifieth he by this whileness?"[2]

Maude shook her head, as if to say that she could not tell. She had resumed her work, the hemming of what she (not very elegantly) called a sudary, and we, euphemistically but tautologically, a pocket handkerchief.

"Ah! 'tis a blessed thing to have a brother!" observed Bertram with irony. "Well!—and what news, sweet Hugh, of olden friends?"

"None overmuch," responded Hugh, "unless it be ol the death of Father Wilfred, of the Priory at Langley."

"Ah me!" exclaimed Bertram regretfully.

"Master Calverley," said Maude, looking up, "do me to wit, of your goodness, if you wot any thing touching the Lady Avice de Narbonne?"

"But so much," answered he, "that she hath taken veil upon herself in the Minoresses' convent at Aldgate, and is, I do hear, accounted of the sisters a right holy and devout woman."

"Marry, I am well fain to hear so good news," said Maude.

"Good news, Mistress Maude! forsooth, were I lover or kinsman of the fair lady, I would account them right evil news," commented Bertram, in a tone of some surprise.

"Methinks I conceive what Mistress Maude signifieth," quietly observed Hugh. "She accounteth that the Lady

<hr>

[1] Persuaded.   [2] Whirling, turning round.

Avice shall find help and comfort in the Minoresses' house."

"Aye, in very deed," said Maude, "the which methinks she could never have found without."

"God have it so!" answered Hugh, gently. "Yet I trust, Mistress Maude, that our Lord may be found without convent cell, as lightly[1] as within it."

"Be these all thy news, sweet Hugh?" inquired Bertram. "Is nought at work in the outer world?"

"Matters be reasonable peaceful at this present. But methinks King Henry sitteth not over delightsomely on his throne, seeing he hath captivated[2] the four childre of my sometime Lord of March, and shut them close in the Castle of Wirdsor."

"Hath he so?" asked Bertram, with interest. "Poor hearts!"

"Be they small childre?" said Maude, compassionately."

"The Lady Anne, that is eldest, hath but nine years, I do hear."

"Aye me, Master Calverley! Have they any mother?"

"Trust me, aye!" broke in Bertram. "Why, have you forgot that my Lady of March is sister unto the Duchess' Grace of York?"

"And is she prisoned with the childre?"

"Holy Mary! the King's Grace lacketh not her," said Bertram.

"She was dancing at the Court a few weeks gone," returned Hugh rather drily, "with her servant,[3] the Baron of Powys, a waiting upon her; and so was likewise the Lady Elizabeth, my Lord of Exeter his widow, with the

---

[1] Easily.   [2] Captured.   [3] Lover.

Lord Fanhope. Men say there shall be divers weddings at Court this next summer, and these, as I reckon, among them."

"Ah! the Lady Elizabeth's Grace danceth right well!" said Bertram sarcastically. "Marry, Robin Falconer, of my Lord's Grace of York's following, which bare hither certain letters this last month, told me they had dances at Court in Epiphany octave, when we rade for our lives from Oxford; and that very night my Lord's Grace of Exeter was beheaden at Pleshy, his wife, the Lady Elizabeth, was at the cushion dance and singing to her lute in the Lady Blanche[1] her chamber, where all the Court was gathered."

"Aid us, our Lady of Pity!" whispered Maude in a shocked voice.

"There be some women hard as stones!" pursued Bertram disgustedly.

For men knew the Lady Elizabeth well in those days, as fairest and gayest of the Princesses. She was King Henry's favourite sister, though that royal gentleman showed his favour rather oddly, by granting her a quantity of damaged goods of her late husband, among which were sundry towels, "used and torn." During the terrible struggle which had just occurred, she had sided with her brother, against King Richard, of whom her husband Exeter was a fervent partisan. Perhaps such vacillation as was occasionally to be seen in Exeter's conduct may be traced to her influence. The night that King Richard was taken, she "made good cheer," though the event was almost equivalent to the signing of her husband's death-warrant. I doubt if we must not class

[1] The Princess Royal.

this accomplished and beautiful Elizabeth among the most heartless women whose names have come down to us on the roll of history. And where a woman is heartless, she is heartless indeed.

"Forsooth, Master Lyngern, methinks I wis what you mean by women hard as stones," observed Maude with a slight shudder. "They do give me alway the horrors."

"Think you there is naught of the stone in the Lady Custance?" said Hugh in a low voice.

Maude energetically repudiated the imputation.

"She a stone? nay!—she is a butterfly," said Bertram.

"And, pray you, which were better to have a stone or a butterfly to your wife?" asked Hugh, laughingly.

"The stone, in good surety," said Bertram. "I were allgates[1] afeard of hurting the butterfly."

"Very well," responded Hugh, rather drily; "but the stone might hurt thee."

The summer passed very quietly at Cardiff, except for one incident. Maude spent it in learning to read, for which she had always had a strong wish, and now coaxed Father Ademar to teach her. The confessor was a Lollard, and was therefore not deterred by any fear of her becoming acquainted with forbidden books. He willingly complied with Maude's wish.

The incident which disturbed the calm was a hostile visit of Owain Glyndwr, who appeared with a large force on the tenth of July, and held the Church of St. Mary against all comers, until driven out with great slaughter. On the very morning of his appearance, the last baby came to Cardiff Castle a baby which would never see its father. The Bishop of Llandaff, who was

---

[1] Always.

a guest in the Castle, was obliged to reconsecrate the church before the child could be christened. It was not till late in the evening that the little lady was baptized by the name of Isabel, after the dead Infanta. She might have been born to illustrate Bertram's observations, for her heart was as hard as a stone, and as cold.

When Maude became able to read well, she was installed in the post of daily reader to the Dowager. Constance had never cared for books; but the old lady, who had been a great reader for her time, missed her usual luxury now that age was dimming her eyes, and was very glad to employ Maude's younger sight. The book was nearly always one of Wycliffe's, and the reading invariably closed with a chapter of his Testament. Now and then, but only now and then, she would ask for a little poetry—taking by preference that courtly writer whom she knew as a great innovator, but whom we call the father of English poetry. But she was very particular which of his poems was selected. The Knight's, the Squire's, the Man of Law's, the Prioress's, and the Clerk's Tales, were all that she would have of that book by which we know Geoffrey Chaucer best. She liked better the graceful fairy tale of the Flower and the Leaf, written for the deceased Lollard Queen; and best of all that most pathetic lamentation for the Duchess Blanche of Lancaster, whom Elizabeth Le Despenser had known personally in her youth. Maude would never have suspected the Dowager of the least respect for poetry; and she was surprised to watch her sit by the open casement, dreamily looking out on the landscape, while she read to her of the "white ycrowned Queen" of the Daisy, or of the providential interpositions

oy which " Crist unwemmèd kept Custance," or oftener
yet—

> " But what visàge had she thereto ?
> Alas, my heart is wonder woe
> That I ne can discriven it
> Me lacketh both English and wit . . .
> For certes Nature had such lest
> To make that fair, that truly she
> Was her chief patron of beautè,
> And chief ensample of all her work
> And monstre[1]   for be 't ne'er so derk,
> Methinkth I see her evermo' !"

But this, as has been said, was only now and then.
The words which were far more common were Wycliffe's;
and those which were invariable were Christ's.

When Maude began this work, she had not the re-
motest idea of changing her faith, nor even of inquiring
into the grounds on which it rested. She entertained
no personal prejudice against the Lollards, with whom
she associated her dead mistress the Infanta, and her
young murdered master; but she vaguely supposed their
doctrines to be somehow unorthodox, and considered herself as good a " Catholic" as any one. She noticed that
Father Ademar gave her fewer penances than Father
Dominic used to do ; that he treated her mistakes as
mistakes only, and not as sins , that generally his ideas
of sin had to do rather with the root of evil in the heart
than with the diligent pruning of particular branches;
that he said a great deal about Christ, and not much
about the saints. So Maude's change of opinion came
over her so gradually and noiselessly that she never
realized herself to have undergone any change at all
until it was unalterable and complete.

[1] Then employed in the sense in which we now use *phœnix.*

The realisation came suddenly at last, with a passing word from Dame Audrey, the mistress of the household at Cardiff.

"Nay," she had said, a little contemptuously, in answer to some remark: "Mistress Maude is too good to consort with us poor Catholics. She is a great clerk, quotha! and hath Sir John de Wycliffe his homilies and evangels at her tongue's end. Marry, I count in another twelvemonth every soul in this Castle saving me shall be a Lollard."

Maude was startled. Was the charge true that she was no longer a "Catholic," but a Lollard? And if so, in what did the change consist of which she was herself unconscious?

That afternoon, when she sat down to read to the Dowager as usual, Maude asked timidly—

"Madam, under your Ladyship's good leave, there is a thing I would fain ask at you."

"Ask freely, my maid," was the kindly answer.

"Might it like you to arede me, Madam, of your grace —in what regard, and to what greatness, the Lollards do differ from the Catholics?"

The Dowager smiled, but she looked a little surprised.

"A short question, forsooth, my maid, the which to answer shortly should lack sharper wit than mine. But I will give thee to wit so far as I can. We do believe that all things which be needful for a Christian man to know, be founden in God's Word, yclept Holy Scripture: so that all other our differences take root in this one. For the which encheson[1] we do deny the Pope to have right and rule over this our Church of England, which

———
[1] Reason.

lieth not in his diocese, neither find we in Holy Scripture that the Bishop of Rome should wield rule over other Bishops ; but that in every realm the King thereof should be highest in estate over the priests as over any other of his subjects. Wherefore likewise we call not upon the saints, seeing that Holy Scripture saith 'oo God and a Mediatour is of God and of men, a man, Crist Jesu :' neither may we allow the holy bread of the blessed Sacrament of the Altar to be the very carnal flesh of our Saviour Christ, there bodily present, seeing both that Paul sayeth of it 'this breed' after that it be consecrate, and moreover that our own very bodily senses do deny it to be any other matter. So neither will any of us use swearing, which is utterly forbid in God's Word ; neither hold we good the right of sanctuary, ne the power of the Pope's indulgence, ne virginity of the priesthood   seeing that no one of all these be bidden by Holy Scripture."

The old lady paused, and cut off her loose threads before she continued, in a rather more constrained voice.

"Beyond all these," she then added, "there be other matters wherein certain of us do differ from other. To wit, some of us do love to sing unto symphony[1] the praise and laud of God ; the which othersome (of whom am I myself) do account to be but a vain indulgence of the flesh, and a thing unmeet for its vanity to be done of God's servants dwelling in this evil world. Some do hold that childre ought not to be baptized, but only them that be of age to perceive the signification of that holy rite : herein I see not with them. Likewise there be othersome that would have the old prayers for to abide,

[1] Music.

being but a form of words; while other (of whom be I) do understand such forms to be but things dead and dry, and we rather would pray unto our Lord with such words as He in the instant moment shall show unto us—the which (nowise contaking[1] other) we do nathless judge to be more agreeable with Holy Scripture. But wherefore wouldst know all this, my maid?"

Maude's answer was not a reply according to grammar, but it showed her thoughts plainly enough. She had been carefully comparing her own inward convictions with the catalogue as it proceeded. She certainly could see no harm either in infant baptism or sacred music: as to the question of forms of prayer, she had never considered it. But on all the other points, though to her own dismay, she found herself exactly in agreement with the description given by the Dowager.

"Then I *am* a Lollard, I account!" she said at last, with a sigh.

"And what if so, my maid?" quietly asked the old lady.

"Good Madam, can I so be, and yet be in unity with the Catholic Church?" said Maude in a tone of distress. "Methinks 'tis little comfort to be not yet excommunicate, if I do wit that an' holy Church knew of mine errors, she should cut me away as a dry branch. And yet" and a very puzzled, troubled look came into Maude's face—"what I crede, I crede; ne can I thereof uncharge[2] me."

"My maid," said the Dowager earnestly, looking up, "the true unity of the Church Catholic is the unity of Christ. He said not 'Come into the Church,' but 'Come

---

[1] Reproaching.   [2] Disburden.

to Me.' He that is one with Christ cannot be withoutenside Christ's Church."

No more was said at that time; but what she had heard already left Maude's mind in a turmoil. She next, but very cautiously, endeavoured to ascertain the opinions of her mistress. Constance made her explain her motive in asking, and then laughed heartily.

"By St. Veronica her sudary, what matter? Names be but names. So long as a man deal uprightly and keep him from deadly sin—call him Catholic, call him Lollard—is he the worser man? There be good and ill of every sort. I have known some weary tykes[1] that were rare Catholics; and I once had a mother that is with God and His angels now, and men called her a Lollard."

Evidently Constance's practical religion was summed up in the childish phrase—"Be good." An excellent medicine—if the patient were not unable to swallow.

Maude tried Bertram next, and felt, to use her own phrase, more "of a bire"[2] than ever. For she found him nearly in the same state of mind as herself, but advanced one step further. Convinced that the true meaning of Lollardism was plain adhesion to Holy Scripture, he was prepared to accept the full consequences. He had not only been thinking for himself, but talking with Hugh Calverley: and Hugh, like his father, was a Lollard of the most extreme type.

"It seemeth me, Mistress Maude," he said boldly, "less dread to say that the Church Catholic must needs have erred, than to say that God in His Word can err."

"But the whole Church Catholic!" objected Maude

---

[1] Really, a sheep-dog; used as a term of reproach.   [2] Confused.

in a most troubled voice. "All the holy doctors and bishops that have ever been—yea, and the very Fathers of the Church!"

"'Nyle ye clepe to you a fadir on erthe,'" replied Bertram gravely.

"But, Master Lyngern, think you, the Holy Ghost dwelleth in the priests, and so He doth not in slender folk like to you and me."

"Aye so?" answered he, with a slight curl of his lip. "He dwelleth in such men as my Lord of Canterbury, trow? Our Lord saith the tree is known by his fruits. It were a new thing, mereckoneth, for a man to be indwelt of the Holy Ghost, and to bring forth fruits of the Devil."

"But our Lord behote[1] to dwell in His Church alway," urged Maude, though she was arguing against herself.

"He behote to dwell in all humble and faithful souls —they be His Church, Mistress Maude. I never read in no Scripture that He behote to write all the Pope's decretals, nor to see that no Archbishop of Canterbury should blunder in his pastorals."

"But the Church, Master Lyngern—*the Church* cannot err! Holy Scripture saith it."

"Aye so?" said Bertram again. "Where?"

Maude was obliged to confess that she did not know where; she had "alway heard say the same;" but finding Bertram rather too much for her in argument, she carried her difficulty to Father Ademar when she next went to confession. She would never have propounded such a query to Father Dominic at Langley, since it would most certainly have ensured her a severe scolding and

---

[1] Promised.

some oppressive penance ; perhaps to lie flat on the threshold of the chapel and let every one pass over her, perhaps to lick the dust all round the base of the Virgin's pedestal. And Maude's own private conviction was that penances of this kind never did her the least good. Father Dominic told her that they humbled her. It was true they made her feel humiliated ; but was that the same as feeling humble ? They also made her feel irritated and angry—with whom, or with what, she hardly knew ; but certainly with some person or thing outside of herself. But they never made her think that she had done wrong—only that she had been misunderstood and badly used.

Matters were very different with Father Ademar. He was so quiet and gentle that Maude never felt afraid of him. Confession to Father Dominic bore the awful aspect cast over a visit to a dentist's surgery ; but confession to Father Ademar was (at least to Maude) merely talking over her difficulties with a friend. He often said, " Pray our Lord to grant thee wisdom in this matter," but he never said, " Repeat fifty Aves and ten Paternosters." And when Maude now laid her troubles before him as lucidly as she could, he gave her an answer which, she thought at first, did not touch the case at all, and yet which in the end settled every difficulty connected with it.

" Daughter," said the Lollard priest, "there is another question which must be first answered. Thou hast taken up the golden rod by the wrong end. Turn it around and have the other ensured ; then we will talk of this."

" What other question, Father ?"

" The same that our Lord asked of the sick man at

the cistern[1]—'Wilt thou be made whole?' Art thou of the unity of Christ? art thou one with Him? Hast thou closed with Him? Wist thou that 'He loved *thee*, and gave Himself for thee?' For without thou be first ensured of this, it shall serve thee but little to search all the tomes of the Fathers touching the unity of the Church."

"But if I be in the true Church, Father, I must needs be of the unity of Christ."

"Truth," said Father Ademar, in his quietest manner. "Then turn the matter about, as I bade thee, and see whether thou art in Christ. So shalt thou plainly see thyself to be in the true Church."

Maude was silenced, but at first she was not convinced. Ademar did not press her answer. He left her to decide the question for herself. But many months passed away, fraught with many struggles and heart searchings and deep studies of Wycliffe's Bible, before Maude was able to decide it. Bertram, whose mental nature was less self-conscious and analytical than hers, was at peace long before she was. But the day came at last when Maude was able to answer Ademar's question—when she could say, "Father, I am of the true Church, because I am one with Christ."

The life at Cardiff Castle was very quiet—much too quiet to please Constance, who was again becoming extremely restless. They heard of wars and rumours of war conspiracy after conspiracy, all more or less futile : some to free King Richard, whom a great number believed to be still living ; some to release and crown the little Earl of March, yet a close prisoner in Windsor

<hr>

[1] Pool.

Castle; some to depose or assassinate Henry. But they were all to the dwellers in Cardiff Castle like the sounds of distant tempest, until the summer of 1402, when two terrible events happened almost simultaneously, and one at their very doors. Owain Glyndwr, the faithful Welsh henchman of King Richard, took and burnt Cardiff in one of his insurrectionary marches; sparing the Castle and one of the monasteries on account of the loyalty (to Richard) of their inmates; and about the same time Hugh Calverley came one day from Bristol, to summon the Princess to come immediately to Langley. Her father was dying.

Constance reached Langley in time to receive his last blessing. He died in the same quiet, apathetic manner in which he had lived—his intellect insufficient to realise all the mischief of which he had been guilty, but having realised one mistake he had made—his second marriage. He desired to be buried in the Priory Church at Langley, by the side of his "dear wife Isabel," whose worth he had never discovered until she was lost to him for ever.

It was on the first of August that Edmund of Langley died. After his funeral, the Duchess Joan—now a young woman of nineteen—intimated her intention of paying a visit to Court, as soon as her first mourning was over, and blandishingly hoped that her dear daughter would do her the pleasure of accompanying her. Maude would have liked her mistress to decline the invitation, for she would far rather have gone home. But Constance accepted it eagerly. It was exactly what she wished. They reached Westminster Palace just after the King had returned from his autumn progress, and he expressed a hope that his aunt and cousin would stay with him long enough to be present at the approaching ceremony of his second marriage with the Duchess Dowager of Bretagne.

It was the evening after their arrival at Westminster, and Maude sat on a stool in the great hall, every now and then recognising and addressing some acquaintance of old time. On the daïs was a brilliant crowd of royal and semi-royal persons, among whom Constance sat engaged in animated conversation, and evidently enjoying herself. Maude knew most of them by sight, but as her eyes roved here and there, they lighted on a young man coming up towards the daïs whom she did not know. He stopped almost close to her, to speak to Aumerle, now Duke of York, so that Maude had time and opportunity to study him.

He was dressed in the height of the fashion. In the present day his costume would be thought supremely ridiculous for a man ; but when he wore it, it was considered perfectly enchanting. It consisted of a gown—similar to a long dressing-gown, nearly touching the feet —of blue velvet, spangled with gold fleur de lis, and lined with white satin ; an under tunic (equivalent to a waistcoat) of bright apple-green satin, with wide sweeping sleeves of the same, cut at the edge into imitations of oak-leaves. Under these were tight sleeves of pink velvet, edged at the wrist by white frills, and a similar white frill finished the gown at the neck. His boots were black velvet, with white buttons ; they were about a yard long, tapering to a point, and were tied up to the garter by silver chains, a pattern resembling a church window being cut through the upper portion of the boot.

These very fashionable and most uncomfortable articles were known as cracowes, having come over from Germany with the late Queen Anne. In the young man's hand was a black velvet cap, covered by a spreading plume of apple-green feathers. Round the waist, outside the gown, was a tight black velvet band, to which was fastened the scabbard of a golden-hilted sword.

This extremely smart young gentleman was Sir Edmund de Holand, Earl of Kent,—brother and heir of the Duke of Surrey, and brother also of Constance's step-mother. He was a true Holand in appearance, nearly six feet in height, most graceful in carriage, very fair in complexion, his hair a glossy golden colour, with a moustache of similar shade. His age was just twenty-one. He was pre-eminently handsome—surpassing even Surrey. His eyes were of the softest blue, clear and bright; his voice soft, musical, and insinuating.

I am careful to describe the Earl of Kent fully, because he is about to become a prominent person in the story, and also because he had absolutely nothing to recommend him beyond his physical courage, his taste in dress, his fascinating manners, and his very handsome person. These points have to be dwelt upon, since his virtues lay entirely in them.

Kent and York conversed in a low tone for some minutes. When the subject seemed exhausted, York turned quickly round to his sister, as if a sudden idea had occurred to him.

"Lady Custance! You remember my Lord of Kent, trow?—though methinks you have scarce met together sithence we were all childre."

Constance lifted up her eyes, and offered her hand to

Kent's kiss of homage.   Aye, to her utter misery and undoing, like Elaine,

> ——" she lifted up her eyes,
> And loved him, with that love which was her doom."

Not worth such love as that, Constance! Not worth one beat of that true heart which was stilled at Bristol, and which now lies, dust to dust, in Tewkesbury Abbey. This man will not love you as he did, to the end. He will only give you what love he can spare from himself, for he is his own most cherished treasure. And it will be—as, a few hours later, you whisper to yourself, pulling the petals from a white daisy—"*un peu beaucoup—point du tout:*"—a little yesterday, intense to-day, and none at all to-morrow.

Constance and Kent saw a good deal of each other during her visit to Westminster. Her brother of York evidently furthered his suit to the utmost of his power. Maude, who had learned utterly to distrust the Duke of York, set herself to consider what his reason could be. That York rarely did any thing except with some ulterior and selfish object, she was satisfied. But the more she thought about the matter, the further she found herself from arriving at any conclusion. The secret was to be revealed to her before long. The plotting brain of the Prince was busy as usual in the concoction of another conspiracy, and to forward his purposes on this occasion he intended to make a catspaw of his sister. The plot was not yet quite ripe; but when it should be, for Constance to be Kent's wife would make her all the more eligible as a tool.

The ceremonies attendant on the royal marriage were

over; the King was about to take the field against another
insurrection of Glyndwr, and the Earl of Kent had undertaken to guard him to Shrewsbury. Maude, in close
attendance on her mistress, heard the parting words
between Kent and Constance.

"You will render me visit at Cardiff, my Lord ?"

"Sweet Lady, were it possible I could neglect such
bidding ?"

Constance journeyed in the royal train for a distance,
and turned off towards Cardiff, when their ways parted.

Her manner when she arrived at home was particularly affectionate, both to the Dowager and her children,
of whom little Richard was now eight years old, while
Isabel had just reached four. The keen eyes of the
old lady—much sharper mentally than physically—soon
discerned the presence of some new element in her
daughter-in-law's mind. She closely questioned Maude
as to what had happened, or was about to happen ; and
after a minute's hesitation, Maude told her all she knew
and feared. For some time after receiving this information, Elizabeth Le Despenser sat gazing uneasily from
the lattice, with unwontedly idle hands.

"Sister's son unto our adversary !" she murmured to
herself at last. "Whither shall this tend ? Verily, there
is One stronger than Thomas de Arundel. Is He leading
us blind by a way that we know not ? for in very sooth
I cannot discern the way. If so it be, then—Lord, lead
Thou on !"

Kent paid his visit to Cardiff in the winter, accom
panied by Constance's pet brother, Lord Richard of
Conisborough, who had been promoted to his father's
old dignity of Earl of Cambridge. It was the first time

that the Dowager had seen either; and she afterwards communicated her impressions of the pair to Maude, as they sat together at work.

"As touching the Lord Richard, he is gent and courteous enough; he were no ill companion, an' he knew his own mind a little better. Mayhap three of him, or four, might make a man amongst them."

For Cambridge, though in a much fainter degree, reflected his father's character by finding it very difficult to say no.

"And what thinks your Ladyship of my Lord of Kent?" asked Maude with some anxiety.

The Dowager shook the loose threads from her work with a peculiar little laugh.

"Marry, my maid, what think I of my Lord of Kent his barber, and his tailor?" said she; "for they made my Lord of Kent betwixt them. He is not a man of God's making."

"But think you, Madam, he is to be trusted or no?"

"Trusted! for what? To oil his golden locks, and perfume well his sudary, and have his sleeves of the newest cutting? Aye, forsooth, and that right worthily!"

"I meant," explained Maude, "to have a care of our Lady."

"Maybe he shall keep her in ointment for her hair," returned the Dowager.

The Earl of Kent returned to Court, and for some time stayed there. He was rather too busy to prosecute his wooing. The Lord Thomas of Lancaster, one of the King's sons, was projecting and executing an expedition from Calais to Sluys, and he took Kent with him; so that, with one or another obstacle arising, Constance's second marriage was not quite so quick in coming as Maude had expected. But at last it did come.

The Duke of York and his Duchess—not long married—and the Earl of Cambridge, journeyed to Cardiff for their sister's wedding. The Duchess of York, though both an heiress and a beauty, left no mark on her time. She was by profession at least a Lollard; and since Lollardism was not now walking in silver slippers, this says something for her. But in all other respects she appears to have been one of those beautiful, mindless women whom clever men frequently marry. Perhaps no woman with a decided character of her own would have ventured on such a husband as Edward Duke of York.

It was a mild winter day, and a picnic was projected in the woods near Cardiff. The wedding was to take place in about a week. Maude rode on a pillion to the scene where the rustic dinner was to be behind Bertram Lyngern, who seemed in a particularly bright and amiable mood. When a woman rode on a pillion, it must be remembered that she was in a very insecure position; and it was an absolute necessity for the fair rider to clasp her arms round the waist of the man who sat before her, and, when the road was rough, to cling pretty tightly. It was therefore desirable that the pair should be at least reasonably civil to one another, and should not get on quarrelsome terms. There was little likelihood of Maude's quarrelling with Bertram, her friend of twenty years' standing; but she did not share his evident light heartedness as he rode carolling along, now breaking out into a snatch of one song, and now of

another, and constantly interrupting himself with playful remarks.

> "'Sitteth all still, and hearkeneth to me:
> The King of Almayne, by my léauté,
> Thritti thousand pound asked he ——'

—A squirrel, Mistress Maude! shall I catch it?

> "'*Dame avec l'œil de beauté* ——'

So, my good lad, softly! so, Lyard! How clereful a
day! Nigh as soft as summer.

> "'Summer is ycomen in—
> Merry sing, cuckoo!
> Groweth glede, and bloweth mead,
> And springeth wood anew.'

Be merry, Mistress Maude, I pray you! you mope not,
surely?"

"I scarce know, Master Lyngern. Mayhap so."

"Shame to mope on such a day!" said Bertram, springing from the saddle, and holding his hand to help Maude
to jump down also. "There hath not been so fair a morrow this month gone."

He was soon busy unpacking the sumpter-mules' bags,
with two or three more ; and dinner was served under the
shade of the trees, without any consideration of cere
mony. Our fathers spent so much of their time out of
doors, and dressed for the season so much more warmly
than we do, that they chose days for picnics at which
we should shudder. After dinner Maude wandered
about a little by herself, and at length sat down at the
foot of a lofty oak. She had not been there many
minutes before she saw Constance and York coming
slowly towards her, evidently in earnest conversation.

"Lo' you here, Ned!" said Constance eagerly, when she caught sight of Maude. "Here is one true as steel. I ˙ that you say must have no eavesdroppers, sit we on the further side of this tree; and Maude, hold where thou art, and if any come this way, give a privy pluck at my gown, and we will speak other."

They sat down on the other side of the oak.

"Custance," began her brother, "I misconceive not, trow, to account thee yet true to the cause of King Richard, be he where he may?"

York knew, as certainly as he knew of his own existence, that Richard had been dead five years. But it suited his purpose to speak doubtfully.

"Certes, Ned, of very inwitte!"[1]

"Well. And if King Richard were dead, who standeth next heir?"

"My Lord of March, no manner of doubt."

"Good again. Then we thus stand : King Henry that reigneth hath no right ; and the true King is shut up in Pomfret, or, granting he be dead, is then shut up in Windsor."

"Well, Ned ?"

"Shall we—thou and I—free young March and his brother and sisters ?"

"Thou and I !"

She was evidently doubtful. Edward took a stronger bolt from his quiver.

"Custance, Dickon loves Anne Mortimer."

That was a different matter. If Dickon wanted Anne Mortimer or anything else, in his sister's eyes, he must have it. To refuse to help Ned was one thing, but to refuse to help Dickon was quite another.

---

[1] Most heartily.

"But how should we win in ?"

Edward drew a silver key from his pocket.

"I gat this made of a smith, Custance, a year gone. 'Tis a key for my strong-room at Langley, the which was lost with other my baggage fording the Thames, and I took the mould of the lock in wax, and gave it unto the smith."

He looked in her face, pausing a little between the sentences, to make sure that she understood him; and he saw by her eyes that she did. The very peril and uncertainty involved in such an adventure gave it a charm for her.

"When, Ned ?"

"When I send word."

"Very well. I will be ready."

Before Edward could reply, Bertram Lyngern's horn sounded through the forest, saying distinctly to all who heard it, "Time to go home!" The three rose and walked towards the trysting-place, both Constance and Maude possessed of some ideas which had never presented themselves to them before.

Bertram and Maude rode back as they had come. Maude was very silent, which was no wonder; and so, for ten minutes, was Bertram. Then he began :

"How liked you this forest life, Mistress Maude ?"

"Well, Master Lyngern, and I thank you," said she absently.

"And to-morrow is a week our Lady's Grace shall wed ?"

"Why, Master Lyngern, you know that as well as I."

Maude wished he would have left her to her own

thoughts, from which his questions were no diversion in any sense.

"Mistress Maude, when will you be wed?"

The diversion was effected.

"I, Master Lyngern! I am not about to wed."

"Are you well avised of that, Mistress Maude?"

"Marry, Master Lyngern!" said Maude, feeling rather affronted.

"If you will take mine avisement, you will be wed likewise," said Bertram gravely

"What mean you, Master Lyngern?"

Maude was really hurt. She liked Bertram, and here he was making fun of her, without the least consideration for her feelings.

"Marry, I mean that same," responded Bertram coolly. "Would it like you, Mistress Maude?"

"Methinks you had better do me to wit whom your avisement should have me to wed," said Maude, standing on her dignity, and manufacturing an angry tone to keep herself from crying. She would certainly have released her hold of Bertram, and have sat on her pillion in indignant solitude, if she had not felt almost sure that the result would be a fall in the mud. Bertram's answer was quick and decided.

"Me!"

Maude would have answered with properly injured dignity if she could ; but a disagreeable lump of something came into her throat which spoilt the effect.

"Thou hadst better wed me, Maude," said Bertram coaxingly, dropping his voice and his conventionalities together. "There is not a soul loveth thee as I do ; and thou likest me well."

"I pray you, Master Lyngern, when said I so much?" responded Maude, stung into speech again.

"Just twenty years gone, little Maude," was the gentle answer.

Bertram's voice had changed from its bantering tone into a tender, quiet one, and Maude felt more inclined to cry than ever.

"Is that saying truth no longer, Maude?"

Maude's conscience whispered to her that she must not say any thing of the sort. Still she thought it only proper to hold out a little longer. She was silent; and Bertram, who thought she was coming round, let her alone for a short time. The grey towers of Cardiff slowly rose to view, and in a few seconds more they would no longer be alone.

"Well, Maude?" asked Bertram softly. "Is it aye or nay?"

"As you will, Master Lyngern."

This was Bertram's wooing; and Maude wondered, when she was alone, if any woman had been so wooed before.

Constance expressed the greatest satisfaction when she heard of her bower woman's approaching marriage; but one item of Bertram's project she commanded altered —namely, that Maude's nuptials should not take place on the same day as her own.

"Why, Maude!" she said, "if our two weddings be one day, I shall have but an half day's rejoical, and thou likewise! Nay, good maid! we will have each her full day, and a bonfire in the base court, and feasting, and dancing to boot. Both on one day, quotha! marry, but that were niggardly."

So Maude was married on the Saturday previous to her mistress. She was dressed in lilac damask, trimmed with swansdown, and her hair, for the last time in her life, streamed over her shoulders and fell at its own sweet will. Matrons always tucked away their hair in the dove-cote, while widows were careful not to show a single lock. Bertram exhibited extraordinary splendour, for he was generally rather careless about his dress. He wore a red damask gown, trimmed with rabbit's fur; a bright blue under-tunic; a pair of red boots with white buttons; and he bore in his hand a copped hat of blue serge. The copped hat had no brim, and was about a foot and a half in height. Bertram's appearance, therefore, to say the least, was striking.

When the ceremony was just completed, without any previous intimation, the Duke of York, who was present, drew his sword, and lightly struck the shoulder of the bridegroom, before he could rise from his knees.

"Rise, Sir Bertram Lyngern!"

So Maude became entitled at once to the honourable prefix of "Dame."

The grander wedding was on the following Thursday. The Earl of Kent's costume baffles description. Suffice it to say that it cost two thousand pounds. The royal bride doffed her widow's weeds, and appeared in a crimson silk deeply edged with ermine, low in the neck, but with long sleeves to the wrist. She wore the dove cote, and over it an open circlet of gold and gems, to mark her royal rank.

At the threshold of Constance's bower, after the ceremony, the old Lady Le Despenser met the Earl and Countess of Kent.

"The Lord bless you, fair daughter!" she said, laying her hands on the bowed head of the bride.

But a little later the same evening, she said unexpectedly, "Aye me! I am but a blind thing, Dame Maude; yet this match of the Lady Custance doth sorely misgive me."

At the other end of the room, the Duke of York was saying, "You will visit me at Langley, fair sister, this coming spring?"

"With a very good will, Ned."

It only remains to be noted that Father Ademar officiated at both marriages; and that as in those days people went home for the honeymoon, not away from it, the Earl and Countess set out from Cardiff in a few days for Brockenhurst, the birthplace and favourite residence of the young Earl. The children were left with their grandmother; they were to follow, in charge of Maude and Bertram, to Langley, where their mother intended to rejoin them. Maude continued to be bower-woman to her mistress; but some of the more menial functions usually discharged by one who filled that office, were now given to a younger girl, who bore the name of Eva de Scanteby.

It was in the evening of a lovely spring day that Constance, accompanied by Kent, rejoined Maude and her children at Langley.

CHAPTER IX.

PLOT AND COUNTERPLOT.

"He that hath a thousand friends hath not a friend to spare,
And he that hath one enemy shall find him everywhere."

ON the evening of Constance's arrival at Langley,
two men sat in close conference in the Jerusalem
Chamber of the Palace of Westminster. One of them
was a priest, the other a layman. The first priest, and
the first layman, in the realm; for the elder was
Thomas de Arundel, Archbishop of Canterbury, and
the younger was Henry of Bolingbroke, King of England.

The Archbishop was a tall, stout, portly man, with a
round, fair, fat face, on which sat an expression of ex
treme self-complacency. A fine forehead, both broad
and high, though slightly too retreating, surmounted a
pair of clear, bright grey eyes, a well-formed nose, and
lips in which there was no weakness, but they were
just a shade too smiling for sincerity. Though his age
was only fifty one, his hair was snow-white. Of course
his face was closely shaven; for it is an odd fact that the
higher a man's sacerdotal pretensions rise, the more
unlike a man he usually makes himself—resembling

the weaker sex as much as possible, both in person and costume. This man's sacerdotal pretensions ran very high, and accordingly his black cassock fell about his feet like a woman's dress, and his face was guiltless of beard or whisker.

The age of the King was thirty eight, and he was one of the tallest men in his kingdom. The colour of his hair, whiskers, and small forked beard, was only one remove from black. Dark pencilled eyebrows, of that surprised shape which many persons admire, arched over keen liquid dark eyes. The general type of the features was Grecian; their regularity was perfect, but the nose was a trifle too prominent for pure Grecian. About the set of the lips, delicately as they were cut, there was a peculiarity which a physiognomist might have interpreted to mean that when their owner had once placed a particular end before him, no considerations of right on the one hand, or of friendship on the other, would be allowed to interfere with its attainment. This was a very clever man, a very sagacious, far seeing man, a very handsome man, a very popular man; yet a man whom no human heart ever loved, and who never loved any human being—a man who could stand alone, and who did stand alone, to the hour when, "with all his imperfections on his head," he stood before the bar of God.

"The match is no serviceable one," said the Archbishop.

"Truth to tell," replied the King a little doubtfully, "I scarce do account my cousin herself an heretic:— yet I wis not—she may be. But she hath been rocked in the heresy in her cradle, and ever sithence hath been within earshot thereof. You wot well, holy Father, what her lord was; and his mother, with whom she hath dwelt these ten years or more, is worser than himself. Now it shall never serve to have Kent lost to the Church her cause. You set affiance on him, I know, and I the like: and if he be not misturned, methinks he may yet prove a good servant. But here is this alliance cast in our way! I know they be wed without my licence: yet what should it serve to fine or prison him? To prison her might be other matter; but we cannot touch her. So this done should not serve our turn. Father, is there any means that you can devise to break this marriage?"

"The priest that wed them is a Gospeller," returned the Archbishop with a peculiar smile.

"A priest in full orders," objected the King, "of good life and unblemished conversation. Even you, holy Father, so fertile in wise plans, shall scarce, methinks, be able to lay finger on him."

"Scantly; without he were excommunicate of heresy at the time this wedding were celebrate."

"Which he was not," answered the King rather impatiently. "Would to Saint Edmund he had so been! It were then no marriage."

The Archbishop made no reply in words, but drawing towards him a sheet of paper which lay upon the table, he slowly traced upon it a date some two months previous—the date of the Sunday before Constance's marriage. The King watched him in equal silence, with knitted brows and set lips. Then the two conspirators' eyes met.

"Could that be done?" asked the royal layman, under his breath.

"Is it not done, Sire?" calmly responded the priestly villain, pointing to the paper.

The King was silent for a minute; but, unprincipled as he was, his conscience was not quite so seared as that of Arundel.

"The end halloweth the means, trow?" he said inquiringly.

"All means be holy, Sire, where the end is the glory of God," replied Arundel, with a hypocritical assumption of piety. "And the glory of God is the service and avancement of holy Church."

Still Henry's mind misgave him. His conscience appears at times to have tortured him in his later years, and he shrank from burdening it yet further.

"Father, if sin be herein, you must bear this burden!"

"I have borne heavier," replied Arundel with a cynical smile.

And truly, to a man upon whose soul eleven murders lay lightly, an invalidated marriage was likely to be no oppressive weight.

"Yet even now," resumed the King, again knitting his brows uneasily, "methinks all hardships be scarce vanished. Our good cousin of Kent is he that should not be turned aside from his quarry[1] by a brook in his way."

"Not if an eagle arose beyond the heron he pursued?" suggested Arundel, significantly.

"Ha!" said the King.

"He is marvellous taken with beauty," resumed his priestly counsellor. "And the Lady Custance is not the sole woman in the world."

[1] Object of pursuit; a hunting phrase.

"You have some further thought, Father," urged Henry.

"Methinks your Grace hath a good friend in the Lord Galeas, Duke of Milan?"

"Aye, of olden time," answered the King, with a sigh. Was it caused by the regretful thought that if he could bring back that olden time, when young Henry of Bolingbroke was learning Italian at Milan and Venice, he might be a happier man than now?

"He hath sisters, methinks, that bear high fame for fair and lovesome?"

"None higher in Christendom."

"And the youngest born, the Lady Lucy, I take it, is yet unwed?"

"She is so."

"And cometh not behind her sisters for beauty?"

"She was but a little child when I was at Milan," said the King, "but I hear tell of her as fairest of all the fair Visconti."

"Were it impossible, Sire, that the lady, in company of her young brothers, should visit your Highness' Court?"

Henry readily owned that it was by no means impossible, if he were to ask it: but he reminded the Archbishop that the Duke of Milan was poor, though proud; and that while he would consider the Princess Lucia eternally disgraced by marrying beneath her, he probably would not scruple to sell her hand to the highest bidder of those illustrious persons who stood on the list of eligibles. And Kent, semi-royal though he were, was not a rich man, his family having suffered severely from repeated attainders.

"And what riches he hath goeth in velvet and ouches,"[1] said the Archbishop, with his cold, sarcastic smile. "Well —if the Duke's Grace would fain pick up ducats even in the mire, mayhap he shall find them as plenty in England as otherwhere. Your Highness can heald[2] gold with any Prince in Italy. And when the lady is hither, 'twere easy to bid an hunting party, an' your Grace so list. My cousin of Kent loveth good hawking."

Again that keen, cruel smile parted the priestly lips.

"Moreover, Sire, she must be a Prince's daughter, or my cousin, who likewise loveth grandeur and high degree, may count the cost ere he swallow the bait. The Lady Custance is not lightly matched for blood."

"You desire this thing, holy Father?"

The eyes of the two evil counsellors met again.

"It were an holy and demeritous work, Sire," said the priest.

"Be it as you will," returned Henry hastily. "But mind you, holy Father! you bear what there may be of sin."

"I can carry it, Sire!"

The royal and reverend conspirators parted; and the Archbishop, mounting his richly caparisoned mule (an animal used by priests out of affected humility, in imitation of the ass's colt on which Christ rode into Jerusalem), rode straight to Coldharbour, the town residence of his niece, Joan Duchess Dowager of York. He found her at work in the midst of her bower-women; but no sooner did she hear the announcement of her Most Reverend uncle, than she hurriedly commanded them all to leave the room.

<hr>

[1] Jewellery.   [2] Pour forth.

"Well?" she said breathlessly, as soon as they were alone.

"Thy woman's wit hath triumphed, Joan. 'Twas a brave thought of thine, touching the Lady Lucy of Milan. The King fell in therewith, like a fowl into a net."

"Nay, the Lady Lucy was your thought, holy Father; I did but counsel to tempt him with some other. Then it shall be done?"

"It shall be done."

"Thanks be to All-Hallows!" cried the Duchess, with mirth which it would scarcely be too strong a term to call fiend-like. "Now shall the proud minx be brought to lower her lofty head! I hate her!"

"'Tis allowed to hate an heretic," said the Archbishop calmly. "And if the Lady Le Despenser be no heretic, she hath sorely abused her opportunities."

"She shall never be Nym's true wife!" cried the Duchess fierily. "I will not have it! I would sooner follow both her and him to the churchyard! I hate, I hate her!" ·

"Thou mayest yet do that following, Joan. But I must not tarry. Peace be with thee!"

Peace!—of what sort? We are told, indeed, of one who is like a strong man armed, and who keepeth his goods in peace. And the dead sleep peacefully enough —not only dead bodies, but dead souls.

The Earl and Countess of Kent had been about a week at Langley, when a letter arrived from the King, commanding the attendance of the Earl at Court, as feudal service for one of his estates held on that tenure. The Countess was not invited to accompany him. The Duke of York seized his opportunity, for his plot was fully ripe, and suggested that she should obtain the royal permission to pay a visit to Windsor, where the hapless heirs of March were imprisoned. Permission to do so was asked and granted, for the King never suspected his cousin of any sinister intention.

The Earl set out first for Westminster. Constance stood at her lattice, and waved a loving farewell to him as he rode away, turning several times to catch another glimpse of her, and to bend his graceful head in yet another farewell. He had not quite recovered from the glamour of his enchantment.

"Farewell!" said the Princess at last, though her husband was far beyond hearing. "Hark, Maude, to the Priory bells—dost hear them? What say they to thee? I hear them say—'He will come he will come —safely back again!'" And she sang the words in the tone of the chime.

Maude was silent. A dark, sudden presentiment seemed to seize upon her of unknown coming evil, and to her ear also the bells had a voice. But they rang "He will come he will come never any more!"

The bells told the truth—to one of them.

The Duke of York escorted his sister to Windsor. She was accompanied by Bertram and Maude, Eva, and several minor domestics. He left her full directions how to proceed, promising to meet her with a guard of men a few miles beyond Eton, and go with her overland as far as Hereford. The final destination of Constance and her recaptured charges was to be her own home at Cardiff, but a rather roundabout way was to be taken to baffle the probable pursuers. York promised to let Kent know of the escapade through one of his squires on the morning of their departure from Windsor, with orders to join them as quickly as possible by sea from Bideford. At Cardiff the final stand was to be made, in favour of Richard, if living—of March if he were proved to be dead. The evening of a saint's day, about ten days later, was selected for the attempted rescue; in the hope that the sentinels, having honoured the saint by extra feasting and potations, might be the less disposed to extra vigilance.

The first point to be ascertained was the exact rooms in the Castle occupied by the youthful captives. This was easily found out by Bertram. He and Maude were the sole confidants of their mistress's secret. The second scene of the drama—which might turn either to comedy or tragedy—was to obtain a mould of the lock in wax. This also was done by Bertram, who further achieved the third point—that of procuring false keys from a smith. Constance, whose ideas of truth were elastic and accommodating, had instructed her messenger to say that the keys had been lost, and the new ones were wanted to replace them; but Bertram kept a conscience which declined to be burdened with this falsehood, and accordingly he merely reported that the person who had sent him required duplicates of the keys.

No idea of wrongfulness in aiding the plot ever occurred either to Bertram or Maude. In their eyes King Henry was no king at all, but a rebel, a usurper, and a murderer; and the true King, to whom alone their fealty was due, was (if Richard were dead) the boy unjustly confined in Windsor Castle. To work his freedom, therefore, was not a bad deed, but a good one; nor could it fairly be called treachery to circumvent a traitor.

The keys were safely secreted in Constance's jewel-box until the night appointed for the rescue came.

It proved to be fair, but cloudy, with a low damp mist filling the vale of the Thames. Bertram took no one into his confidence but his own squire, William Maydeston, whom he posted in the forest, at a sufficient distance from the Castle, in charge of the four horses necessary to mount the party.

The Princess went to bed as usual—about eight o'clock, for she kept late hours for her time   with Maude and Eva in attendance. Both were dismissed; and Eva at least went peacefully to sleep, in happy ignorance of the kind of awakening which was in store for her. At half-past ten, an hour then esteemed in the middle of the night, Maude, according to instructions previously received, softly opened the door of her lady's bed-chamber. She found her not only risen, but already fully equipped for her journey, and in a state of feverish excitement. She came out at once, and they joined Bertram, who was waiting in the corridor outside. The little trio of plotters crept slowly down the stairs, and across the court yard to the foot of the Beauchamp Tower, within which the children were confined. It was necessary to use the utmost caution, to avoid being heard by the sentinels. Bertram fitted the false key into the great iron lock of the outer door. The door opened, but with such a creak that Maude shuddered in terror lest the sentinels should hear it. She was reassured by a peal of laughter which came from beyond the wall. The sentinels were awake, but were making too much noise themselves to be easily roused to action. Then the party went silently up into the Beauchamp Tower, unlocked the door which they sought, and leaving Bertram outside it to give an alarm if necessary, Constance and Maude entered the first of the two rooms.

A white, frightened face was the first thing they saw. In the outer chamber, as the less valuable pair of prisoners, slept the sisters, Anne and Alianora Mortimer, whose ages were fifteen and eleven. Alianora, the younger, slept quietly; but Anne sat up, wide awake, and said in a tremulous voice which she tried in vain to render firm—

"What is it? Are you a spirit?"

Constance was by her side in a moment, and assured the girl at least of her humanity by taking Anne's face between her hands. She looked on it with deep interest; for this was the face that Dickon loved. A soft, gentle face it was, which would have been pretty if it had been less thin and wan with prison life, and less tired with suspense and care. To her

> " The future was all dark,
> And the past a troubled sea,
> And Memory sat in her heart,
> Wailing where Hope should be."

For Anne Mortimer was one of those hapless girls who are not motherless, but what is far worse, un mothered. Her father, who lay in his bloody grave in Ireland, she had loved dearly; but her mother was a mere stranger somewhere in the world, who had never cared for her at all. To the younger ones Anne herself had been the virtual mother; they had been tended by her fostering care, but who save God had ever tended her? Thus, from the time of her father's death, when she was eight years old, Anne's life had been a flowerless, up hill road, with nothing to look forward to at the end. Was it any wonder that the face looked worn with care, though only fifteen years had passed over it?

The sole breaks to the monotony of this weary life occurred when the Court was at Windsor. Then the poor little prisoners were permitted to come out of durance, and—still under strict surveillance to join the royal party. These times were delightful to the younger three, but they would have been periods of unmixed pain to Anne, if it had not been for the presence and uniform kindness of one person. She shuddered within herself when the King or his Mentor the Archbishop addressed her, shrinking from both with the instinctive aversion of a song bird to a serpent; but Richard of Conisborough spoke as no one else spoke to her—so courteously, so gently, so kindly, that no room was left for fear. No one had ever spoken so to this girl since her father died. And thus, without the faintest sus picion of his feelings towards her, the lonely maiden's imagination wove its sweet fancies around this hero of her dreams, and she began unconsciously to look forward to the time when she should meet him again. Well for her that it was so! for she was a "pale meek blossom " unsuited for rough blasts, and the only ray of sunshine which was ever to fall across her life lay in the love of Richard of Conisborough.

"Who is it?" Anne repeated, in a rather less frightened tone.

"Hast thou forgot me, Nannette?" said Constance

affectionately. "I am the Lady Le Despenser—thine aunt now, the wife of thine uncle of Kent."

"Oh!" responded Anne, with a long-drawn sigh of relief. The tone said, "How delightful!" "I thought you were a ghost."

"Well, so I am, but within the body," whispered Constance with a little laugh.

"That makes all the difference," said Anne, whose response did not go beyond a faint smile. "Has your Ladyship then won allowance to visit us?"

Her voice expressed some surprise, for certainly the middle of the night was a singular time for a visitor to choose for a call.

"Nay, sweet heart. I come without allowance—hush! to bear you all away hence. Wake thy sister, and arise both, and busk[1] you quickly. Where be thy brothers?"

"In the inner cowche."[2]

Constance desired Maude to hasten the girls in dressing, which must be done by the fitful moonlight, as best it could, and went herself into the inner chamber. Both the boys were asleep. They were Edmund, the young Earl, whose age was nearly thirteen, and his little brother Roger, who was not yet eight. Constance laid her hand lightly on the shoulder of the future King.

'Nym!" she said. "Hush! make no bruit."

The boy was sleeping too heavily to be roused at once; but his little brother Roger awoke, and looked up with two very bright, intelligent eyes.

"Are we to be killed?" he wanted to know; but his query was not put in the frightened tone of his sister.

[1] Dress.   [2] Bedroom.

"Not so, little one.　Wake thy brother, and rise quickly."

"'Tis no light gear to wake Nym," said little Roger. "You must shake him."

Constance put the advice in practice, but Edmund only gave a grunt and turned over.

"Nym!" said his little brother in a loud whisper. "Nym! wake up."

Edmund growled an inarticulate request to be "let be."

"Then you must pinch him,' said little Roger. "Nip him well　be not afeard."

Constance, extremely amused, acted on this recommendation also.　Edmund gave another growl.

"Nay, then you must needs slap him!" was the third piece of advice given.

Constance laughingly suggested that the child should do it for her.　Little Roger jumped up, boxed his brother's ears in a decided manner, and finally, burying his small hands in Edmund's light curly hair, gave him a dose of sensation which would have roused a dormouse.

"Is he in this wise every morrow?" asked Constance.

"Master Gaoler bringeth alway a wet mop," said little Roger confidentially. "Wake up, Nym! If thou fallest to sleep again, I must tweak thee by the nose!"

This terrible threat seemed to be nearly as effectual as the mop.　Edmund stretched himself lazily, and in very sleepy accents desired to know what his brother could possibly mean by such wanton cruelty.

"Where is thy breeding, churl, to use such thewis [1] with a lady?" demanded little Roger in a scandalised voice.

[1] Manners.

"Lady! where is one?" murmured Edmund, whose eyes were still shut.

"Methinks thou art roused now, Nym," said Constance. "But when thou shalt be a knight, I pity thy squire. Haste, lad, rise and busk thee in silence, but make as good speed as ever thou canst. Roger, see he turneth not back to sleep. I go to thy sisters."

"Nay, but he will, an' you pluck him not out of bed!" said little Roger, who evidently felt himself unfit to cope with the emergency.

"Thou canst wring him by the nose, then," said Constance, laughing. "Come, Nym! turn out—quick!"

Edmund turned over on his face, buried it in the pillow, and tacitly intimated that to get up at the present moment was an impossibility.

"He'll have another nap!" said little Roger, in the mournful tone of a prophet who foresaw the speedy accomplishment of his tragical predictions.

"But he must not!" exclaimed Constance, returning.

"Then you must pluck him out, and set him on the floor," repeated little Roger earnestly. "'Twill be all I can do to let him to[1] get in again then—without you clap his chaucers[2] about his ears," he added meditatively, as if this expedient might possibly answer.

Constance took the future master of England by his shoulders, and pulled him out of bed without any further quarter. The monarch elect grumbled exceedingly, but in so inarticulate a style that very little could be understood.

"Now, Nym!" said Constance warningly to her refractory and dilatory nephew, "if thou get into bed again,

[1] Hinder him from.   [2] Slippers.

we will leave thee behind, and crown Roger, that is worth ten of thee. By my Lady St. Mary! a pretty King thou wilt make!"

"Eh?" inquired Edmund, brightening up.

"Let be. Go on and busk thee. Roger! if he is not speedy, come to the door and say it."

Constance went back to the girls. She found Anne nearly ready, but Alianora, who apparently shared the indolent disposition of her elder brother, was dressing in the most deliberate manner, though Maude and Anne were both hastening her as much as they could.

"Now, Nell!" said Constance, employing the weapon which had proved useful with Edmund, "if thou make not good speed, we will leave thee behind."

"Well, what if so?" demanded Alianora coolly, tying a string in the most leisurely style.

"If I have not as great a mind to leave you both behind!"—cried Constance in an annoyed tone. "I will bear away Nan and Roger, and wash mine hands of you!"

"Please, I'm ready!" announced little Roger in a whisper through the crack of the door, in an incredibly short space of time.

"Why wert thou not the firstborn?" exclaimed the Princess. "I would thou hadst been! What is Nym about?"

"Combing his hair," said Roger, glancing back at him, "and hath been this never so long."

Constance dashed back into the room with one of her quick, impulsive movements, snatched the comb from his dilatory young Majesty, smoothed his hair in a second, ordered him to wash his hands, and to put on his gown and tunic, and stood over him while he did it.

"The saints have mercy on thee, Nym, and send thee a wise council!" said she, half in earnest and half in jest. "The whole realm will go to sleep else."

"Well, they might do worser," responded Edmund calmly.

The two sluggards we.e ready at last, but not before Constance had lost her temper, and had noticed the unruffled endurance of Anne.

"Why, Nan, thou hast patience enough!" she said.

"I have had need these seven years," answered the maiden quietly.

"Now, Maude, take thou Lord Roger by the hand; and Nan, take thy sister. Nym, thou comest with me. Lead on, Sir Bertram; and mind all of you—no bruit, not enough to wake a mouse!"

"It would not wake Nym, then!" said little Roger.

They crept down the stairs of the Beauchamp Tower as slowly and cautiously as they had come. Down to the little postern gate, left unguarded by the careless sentinel, who was carousing with his fellows on another side of the Castle; out and away to the still glade in Windsor Forest, where Maydeston stood waiting with the horses, all fitted with pillion and saddle.

"Here come we, Maydeston!" exclaimed Bertram. "Now, Madam, an' it like your Grace to mount with help of Master Maydeston, will it list you that I ride afore?"

For it was little short of absolute necessity that the gentleman should be seated on his saddle before the lady mounted the pillion.

"Nay—the King that shall be, the first!" said Constance.

Bertram bowed and apologised. He was always in the habit of giving precedence to his mistress, and he really had forgotten for a moment that the somnolent Nym was to be regarded as his Sovereign. So his future Majesty, with Bertram's assistance, mounted the bay charger, and his sister Alianora was placed on the pillion behind him.

The next horse was mounted by Constance, with Bertram before her; the third by little Roger, very proud of his position, with Maude set on the pillion in charge of her small cavalier, and the bridle firmly tied to Bertram's saddle. Last came Maydeston and Anne. They were just ready to start when Constance broke into a peal of merry laughter.

"I do but laugh to think of Eva's face, when she shall find neither thee nor me,' she said to Maude, "and likewise his Highness' gaolers, waking up to an empty cage where the little birds should be."

Maude's heart was too heavy and anxious about the issue of the adventure to enable her to reply lightly.

Through the most unfrequented bridle-paths they crept slowly on, till first Windsor, and then Eton, was left behind. They were about two miles beyond Eton, when a hand was suddenly laid on Constance's bridle, and the summons to "Stand and deliver!" jestingly uttered in a familiar and most welcome voice.

"Ha, Dickon! right glad am I to hear thee!" cried his sister.

"Is all well, Custance?"

"Sweet as Spanish must.[1] But where is Ned?"

"Within earshot, fair Sister," said Edward's equally

---

[1] New wine.

well known and deeper tones. "Methinks a somewhat other settlement should serve better for quick riding, though thine were well enough to creep withal. Sir Bertram, I pray you alight you shall ride with your dame, and I with the Lady Countess. Can you set the Lord Roger afore? Good! then so do. Lord Sele! I pray you to squire the Lady Alianora's Grace. His Highness will ride single, as shall be more to his pleasure. Now, Dickon, I am right sorry to trouble thee, but mefeareth I must needs set thee to squire the Lady Anne."

Semi-sarcastic speeches of this kind were usually Edward's nearest approach to fun. The fresh arrangement was made as he suggested; and though little Roger would not have acknowledged it publicly on any consideration, yet privately he felt the change in his position a relief. Lord Richard of Conisborough was the last of the illustrious persons to mount, and his squire helped Anne Mortimer to spring to her place behind him. The only notice which Richard outwardly took of her was to say, as he glanced behind him—

"We ride now at quick gallop; clasp me close, Lady Anne."

They were off as soon as he had spoken at such a gallop as Anne had never ridden in all her life. But she felt no fear, for the one person in the world whom she trusted implicitly was he who sat before her.

During part of the way, they followed the same route which Le Despenser and Bertram had taken five years before; and Bertram found a painful interest in pointing out to Maude the different spots where the incidents of the journey had happened. Meanwhile a dialogue was passing between Edward and Constance which the former had expected, and had made his arrangements for the journey with the special view that her queries on that topic should be answered by no one but himself.

"Ned, hast seen my Lord ?'

"But once sithence I saw thee."

"How is it with him ?"

"Passing well, for aught I know."

"Thou didst him to wit of all this matter ?"

"Said I not that I so would ?"

"But didst thou ?" she repeated, noting the evasion.

"I did so."

In saying which, Edward told a deliberate falsehood.

"And when will he be at Cardiff ?"

"When the wind bloweth him thither," said the Duke drily.

"Now, Ned !"

"Nay, Custance what know I more than thou ? The winds be no squires of mine."

"But he will come with speed ?"

"No doubt."

"Sent he no word unto me ?"

"Oh, aye—an hogshead full !"

"Ned, thou caitiff ![1]—what were they ?"

"Stuff and folly."

"Thou unassoiled villain, tell me them this minute, or——"

"Thou wilt drop from the pillion ? By all means, an' it so like thee. I shall but be left where I am."

"Ned ! I will nip thee like a pasty, an' thou torment me thus."

[1] Miserable wretch.

"Forsooth, Custance, I charged no memory of mine with such drastis."[1]

"Drastis!"

"I cry thee mercy—cates[2] and honey, if thou wilt have it so. 'Twas all froth and thistle-down."

"I have done, Ned. I will not speak to thee again this month."

"And wilt keep that resolve—ten minutes? By 'r Lady, I am no squire of dames, Custance. Prithee, burden not me with an heap of fond glose."[3]

"By Saint Mary her hosen, but I would my Lord had chosen a better messenger!"

Constance was really vexed. Edward himself was in a little difficulty, for he had only been amusing himself with his sister's anxieties. In reality, he was charged with no message, and he did not want the trouble of devising one suitable to Kent's character.

"By Saint Mary her galoches,"[4] he said jocularly, "what wouldst have of me, Custance? I cannot carry love-letters in mine head."

"But canst not tell me one word?"

Edward would have given a manor if she would have been quiet, or would have passed to some other topic. But he said—

"Lo' you, Custance! I cannot gallop and talk."

"Hast found that out but now?" was the ironical response.

"Well, if thou must needs have a word," replied he testily, "he said he loved thee better than all the world. Will that do?"

---

[1] Dross, rubbish.   [2] Delicates = good things.
[3] Foolish flattery.   [4] Loose overshoes.

"Aye, that shall serve," said Constance in a low voice.

So it might have done—had it been true.

There was silence for half an hour; when Edward said in his gravest tone—

"Custance! I would fain have thee hearken me."

"For a flyting?" demanded his sister in a tone which was not at all grave. "Thy voice hath sound solemn enough for a justiciary."

"*Niñerias*,[1] Custance! I speak in sober earnest."

"Say on, my Lord Judge!"

"When I have seen thee in safety, I look to turn back to the Court."

"Sweet welcome thou shalt find there!"

"Maybe—if I scale yet again the walls of Eltham Palace, where the King now abideth—as I sought in vain to do this last Christmas."

"Scale the walls!—What to do, Ned?"

"What thinkest, Custance?"

"Ned! surely thou meanest not to take the King's life? caitiff though he be!"

"Nay," said Edward slowly; "scantly that, Custance —without I were forced thereto. It might be enough to seize him and lock him up, as he did to our Lord, King Richard."

"I will have no hand in murder, caitiff!"

Constance spoke too sternly to be disregarded. And it was in her nature to have turned back to Windsor that moment, had she been left without reassurance that all would go right.

"Softly, fair Sister!—who spake of so horrid a thing?

[1] Nonsense!

Most assuredly I mean no such, nor have any intent thereto."

"Scale walls at thy pleasure," she said in a calmer tone, "and lock Harry of Bolingbroke under forty keys if thou list : I will not let thee. But no blood, Ned, or I leave thee and thy gear this minute."

"Fair sister Custance, never had I no such intent, by All Hallows ! "

"Have a care ! " she said warningly.

After that they galloped in silence.

The journey went on till the Welsh Marches were reached, of which the Earl of March was lord. Edmund began to hold his head higher, for he knew that the Welsh loyalists were ready to welcome him as King. Little Roger innocently asked if he would be Prince of Wales when his brother was King of England ; because in that case, he would pull down some of the big hills which it took so long to climb. At last only one day's march lay between them and the Principality.

And on that morning Edward left them. Constance could not understand why he did not go with them to Cardiff. He was determined not to do so; and to the disappointment of every one, he induced his brother to accompany him. Richard would rather have stayed; but he had been too long accustomed to obey the stronger will of his brother to begin the assertion of his own. The yielding character which he had inherited from his father prevailed ; and however unwillingly, he followed Edward.

On the morning of that last day's march, they had to traverse a narrow rocky pass. The path, though rough and stony, was tolerably level ; and feeling themselves almost safe, they slackened their pace. They had just been laughing at some remark of little Roger's, and they were all in more or less good spirits, feeling so near the end of their perilous journey; when all at once, in a turn of the pass, the leading horse came to a sudden halt.

"Stand, in the King's name!"

Before them was a small, compact body of cavalry; and at their head, resplendent in official ermine, Sir William Hankeford, Judge of the King's Bench.

Resistance and flight were equally impossible. Constance addressed herself to the old man whom she had cheated five years before, and who, having subsequently discovered her craftiness, had by no means forgotten it.

"Sir William, you will do your commission; but I pray you remember that here be five of the King your master's cousins, and we claim to be used as such."

The old Judge's eyes twinkled as he surveyed the royal lady.

"So, Madam! Your Ladyship hath the right: my commission I shall do, and set the King my master's cousins in safe keeping—with a chimney-board clapped to the louvre."[1]

Constance fairly laughed.

"Come, Sir, I should scantly play the same trick on you twice."

"No, Madam, I will have a care you no do."

"And for what look we, Sir William? May we know?"

"Madam," said Hankeford drily, "you may look for what you shall find, and you may know so much as you be told."

---

[1] Chimney.

"We may bid farewell, trow?"

"So it lie not over too much time."

"Well! needs must, Nym," said Constance, turning to the boy who had so nearly worn the crown of England. "And after all, belike, it shall be worser for me than thee."

"Nym won't care," spoke up little Roger boldly, "if my master yonder will let him lie till seven of the clock of a morrow."

"Till nine, if it like him," said Sir William.

"Then he'll be as happy as a king!" added little Roger.

"Nay, you be all too young to care overmuch—save Nan," responded Constance, looking at Anne's white troubled face. "Poor maid! 'tis hard for thee."

"I can bear what God sendeth, Madam," said Anne in a low voice.

"Well said, brave heart!" answered Constance, only half understanding her. "The blessed saints aid thee so to do!—Now, Sir William, dispose of us."

Hankeford obeyed the intimation by separating them into two bands. Constance, Bertram, and Maude, he placed in the care of Elmingo Leget, an old servant of the Crown, with orders to conduct them direct to London, where Constance guessed that she at least was to undergo trial. The four young Mortimers he took into his own charge, but declined to say what he was going to do with them. The three officers of the Duke of York were desired to return to their master, the old Judge cynically adding that they could please themselves whether they told him of the recapture or not; while Maydeston was as cynically informed that Sir William saw no sufficient reason wherefore the King's Grace should be at the charges of his journey home, but that he might ride in the company if he listed to pay for the lodgings of his beast and his carcase. To which most elegant intimation Maydeston replied that he was ready to pay his own expenses without troubling his Majesty, and that he did prefer to keep his master company.

So the little group of friends were parted, and Constance began her return journey to London as a prisoner of state.

But what was happening at Cardiff? And where was the Earl of Kent?

We shall see both in the next chapter.

CHAPTER X.

HOW THE ROSE WAS GRAFTED.

"To drive the deer with hound and horne
Earl Percy took his way;
The child may rue that is unborne
The hunting of that day."
—*Ballad of Chevy Chase.*

"WILLEMINA!" said the old Lady Le Despenser to her bower-maiden, "what horn was that I heard but now without?"

"Shall I certify your Ladyship?" asked Willemina, rising and gathering together the embroidered quilt on which she was working.

"Aye, child," said the Dowager; "so do."

But when Willemina came back, she looked very important.

"Madam, 'tis a sumner from my Lord's Grace of Canterbury, that beareth letter for Sir Ademar. Counteth your Ladyship that he shall be made bishop or the like?"

"With Harry of Bolingbroke in the throne, and Thomas de Arundel bearing the mitre?" responded the old lady with a laugh. "Marry, my maid, that were a new thing."

"Were it so, Madam?" asked Willemina innocently. "Truly, Sir Ademar is well defamed[1] of all around here."

"This is not the world, child!" said the Dowager. "'Tis more like— Well, Sir Ademar? Hath my Lord's Grace—*Jésu, pour ta pité!*"

Ademar had walked quietly into the room, and placed a paper in the hands of the Dowager. It was a solemn writ of excommunication against Ademar de Milford, clerk in orders, and it was dated on the Sunday which had intervened between the marriage of Maude and that of Constance. All official acts of Ademar since that day were invalidated. Maude's marriage, therefore, was not affected, but Constance was no longer Countess of Kent.

"Sir Ademar, this is dread!" exclaimed the old lady in trembling accents. "What can my Lord's Grace have against you? This this toucheth right nearly the Lady, our daughter Christ aid her of His mercy!"

"Maybe, Madam, it were so intended," said Ademar shrewdly. "For me, truly I wis little what my Lord hath against me—saving that I see not in all matters by his most reverend eyes. I know better what *the* Lord hath against me yet what need I note it, seeing it is cancelled in the blood of His Son?—But for our Lady—ah me!"

"Sir Ademar!" and the dark sunken eyes of the Dowager looked very keenly into his—"arede me your thought—is my Lord of Kent he that should repair this wrong, or no?"

Ademar's voice was silent; but his eyes said, "No!"

"God comfort her!" murmured the old lady, turning

____
[1] Has a good reputation.

away. "For, ill as she should brook the loss of him, yet methinks, if I know her well, she might bear even that lighter than the witting that her name was made a name of scorn for ever."

"Lady," said Ademar, quietly, "even God can only comfort them that lack comforting."

She looked at him in silence. Ademar pointed out of the window to two little children who were dancing merrily on the shore, and laughing till they could scarcely dance.

"How would you comfort them, Madam?"

"They need it not," she murmured, absently.

"In verity," said Ademar; "neither wasteth our Lord His comfort on them that dance, nor His pitifulness on them that be at ease. And I have seen ere now, Madam, that while He holdeth wide the door of His fold for all His sheep to enter in, yet there be some that will not come in till they be driven. Yea, and some lack a sharp rap of the shepherd's rod ere they will quit the wayside herbage."

"And you think she feedeth thereby?"

"I think that an' she be of the sheep, she must be fetched within; and maybe not one nor two strokes shall be spent in so doing."

"Amen, even if so! But this rap hath fallen on the tenderest side."

"The Shepherd knoweth the tender side, Madam; and lo' you, that so doing, He witteth not only where to smite with the rod, but where to lay the plaister."

"And you, Sir Ademar—lack you no plaister?"

"Madam, I have but received a gift. 'For it is *ghouun*[1]

[1] Given.

to you for Christ, that not oonli ghe[1] bileuen in him, but also that ghe suffren for him.'"

"Can you so take it, it is well."

And the old lady turned aside with a sigh.

"Aye," said the Lollard priest, "it was well with the Shunammite gentlewoman. And after all, it is but a little while ere our Lord is coming. 'Tis light gear to watch for the full day, when you see the sun gilding the crests of the mountains."

"Yet when you see *not* the sun——?"

"Then, Lady, you long the more for his coming."

There was no slight stir that morning on Berkhamsted Green. The whole Court was gathered there, fringed on its outskirts by a respectful and admiring crowd of sight-seers. Under a spreading tree sat the King, on a fine black charger, a hooded hawk borne upon his wrist. Close beside him was a little white palfrey, bearing a lady, and on her wrist also was a hooded hawk. They were apparently waiting for somebody. In front, the Prince of Wales, being of an active turn of mind, was amusing himself by making his horse prance and curvet all about the green, and levelling invisible lances at imperceptible foes to the intense interest of the outside crowd.

"Late, late, my Lord of Kent!" he cried lightly, as a bay charger shot past him, its rider doffing his plumed cap.

Kent merely bowed again in answer, and rode rapidly up to the King.

"Better late than never, fair Cousin!" was Henry's

[1] Ye.

greeting. "We will forth at once. Will you ride by our fair guest?—The Lady Lucy of Milan!"

The lady who sat on the white palfrey turned her face towards the Earl of Kent, and, slightly blushing and smiling, spoke a few words of courteous French, indicating her acceptance of his society for the day.

She was the most beautiful woman whom Kent had ever seen. Her figure was very slight, and her carriage easy and graceful; her age was about twenty. Glossy, luxuriant hair, of the deepest black, shaded a delicate face, in shape midway between round and oval, the features of which, though very regular, could not strictly be termed either Roman or Grecian, for the nose was too straight for the former, while the forehead was too prominent and too fully developed for the latter. Her eyes were usually cast down, so that they were rarely seen; but when she raised them, they showed themselves large, lustrous, and clear, of a rich, deep, gleaming brown. Her complexion was formed neither of lilies nor roses; it was that pure, perfect cream-colour, which one William Shakspere knew was beautiful, though some of his commentators have rashly differed from him. Add to this description a low, musical voice, strangely clear for her nationality, and a smile of singular fascination,— and it will not seem strange that Kent fell into the snare laid for him, and had no eyes thenceforward but for Lucia Visconti.

The King kept all day near his decoy and his victim. He never interfered with their conversation, but when it languished he was always at hand to supply some fresh topic. They spoke French, which was understood and employed fluently by all three; but Kent knew no

Italian, and Lucia no English. The King spoke Lucia's language well—a fact which greatly assisted an occasional "aside." But Lucia was only half aware of the state of affairs, and it would not have suited Henry's purpose to inform her too fully. She knew that she was expected to make herself agreeable to the Earl of Kent, and that he was a cousin and favourite of the King—so far as a man of Henry's stamp can be said to have had any favourites. But of the plot for which she was made the innocent decoy, she had not the faintest idea.

The shades of evening began to fall at last, and the royal bugle-horn was sounded to call the stragglers home.

Kent and Lucia were riding together. They had reached a fork in the road, where the right-hand path branched off to Berkhamsted, and the left to Langley. And all at once there arose before Kent's soul a haunting memory—a memory which was to haunt him for many a day thereafter; and between his eyes and the fair face of the Italian Princess came another face, shaded with soft light hair, and lighted by sapphire eyes, which, he thought, were probably watching even now from the oriel window at Langley. He checked his horse, and wavered irresolutely for an instant.

He did not know that Constance was no longer at Langley. He did not know that at the very moment when he paused at the cross roads, she was passing the threshold of the Tower as a prisoner of state. For that one moment Kent's better angel strove with his weak nature. But the phase of "*beaucoup*" was over, and "*point du tout*" was beginning.

Lucia saw the momentary irresolution. She touched

her palfrey lightly with the whip, and turned her splendid eyes on her votary.

"This way, Monseigneur—come!"

The struggle was over. Kent spurred on his charger, and followed his enchantress.

There was another scene enacting at the same time, and not far away. The Duke of York and Lord Richard of Conisborough were riding home to Langley. The brothers were very silent; Richard because he was sad and anxious, Edward because he was vexed and sullen. They had just heard of their sister's arrest.

The portcullis at Langley was visible, when Edward smote his hand on the pommel of his saddle a much more elaborate structure than gentlemen's saddles now —with a few words of proverbial Spanish.

"Patience, and shuffle the cards! I may yet go to Rome, and come back Saint Peter."

Richard lifted his mournful eyes to his brother's face.

"Ned!" he said in a low voice, "it were better to abide a forest hind, methinks, than to come back Jude the Iscariot."

"What meanest, Dickon?"

"Take no heed what I meant, so it come not true."

"So what come not true?" Edward's voice, at any rate, expressed surprise and perplexity.

"If thou wist not, Ned, I am thereof fain."

"Save thee All Hallows, Dickon! I can no more arede thy speech than the man in the moon."

"So better, brother mine."

They rode on for a little while without further words. Just before they came within earshot of the porters, Richard added quietly—

"I marvel at times, Ned, if it shall not seem strange one day that we ever set heart overmuch on anything, save only to have 'washen our stolis in the blood of the Lamb, that the power of us be in the tree of life, and enter by the gates into the city.'"

"When art thou shorn priest?" asked Edward cynically.

"I will do thee to wit in time to see it," said Richard more lightly, as they rode across the drawbridge at Langley.

How far did Edward play the traitor in this matter of the attempted rescue of the Mortimers? It cannot be said distinctly that he did at all; but he had played the traitor on so many previous occasions—he had assisted in hatching so many conspiracies for the mere object of denouncing his associates—that the suspicion of his having done so in this instance is difficult to avoid. And the strangest point of all is, that to the last hour of his life this man played with Lollardism. He used it like a cloak, throwing it on or off as circumstances demanded. He spent his life in deceiving and betraying every friend in turn, and at last told the truth in dying, when he styled himself "of all sinners the most wicked."

Three days after that evening, the House of Lords sat in "Parliament robes," in Westminster Hall. But the King was not present: and there were several peers absent, in attendance on His Majesty; among them the Duke of York, the Earl of Cambridge, and the Earl of Kent. The House had met to try a prisoner: and the prisoner was solemnly summoned by a herald's voice to the bar.

"Custance of Langley, Baroness of Cardiff!"

Forward she came, with firm step and erect head, clad in velvet and ermine, as beseemed a Princess of England: and with a most princess-like bend of her stately head, she awaited the reading of the charge against her.

The charge was high treason. The prisoner's answer was a simple point-blank denial of its truth.

"What mean you?" demanded the Lords. "No did you, by means of false keys, gain entrance into the privy chambers of our Lord the King in the Castle of Windsor?"

"I did so."

"How gat you those false keys?"

"From a blacksmith, as you can well guess."

"From what smith?"

"I cannot tell you; for I know not."

"Through whom gat you them?"

"I gat them, and I used them: that is enough."

"Through whom gat you them?"

"Fair Lords, you get no more of me."

"Through whom gat you them?" was repeated the third time.

The answer was dead silence. The question was repeated a fourth time.

"My Lords, an' ye ask me four hundred times, I will say what I say now: ye get no more of me."

"We have means to make men speak!" said one of the peers, threateningly.

"That may be; but not women."

"They can talk fast enough, as I know to my cost!" observed the lord of a very loquacious lady.

"Aye, and hold their peace likewise, as I will show you!" said Constance.

"Is it not true," enquired the Chancellor further, "that you stale away out of the Castle of Windsor the four childre of Roger Mortimer, sometime Earl of March?"

"It is very true."

"And wherefore did you so?"

"Because I chose it!" she said, lifting her head royally.

"Madam, you well wot you be a subject."

"I better wot you be," returned the unabashed Princess.

"And who aided and counselled you thereto?" asked the Chancellor—who was the prisoner's own cousin, Henry Beaufort, Bishop of Lincoln, and brother of the King.

"I can aid myself, and counsel myself," answered the prisoner.

"My question is not answered, Dame."

"Aye so, Sir. And 'tis like to abide thus a while longer."

"I must know who were your counsellors. Name but one man."

"Very well. I will name one an' you press me so to do."

"So do.

"Sir Henry de Beaufort, Chancellor of England."

A peal of laughter rang through the House.

"What mean you, Madam?" sternly demanded the affronted Chancellor.

"Marry, my Lord, you pressed me to name a man— and I have named a man."

The merriment of the august assembly was not decreased by the fact that the Chancellor was rather unpopular.

"Are you of ability, Madam, to declare unto us right-wisely that neither of my Lords your brothers did aid you in this matter?"

"I have passed no word, Sir, touching either of my brothers."

"The which I do now desire of you, Dame."

"Do you so, my Lord? I fear your Lordship may weary of waiting."

"I will wait no longer!" cried Beaufort, angrily and impatiently. "I—— "

"Say you so, Sir?" responded the Princess in her coolest manner. "Then I bid your Lordship a merry morrow.—I am ready, Master Gaoler."

"I said not we were ready, Madam!" exclaimed Beaufort.

"No did, Sir? Then I cry your Lordship mercy that I misconceived you."

"Dame, I demand of you whether your brothers gave unto you no aid in this matter?"

Constance was in a sore strait. She did not much care to what conclusion the House came as concerned Edward: he was the prime mover in the affair, and richly deserved any thing he might get, irrespective of this proceeding altogether. But that any harm should come to Richard was a thought not to be borne. She was at her wits' end what to answer, and was on the point of denying that either had assisted her, when the Chancellor's next remark gave her a clue.

"If ne my Lord of York ne my Lord of Cambridge

did aid you, how cometh it to pass that three servants of the Duke's Grace were with you in your journey ? "

"Ask at their master, not me," said Constance coolly.

"'Tis plain, Madam, that his Grace of York did give you aid, methinks."

"You be full welcome, Sir Keeper, to draw your own conclusions."

"Lo' you, my Lords, the prisoner denieth it not !— And my Lord of Cambridge — what part took he. Lady ? "

"Never a whit, Sir," answered Constance audaciously.

"May I crede you, mewondereth ? "

"You did but this moment, my Lord. If my word be worth aught in the one matter, let it weigh in the other."

The Chancellor meditated a minute, but he could not deny the justice of the plea.

"Moreover, Lady, we heard "—how had they heard it ?—"that some trial were to be made of scaling the walls of the King's Grace's Palace of Eltham."

Constance grew paler. If they had heard this of Edward, what might they have heard of Richard's presence in the journey to Hereford ?

"Have you so, Sir ? " she answered, losing none of her apparent coolness.

"We have so, Madam ! " replied Beaufort sternly; "and moreover of conspiration to steal away his Highness' person, and prison him—if not worser matter than this."

"Not of my doing," said Constance.

"How far you were privy thereto or no, that I leave. But can you deny that it were of my Lord of York his doing ? "

"I was not there," she quickly rejoined. "How then wis I?"

"Can you deny that my Lord of Cambridge was therein concerned?"

"I can!" cried Constance in an agony   too hastily.

"Oh, you can so?" retorted Beaufort, seeing and instantly pressing his advantage. "Then you do wis thereof something?"

She was silent.

"My Lord of York—he was there, trow?"

No answer.

"He was there?"

"Sir Keeper, I was not there. What more can I say?"

"Who was there, Dame?—for I am assured you know."

"Who was where?" retorted the Princess satirically. "If no man scaled the Palace walls, how ask you such questions?"

"Nay, ask that at your Ladyship's own conscience; for it was not I, but you, that said first you were not there."

She was becoming entangled in the meshes.

"Lock you up whom your Lordship will!" she exclaimed. "The truth of all I have said can be proven, and thereto I do offer Master Will Maydeston mine esquire, which shall prove my truth with his body against such as do accuse me.[1]   And further will I say nought."

"But you must needs have had further aid, Lady."

"Aye so, Sir?"

"Most surely. Who were it, I demand of you?"

"I have said my saying."

___

[1] By duel; a resource then permitted by law.

"And you do deny, Madam, to further justice?"

"Right surely, without justice were of my side."

What was to be done with such a prisoner? Beaufort at last gave up in despair the attempt to make her criminate her accomplices any further, though he could hardly avoid guessing that Bertram and Maude had helped her more or less. The sentence pronounced was a remarkably light one, so far as Constance was concerned. In fact, the poor smith, who was the most innocent of the group, suffered the most. How he was found can but be guessed; but his life paid the forfeit of his forgery. The Princess was condemned to close imprisonment in Kenilworth Castle during the King's pleasure. Maude was sentenced to share her mistress's durance; and Bertram's penalty was even easier, for he was allowed free passage within the walls, as a prisoner on parole.

It was in the beginning of March that the captive trio, in charge of Elmingo Leget, arrived at Kenilworth. Two rooms were allotted for the use of Constance and Maude. The innermost was the bedchamber, from which projected a little oratory with an oriel window; the outer, the "withdrawing chamber," which opened only into a guardroom always occupied by soldiers. Bertram was permitted access to the Princess's drawing-room at her pleasure, and her pleasure was to admit him very frequently. She found her prison-life insufferably wearisome, and even the scraps of extremely local news, brought in by Bertram from the courtyard, were a relief to the monotony of having nothing at all to do. She grew absolutely interested in such infinitesimal facts as the arrival of a barrel of salt sprats, the sprained ankle of Mark Milksop[1] of the garrison, the Governor's new crimson damask gown, and the solitary cowslip which his shy little girl offered to Bertram "for the Lady."

But having nothing to do, by no means implied having nothing to think about. On the contrary, of that there was a great deal. The last items which Constance knew concerning her friends were, that Kent had been told of her flight from Windsor (if York's word could be trusted); that her children were left at Langley; and that her admissions on her trial had placed York in serious peril, for liberty if not life. As to the children, they were probably safe, either at Langley or Cardiff; yet there remained the possibility that they might have shared the fate of the Mortimers, and be closely confined in some stronghold. It was not in Isabel's nature to fret much over any thing; but Richard was a gentle, playful, affectionate child, to whom the absence of all familiar faces would be a serious trouble. Then what would become of Edward, whom she had tacitly criminated? What would become of Richard, the darling brother, whom not to criminate she had sacrificed truth, and would have sacrificed life? And, last and worst of all, what had become of Kent? If he had set out to join her, the gravest suspicion would instantly fall on him. If he had not, and were ignorant what had befallen her, Constance—who did not yet know his real character—pictured him as tortured with apprehension on her account.

"O Maude!" she said one evening, "if I could know what is befallen my Lord, methinks I might the lighter bear this grievance!"

---

[1] A genuine surname of the time.

Would it have been any relief if she could have known—if the curtain had been lifted, and had revealed the cushion-dance which was in full progress in the Lady Blanche's chamber at Westminster, where the Earl of Kent, resplendent in violet and gold, was dropping the embroidered cushion at the feet of the Princess Lucia?

"Dear my Lady," said Maude in answer, "our Lord wot what is befallen him."

"What reck I, the while I wis it not?"

And Maude remembered that the thought which was a comfort to her would be none to Constance. The reflection that God knows is re-assuring only to those who know God. What could she say which would be consoling to one who knew Him not?

"Maude," resumed her mistress, "'tis my very thought that King Harry, my cousin, doth this spite and ire against me, to some count,[1] because he maketh account of me as a Lollard."

Maude looked up quickly; but dropped her eyes again in silence.

"Thou wist I have dwelt with them all my life," proceeded Constance. "My Lord that was, and my Lady his mother, and my Lady my mother—all they were Lollards. My fair Castle of Llantrissan to a shoe-latchet, but he reckoneth the like of me!"

"Would it were true!" said Maude under her breath.

"'Would it were true!'" repeated Constance, laughing. "Nay, by the head of St. John Baptist, but this Maude would have me an heretic! Prithee, turn thy wit to better use, woman. I may be taken for a Gospeller, yet not be one."

---

[1] Extent.

"But, sweet Lady," said Maude, earnestly, "wherefore will ye take the disgrace, and deny yourself of the blessing?"

"When I can see the blessing, Maude, I will do thee to wit," replied Constance, laughingly.

"Methinks it is scarce seen," returned Maude, thoughtfully. "Madam, you never yet saw happiness, but ye have felt it, and ye wit such a thing to be. And I have felt the blessing of our Lord's love and pity, though ye no have."

"Fantasies, child!" said Constance.

"If so be, Dame, how come so many to know it?"

"By reason the world is full of fantastical fools," answered Constance, lightly. "We be all nigh fools, sweeting—big fools and little fools—that is all."

Maude gave up the attempt to make her understand. She only said, "Would your Grace that I read unto you a season?" privately intending, if her offer were accepted, to read from the gospel of St. Luke, which she had with her. But Constance laughingly declined the offer; and Maude felt that nothing more could be done, except to pray for her.

Time rolled away wearily enough till the summer was drawing to its close. And then a new interest awoke for both Maude and her lady. For the leaves were just beginning to droop on the trees around Kenilworth Castle, when the disinherited heiress of Kent, a prisoner from her birth, opened her eyes upon the world which had prepared for her such cold and cruel welcome.

There was plenty to do and to talk about after this. Constance was perplexed what name to give her baby. She had never consulted any will but her own before, for she had not cared about pleasing Le Despenser. But she wanted to please Kent, and she did not know what name would gratify him. At length she decided on Alianora, a name borne by two of his sisters, of whom the eldest, the Countess of March, she believed to be his favourite sister.

A few weeks after the birth of Alianora, on a close, warm autumn afternoon, Constance was lying on her bed to rest, feeling languid and tired with the heat; and Maude sat by the window near her, singing softly to the baby in her arms. Hearing a gentle call from Bertram outside, Maude laid the child down and opened the door. Bertram was there, in the drawing-room, and with him were two sisters of St. Clare, robed in the habit of their order.

"These holy sisters would have speech of the Lady," explained Bertram. "May the same be?"

Certainly it might, so far as Constance was concerned. She was so weary of her isolation that she would have welcomed even the Duchess Joan. She bade the immediate admission of the nuns, who were evidently provided with permission from the authorities. They were both tall women, but with that item the likeness began and ended. One was a fair-complexioned woman of forty years,—stern-looking, spare, haggard-faced, in whose cold blue eyes there might be intelligence, but there was no warmth of human kindness. The other was a comfortable-looking girl of eighteen, rosy-cheeked, with dark eyes and hair.

"Christ save you, holy sisters!" said Constance as they approached her. "Ye be of these parts, trow?"

"Nay," answered the younger nun, "we be of the

House of Minoresses beyond Aldgate; and though thine eyes have not told thee so much, Custance, I am Isabel of Pleshy."

"Lady Isabel of Pleshy! Be right welcome, fair cousin mine!"

Isabel was the youngest daughter of that Duke of Gloucester who had been for so many years the evil angel of King and realm. Constance had not seen her since childhood, so that it was no wonder that she failed to recognize her. Meanwhile Maude had turned courteously to the elder nun.

"Pray you, take the pain to sit in the window."

"I never sit," replied the nun in a harsh, rasping voice.

"Truly, that is more than I could say," observed Maude with a smile. "Shall it like you to drink a draught of small ale?"

"I never drink ale."

This assertion would not sound strange to us, but it was astounding to Maude.

"Would you ipocras and spice rather?"

"I never eat spice."

"Will you eat a marchpane?"

"I never eat marchpane."

Maude wondered what this impracticable being did condescend to do.

"Then a shive of bread and tryacle?"

"Bread, an' you will: I am no babe, that I should lack sugar and tryacle."

Maude procured refreshments, and the elder nun, first making the sign of the cross over her dry bread, began to eat; while Lady Isabel, who evidently had not reached an equal height of monastic sanctity, did not refuse any of the good things offered. But when Maude attempted further conversation, the ascetic and acetic lady, intimating that it was prayer-time, and she could talk no more, pulled forth a huge rosary of wooden beads, from which the paint was nearly worn away, and began muttering Ave Marys in apparently interminable succession.

"Now, Isabel," said Constance, "prithee do me to wit of divers matters I would fain know. Mind thou, I have been shut up from all manner of tidings, good or ill, sithence this last March, and I have a sumpter-mule's load of questions to ask at thee. But, first of all, how camest thou hither?"

"Maybe thou shalt find so much in the answers to thy questions," replied Isabel– a smile parting her lips which had in it more keenness than mirth.

"Well, then, to fall to: Where *is* my Lord?"

"In Tewkesbury Abbey, as methought."

"A truce to thy fooling, child! Thou wist well enough that I would say my Lord of Kent."

"How lookest I should wit, Custance? We sisters of St. Clare be no newsmongers. — Well, so far as I knowledge, my Lord of Kent is with the Court. I saw him at Westminster a month gone."

"Is it well with him?"

"Very well, I would say, from what I saw."

Constance's mind was too much engrossed with her own thoughts to put the right interpretation on that cold, mocking smile which kept flitting across her cousin's lips.

"And wist where be my little Dickon, and Nib?"[1]

"At Langley, in care of Philippa, our fair cousin."[2]

---

[1] Isabel.   [2] Then synonymous with relative.

"Good.   And Dickon my brother?"

"I scantly wis—marry, methinks with the Court, at this present."

"And my brother Ned?"

"In Pevensey Castle."

"What, governor thereof?"

But Constance guessed her cousin's answer.

"Nay,—prisoner."

"For this matter?"

"Aye, for the like gear thyself art hither."

"Truly, I am sorry.   And what came of our cousins of March?"

"What had come aforetime."

"They be had back to their durance at Windsor?"

"Aye."

"And what did my Lord when thou sawest him? Arede me all things touching him.   What ware he? —and what said he?—and how looked he?   Knew he thou shouldst see me?—and sent he me no word by thee?"

"Six questions in a breath, Custance!"

"Go to—one after other.   What ware he?"

"By my mistress St. Clare! how should I wit?   An hundred yards of golden baudekyn, and fifty of pink velvet; and pennes[1] of ostriches enough to set up a peltier[2] in trade."

"And how looked he?"

"As his wont is—right goodly, and preux[3] and courteous."

"Aye so!" said Constance tenderly.   "And knew he thou shouldst see me?"

_____

[1] Plumes.   [2] Furrier.   [3] Brave.

"I am not well assured, but methinks rather aye than nay."

"And what word sent he by thee ?"

"None."

"What, not one word ?"

"Nay."

Constance's voice sank to a less animated tone.

"And what did he ?"

"They were about going in the hall to supper."

"Handed he thee ?"

"Nay, my cousin the King's Grace handed me."

"Then who was with my Lord ?"

"The Lady Lucy of Milan."

"Lucy of Milan !—is she not rarely beauteous ?"

"I wis nought about beauty. If it lie in great staring black eyes, and a soft, debonere[1] manner, like a black cat, belike so."

For the first time, Constance fairly noticed Isabel's peculiar smile. She sat up in her bed, with contracted brow.

"Isabel, there is worser behind."

"There is more behind, Custance," said Isabel coolly.

"Speak, and quickly !"

"Well, mayhap better so. Wit thou then, fair Cousin, that thy wedding with my Lord of Kent is found not good, sith— "

"Not good!" Constance said, or rather shrieked. "God in Heaven have mercy ! not good !"

"Not good, fair Cousin mine," resumed Isabel's even tones, "seeing that the priest which wedded you was

---

[1] Amiable, pleasant.

ere that day excommunicate of heresy, nor could lawfully marry any."

Maude's face grew as white as her lady's, though she gave no audible sign of her terrible apprehension that her marriage was invalid also. Isabel, who seemed to notice nothing, yet saw everything, turned quietly to her. And though the sisters of St. Clare might be no newsmongers, the royal nun had evidently received full information on that subject.

"There is no cause for your travail,[1] Dame Lyngern, she said calmly. "The writ bare date but on Sunday, and you were wed the even afore; so you be no wise touched.—Marry, Custance, thou seest that so being, my Lord of Kent—and thou likewise—be left free to wed; wherefore it pleased the King's Grace, of his rare goodness, to commend him unto the Lady Lucy of Milan by way of marriage. They shall be wed this next January."

Isabel spoke as quietly as people generally do who are not personally concerned in the calamity they proclaim. But perhaps she hardly anticipated what followed. Her eyes were scarcely ready for the sight of that white livid face, quivering in every nerve with human agony, nor her ears for the fierce cry which broke from the parched bloodless lips.

" Thou liest!"

Isabel shrank back with a look of uneasy apprehension in her round rosy face.

"Nay, burden not me withal, Custance! 'Tis no work of mine. I am but a messenger."

---

[1] Trouble, vexation.

"Poor fool·! I shall not harm thee! But whose messenger art?"

"The King's Grace himself bade me to see thee."

"And tell me *that?*"

"He bade me do thee to wit so much."

"'So much'—how much? What I have heard hath killed me. Hast yet ill news left to bury me withal?"

"Only this, Custance," replied her cousin in a deprecating tone, "that sithence, though it were not good by law of holy Church, yet there was some matter of marriage betwixt thee and my Lord of Kent; and men's tongues, thou wist, will roll and rumble unseemlily,—it seemed good unto his Highness that it should be fully exhibit to the world how little true import were therein; and accordingly he would have thee to put thine hand to a paper, wherein thou shalt knowledge that the marriage had betwixt you two was against the law of holy Church, and is therefore null and void. If thou wilt do the same, I am bid to tell thee thou shalt have free liberty to come forth hence, and all lands of thy dower restored."

"Art at an end?"

"Aye; therewith closeth my commission."

"Then have back at thy leisure, and tell Harry of Bolingbroke from me that I defy him and Satan his master alike. I will set mine hand to no such lie, as there is a Heaven above me, and beneath him an Hell!"

"Custance!" remonstrated her cousin in a scandalised tone.

But Constance lifted her head, and flung up her hands towards heaven.

"O God of Paradise!" she cried, "holy and true, just in Thy judgments, look upon us two—this King and me—and betwixt us judge this day! Look upon us, Lady of Pity, Lily of Christendom, and say whether of us two is the sinner! O all ye Angels, all ye Saints in Heaven! that sin not, but plead for us sinners,— plead ye this day with God that He will render to each of us two his due, as he hath demerited! Before you, before holy Church, before God in Heaven, I denounce this man Harry of Bolingbroke! Render unto him, O Lord! render unto him his desert!"

"Custance, thou mayest better take this matter more meekly," observed Isabel with quiet propriety, very different from her cousin's tone and mien of frenzied passion. "I have told thee truth, and no lie. What should it serve? The priest is excommunicate, and my Lord of Kent shall wed the Lady Lucy, and the King will have thine hand thereto, ere thou come forth."

"Not if I die here a thousand times!"

"I do thee to wit, Custance, that there is grave doubt cast of thy truth and fealty——"

"To Harry of Bolingbroke?" she asked contemptuously. "When lent I *him* any?"

"Custance!—Of thy truth and fealty unto holy Church our mother. Nor, maybe, shall she be over ready to lift up out of the mire one whom all the holy doctors do esteem an heretic."

"What, I?"

"Thou."

"I never was an heretic yet Isabel, but I do thee to wit thou goest the way to make me so. As to holy

Church, she never was my mother.   I can breathe
without her frankincense, belike, and maybe all the
freer."

"Alas, Custance! Me feareth sore thou art gone a
long way on that ill road, else hadst thou never spoken
such unseemly words."

"Be it so!" said Constance, with the recklessness
of overwhelming misery.   "An heretic's daughter, and
an heretic's widow—what less might ye look for?   If
thou hast mangled mine heart enough to serve thee,
Isabel, I would thou wert out of my sight!"

"Fair Cousin, I do ensure thee mine own lieth bleeding for thy pain."

"Aye, forsooth! I see the drops a-dripping!" said
Constance in bitter mockery.   "Marry, get thee hence—
'tis the sole mercy thou canst do me."

"So will I ; but, Custance, I ensure thee, I am
bidden to abide hither the setting of thine hand to
that paper."

"Then haste and bid measure be taken for a coffin,
for one shall lack either for thee or me ere thou depart!"

"Alack, alack!"

But Isabel rose and withdrew, signing to her companion to follow.   The elder nun, who had not yet
finished her rosary, stopped in the middle of a Paternoster, and obeyed.

"Leave me likewise, thou, Maude," said Constance, in
a voice in which anguish and languor strove for the pre-
dominance.

"Dear my Lady, could I not——?" Maude began
pityingly.

"Nay, my good Maude, nought canst thou do. Unless

it *were* true that God would hearken prayer, and then, perchance—"

"Trust me for that, Lady mine !—Take I the babe withal ? "

"Poor little maid !—Aye,—take her to thee."

Maude followed the nuns into the drawing-room. She found the beadswoman still busy, on her knees in the window. and Isabel seated in the one chair sacred to royalty.

"'Tis a soft morrow, Dame Lyngern," complacently remarked the lady whose heart lay bleeding. "Be that your little maid ?"

Maude's tone was just a little stiff.

"The Lady Alianora de Holand, Madam."

"Ah ! our fair cousin her babe ?—Poor heart !"

Maude was silent.

"Verily, had I wist the pain it should take us to come hither," pursued Isabel, apparently quite careless about interrupting the spiritual labours of her sister nun, "me-thinks I had prayed my Lord the King to choose another messenger. By the rainfall of late, divers streams have so bisched[1] their banks, that me verily counted my mule had been swept away, not once ne twice. It waked my laughter to see how our steward, that rade with us, strave and struggled with his beast."

Maude's heart was too heavy to answer ; but Isabel went on chattering lightly, to a murmured under-current of "*Ora pro nobis,*" as bead after bead, in the hands of the kneeling nun, pursued its fellow down the string of the rosary. Maude sat on the settle, with the sleeping child in her arms, listening as if she heard not, and

____
[1] Overflowed.

feeling as though she had lost all power of reply. At last the rosary came to its final bead, and, crossing herself, the elder nun arose.

"Sister, I pray you of your Paternoster, sith you be terminate," said Isabel, holding out her hand. "Mine brake, fording the river astont,[1] and half the beads were gone ere I could gather the same. 'Tis pity, for they were good cornelian."

The rosary changed hands, and Isabel began to say her prayers, neither leaving her chair nor stopping her conversation.

"'Twas when we reached the diversory[2] last afore Stafford, Dame Lyngern—*Janua Cœli, ora pro nobis !*—we were aware of a jolly debonere pardoner,[3]—*Stella Matutina, ora pro nobis !*—that rade afore, on a fat mule, as well-liking as he—*Refugium Peccatorum, ora pro nobis!*—and coming anigh us, quoth he to me, that first rade—*Regina Angelorum, ora pro nobis !*—' Sister,' quoth my master the pardoner——."

"Sister Isabel, you have dropped a bead !" snapped the elder nun.

"Thanks, Sister Avice.—By my Lady Saint Mary ! where was I ? Oh aye !—*Regina Patriarcharum, ora pro nobis !* Well, Dame Lyngern, I will do you to wit what befell."

But Maude's eyes and attention were riveted.

"Be there two Avices in the Priory at Aldgate?—crying your Ladyship mercy."

"Nay, but one," said Isabel. "Wherefore, Dame ?"

---

[1] Near.   [2] Inn.

[3] An officer of the Bishop's Court, whose business was to carry to their destination written absolutions and indulgences.

"But—this is not my Avice ," faltered Maude.

"I am St. Clare's Avice, and none other," said the nun stonily.

"But—Avice de Narbonne ?"

"Avice de Narbonne I was; and thou wert Maude Gerard."

"Christ's mercy on thee !"

"What signifiest ?" responded Avice, sternly. "I am an holy sister, and as Sister Isabel shall certify unto thee, am defamed for holiest of all our house."

"Aye so," admitted Isabel.

"I am sorry for thee, Cousin !" whispered Maude, her eyes full of tears.

"Sorry !" said Isabel.

"Sorry !" repeated Avice. "When I have ensured mine own salvation, and won mine husband's soul from Purgatory, and heaped up great store of merit belike! —Woman, I live but of bread and water, with here and there a lettuce leaf; a draught of milk of Sundays, but meat never saving holydays. I sleep never beyond three hours of a night, and of a Friday night not at all. I creep round our chapel on my bare knees every Friday morrow and Saturday even, and do lick a cross in the dust at every shrine. I tell our Lady's litany morrow and even. Sorry ! When every sister of our house doth reckon me a very saint !"

A vision rose before Maude's eyes, of a man clad in blue fringes and phylacteries, who stood, head upright, in the Holy Place, and thanked God that he was not as other men. But she only said,—

"O Avice !—what doth God reckon thee ?"

Isabel stared at her.

"The like, of force!" said Avice, with a sneer.

"Avice, I deemed thee once not far from the kingdom of God. But I find thee further off than of old time."

"Thou art bereft of thy wits, sure!" said Avice, contemptuously.

"By the Holy Coat of Treves, but this passeth[1]!" exclaimed Isabel, looking decidedly astonished.

"This world is no garden of pleasance, woman!" resumed Avice, harshly. "We must needs buy Heaven, and with heavy coin."

"Buy thou it, an' thou canst," said Maude, rocking the child to and fro, while one or two tears fell upon its little frock. "For me, I thank our Lord that He hath paid down the price."

She rose, for the child was beginning to cry, and walked to the window to try and engage its attention.

"A Gospeller, by my troth!" whispered Isabel, with a shrug of her shoulders.

"Maude was alway given unto Romaunts and the like fooling!" responded Avice as scornfully as before.

[1] Surpasses expectation or reason.

CHAPTER XI.

THE ROUGH NIGHT WIND.

" Whan cockle-shells ha'e siller bells,
And mussels grow on every tree,—
Whan frost and snaw shall warm us a',—
Then shall my luve prove true to me !"
                              —OLD BALLAD.

IT was the evening of the third day succeeding Isabel's visit, and while she and Avice were seated in the banquet-hall with the Governor and his family, the scene lit up by blazing pine torches, a single earthen lamp threw a dull and unsteady light over the silent bed-chamber of the royal prisoner. The little Alianora was asleep in her cradle, and on the bed lay her mother, not asleep, but as still and silent as though she were. Near the cradle, on a settle, sat Maude Lyngern, trying with rather doubtful success to read by the flickering light.

Constance had not quitted her bed during all that time. She never spoke but to express a want or reply to a question. When Maude brought her food, she submitted to be fed like an infant. Of what thoughts were passing in her mind, she gave no indication.

At last Maude came to the conclusion that the spell of silence ought to be broken. The passionate utterances which Isabel's news had evoked at first were better than this dead level of silent suffering. But she determined to break it by no arguments or consolations of her own, but by the inspired words of God. She felt doubtful what to select; so she chose a passage which, half knowing it by heart, would be the easier to make out in the uncertain light.

"'And oon of the Farisees preiede[1] Jhesus that he schulde ete with him; and he entride into the hous of the Farisee, and sat at the mete. And lo, a synful woman that was in the cytee, as sche knewe that Jhesus sat *at the mete in the* hous of the Farisee, she broughte an alabastre box of oynement, and sche stood bihynde bisidis hise feet, and bigan to moiste hise feet with teeris, and wypide with the heeris of hir heed, and kiste hise feet, and anoyntide with oynement. And the Farisee seyng[2] that had clepide him seide within himsilf, seiyinge, if this were a profete, he schulde wete who and what maner womman it were that touchide him, for sche is a synful womman. And Jhesus answerde and seide to him, Symount, I han sum thing to seye to thee. And he seide, Maistir, seye thou. And he answerde, Tweye dettouris weren to oo lener[3]; and oon oughte fyve hundrid pens[4] and the tother fifty. But whanne thei hadden not wherof thei schulen yelde,[5] he forgaf to bothe. Who thanne loueth him more? Symount answerde and seide, I gesse that he to whom he forgaf more. And he answeride to him, Thou hast demed[6] rightly. And he turnide to the womman, and seyde to Symount, Seest thou this womman? I entride into thin hous, thou gaf

---

[1] Prayed.   [2] Seeing.   [3] One lender.
[4] Pence.   [5] Yield = pay.   [6] Doomed = judged.

no watir to my feet; but this hath moistid my feet with teeris, and wipide with her heeris. Thou hast not gouen to me a cosse[1]; but this, sithen sche entride, ceeside not to kisse my feet. Thou anointidst not myn heed with oyle; but this anointide my feet with oynement. For the which thing I seye to thee, manye synnes ben for-giuen to hir, for sche hath loued myche; and to whom is lesse forgyuen to hir, he loueth lesse. And Jhesus seyde to hir, Thi synnes ben forgiuen to thee. And thei that saten togider at the mete bigunnen to seye withinne hemsilf,[2] Who is this that forgyveth synnes? But he seide to the womman, Thei feith hath maad thee saaf; go thou in pees.' "

Maude added no words of her own. She closed the book, and relapsed into silence. But Constance's solemn stillness was broken at last.

" 'He seide to the womman!'—Wherefore no, having so spoken to the Pharisee, have left[3]?"

" Nay, dear my Lady," answered Maude, "it were not enough. So dear loveth our good and gentle Lord, that He will not have so much as one of His children to feel any the least unsurety touching His mercy. Wherefore He were not aseeth[4] to say it only unto the Pharisee; but on her face, bowed down as she knelt behind Him, He looked, and bade her to be of good cheer, for that she was forgiven. O Lady mine! 'tis great and blessed matter when a man hath God to his friend!"

" Thy words sound well," said the low voice from the bed. "Very well, like the sound of sweet waters far away."

<hr>

[1] Kiss. [2] Themselves. [3] Concluded. [4] Contented.

"Far away, dear my Lady?"

"Aye, far away, Maude,—without[1] my life and me."

"Sweet Lady, if ye will but lift the portcullis, our Lord is ready and willing to come within. And whereinsoever He entereth, He bringeth withal rest and peace."

"Rest! Peace! Aye so. I guess there be such like gear some whither—for some folks."

"They dwell whereso Christ dwelleth, Lady mine."

"In Paradise, then! I told thee it were far hence."

"Is Paradise far hence, Lady? I once heard say Father Ademar that it were not over three hours' journey at the most; for the thief on the cross went there in one day, and it were high noon ere he set out."

Maude stopped sooner than she intended, suddenly checked by a moan of pain from Constance. The mere mention of Ademar's name seemed to evoke her overwhelming distress, as if it brought back the memory of all the miserable events over which she had been brooding for three days past. She rocked herself from side to side, as though her suffering were almost unendurable.

"If he could come back! O Maude, Maude! if only he could come back!"

"Sweet Lady, an' he were hither, methinks Father Ademar——"

"No, no not Father Ademar. Oh, if I could rend the grave open!—if I could tear asunder the blue veil of Heaven! I set no store by it all then; but now—! He would forgive me: he would not scorn me! He would not count me too vile for his mercy. O my Lord, mine own dear Lord! you would never have served me thus!"

<hr>

[1] Outside.

And down rained the blessed tears, and relieved the dry, parched soil of the agonised heart. She lay quieter after that torrent of pain and passion. The terrible spell of dark silence was broken ; and Maude knew at last, that through this bitterest trial she had ever yet experienced, the wandering heart was coming home at least to Le Despenser.

Was it needful that she should pass through yet deeper waters, before she would come home to God ?

The leaves were carpeting the ground around Kenilworth, when Constance granted a second interview to her cousin Isabel. There was more news for her by that time. Edward had been once more pardoned, and was again in his usual place at Court. How this inscrutable man procured his pardon, and what sum he paid for it, in cash or service, is among the mysteries of the medieval "back-stairs." He had to be forgiven for more than Constance knew. Among his other political speculations, he had been making love to the Queen ; a fact which, though there can be little doubt that it was a mere piece of policy on his part, was unlikely to be acceptable to the King. But the one item which most closely concerned his sister was indicated in plain terms by his pardon—that she need look for no help at her brother's hands until she too "put herself in the King's mercy."

The King's mercy! What that meant depended on the King. In the reign of Richard of Bordeaux, that prisoner must be heavily charged to whom it did not mean at least a smile of pardon—not unfrequently a grant of lands, or sometimes a coronet. But in the reign of Henry of Bolingbroke, it meant rigid justice, as he understood justice. And his mercy, to any Lollard, convicted or suspected, usually meant solitary confinement in a prison cell. What inducement was there for Constance to throw herself on such mercy as that? Nor was she further encouraged by hearing of another outbreak on behalf of King Richard or the Earl of March, headed by Archbishop Scrope and Lord Mowbray, and the heads of the ringleaders had fallen on the scaffold.

Isabel had sat and talked for an hour without winning any answer beyond monosyllables. She was busy with her rosary—a new coral one —while she unfolded her budget of ncws, and tried to persuade her cousin into compliance with the King's wish. The last bead was just escaping from her fingers with an Amen, when Constance turned to her with a direct question.

"Now speak plainly, fair Cousin; what wouldst have me to do?"

"In good sooth, to put thee in the King's mercy."

"In *his* mercy!" murmured the prisoner significantly. "The which should be wist how much?"

"Truly, to free thee hence, and thou shouldst go up to London to wait upon his Grace."

"And then ——?"

Isabel knew what the King intended to exact, but the time was not yet come to say too much, lest Constance should be alarmed and draw back altogether. So she replied evasively—

"Then his Highness should restore to thee thy lands, on due submission done."

"And yield me back my childre?"

"Most surely."

A knot was tied upon Isabel's memory, unknown to her cousin. If Constance cared much for her children, they might prove a most effective instrument of torture.

"Well!—and then?"

"Nay, ask at thine own self. Me supposeth thou shouldst choose to return to thine own Castle of Cardiff. But if it pleased thee rather to abide in the Court, I cast no doubt——"

"Let be!—and then?"

"Then, in very deed," resumed Isabel, warming with her subject, "thou shouldst have chance to make good alliance for Nib and Dickon, and see them well set in fair estate."

"Ah!—and then?"

"Why, then thou mayest match thy grandchildre yet better," answered Isabel, laughing.

"And after all, Isabel," returned Constance, in a manner much graver than was usual with her, "there abideth yet one further *then* death, and God's judgment."

"Holy Mary aid us!—avaunt with such thoughts!"

"Canst thou avaunt with such thoughts, child?" said Constance, with a heavy sigh. "Ah me! they come unbidden, when the shadows of night be over the soul, and the thick darkness hath closed in upon the life. And I, at the least, have no spell to bid them avaunt. If holy Mary aid thee in that avoidment, 'tis more than she doth for me."

Isabel seemed at a loss for a reply.

"I have had no lack of time for thought, fair Cousin, while I yonder lay. And the thought would not away, —when we stand together, I and Harry of Bolingbroke, at that Bar of God's judgment, shall I desire in that day that I had said aye or nay to him now?"

"Forsooth, Custance, I am not thy confessor. These be priests' matters—not gear for women like thee and me."

"What, child! is thy soul matter for the priest's concernment only? Is it not rather matter for thee—thee by thyself, beyond all priests that be? Thou and the priest may walk handed [1] up to that Bar, but methinks he will be full fain to leave thee to bide the whipping."

"Nay, in very deed, Custance, thou art a Lollard, else hadst thou never spoken no such a thing!"

"What, be Lollards the only men that have a care for their own souls? But be it as thou wilt what will it matter *then?* Isabel, in good sooth I have sins enough to answer for, neither will I by my good-will add thereto. And if it be no sin to stand up afore God and men, and swear right solemnly unto His dread face that I did not that which I did before His sun in Heaven good lack! I do marvel what sin may be. There is no such thing as sin, if it be no sin to swear to a lie!"

"But, Custance, the King's Highness asketh not thee to deny that thou wert wed unto my Lord of Kent, but only to allow openly that the same were not good in law."

"Can a law go backwards-way?"

"Fair Cousin, the priest was excommunicate afore."

"God wot if he were!" said Constance shrewdly. "Bishops use not to leave their letters tarry two months on the road, child. There have been riddles writ ere now; aye, and black treachery done—by shaven crowns

---

[1] Walk hand in hand.

too. Canst thou crede that story? 'Tis more than I can."

"Constance, I do ensure thee, the King's Grace sware unto me his own self, by the holy Face of Lucca, and said, if thou didst cast any doubt of the same, my Lord Archbishop should lay to pledge his corporal oath thereon."

"His corporal oath ensure me! nay, nor an' he sware by Saint Beelzebub!" cried Constance in bitter scorn. "I have heard of a corporal oath ere now, child. I know of one that was taken at Conway, by an old white-haired man,[1] whose reverend head should have lent weight to his words: but they were words, and nought else. How many days were, ere it was broken to shivers? I tell thee, Nib, Harry of Bolingbroke may swear an' it like him by every saint in the calendar from Aaron to Zachary; and when he is through, my faith in his oaths will go by the eye of a needle. Why, what need of oath if a man be but true? If I would know somewhat of Maude yonder, I shall never set her to swear by Saint Nicholas; I can crede her word. And if a man's word be not trustworthy, how much more worth is his oath?"

"But, Custance! the King's Grace and my Lord Arch-bishop——"

"How thou clarifiest[2] the King's Grace! Satan ruleth a wider realm than he, child, but I would not trust his oath. What caused them to take account that I should not believe them, unless their own ill consciences?"

---

[1] The Earl of Northumberland, to induce King Richard to place himself in the power of his cousin Henry.　　　[2] Glorifiest.

Isabel was silent.

"Isabel!" said her cousin, suddenly turning to her, "have they *his* oath for the same?"

"Whose, Custance?—my Lord of Kent?"

Constance nodded impatiently.

"Oh, aye."

"He hath allowed our wedding void in law?"

"Aye so."

"What manner of talk held his conscience with him, sithence, mewondereth?" suggested Constance, in a low, troubled voice. "But maybe, like thee, he accounteth if but priest's gear."

"Marry, 'tis far lighter travail. I list not to carry mine own sins: I had the liefer by the worth of the Queen's Highness' gems they were on the priest's back."

"Ah, Nib!—but how if God charge them on thy back at the last?"

"Good lack! a white lie or twain, spiced with a little matter of frowardness by times! My back is broad enough."

"I am fain to hear it, for so is not mine."

"Ah! thou art secular—no marvel."

"Much thanks for thy glosing,[1] mine holy sister!" said Constance sarcastically. "The angels come down from Heaven, to set thee every morrow in a bath of rose water, trow? While I, poor sinner that I am, having been twice wed, may journey to Heaven as best I can in the mire. 'Tis well, methinks, there be some secular in the world, for these monks and nuns be so holy that elsewise there were no use for God's mercy."

"Nay, Custance!"

----

[1] Flattery.

"Well, have it as thou wilt, child! What matter?" returned her cousin with a weary air. "I am no doctor of the schools, to break lances with thee. Only methinks I have learned, these last months, a lesson or twain, which maybe even thy holiness were not the worser to spell over. Now let me be."

Isabel thought that the victim was coming round by degrees, and she wisely forbore to press her beyond the point to which she chose to go of herself. So the interview ended. It was not till October that they met again.

Maude fancied that Avice eschewed any renewal of intercourse with her. She kept herself strictly secluded in the chamber which had been allotted to the nuns; and since Maude had no power to pass beyond the door of the guard room, the choice lay in Avice's own hands. At neither of the subsequent interviews was she present.

"Well, fair Cousin! what cheer?" was Isabel's greeting, when she presented herself anew.

"Thus much," replied Constance; "that, leave given, I will go with thee to London.'

"Well said!" was the answer, in a tone which intimated that it was more than Isabel expected.

"But mark me, Isabel! I byhote[1] nought beyond."

"Oh aye!—well and good."

"And for thus much yielding, I demand to have again the keeping of my childre."

"Good lack! thou treatest with the King's Grace as though thou wert queen of some land thyself," said Isabel, with a little laugh. "Verily, that goeth beyond my commission: but methinks I can make bold to say

[1] Promise.

thus much: that an' thou come with me, they shall be suffered at the least to see thee and speak with thee."

Constance shook her head decidedly.

"That shall not serve."

"Nay, then, we be again at a point. I can but give mine avisement unto thee to come thither and see."

The point was sturdily fought over on both sides. Isabel dared promise nothing more than that Constance should be allowed to see her children, and that she herself would do her utmost to obtain further concessions. At last it was settled that the King should be appealed to, and the request urged upon him by his emissary, by letter. Isabel, however, was evidently gifted with no slight ambassadorial powers; for when she selected Bertram Lyngern as her messenger, the Governor did not hesitate to let him go.

But Bertram's projected journey never took place, for a most unexpected event intervened to stop it.

It was the seventh of November, and a warm, close, damp day, inducing languor and depression in any person sensitive to the influence of weather. Constance and Maude had received no visit that day from any one but Bertram, who was busy preparing for his journey. There were frequent comers and goers to Kenilworth Castle, so that the sound of a bugle-horn without was likely to cause no great curiosity; nor, as Constance's drawing room window opened on a little quiet corner of the inner court-yard, did she often witness the arrival of guests. So that three horns rang out on that afternoon without awakening more than a passing wonder "who it might be;" and when an unusual commotion was heard in the guard-room, the cause remained unsurmised. But when the door of the drawing-room was opened, a most unexpected sight dawned on the eyes of the prisoners. Unannounced and completely unlooked-for, in the doorway stood Henry of Bolingbroke, the King.

It was no wonder that Maude's work dropped from her hands as she rose hastily; nor that Constance's eyes passed hurriedly on to see who composed the suite. But the suite consisted of a solitary individual, and this was her ubiquitous brother, Edward of York.

"God give you good even, fair Cousin!" said Henry, with a bend of his stately head. His manners in public, though less really considerate, were stiffer and more ceremonious than those of his predecessor. "You scantly looked, as methinks, for a visit of ours this even?"

· "Your Highness' servant!" was all that Constance said, in a voice the constrained tone of which had its source rather in coldness than in reverence.

"Christ save thee, Custance!" said Edward, sauntering in behind his royal master. "Thou hast here a fine look out, in very deed."

"Truth, Ned; and time to mark it!" rejoined his sister.

· The door opened again, and with a lout[1] of the deepest veneration, Isabel made her appearance.

"I pray you sit, ladies," commanded the King.

The Princesses obeyed, but Maude did not consider herself included. The King took the isolated chair with which the room was provided.

"An' you be served, our fair Cousins," he remarked, "we will to business, seeing our tarrying hither shall be

---

[1] The old English courtesy, now considered rustic.

but unto Monday; and if your leisure serve, Lady Le Despenser, we would fain bear you with us unto London. Our fair cousin Isabel, as methinks, did you to wit of our pleasure?"

What was the occult power within this man—whom no one liked, yet who seemed mysteriously to fascinate all who came inside the charmed circle of his personal influence? Instead of answering defiantly, as she had done to Isabel, Constance contented herself with the meek response—

"She so did, Sire."

"You told her all?" pursued the King, turning his keen eyes upon Isabel.

"To speak very truth, Sire," hesitated Isabel, "I did leave one little matter."

She seemed reluctant to confess the omission; and Constance's face paled visibly at this prospect of further sorrow in store.

"Which was that, fair Cousin?"

Henry was a perfect master of the art of expressing displeasure without any use of words to convey it. Isabel knew in an instant that he considered her to have failed in her mission.

"Under your gracious leave, my Liege," she said deprecatingly, "had your Grace seen how my fair cousin took that which I did say, it had caused you no marvel that I stayed ere more were spoken."

"We blamed you not, fair Cousin," responded Henry coldly. "What matter left you unspoken?"

"An' it like your Grace to pardon me, touching her presence desired——"

"Enough said. All else spake you?"

"All else, your Highness' pleasure served," answered Isabel meekly.

"My 'presence desired'!" broke in Constance. "What meaneth your Grace, an' it like you? Our fair cousin did verily arede[1] me that your Grace commandeth mine appearing in London; and thither I had gone, had it not pleased your Grace to win hither."

"So quoth she; but this was other matter," calmly rejoined the King. "Our Council thought good, fair Cousin, that you should be of the guests bidden unto the wedding of our cousin of Kent with the fair Lady Lucy of Milan."

For one instant after the words were spoken, there was dead silence through the room—the silence which marks the midst of a cyclone. The next moment, Constance rose, and faced the man who held her life in his hands. The spell of his mysterious power was suddenly broken; and the old fiery spirit of Plantagenet, which was stronger in her than in him, flamed in her eyes and nerved her voice.

"You meant *that?*" she demanded, dropping etiquette.

"It hath been reckoned expedient," was the calm reply.

"Then you may drag me thither in my coffin, for alive will I never go!"

"This, Custance, to the King's Highness' face!" deprecated her pardoned and (just then) subservient brother.

"To his face? Aye,—better than behind his back!" cried the defiant Princess. "And to thy face, Harry of Bolingbroke, I do thee to wit that thou art no king of mine, nor I owe thee no allegiance! Wreak thy will on me for saying it! After all, I can die but once; and I

[1] Tell.

can die as beseems a King's daughter; and I would as lief die and be rid of thee as 'bide in a world vexed with thy governance."

"Custance! Custance!" cried Edward and Isabel in concert.

"Let be, fair Cousins," answered the cool unmoved tones of the King. "We can make large allowance for our cousin's words—they be but nature."

This astute man knew how to overlook angry words. And certainly no words he could have used would have vexed Constance half so much as this assumption of calm superiority.

"Speak your will, Lady," he quietly added. "To all likelihood it shall do you some relievance to uncharge your mind after this fashion; and I were loth to let you of that ease. For us, we are used to hear our intent misconceived. But all said, hear our pleasure."

Which was as much as to say with contemptuous pity,—Poor captive bird! beat your wings against the iron bars of your cage as much as you fancy it; they are iron, after all.

"Fair Cousin," resumed the King, "you must be at this wedding, clad in your widow's garb; and you must set your hand to the paper which our cousin Isabel holdeth. Know that if you be obedient, the custody and marriage of your son, with all lands of your sometime Lord, shall be yours, and you shall forthwith be set at full liberty, nor word further spoken touching past offences. But you still refusing, then every rood of your land is forfeit, and the marriages and custody of all your childre shall be given unto our fair aunt, the Duchess Dowager of York. We await your answer."

It was not in words that the answer came at first.
Only in an exceeding bitter cry—

> "As of a wild thing taken in a trap,
> Which sees the trapper coming through the wood."

Constance saw now the full depth of misery to which
she was doomed. The utmost concession hitherto wrung
from her was that she would go to London and confront
the King. And now it was calmly required of her that
she should not only sign away her own fair name, but
should confront Kent himself—should sit a quiet spectator of a ceremony which would publicly declare the
invalidity of her right to bear his name—should by her
own act consign her child to degradation and penury—
should be a witness and a consenting party to the utter
destruction of all her hopes of happiness. She knew
that the lark might as well plead with the iron bars as
she with Henry of Bolingbroke. And the penalty of
her refusal was not merely poverty and homelessness.
She could have borne that; indeed, the sentence about
the estates passed by her, hardly noted. The bitterest
sting lay in the assurance thus placidly given her, that
her loving little Richard would be consigned to the keeping of a woman whom she knew to hate her fiercely—
that he would be taught to hate and despise her himself.
He would be brought up as a stranger to her; he would
be led to associate her name with scorn and disgrace.
And how was Joan likely to treat the children, when she
had perpetually striven to vex and humiliate the mother?

The words came at last. But they were of very different character from those which had preceded them.

"Grant me one further mercy, Sire," she said in a low

voice, looking up to him :—"the one greater grace of death "

"Fair Cousin, we would fain grant you abundant grace, so you put it not from you with your own perversity. We have proffered unto you full restorance to our favour, and to endow you with every of your late Lord's lands, on condition only of your obedience in one small matter. We take of you neither life nor liberty."

"Life ? no! only all that maketh life worthy the having."

"We wist not, fair Cousin, that our cousin of Kent were so precious," replied the King, with the faintest accent of satire in his calm, polished voice.

But Constance, like a spring let loose, had returned to her previous mood.

"What, take you nought from me but only him ?" she cried indignantly. "Is it not rather mine own good name whereof you would undo me? Ye have bereaved me of him already. I tare him from mine heart long ago, though I tare mine own heart in the doing of it. He is not worth the love I have wasted on him, and have repreved[1] thereof one ten thousand times his better! God assoil[2] my blindness !—for mine eyes be opened now. But you, Sire, —you ask of me that I shall sign away mine own honourable name and my child's birthright, and as bribe to bid me thereunto, you proffer me my lands! What saw you ever in Custance of Langley to give you the thought that she should thus lightly sell her soul for gold, or weigh your paltry acres in the balances against her truth and honour ?"

Every nerve of the outraged soul was quivering with

---

[1] Denied, rejected.　　　[2] Forgive.

excitement. In the calm even tones which responded, there was no more excitement than in an iceberg.

"Fair Cousin, you do but utterly mistake. The matter is done and over; nor shall your 'knowledgment thereof make but little difference. 'Tis neither for our own sake, neither for our cousin of Kent, but for yours, that we would fain sway you unto a better mind. Nor need you count, fair Cousin, that your denial should let by so much as one day our cousin of Kent his bridal with the Lady Lucy. We do you to wit that you stand but in your own light. Your marriage is annulled. What good then shall come of your 'knowledgment, saving your own easement? But for other sake, if ye do persist yct in your unwisdom, we must needs make note of you as a disobedient subject."

There was silence again, only broken by the quiet regular dripping of the water clock in a corner of the room. Silence, until Constance sank slowly on her knees, and buried her face upon the cushion of the settle.

"God, help me; for I have none other help!" sobbed the agitated voice. "Help me to make this unceli[1] choice betwixt wrong and wrong, betwixt sorrow and sorrow!"

A less impulsive and demonstrative woman would not have spoken her thoughts aloud. But Constance wore her heart upon her sleeve. What wonder if the daws pecked at it?

"Not betwixt wrong and wrong, fair Cousin," responded the cool voice of the King. "Rather, betwixt wrong and right. Nor betwixt sorrow and sorrow, but betwixt sorrow and pleasance."

[1] Miseiable.

With another sudden change in her mood, Constance lifted her head, and asked in a tone which was almost peremptory—

"Is it the desire of my Lord himself that I be present?"

To reply in the affirmative was to lie; for Kent was entirely innocent and ignorant of the King's demand. But what mattered a few lies, when Archbishop Arundel, the fountain of absolution, was seated in the banquet-hall? So Henry had no scruple in answering unconcernedly

"It is our cousin of Kent his most earnest desire."

"And yet once more," she said, fixing her eyes upon him, as if to watch the expression of his face while she put her test-question. "Yonder writ of excommunication :—was it verily and indeed forth against Sir Ademar de Milford, the Sunday afore I was wed?"

Did she expect to read any admission of fraud in that handsome passionless face? If she did, she found herself utterly mistaken.

"Fair Cousin, have ye so unworthy thoughts of your friends? Certes, the writ was forth."

"My friends! where be my friends?—The writ was forth?"

"Assuredly."

"Then wreak your will—you and Satan together!"

"How conceive we by that, fair Cousin?" inquired the King rather satirically.

"Have your will, man!" she said wearily, as if she were tired of keeping measures with him any longer. "Things be sorely acrazed in this world. If there be an other world where they be set straight, there shall be some travail to iron out the creases."

"Signify you that you will sign this paper?"

Isabel passed the paper quietly to Henry.

"What matter what I signify, or what I sign? If my name must needs be writ up in black soot, it were as well done on that paper as an other."

The King laid the document on the table, where the standish was already, and with much show of courtesy, offered a pen to his prisoner. She knelt down to sign, holding the pen a moment idle in her fingers.

"What a little matter art thou!" she said, soliloquising dreamily. "A grey goose quill! Yet on one stroke of thee all my coming life hangeth."

The pen was lifted to sign the fatal document, when the proceedings were stopped by an unexpected little wail from something in Maude's arms. Constance dashed down the quill, and springing up, took her little Alianora to her bosom.

"Sign away thy birthright, my star, my dove! Wretched mother that I am, to dream thereof! How could I ever meet thine innocent eyes again? I will not sign it!"

"As it like you, fair Cousin," was the quiet response of that voice gifted with such inexplicable power. "For us, we have striven but to avance you unto your better estate. 'Tis nought to us whether ye sign or no."

She hesitated; she wavered; she held out the child to Maude.

"I would but add," observed the King, "that yonder babe is no wise touched by your signing of that paper. Her birthright is gone already; or more verily, she had never none to go. Your name unto yon paper maketh no diversity thereabout."

Still the final struggle was terrible. Twice she resumed the pen ; twice she flung it down in passionate though transient determination not by her own act to alienate her child's inheritance and blot her own fair name. But every time the memory of her favourite, her loving little Richard, rose up before her, and she could not utter the refusal which would deprive her of him for ever. Perhaps she might even yet have held out, had the alternative been that of resigning him to any person but Joan. But the certain knowledge that he would be taught to despise and hate her was beyond the mother's power to endure. At last she snatched up the pen, and dashed her name on the paper. It was signed in regal form, without a surname.

"There!" she cried passionately : "behold all ye get of me! If I may not sign 'Custance Kent,' content you with 'Custance.' Never 'Custance Le Despenser!' My Loid was true to his heart's core ; and never sign I *his* name to a dishonour and a lie!—O my Dickon, my pretty, pretty Dickon! thou little knowest the price thine hapless mother hath paid for thee this day!"

Henry IV. was not a man who loved cruelty for its own sake : he was simply a calculating, politic one. He never wasted power on unnecessary torture. When his purpose was served, he let his victim go.

"Fully enough, fair Cousin!" he said with apparent kindness. "You sign as a Prince's daughter—and such are you. We thank you right heartily for this your wise submission, and as you shall shortly see, you shall not lose thereby."

Not another word was said about her presence at the wedding. That would come later. His present object was to get her to London. The evening of the 17th of November saw them at Westminster Palace.

During the journey, Avice carefully avoided any private intercourse with Maude. The latter tried once or twice to renew the interrupted conversation; but it was either dinner-time, or it was prayer time, or there was some excellent reason why Avice could not listen. And at last Maude resigned the hope. They never met again. But one winter day, eighteen years later, Maude Lyngern heard that Sister Avice, of the Minoresses' house at Aldgate, had died in the odour of sanctity; and that the sisters were not without hope that the holy Father might pronounce her a saint, or at least "beata." It was added that she had worn herself to a skeleton by fasting, and for three weeks before her death had refused all sustenance but the sacrament, which she received daily. And that was the last of Cousin Hawise.

We return from this digression to Westminster Palace.

News met them as they stepped over the threshold— news of death. Alianora, Countess of March, sister of Kent, and mother of the Mortimers, had died at Powys Castle.

When Constance reached the chamber allotted to her at Westminster, she found there all the personal property which she had left at Langley twelve months earlier.

"Maude!" she said that night, as she laid her head on the pillow.

"Lady?" was the response.

"To morrow make thou ready for me my widow's garb. I shall never wear any other again."

"Aye, Lady," said Maude quietly.

"And—hast here any book of Sir John de Wycliffe?"

"The Evangel after Lucas, Lady."

"Wilt read me to sleep therewith?"

"Surely, Lady mine."

"Was it thence thou readst once unto me, of a woman that was sinful, which washed our Lord's feet?"

"Aye so, Madam."

"Read that again."

The words were repeated softly in the quiet chamber, by the dim light of the silver lamp. Maude paused when she had read them.

"When thou and I speak of such as we love, Maude, we make allowance for their short-comings. 'She did but little ill,' quoth we, or, 'She had sore provoking thereto,' and the like. But he saith, 'Manye synnes ben forgiuen to hir'—yet not too many to be forgiven!"

"Ah, dear my Lady," said Maude affectionately, "methinks our Lord can afford to take full measure of the sins of His chosen ones, sith He hath, to bless them, so full and free forgiveness."

"Yet that must needs cost somewhat."

"Cost!" repeated Maude with deep feeling. "Lady, the cost thereof to Him was the cross."

"But to us?" suggested Constance.

"Is there any cost to us, beyond the holding forth of empty hands to receive His great gift? I count, Madam, that as it is His best glory to give all, so it must be ours to receive all."

"O Maude!" she wailed with a weary sigh, "when can I make me clean enough in His sight to receive this His gift?"

"Methinks, Lady mine, this woman which came into the Pharisee's house was no cleaner ne fairer than other women. And, tarrying to make her clean, she might have come over late. Be not the emptiest meetest to receive gifts, and the uncleanest they that have most need of washing ?"

"The most need,—aye."

"And did ever an almoner 'plain that poor beggars came for his dole,—or a mother that her child were too much bemired to be cleansed ?"

"Is there woman on middle earth this night, Maude, poorer beggar than I, or more bemired ?"

"Sweet Lady !" said Maude very earnestly, "if you would but make trial of our Lord's heart toward you ! 'Alle ye that traveilen and ben chargid, come to Me'— this is His bidding, dear my Lady ! And His promise is, 'I will fulfille you'—'ye schal fynde reste to your soulis.'"

"I would come, if I knew how !" she moaned.

"Maybe," said Maude softly, "they which would come an' they knew how, do come after His reckoning. Howbeit, this wis I,—that an' your Ladyship have will to come unto Him, He hath full good will to show you the way."

There was no more said on either side at the time. But if ever a weary, heavy-laden sinner came to Christ, Constance Le Despenser came that night.

The next day she resumed her widow's garb. At that period the weeds of widowhood were pure white, the veil bound tightly round the face, a piece of embroidered linen crossing the forehead, and another the chin, so that the only portion of the face visible was from the eyebrows to the lips. Indeed, the head dress of a widow and that of a nun were so similar that inexperienced eyes might easily mistake one for the other. The costume was not by any means attractive.

The hour was yet early when the Duchess of York was announced; and when the door was opened, the little Richard, whose presence had been purchased at so heavy a cost, sprang into his mother's arms. His little sister, who followed, was shy and hung back, clinging close to the Duchess. The year which had elapsed since she had seen Constance and Maude seemed to have obliterated both from her recollection. With all her faults, Constance was an affectionate mother, with that sort of affection which developes itself in petting; and it pained her to see how Isabel shrank away from her. The only comfort lay in the hope that time would accustom her to her mother again; and beyond the mere affection of·custom, Isabel's nature would never reach.

It soon became evident that King Henry meant to keep his word. Two months after her arrival at Westminster, Constance received a grant of all her late husband's goods forfeited to the Crown; and five days later was the marriage of Edmund of Kent and Lucia of Milan.

They were married in the Church of St. Mary Overy, Southwark, the King himself giving the bride. The Queen and the whole Court were present; but Kent never knew who was present or absent; his eyes and thoughts were absorbed with Lucia. He never saw a white draped figure which shrank behind the Queen, with eyes unlifted from the beginning of mass to the end. So, on that last occasion when the separated pair met, neither saw the face of the other.

But Constance was not left to pass through her

terrible ordeal alone. As the Queen's procession filed into the church, Richard of Conisborough placed himself by the side of his sister, and clasped her hand in his. He left her again at the door of her own chamber. No words were spoken between the brother and sister; the hearts were too near each other to need them.

Maude was waiting for her mistress. The latter lay down on the trussing-bed the medieval sofa—and turned her face away towards the wall. Maude quiet'y sat down with her work; and the slow hours passed on. Constance was totally silent, beyond a simple "Nay" when asked if she wanted anything. With more consideration than might have been expected, the King did not require her presence at the wedding banquet; he permitted her to be served in her own room. But the sufferer declined to eat.

The twilight came at last, and Maude folded her needlework, unable to see longer, and doubtful whether her mistress would wish the lamp to be lighted. She had sat idle only for a few minutes when at last Constance spoke   her words having evidently a meaning deeper than the surface.

"The light has died out!" she said.

"In the City of God," answered Maude gently, "'night schal not be there,' for the lantern of it is the Lamb, and He is 'the schynyng morewe sterre.' And He is 'with us in alle daies, into the endyng of the world.'"

"Maude, is not somewhat spoken in the Evangel, touching the taking up on us of His cross?"

"Aye, dear my Lady: 'He that berith not his cross and cometh aftir Me, may not be My disciple.' And moreover :—'He that takith not his cross and sueth[1] Me is not worthi to Me.'"

"I can never be worthy to Him!" she said, with a new, strange lowliness which touched Maude deeply. "But hitherto I have but lain chafing under the cross—I have not taken ne borne it, neither sued Him any whither. I will essay now to take it on me, humbly submitting me, and endeavouring myself to come after Him."

"Methinks, Lady mine, that so doing, ye shall find that He beareth the heavier end. At the least, He shall bear *you*, and He must needs bear your burden with you. Yet in very sooth there is some gear we must needs get by rote ere we be witful enough to conceive the use thereof. The littlemaster[2] witteth what he doth in setting the task to his scholar. How much rather the great Master of all things?"

"Me feareth I shall be slow scholar, Maude. And I have all to learn!"

"Nor loved any yet the learning of letters, Madam. Yet meseemeth, an' I speak not too boldly, that beside the lessons which be especial, that He only learneth,[3] all this world is God's great picture-book to help His children at their tasks. Our Lord likeneth Him unto all manner of gear easy, common matter at our very hands—for to aid our slow wits. He is Bread of Life, and Water for cleansing, and Raiment to put on, and Staff for leaning upon, and Shepherd, and Comforter."

"Enough, now," said Constance, with that strange gentleness which seemed so unlike her old bright, wilful self. "Leave me learn that lesson ere I crave a new one."

---

[1] Followeth.   [2] Schoolmaster.   [3] Teaches.

CHAPTER XII.

FROST AND SNOW.

"Whan bells were rung, and mass was sung,
    And every lady went hame,
Than ilka lady had her yong sonne,
    But Lady Helen had nane."
                                        —OLD BALLAD.

"I HAVE come home, Mother!"

It was Constance who spoke, standing in the hall at Cardiff, wrapped in the arms of the Dowager Lady Le Despenser. And in every sense, from the lightest to the deepest, the words were true. The wanderer had come home. Home to the Castle of Cardiff, which she was never to leave any more; home to the warm motherly arms of Elizabeth Le Despenser, who cast all her worn-out theories to the winds, and took her dead son's hapless darling to her heart of hearts; home to the great heart of God. And the ear of the elder woman was open to a sound unheard by the younger. The voice of that dead son echoed in her heart, repeating his dying charge to her—"Have a care of my Lady!"

"My poor stricken dove!" sobbed the Lady Elizabeth. "Child, men's cruel handling hath robbed thee of much, yet it hath left thee God and thy mother!"

Constance looked up, with tears gleaming in her sapphire eyes, now so much calmer and sadder than of old.

"Aye," she said, the remembrance thrilling through her of the heavy price at which she had bought back her children; "and I have paid nought for God and thee."

"Nay, daughter dear, Christ paid that wyte[1] for thee. We may trust Him to have a care of the quittance.[2]"

The children now claimed their share of notice. Richard kissed the old lady in an energetic devouring style, and proclaimed himself "so glad, Grammer, so glad!" Isabel offered her cheek in her cold unchildlike way. The baby Alianora at once accepted the new element as a perfectly satisfactory grandmamma, and submitted to be dandled and talked nonsense to with pleased equanimity.

"O Bertram!" said Maude that night, "surely our Lady's troubles and travails be now over!"

"It is well, wife, that God loveth her better than thou," was the answer. "He will not leave his jewel but half polished, because the sound of the cutting grieveth thine ears."

"But how could she bear aught more?"

"Dear heart! how know we what any man can bear—aye, even our own selves? Only God knoweth; and we trust Him. The heavenly Goldsmith breaketh none of His gems in the cutting."

The doors of the prison in Windsor Castle were opened that spring to release two of the state prisoners. The dangerous prisoner, Edmund Earl of March, remained in durance; and his bright little brother Roger

---

[1] Forfeit.　　　[2] Receipt.

had been set free already, by a higher decree than any of Henry of Bolingbroke. The child died in his dungeon, aged probably about ten years. Now Anne and Alianora were summoned to Court, and placed under the care of the Queen. They were described by the King as "deprived of all their relatives and friends." They were not quite that; but in so far as they were, he was mainly responsible for having made them so.

The manner in which King Henry provided the purchase money required by the Duke of Milan for Lucia is amusing for its ingenuity. The sum agreed upon was seventy thousand florins; and the King paid it out of the pockets of five of his nobles. One was his own son, Thomas Duke of Clarence; the second and third were husbands of two of Kent's sisters Sir John Neville and Thomas Earl of Salisbury the latter being the son of the murdered Lollard; the fourth was Lord Scrope, whose character appears to have been simple to an extreme; and the last was assuredly never asked to consent to the exaction, for he was the hapless March, still close prisoner in Windsor Castle.

In the summer, Constance received a grant of all her late husband's lands. The Court was very gay that summer with royal weddings. The first bride was Constance's young stepmother, the Duchess Joan of York, who bestowed her hand on Lord Willoughby de Eresby: the second was the King's younger daughter, the Princess Philippa, who was consigned to the ungentle keeping of the far-off King of Denmark. Richard of Conisborough was selected to attend the Princess to Elsinore; but he was so poor that the King was obliged to make all the provision he required for the journey. It was not his own fault that his purse was light : his godfather, King Richard, had left him a sufficient competence ; but the grants of Richard of Bordeaux were not held always to bind Henry of Bolingbroke. But when the Earl of Cambridge returned to Elsinore, he was rewarded for his labours, not with money nor lands, but by a grant of the only thing for which he cared the gift of Anne Mortimer. He was penniless, and so was she. But though poverty was an habitual resident within the doors, love did not fly out at the window.

The year 1408 brought another sanguinary struggle in favour of March's title, headed by the old white haired sinner Northumberland, who fell in his attempt, at the battle of Bramham Moor, on the 29th of February. He had armed in the cause of Rome, which he hoped to induce March to espouse yet more warmly than Henry IV. He probably did not know the boy personally, and imagined him the counterpart of his gallant, fervent father. He was as far from it as possible. Nothing on earth would have induced March to espouse any cause warmly. He valued far too highly his own dearly beloved ease.

Matters dragged themselves along that autumn as lazily as even March could have wished. All over England the rain came down, sometimes in a dashing shower, but generally in an idle dreary dripping from eaves and ramparts. Nothing particular was happening to any body. At Cardiff all was extremely quiet. Constance had recovered as much brightness as she would ever recover, but never any more would she be the Constance of old time.

"Surely our Lady's troubles be over now!" said Maude sanguinely.

On the evening on which that remark was made,—
the fifteenth of September—two sisters of St. Clare sat
watching, in a small French convent, by the dying bed
of a knight. At the siege of Briac Castle, five days
earlier, he had been mortally wounded in the head by a
bolt from a crossbow; and his squires bore him into the
little convent to die in peace. The sufferer had never
fully recovered his consciousness. He seemed but dimly
aware of any thing—not fully sensible even to pain. His
words were few, incoherent, scarcely intelligible. What
the nuns could occasionally disentangle from his low
mutterings was something about "blue eyes," and
"watching from the lattice." The last rites of the
Church were administered, but there could be no confession; a crucifix was held before his eyes, but they
doubted if he recognised what it was. And about sun-
set of that autumn evening he died.

So closed the few and evil days of the vain, weak,
self-loving Kent. His age was only twenty-six; he left
no child but the disinherited Alianora, and his sisters
took good care that she should remain disinherited.
They pounced upon the lands of the dead brother with
an eagerness which would have been rather more decent
had it been a little less apparent; and to the widowed
Lucia, who was the least guilty party to the conspiracy
for which she had been made the decoy, they left little
beyond her wardrobe. She was actually reduced to
appeal to the King's mercy for means to live. Henry
responded to her piteous petition by the offer of his
brother of Dorset as a second husband. Lucia was one
of those women who are born actresses, and whose nature
it is to do things which seem forced and unnatural to

others. She flattered the King with anticipations that she was on the point of complying with his wishes, till the last moment; and then she eloped with Sir Henry de Mortimer, possibly a distant connection of the Earl of March. It may be added, since Lucia now disappears from the story, that she survived her second marriage for fourteen years, and showed herself at her death a most devout member of the orthodox Church, by a will which was from beginning to end a string of bequests for masses, to be sung for the repose of her soul, and of the soul of Kent.

Bertram and Maude, to whom the news came first, scarcely knew how to tell Constance of Kent's death. At last Maude thought of dressing the little Alianora in daughter's mourning, and sending her into her mother's room alone. The gradations of mourning were at that time so distinct and minute that Constance's practised eye would read the parable in an instant. So they broke in that manner the news they dared not tell her.

For the whole day there was no sign from Constance that she had even noticed the hint. Her voice and manner showed no change. But at night, when the little child of three years old knelt at her mother's knee for her evening prayer, said Lollard wise in simple English, they found it had not escaped her. As the child came to the usual " God bless my father and mother," —which, fatherless as she had always been, she had been taught to say,—Constance quietly checked her, and made her say, "God bless my mother" only. And at the close, little Alianora was instructed to add,—" God pardon my father's soul."

Knowing how passionately Constance had once loved Kent, this calm show of indifference puzzled Maude Lyngern sorely. But to the Dowager Lady it was no such riddle.

"Her love is dead, child," she said, when Maude timidly expressed her surprise. "And when that is verily thus, it were lighter to bid a dead corpse live than a dead love."

All this time the Lollard persecution slowly waxed hotter and hotter. Men began to thank God when any "heretics" among their friends were permitted to die in their beds, and to whisper in hushed accents that when the Prince of Wales should be King, whose nature was more merciful than his father's, matters might perchance mend. They little knew what the future was to bring. The worst was not yet over, was not even to come during the reign of Henry of Bolingbroke.

Seeing that Constance was now restored to her lands, and basking in the sunshine of Court favour, it struck Lady Abergavenny, a niece of Archbishop Arundel, who was a politic woman as most of his nieces were that an alliance between her son and Isabel Le Despenser would be a good speculation. And her Ladyship, being moreover a strong-minded woman, whose husband was of very little public and less private consequence, carried her point, and the marriage of Isabel with young Richard Beauchamp took place at Cardiff on the eleventh birthday of the bride.

The ceremony was slightly hastened at the wish of the Dowager Lady Le Despenser. She was anxious not to distress Constance by breaking the news too suddenly to her, but she felt within herself that the golden bowl was nearing its breaking at the fountain, and that the silver cords of her earthly house of this tabernacle were not far from being taken down. She was an old woman, —very old, for a period wherein few lived to old age; she had long outlived her husband, and had seen the funerals of nearly all her children. The greater part even of her earthly treasures were already safe where moth and rust corrupt not, and her own feeling of earnest longing to rejoin them grew daily stronger. It was for the daughter's sake alone that she cared to live now; the daughter to whom men had left only God and that mother. A new lesson was now to be taught to Constance—to rest wholly upon God.

It was very tranquilly at last that Elizabeth Le Despenser passed away from earth. She took most loving leave of Constance, blessed and said farewell to all her children, and charged Bertram and Maude to remain with her and be faithful to her.

Twenty years' companionship, fellowship in sorrow, and fellowship in faith, had effected a complete revolution in the feelings of Constance towards her mother-in law.

"O Mother, Mother!" she sobbed; "what shall I do without you!"

"My child," answered Elizabeth, "had the heavenly Master not seen that thou shouldst well do without me, He had left me yet here."

"You yourself said, Mother, that He had left me but Him and you!"

"Aye, dear daughter; and yet He hath left thee Himself. Every hour He shall be with thee; and every hour of thy life moreover shall be an hour the less betwixt thee and me."

The last thing that they heard her murmur, which had reference to that land whither she was going, was —" Neither schulen they die more."

They laid her in the family vault at Tewkesbury Abbey; and once more there was mourning at Cardiff.

It was only just begun when news came of another death, far more unexpected than hers. Richard of Conisborough and Anne Mortimer were already the parents of a daughter; and two months after the death of the Lady Le Despenser a son was born, who was hereafter to become the father of all the future kings of England. And while the young mother lay wrapped in her first tender gladness over her new treasure, God called her to come away to Him. So she left the little children who would never call her "mother," left the husband who was all the world to her; and fragile White Rose as she was Anne Mortimer "perished with the flowers." She died "with all the sunshine on her," aged only twenty-one years. Perhaps those who stood round her coffin thought it a very sad and strange dispensation of Providence. But we, who know what lay hidden in the coming years, can see that God's time for her to die was the best and kindest time. And indications are not quite wanting, slight though they may be, that Richard of Conisborough was not a political, but a religious Lollard, and that this autumn journey of Anne Mortimer to the unknown land may have been a triumphal entry into the City of God.

The news that Constance had of set purpose cast in her lot with the Lollards was not long in travelling to Westminster. And she soon found that the lot of a

Lollard was no bed of roses. In his anger, Henry of Bolingbroke departed from his usual rule of rigid justice, and revoked the grant which Constance may be said to have purchased with her heart's blood. Her favourite Richard, now a fine youth of sixteen, was taken from her, and his custody, possessions, and marriage were granted to trustees, of whom the chief persons were Archbishop Arundel and Edward Duke of York. This meant that the trustees were to sell his hand to the father of some eligible damsel, and pocket the proceeds; and also to convert to their own use the rents of young Richard's estates until he was of age. The Duke of York was just now a most devout and orthodox person. It was time, for any one who cared to save his life, as Edward did; for a solemn decree against Wycliffe's writings had just been fulminated at Rome; and while Henry of Bolingbroke sat on the throne, England lay at the feet of the Pope. The trustees took advantage at once of the favour done them, and sold young Richard (without consulting Constance) to the Earl of Westmoreland, for the benefit of one of his numerous daughters, the Lady Alianora Neville. She was a little girl of about ten years old, and remained in the charge of her mother, the King's sister. In the April following it pleased the Duke of York to pay a visit to his sister, and to bring her son in his train. Edward was particularly silent at first. He appeared to have heard no news, to be actuated by no motive in coming, and generally to have nothing to say. Richard, on the contrary, was evidently labouring under suppressed excitement of some kind. But when they sat down to supper, York called for Malvoisie, and threw a bomb into the midst of the company by the wish which he uttered as he carried the goblet to his lips.

"God pardon King Henry's soul!"

He was answered by varying exclamations in different tones.

"Aye, Madam, 'tis too true!" broke forth young Richard, addressing his mother; "but mine uncle's Grace willed me not to speak thereof until he so should."

"Harry of Bolingbroke is dead?   Surely no!"

"Dead as a door-nail," said York unfeelingly.

"Was he sick of long time?"

"Long enough!" responded York in the same manner. "Long enough to weary every soul that ministered to his fantasies, and to cause them ring the church bells for joy that their toil was over   Leprosy, by my troth! —a sweet disorder to die withal!"

"Ned, I pray thee keep some measure in speech."

"By the Holy Coat of Treves! but if thou wouldst love to deal withal, Custance, thy tarrying at Kenilworth hath wrought mighty change in thee. Marry, it pleased the Lady Queen to proffer unto me an even's watch in the chamber. 'Good lack! I thank your Grace,' quoth I, 'but 'tis mine uttermost sorrow that I should covenant with one at Hackney to meet with me this even, and I must right wofully deny me the ease that it should do me to abide with his Highness' An honest preferment, to be his sick nurse, by St. Lawrence his gridiron! Nay, by St. Zachary his shoe-strings, but there were two words to that bargain!"

"Then what did your Grace, Uncle?" said Isabel in her cool, grown up style.

"Did? Marry, little cousin, I rade down to Norwich

House, and played a good hour at the cards with my Lord's Grace of Norwich; and then I lay me down on the settle and gat me a nap; and after spices served, I turned back to Westminster, and did her Grace to wit that it were rare cold riding from Hackney."

"Is your Grace yet shriven sithence, Uncle?" inquired young Richard rather comically.

"The very next morrow, lad, my said Lord of Norwich the confessor. I bare it but a night, nor it did me not no disease in sleeping."

"Maybe it should take a heavy sin to do that, fair Uncle," said Isabel with a sneer.

"What wist, such a chick as thou?" returned York, holding out his goblet to the dispenser of Malvoisie.

A little lower down the table, Sir Bertram Lyngern and Master Hugh Calverley were discussing less serious subjects in a more sober and becoming manner.

"Truly, our new King hath well begun," said Hugh. "My Lord of March is released of his prison, and shall be wed this next summer to the Lady Anne of Stafford, and his sister the Lady Alianora unto my Lord of Devon his son; and all faithful friends and servants of King Richard be set in favour; and 'tis rumoured about the Court that your Lady shall receive confirmation of every of his father's grants made unto her."

"I trust it shall so be verily," said Bertram.

"And further yet," pursued Hugh, slightly dropping his voice, "'tis said that the King considereth to take unto the Crown great part of the moneys and lands of the Church."

"Surely no!"

"Aye, so far as my judgment serveth, 'tis so soothly."

"But that were sacrilege!"

"Were it?" asked Hugh coolly.

For the extreme Lollards, of whom he was one, looked upon the two political acts which we have learned to call disestablishment and disendowment, as not only permissible, but desirable. In so saying, I speak of the political Lollards. All political Lollards, however, were not religious ones, nor were all religious Lollards sharers in these political views. John of Gaunt, a strong political Lollard, was never a religious one in his life; while King Richard, who decidedly leaned to them in religion, disliked their politics exceedingly. In fact, it was rather the fervent, energetic, practical reformers who took up with such aims; while those among them who walked quietly with God let the matter alone. Hugh Calverley had been drawn into these questions rather by circumstances than choice. While he was emphatically one that "sighed and that cried for all the abominations that were done in the midst of" his Israel, he was sagacious enough to know that even from his own point of view, the abolition of the hierarchy, or the suppression of the monastic orders, were no more than lopping off branches, while the root remained.

It was perfectly true that Henry V. seriously contemplated the policy of disendowment, which Parliament had in vain suggested to his father. And it continued to be true for some six months longer. The clue has not yet been discovered to the mysterious and sudden change which at that date came over, not only the policy, but the whole character of Henry of Monmouth. Up to that date he had himself been something very like a political Lollard; ever after it he was fervently orthodox. The suddenness of the change was not less remarkable than its completeness. It took place about the first of October, 1413; and it exactly coincides in date with a visit from Archbishop Arundel, to urge upon the reluctant King the apprehension of his friend Lord Cobham. Whatever may have been the means of the alteration, there can be but littl: question as to who was the agent.

The King's confirmation of grants to his cousin Constance occurred before this ominous date; and, revoking the last penalty inflicted, it restored her son to her custody. Richard therefore came home in July, where he remained until September. His attendance was then commanded at Court, and he left Cardiff accordingly.

"Farewell, Madam!" he said brightly, as his mother gave him her farewell kiss and blessing. "God allowing, I trust to be at home again ere Christmas; and fiom London I will seek to bring your Grace and my sisters some gear of pleasance"

"Farewell, my Dickon!" said Constance, lovingly. "Have a care of thyself, fair son. Remember, thou art now my dearest treasure."

"No fear, sweet Lady!"

So he sailed off, waving his hand or his cap from the boat, so long as he could be seen.

A letter came from him three weeks later—a doubtful, uneasy letter, showing that the mind of the writer was by no means at rest concerning the future. The King had received him most graciously, and every one at Court was kind to him; but the sky was lowering ominously over the struggling Church of God—that little section of the Holy Catholic Church, on which the "mother and mistress of all churches" looked down with such supreme contempt. The waves of persecution were rising higher now than to the level of poor tailors like John Badby, or even of priestly graduates like William Sautre.

"Lady, I do you to wit," wrote young Richard, "that as this day, Sir John Oldcastle, Lord Cobham, was put to his trial, and being convinced,[1] was cast[2]; the beginning and end of whose offence is that he is a Lollard confessed, and hath harboured other men of the like opinions. And the said Lord is now close prisoner in the Tower of London, nor any of his kin ne lovers[3] suffered to come anigh him. And at the Court it is rumoured that Sir William Hankeford (whom your Ladyship shall well remember) should be sent into our parts of South Wales, there to put down both heresy and sedition : which sedition, methinks, your Ladyship's favour allowing, shall point at Sir Owain Glendordy[4]; and the heresy so called, both your Ladyship and I, your humble son and servant, do well know what it doth signify. So no more at this present writing ; but praying our Lord that He would have your Ladyship in His good keeping, and that all we may do His good pleasure, I rest."

Twelve days later came another letter, written in a strange hand. It was dated from Merton Abbey, in Surrey, was attested by the Abbot's official cross and seal, and contained only a few lines. But never throughout her troubled life had any letter so wrung the heart of Constance Le Despenser. For those few formal lines

---

[1] Convicted.   [2] Sentenced.   [3] Friends.
[4] The name is usually spelt thus in contemporary records.

brought the news that never again would her eyes be gladdened by her heart's dearest treasure—that the Angel of Death had claimed for his own her bright, loving, fair haired Richard.

No details have been handed down concerning that early and lamented death of the last Lord Le Despenser. We do not even know how the boy died—whether by the visitation of God in sudden illness, or by the fiat of Thomas de Arundel, making the twelfth murder which lay upon that black, seared soul. He was buried where he died, in the Abbey of Merton—far from his home, far from his mother's tears and his father's grave. It was always the lot of the hapless buds of the White Rose to be scattered in death.

There was only one person at Cardiff who did not mourn bitterly for its young Lord. To his sister Isabel, the inheritance to which she now became sole heiress— the change of her title from "Lady Isabel de Beauchamp" to "The Lady Le Despenser"—were amply sufficient compensation to outweigh the loss of a brother. But little Alianora wept bitterly.

"Aye me! what a break is this in our Lady's line!" lamented Maude to Bertram. "God grant it the last, *if* His will is!"

It was only one funeral of a long procession.

The Issue Roll for Michaelmas, 1413–4, bears two terribly significant entries the expenses for the custody of Katherine Mortimer and her daughters, who were "in the King's keeping" and the costs of the funerals of the same persons, buried in St. Swithin's Church, London. This was the hapless daughter of Owain Glyndwr, the wife of Edmund Mortimer, uncle of the

Earl of March. A mother and two or more daughters do not usually require burial together, unless they die of contagious disease. Of course that may have been the case; but the entry looks miserably like a judicial murder.

Stirring events followed in rapid succession. Lord Cobham escaped mysteriously from the Tower, and as mysteriously from an armed band sent to apprehend him by Abbot Heyworth of St. Albans. Old Judge Hankeford made his anticipated visit to South Wales, and ceremoniously paid his respects to the Lady of Cardiff, whose associations with his name were not of the most agreeable order. With the new year came the unfortunate insurrection of the political Lollards, goaded to revolt partly by the fierce persecution, partly by a chivalrous desire to restore the beloved King Richard, whom many of them believed to be still living in Scotland. Wales and its Marches were their head-quarters. Thomas Earl of Arundel—son of a persecutor—was sent to the Principality at the head of an army, to "subdue the rebels;" Sir Roger Acton and Sir John Beverley, two of the foremost Lollards of the new generation, were put to death; and strict watch was set in every quarter for Lord Cobham, once more escaped as if by miracle.

And then suddenly came another death—this time by the distinct and awful sentence of God Almighty. He stooped to disconcert for a moment the puny plans of men who had set themselves in array against the Lord and His Christ. On the chief of all the persecutors, Sir Thomas de Arundel himself, the angel of God's vengeance laid his irresistible hand. Cut off in the blossom of his sin—struck down in a moment by paralysis of the throat, which deprived him of all power of speech or swallowing the dreaded Archbishop passed to that awful tribunal where his earthly eloquence was changed to silence and shame. He died, probably, not unabsolved ; they could still lay the consecrated wafer upon the silent tongue, and touch with the chrism the furrowed brow and brilliant eyes : but he must have died unconfessed—a terrible thing to him, if he really believed himself the doctrines which he spent his life in forcing upon others.

Arundel was dead ; but the infernal generalissimo of the persecutors, who could not die, was ready with a worthy successor. Henry Chichele stepped into the vacant seat, and the fierce battle against the saints went on.

The nephew of the deceased Archbishop, Thomas Earl of Arundel, presented himself at Cardiff early in the year. He lost no time in delicate insinuations, but came at once to his point. Was the Lady of Cardiff ready to give all possible aid to himself and his troops, against those traitors and heretics called Lollards ? The answer was equally distinct. With some semblance of the old fire flashing in her eyes, the Lady of Cardiff refused to give him any aid whatever.

The Earl hinted in answer, with a sarcastic smile, that judging by the rumours which had reached the Court, he had scarcely expected any other conduct from her.

"Look ye for what ye will," returned the dauntless Princess. "Never yet furled I my colours in peace ; and I were double craven if I should do it in war !"

Her words were reported to the relentless hearts at Westminster. The result was an order to seize all the manors of the Despenser heritage, and to deliver them to Edward Duke of York, the King's dearly beloved cousin, by way of compensation (said the grant) for the loss which he had sustained by the death of Richard Le Despenser. But the compensation was estimated at a high figure.

There were some curious contradictory statutes passed this year. A hundred and ten monasteries were suppressed by order of Council, and at the same time another order was issued for the extirpation of heresy. But, as usual, "the blood of the martyrs was the seed of the Church." Wycliffism increased rapidly among the common people. Meanwhile Henry was preparing for his French campaign ; and at Constance the seventeenth General Council of Christendom was just gathering, and John Huss, with the Emperor's worthless safe conduct in his pocket, was hastening towards his prison not much larger than a coffin—in the Monastery of St. Maurice. The Council ended their labours by burning Huss. They would have liked to burn Wycliffe ; but as he had been at rest with God for over thirty years, they took refuge in the childish revenge of disinterring and burning his senseless bones. And "after that, they had no more that they could do."

The day that heard Huss's sentence pronounced in the white walled Cathedral of Constance, Edward Duke of York · accompanied by a little group of knights and squires, one of whom was Hugh Calverley walked his oppressed horse across the draw bridge at Cardiff. Life had agreed so well with York that he had become very fat upon it.   He had no children, his wife never contradicted him, and he did not keep that troublesome article called a conscience; so his sorrows and perplexities were few.   On the whole, he had found treachery an excellent investment—for one life; and York left the consideration of the other to his death-bed.   It may be that at times, even to this Dives, the voice from Heaven mercifully whispered, "Thou fool!"   But he never stayed his chariot-wheels to listen—until one autumn evening, by Southampton Water, when the end loomed full in view, the Angel of Death came very near, and there rose before him, suddenly and awfully, the dread possibility of a life which might not close with a death bed. But it was yet bright summer when he reached Cardiff; and not yet had come that dark, solemn August hour, when Edward Duke of York should dictate his true character as "of all sinners the most wicked."

On this particular summer day at Cardiff, York was, for him, especially gay and bright.   Yet that night in the Cathedral of Constance stood John Huss before his judges; and in the Convent of Coimbra an English Princess,[1] long ago forgotten in England, yet gentlest and best of the daughters of Lancaster, lay waiting for death.   Somewhere in this troublesome world the bridal is always matched by the burial, the festal song by the funeral dirge.   Men and women are always mourning, somewhere.

York's mind was full of one subject, the forthcoming campaign in France.   He was to sail from Southampton with his royal master in August.   Bedford was to be left Regent, the King's brother—Bedford, who, what-

---

[1] Philippa Queen of Portugal, eldest daughter of John of Gaunt.

ever else he were, was no Lollard, and was not likely
to let a Lollard escape his fangs. And on this interesting topic York's tongue ran on glibly—how King Henry
meant to march at once upon Paris, proclaim himself
King of France, be crowned at St. Denis, marry one of
the French Princesses—which, it did not much signify
and return home a conquering hero, mighty enough
to brave even the Emperor himself on any European
battle plain.

A little lower down the table, Hugh Calverley's mind
was also full of one subject.

"Nay," he whispered earnestly to Bertram : "he is
yet hid some whither,—here, in Wales. Men wit not
where ; and God forbid too many should !"

"Then men be yet a-searching for him ?"

"High and low, leaving no stone unturned. God keep
His true servant safe, unto His honour !"

It needs no far-fetched conjecture to divine that they
were speaking of Lord Cobham.

"And goest unto these French wars, sweet Hugh ?"

"Needs must; my Lord's Grace hath so bidden me."

"But thou wert wont to hold that no Christian man
should of right bear arms, neither fight."

"Truth; and yet do," said Hugh quietly. This was
the view of the extreme Lollards.

"Then how shall thine opinion serve in the thick of
fight ?"

"As it hath aforetime. I cannot fight."

"But how then ?" asked Bertram, opening his eyes.

"I can die, Bertram Lyngern," answered the calm,
resolute voice. "And it may be that I should die as
truly for my Master Christ there, as at the martyr's

stake.   For sith God's will hath made yonder noble Lord my master, and hath set me under him to do his bidding, in all matters not sinful, his will is God's will for me ; and I can follow him to yonder battle-plain with as easy an heart and light as though I went to lie down on my bed to sleep   Not to fight, good friend; not to resist nor contend with any man; only to do God's will.   And is that not worth dying for ?"

Bertram made no reply.   But his memory ran far back to the olden days at Langley— to a scriptorius who had laid down his pen to speak of two lads, both of whom he looked to see great men, but he deemed him the greater who was not ashamed of his deed.   And Bertram's heart whispered to him that, knight as he was, while Hugh remained only a simple squire, yet now as ever, Hugh was the greater hero.   For he knew that it would have cost him a very bitter struggle to accept an unhonoured grave such as Hugh anticipated, only because he thought it was God's will.

They parted the next morning.   Edward's last words to his sister were

"Adieu, Custance, I will send thee a fleur de-lis banner as trophy from the fight.   The oriflamme,[1] if the saints will have it so !"

But Hugh's were—"Farewell, dear friend Bertram. Remember, both thou and I may do God's will !"

---

[1] The oriflamme was *the* banner of France, kept in the Cathedral of St. Denis, and held almost sacred.

CHAPTER XIII.

THE GARDEN OF GOD.

I 'M kneeling at the threshold, aweary, faint, and sore ;
I'm waiting for the dawning, for the opening of the door
I'm waiting till the Master shall bid me rise and come
To the glory of His presence, the gladness of His home.

A weary path I've travelled, mid darkness, storm, and strife,
Beaiing many a burden, contending for my life ;
But now the morn is breaking,—my toil will soon be o'er
I'm kneeling at the threshold, my hand is at the door.
    *   *   *   *   *   *   *

O Lord, I wait Thy pleasure ! Thy time and way are best :
But I'm wasted, worn, and weary : my Father, bid me rest !"
—Dr. ALEXANDER.

THE full glory of summer had come at last.   Over Southampton Water broke a cloudless August day. The musical cries of the sailors who were at work on the Saint Mary, the James, and the Catherine, in the offing preparing for the King's voyage to France— came pleasantly from the distance.   From the country farms, girls with baskets poised on their heads, filled with market produce, came into the crowded sea port town, where the whole Court awaited a fair wind.   There was no wind from any quarter that day.   Earth and sea and sky presented a dead calm : and the only place which was not calm was the heart of fallen man. For a few steps from the busy gates and the crowded market is Southampton Green, and there, draped in mourning, stands the scaffold, and beside it the state headsman.

All the Court are gathered here. It is a break in the monotony of existence—the tiresome dead level of waiting for the wind to change.

The first victim is brought out. Trembling and timidly he comes—Henry Le Scrope of Upsal, the luckless husband of the Duchess Dowager of York, Treasurer of the Household, only a few days since in the highest favour. He was arrested, tried, and sentenced in twenty four hours, just a week before. No voice pleads for poor Scrope, a simple, single-minded man, who never made an enemy till now. He dies to-day— " on suspicion of being suspected" of high treason.

The block and the axe are wiped clean of Scrope's blood, and the headsman stands waiting for the Sheriff to bring the second victim.

He comes forward calmly, with quiet dignity; a stately, fair haired man,—ready to die, because ready to meet God. And we know the face of Richard of Conisborough, the finest and purest character of the royal line, the fairest bud of the White Rose. He has little wish to live longer. Life was stripped of its flowers for him four years ago, when he heard the earth cast on the coffin of his pale desert flower. She is in Heaven ; and Christ is in Heaven ; and Heaven is better than earth. So what matter, though the passage be low and dark which leads up to the gate of the Garden of God ? Yet this is no easy nor honourable death to die. No easy death to a man of high sense of chivalrous honour; no light burden, thus to be led forth before the multitude, to a death of shame, on his part undeserved. Perhaps men will know some day how little he deserved it. At any rate, God knows. And whatever shameful end be decreed for the servant, it can never surpass that of the Master. The utmost that any child of God can suffer for Christ, can never equal what Christ has suffered for him.

And so, calm in mien, willing in heart, Richard of Conisborough went through the dark passage, to the Garden of God. But if ever a judicial murder were committed in this world, it was done that day on Southampton Green, when the blood of the Lollard Prince dyed the dust of the scaffold.

The accusation brought against the victims was high treason. The indictment bore falsehood on its face by going too far. It asserted, not only that they had conspired to raise March to the throne—which might perhaps have been believed; but also that they had plotted the assassination of King Henry which no one who knew them could believe; that March, taken into their counsels, had asked for an hour to consider the matter, and had then gone straight to the King and revealed the plot—which no one who knew March could believe. The whole accusation was a tissue of improbabilities and inconsistencies. No evidence was offered; the conclusion was foregone from the beginning. So they died on Southampton Green.

Perhaps Henry's heart failed him at the last moment. For some reason, Richard of Conisborough was spared the last and worst ignominy of a traitor's death—the exposure of the severed head on some city gate. Henry allowed his remains to receive quiet and honourable burial.

The next day a decree was passed, pardoning March for all crimes and offences. The only offence which he had ever committed against the House of Lancaster was his own existence; and for that he could scarcely be held responsible, either in law or equity. But can we say as much for the offence against God and man which he committed on that sixth of August, when he suffered himself to be dragged to the judge's bench, on which he sat with others to condemn the husband of that sister Anne who had been his all but mother?

We shall see no more of Edmund Mortimer. He ended life as he began it—as much like a vegetable as a human being could well make himself. Few Mortimers attained old age, nor did he. He died in his thirty-fourth year, issueless and unwept; and Richard Duke of York, the son of Anne Mortimer and Richard of Conisborough, succeeded to the White Rose's "heritage of woe."

A week after the execution, the King sailed for Harfleur.

The campaign was short, for those days of long campaigns; but pestilence raged among the troops, and cut off some of the finest men. The Earl of Suffolk died before they left Harfleur, and ere they reached Picardy, the Earl of Arundel. But the King pressed onward, till on the night of the 24th of October, he encamped, ready to give battle, near the little village of Azincour, to be thenceforward for ever famous, under its English name of Agincourt.

The army was in a very sober mood. The night was spent quietly, by the more careless in sleep, by the more thoughtful in prayer. The Duke of York was among the former; the King among the latter. Henry is said to have wrestled earnestly with God that no sins of his might be remembered against him, to lead to the discomfiture of his army. There was need for the entreaty. Perchance, had he slept that night, some such ghostly visions, born of his own conscience, might have disturbed his sleep, as those which troubled one of his successors on the eve of Bosworth Field.

When morning came, and the King was at breakfast with his brother Prince Humphrey, the Duke of York presented himself with a request that he might be permitted to lead the vanguard.

Humphrey, who was of a sarcastic turn of mind, amused himself by a few jokes on the obesity of the royal applicant; but the request was granted, and York rode off well pleased.

"Stand thou at my stirrup, Calverley," said York to his squire. "I cast no doubt thou wilt win this day thy spurs; and for me, I look to come off covered with glory."

"How many yards of glory shall it take to cover his Grace?" whispered one of the irreverent varlets behind them.

"Howsoe'er, little matter," pursued the Duke. "I can scantly go higher than I am : wherefore howso I leave the field, little reck I."

Hugh Calverley looked up earnestly at his master.

"Sir Duke," he said, "hath it come into your Grace's mind that no less yourself than your servants may leave this field dead corpses?"

"Tut, man! croak not," said York. "I have no intent to leave it other than alive—thou canst do as it list thee."

Two months had elapsed since that August evening when, terrified by his brother's sudden and violent death, Edward Duke of York had dictated his will in terms of such abject penitence. The effect of that terror was wearing away. The unseen world, which had come very near, receded into the far distance; and the visible world returned to its usual prominence. And York's aim had always been, not "so to pass through things temporal that he lost not the things eternal," but so to pass towards things eternal that he lost not the things temporal. His own choice proved his heaviest punishment: "for he in his life-time received his good things."

It was a terrible battle which that day witnessed at Agincourt. In one quarter of the field Prince Humphrey lay half dead upon the sward; when the King, riding up and recognising his brother, sprang from his saddle, took his stand over the prostrate body, and waving his good battle-axe in his strong firm hand, kept the enemy at bay, and saved his brother's life. In another direction, a sudden charge of the French pressed a little band of English officers and men close together, till not one in the inner ranks could move hand or foot —crushed them closer, closer, as if the object had been to compress them into a consolidated mass. At last help came, the French were beaten off, and the living wall was free to separate into its component atoms of human bodies. But as it did so, from the interior of the mass one man fell to the ground, dead. No one needed to ask who it was. The royal fleurs-de-lis and lions on the surcoat, with an escocheon of pretence bearing the arms of Leon and Castilla the princely coronet surrounding the helmet—were enough to tell the tale. Other men might come alive out of the fight of Agincourt, but Edward Duke of York would only leave it a corpse.

He stands on the page of history, a beacon for all time. No man living in his day better knew the way of righteousness ; no man living took less care to walk in it. During the later years of his life, it seemed as if that dread Divine decree might have gone forth, most awful even of Divine decrees —"Let him alone." He had refused to be troubled with God, and the penalty was that God would not be troubled with him : He would not force His salvation on this unwilling soul. And now, when "behind, he heard Time's iron gates close faintly," it was too late for renewing to repentance. He that was unholy must be unholy still. Verily, he had his reward.

The end of the struggle was now approaching. On every side the French were hemmed in and beaten down. Prince Humphrey had been carried to the royal tent, but the King was still in the field—here, there, and everywhere, as nearly ubiquitous as a man could be— riding from point to point, and now and then engaging in single-handed skirmish. A French archer, waiting for an opportunity to distinguish himself, levelled his crossbow at the royal warrior, while he remained for a moment stationary. In another second the victory of Agincourt would have been turned into a defeat, and probably a panic. But at the critical instant a squire flung himself before the King, and received the shaft intended for his Sovereign. He fell, but uttered no word.

"Truly, a gallant deed, Master Squire!" cried Henry. "Whatso be your name, rise a knight banneret."

"The squire will arise no more, Sire," said the voice of the Earl of Huntingdon behind him. "Your Highness' grace hath come too late; he is dead."

"In good sooth, I am sorry therefor," returned the King. "Never saw I braver deed, ne better done. Well! if he leave son or widow, they may receive our grace in his guerdon. Who is he? Ho, archer! thou bearest our cousin of York his livery, and so doth this squire. Win hither—unlace his helm, and give us to wit if thou know him."

And when the helm was unlaced, and the archer had recognised the dead face, they knew that the Lollard squire, Hugh Calverley, had saved the life of the persecutor at the cost of his own.

He had spoken the simple truth. He could not fight, but he could die. He could not write his name upon the world's roll of glory, but he could do God's will.

The public opinion of earth accounts this a mean and unworthy object. The public opinion of Heaven is probably of a different character.

Nothing was to be done for widow or child, for Hugh Calverley left neither. He was no ascetic; he was merely a man who thought first of how he might please the Lord, and who felt himself least fettered by single life. So there was no love in his heart but the love of Christ, and nothing on earth that he desired in comparison of Him.

And on earth he had no guerdon. Even the royal words of praise he did not live to hear. But on the other side of the dark river passed so quickly, there were the garland of honour, and the palm of victory, and the King's "Well done, good and faithful servant!" Verily, also, he had his reward.

The autumn was passing into winter before the news reached Constance either of the battle of Agincourt or of the murder on Southampton Green. At first she was utterly crushed and prostrated. The old legal leaven, so hard to work out of the human conscience, wrought upon her with tenfold force, and she declared that God was against her, and was wreaking His wrath upon her for the lie which she had told in denying the validity of her marriage. Was it not evidently so? she asked. Had He not first bereft her of her darling, the precious boy whom her sin had preserved to her? And now not only Edward, but the favourite brother, Dickon, were gone likewise. Herself, her stepmother, her widowed sisters in-law,[1] and the two little children of Richard, were alone left of the House of York. The news of Edward's death she bore with comparative equanimity: it was the sudden and dreadful end of Richard which so completely overpowered her.

"Hold thy peace, Maude!" she said mournfully, in answer to Maude's tender efforts to console her. "God is against me and all mine House. We have sinned; or rather, *I* have sinned,—and have thus brought down sorrow and mourning upon the hearts that were dearest to me. I owe a debt; and it must needs be paid, even to the uttermost farthing."

---

[1] Richard of Conisborough married secondly, and probably chiefly with the view of securing a mother for his children, Maude Clifford, a daughter of the great Lollard House of Clifford of Cumberland. She survived him many years.

"But, dear my Lady," urged Maude, not holding her peace as requested, "what do you, to pay so much as one farthing of that debt? Christ our Lord hath taken the same upon Him. A debt cannot be twice paid."

"I do verily trust," she said humbly, "that He hath paid for me the debt eternal; yet is there a debt earthly, and this is for my paying."

"Never a whit!" cried Maude earnestly. "Dear my Lady, not one cross[1] thereof! That which we suffer at the hand of our Father is not debt, but discipline; the chastising of the son, not the work wrung by lash from the slave. 'The children are free.'"

"Aye, free from the curse and the second death," she said, still despondingly; "but from pains and penalties of sin in this life, Maude, not freed. An' I cut mine hand with yonder knife, God shall not heal the wound by miracle because I am His child."

Maude felt that the illustration was true, but she was not sure that it was apposite, neither was she convinced that her own view was mistaken. She glanced at Sir Ademar de Milford, who sat on the settle, studying the works of St. Augustine, as if to ask him to answer for her. Ademar was no longer the family confessor, for the family had given over confessing; but Archbishop Chichele, professing himself satisfied of his orthodoxy, had revoked the now useless writ of excommunication, and the priest had resumed his duties as chaplain. Ademar laid down his book in answer to the appealing glance from Maude's eyes.

"Lady," he said, "how much, I pray you, is owing to

---

[1] Farthing.

your Grace from the young ladies your daughters, for food and lodging?"

"Owing from my little maids!" exclaimed Constance.

"That is it which I would know," replied Ademar gravely.

"From my little maids!" she repeated in astonishment.

"It is written, Madam, in His book, that as one whom his mother comforteth, He comforteth us. Wherefore, seeing that the comfort your Grace looketh for at His hands is to have you afore the reeve for payment of your debts, it setteth me to think that you shall needs use your children likewise."

"Never!" cried Constance emphatically.

"And so say I, Lady," returned Ademar significantly.

"But, Sir Ademar, God doth chastise IIis children!"

"Truly so, Madam, as you yours. But I marvel which is the more sufferer yourself or the child."

He spoke pointedly, for only the day before Isabel had chosen to be very naughty, and had imperatively required correction, which he knew had cost far more to Constance to administer than to her refractory child to receive.

"Then, Sir Ademar, you do think He suffereth when He chastiseth us?" she asked, her voice faltering a little.

"I cannot think, Dame, that He loveth the rod. Only He loveth too well the child to leave him uncorrected."

"O, Sir Ademar!" she cried suddenly "I do trust 'He shall not find need to try me yet again through these childre! I am so feared I should fail and fall. Ah me! weak and wretched woman that I am, I could not bear to see these two forced from me! God help and pardon me; but me feareth if it should come to this yet again, I would do anything to keep them!"

"The Lord can heal the waters, Lady, ere He fetch you to drink them."

"He did not this draught aforetime," she said sadly.

"Maybe," replied Ademar, "because He saw that your Ladyship's disorder needed a bitter medicine."

There was a respite for just one year. But ever after the news of her brother Richard's death, Constance drooped and pined; and when the fresh storm broke, it found her an invalid almost confined to her bed. It began with a strong manifesto from Archbishop Chichele against the Lollards. Then came a harshly-worded order for all landed proprietors in the Marches of South Wales to reside on their estates and "keep off the rebels." One of these was specially directed to Constance Le Despenser.

But who were the rebels? Owain Glyndwr had died twelve months before. It could not mean him; and there was only one person whom it could mean. It meant Lord Cobham, still in hiding, whom Lord Powys was in the field to capture, and on whose head a rich reward was set. The authorities were trembling in fear of a second outbreak under his guidance. Bertram gave the missive to Maude, who carried it to Constance. Disobedience was to be visited by penalty; and how it was likely to be punished in her case, Constance knew only too well. She received it with a moan of anguish.

"My little maids! my little, little maids!"

She said no more: she only grew worse and weaker.

Then Lord Powys, in search for the "rebels," marched up and demanded aid. He was answered by silence: and he marched on and away, helped by no hand or voice in Cardiff Castle.

"I must give them up!" Constance whispered to Maude, in accents so hopelessly mournful that it wrung her tender heart to hear them. "I cannot give Him up!"

For just then, in the eyes of every Lollard, to follow Lord Cobham was equivalent to following Christ. ·

Weaker and weaker she grew now; always confined to bed; worse from day to day.

And at last, on the 28th of November, 1416, the ominous horn sounded without the moat, and the Sheriff of the county, armed with all the power of the law, entered the Castle of Cardiff, to call the Lady Le Despenser to account for her repeated and contumacious neglect of the royal command.

"Lady mine," said Maude, tenderly, kneeling by her, "the Sheriff is here."

"It is come, then!" replied Constance very quietly. "Bring my little maids to me. Let me kiss them once more ere they tear them away from me. God help me to bear the rest!"

She kissed them both, and blessed them fervently, bidding them "be good maids and serve God." Then she lay back again in the bed, and softly turned her face to the wall so that the intruders would not see it.

"The Sheriff may enter in," she said in a low voice. "Lord, I have left all, and have followed Thee!"

Does it seem a small matter for which to sacrifice all ?

The balances of the Sanctuary are not used with weights of earth.

The Sheriff came in. Maude stood up boldly, indignantly, and demanded to know wherefore he had come. The answer was what she expected.

"To seize the persons of the Lady Le Despenser and her daughters, accused of disobedience to the law, and perverse contumacy, in that she did deny to aid with money and men the search for one John Oldcastle, a prison-breaker convict of heresy and sedition."

"Is he taken?" said Bertram almost involuntarily.

"Nay, not so yet; but the good Lord Powys is now a-hunting after him. He that shall take him shall net a thousand marks thereby, and twenty marks by the year further."

Maude drew a long sigh.

"Much good do they him!" exclaimed Bertram ironically.

Maude went back to the bed and spoke to her mistress.

"Lady, heard you what he said?"

There was no answer, and Maude spoke again. Still the silence was unbroken. She touched the shoulder, and yet no response.

"An' it like you, Madam, you must arise and come with me," said the Sheriff bluntly, as Maude bent over the sufferer. Then, with a low moan, she sank on her knees by the bedside, and a cry which was not all bitterness broke from her.

"'And thus hath Christ unwemmed kept Custance'!"

"What matter, wife?" said Bertram in a tone of sudden apprehension.

"No matter any more!" replied Maude, lifting her

white face. "Master Sheriff, she was dying ere you came to prison her,—on a sendel[1] thread hung her life: but ere you touched her, God snapped yon thread, and set her free."

Aye, what matter?—though they seized on the poor relic of mortality which had once been Constance Le Despenser?—though the mean vengeance was taken of leaving her coffin unburied for four dreary years? "After that, they had no more that they could do." It was only the withered leaves that were left in their hands; the White Rose was free.

"What shall become of the young ladies, Master Sheriff?"

"Nay," growled the surly official, "the hen being departed, I lack nought of the chicks. They may go whither it list them; only this Castle and all therein is confiscate."

Maude turned to Isabel, now a tall statuesque maiden of sixteen years.

"I shall send to my Lord, of force," she answered coldly, "and desire that he come and fetch me hence."

"And your sister, the Lady Alianora?"

The child was kneeling by the side of her dead mother, wrapped in unutterable grief. Isabel cast a contemptuous glance upon her.

"No sister of mine!" she said in the same tone. "I cannot be burdened with nameless childre."

For an instant Maude's indignation rose above both her discretion and her sorrow. She cried—"Girl, God pardon you those cruel words!"—but then with a strong effort she bridled her tongue, and sitting down

[1] A linen cloth of the finest quality.

by the bed, drew the sobbing child's head upon her bosom.

"My poor homeless darling! doth none want thee, my dove?—not even thine own mother's daughter?—Bertram, good husband, thou wilt not let[1] me?—Sweet, come then with us, and be our daughter—to whom beside thee God hath given none. Meseemeth as though He now saith, 'Take this child and nurse it for Me.' Lord, so be it!"

At the end of those four years, men's revenge was satiated, and permission was given for the funeral of the unburied coffin. But they laid her, as they had laid her son, far from the scene of her home, and from the graves of her beloved. The long unused royal vault in the Benedictine Abbey of Reading, in which the latest burial had taken place nearly two hundred years before, was opened to receive its last tenant. There she sleeps calmly, waiting for the resurrection morning.

Three historical tableaux will complete the story.

First, a quiet little village home, where a knight and his wife are calmly passing the later half of life. The knight was rendered useless for battle some years ago by a severe wound, resulting in permanent lameness. In the chimney corner, distaff in hand, sits the dame,—a small, slight woman, with gentle dark eyes, and a meek, loving expression, which will make her face lovely to the close of life. Opposite to her, occupied with another distaff, is a tall, fair, queenly girl, who can surely be no daughter of the dame. By the knight's chair, in hunting costume, stands a young man with a very open,

---

[1] Hinder.

pleasant countenance, who is evidently pleading for some favour which the knight and dame are a little reluctant to grant.

"Sir Bertram, not one word would she hear me, but bade me betake me directly unto yourself. So here behold me to beseech your gentleness in favour of my suit." ·

"Lord de Audley," said the knight, quietly, "this is not the first time by many that I have heard of your name, neither of your goodness You seek to wed my daughter. But I would have you well aware that she hath no portion: and what, I pray you, shall all your friends and lovers say unto your wedding of a poor knight's portionless daughter?"

"Say! Let them say as they list!" cried the young man. "For portion, I do account Mistress Nell portion and lineage in herself. And they be sorry friends of mine that desire not my best welfare. Her do I love, and only her will I wed."

Bertram looked across at his wife with a smile.

"Must we tell him, Dame?"

"I think we may, husband."

"Then know, Lord James de Audley, that you have asked more than you wist. This maid is no daughter of mine. Wedding her, you should wed not Nell Lyngern, a poor knight's daughter; but the Lady Alianora de Holand, Countess of Kent, of the royal line, whose mother was daughter unto a son of King Edward. Now what say you?"

The young man's face changed painfully.

"Sir, I thank you," he said in a low voice. "I am no man fit to mate with the blood royal. Lady

Countess, I cry you mercy for mine ignorance and mine unwisdom."

"Tarry yet a moment, Lord de Audley," said Bertram, smiling again ; for the girl's colour came and went, the distaff trembled in her hand, and her eyes sought his with a look of troubled entreaty. "Well, Nell ?—speak out, maiden mine !"

"Father !" she said in an agitated voice, "he loved Nell Lyngern !"

"Come, Lord James," said Bertram, laughing, "methinks you be not going empty away. God bless you, man and maid !—only, good knight and true, see thou leave not to love Nell Lyngern."

The picture fades away, and another comes on the scene.

The bar of the House of Lords. Peers in their Parliament robes fill all the benches, and at their head sits the Regent,—Prince Humphrey, Duke of Gloucester, the representative Rationalist of the fifteenth century. He was no Papist, for he disliked and despised Romish superstitions; yet no Lollard, for he was utterly incapable of receiving the things of the Spirit of God. Henry V. now lies entombed at Westminster, and on the throne is his little son of nine years old, for whom his uncle Humphrey reigns and rules. There comes forward to the bar a fair-haired, stately woman, robed in the ermine and velvet of a countess. She is asked to state her name and her business. The reply comes in a clear voice.

"My name is Alianora Touchet, Lady de Audley; and I am the only daughter and heir of Sir Edmund de Holand, sometime Earl of Kent, and of Custance his wife, daughter unto Sir Edmund of Langley, Duke of York. I claim the lands and coronets of this my father—the earldom of Kent, and the barony of Wake de Lydel."

Her evidences are received and examined. The case shall be considered, and the petitioner shall receive her answer that day month. She bows and retires.

And then down from her eyrie, like a vengeful eagle, swoops the old Duchess Joan of York—the sister of Kent, the step-mother of Constance who has two passions to gratify, her hatred to the memory of the one, and her desire to retain her share of the estates of the other. She draws up her answer to the claim,—astutely disappearing into the background, and pushing forward her simpler sister Margaret, entirely governed by her influence, as the prominent objector. She forgets nothing. She urges the assent and consent of Henry IV. to the marriage of Lucia, the presence of Constance at the ceremony, and every point which can give weight to her objection. She prays, therefore—or Margaret does for her—that the claim of the aforesaid Alianora may be adjudged invalid, and the earldom of Kent extinct.

Lady Audley reappears on the day appointed. It is the same scene again, with Duke Humphrey as president; who informs her, with calm judicial impartiality, that her petition is rejected, her claim disallowed, and her name branded with the bar sinister for ever. But as she leaves the bar, denied and humiliated, her hand is drawn gently into another hand, and a voice softly asks her—" Am not I better to thee than ten coronets ? "

And so they pass away.

The second dissolving view has disappeared ; and the last slowly grows before our sight.

A dungeon in the Tower of London.   There is only a solitary prisoner,—a man of fifty years of age, mode rate in stature, but very slightly built, with hands and feet which would be small even in a woman.   His face has never been handsome; there are deep furrows in the forehead, and something more than time has turned the brown hair grey, and given to the strongly-marked features that pensive, weary look, which his countenance always wears when in repose.   Ask his name of his gaolers, and they will say it is " Sir Henry of Lancaster, the usurper;" but ask it of himself, and a momentary flash lights up the sunken eyes as he answers, " I am the King."

Neither Pharisee nor Sadducee is Henry the Sixth. He is not a Lollard, simply because he never knew what Lollardism was.   During his reign it lay dormant —the old Wycliffite plant violently uprooted, the new Lutheran shoots not yet visible above the ground.   He was one of the very few men divinely taught without ostensible human agency,—within whom God is pleased to dwell by His Spirit at an age so early that the dawn of the heavenly instinct cannot be perceived.   From the follies, the cruelties, and the iniquities of Romanism he shrank with that Heaven born instinct ; and by the dim flickering light which he had, he walked with God. His way led over very rough ground, full of rugged stones, on which his weary feet were bruised and torn. But it was the way Home.

And now, to night, on the 22nd of May, 1471, the

prisoner is very worn and weary. He sits with a book before him—a small square volume, in illuminated Latin, with delicately-wrought borders, and occasional full-page illuminations ; a Psalter, which came into his hands from those of another prisoner in like case with himself, for the book once belonged to Richard of Bordeaux.[1] He turns slowly over the leaves, now and then reading a sentence aloud :—sentences all of which indicate a longing for home and rest.

"'My soul is also sore vexed ; but Thou, O Lord, how long ?'

"'Lord, how long wilt Thou look on ? Rescue my soul from their destructions, mine only one from the lions.'

"'And now, Lord, what wait I for ?'

"'Who shall give me wings like a dove ?—and I will flee away, and be at rest !'"[2]

At last the prisoner closed the book, and spoke in his own words to his heavenly Friend the only friend whom he had in all the world, except the wife who was a helpless prisoner like himself.

"Lord God, Thy will be done ! Grant unto me patience to await Thy time ; but, O fair Father, I lack rest !"

And just as his voice ceased, the heavy door rolled back, and the messenger of rest came in.

He did not look like a messenger of rest. But all God's messengers are not angels. And there was little indeed of the angel in this man's composition. His figure would have been tall but for a deformity which

---

[1] The Psalter is still extant, in the British Museum : Cott. MS. Domit. A. xvii.   [2] Vulgate version.

his enemies called a hump back, and his friends merely an overgrown shoulder; and his face would have been handsome but for its morose, scowling expression, which by no means betokened an amiable character.

The two cousins stood and looked at each other. The prisoner was the grandson of Henry of Bolingbroke, and he visitor was the grandson of Richard of Conisborough.

There were a few words on each side—contemptuous taunts, and sharp accusations, on the one side,—low, patient replies on the other. Then came a gleam of something flashing in the dim light, and the dagger of the visitor was sheathed in the pale prisoner's heart.

At rest, at last: safe, and saved, and with God.

It was a cruel, brutal, cold-blooded murder. But was it nothing else? Was there in it no operation of those Divine wheels which "grind slowly, yet exceeding small?"—no visitation, by Him to whom vengeance belongeth, of the sins of the guilty fathers upon the guiltless son—vengeance for the broken heart of Richard of Bordeaux, for the judicial murder of Richard of Conisborough, for the dreary imprisoned girlhood of Anne Mortimer, and—last, not least—for the long, slow years of moral torture, ending with the bitter cup forced into the dying hand of the White Rose of Langley?

HISTORICAL APPENDIX.

THE condensed biographical sketches which follow, of such persons as figure principally in the story, will help to show to those who wish to read it intelligently, how much of it is genuine history. They will see that the tale is mainly constructed on a succession of hypotheses, but that every hypothesis rests on a substratum of fact, however slender, and in many cases on careful weighing and comparison of a number of facts together. Some of these conjectures are perhaps the only ones which will fully and satisfactorily account for the sequence of events. For convenience of reference, the names are arranged in alphabetical order.

ARUNDEL, THOMAS DE, ARCHBISHOP OF CANTERBURY,
Third son of Richard the Copped Hat, ninth Earl of Arundel, and Alianora of Lancaster; born 1352 3. Bishop of Ely, 1374; translated to York, of which see consecrated Archbishop, April 3rd, 1388, on the expulsion of Archbishop Neville. In 1390 he joined with Archbishop Courtenay of Canterbury in refusing assent to statutes passed in restraint of the Pope's prerogative. In the winter of 1394-5 he went over to Ireland with the special purpose of exciting King Richard's jealousy and suspicion against the political Lollards, after

having for two years professed to favour them himself. He was translated to Canterbury on the death of Courtenay, and consecrated Archbishop, January 11th, 1397. On September 19th of the same year, Arundel was commanded to keep his house; and the day after was solemnly impeached by the House of Commons of high treason, "he having in the eleventh year of the King [1387-8] counselled the said Duke [Thomas of Gloucester] and Earl [Richard of Arundel, his brother], to take on themselves royal power." (*Rot. Parl.*, III. 353.) The Commons entreated on the 25th that the Archbishop might be banished. The decree of banishment was issued, and he was ordered to sail from Dover, on the 29th of that month. His see was declared vacant, and Roger Walden was elected Archbishop in his stead. But Arundel came back, landing at Ravenspur with Henry of Bolingbroke, July 4th, 1399; and Roger Walden sank into such instant and complete oblivion that some well informed writers have dogmatically asserted that there never was an Archbishop of that name. In October, 1404, Arundel signalised himself by a violent quarrel with the Speaker in full Parliament. He issued his rigid "constitution" against the Lollards in 1409; and he was the principal agent in the persecution of Lord Cobham. He died February 20th, 1414, lingering for a few days after a paralytic stroke, as stated in the story. His age was 61. The mantle of this cleverest man of his day—clever for evil—descended, a hundred years later, upon Stephen Gardiner. Any believer in transmigration could feel no doubt that the soul of the one man inhabited the other.

CAMBRIDGE, RICHARD PLANTAGENET, EARL OF ("Dickon"), Third and youngest child of Edmund Duke of York and his first wife Isabel of Castilla: born at Conisborough Castle, Yorkshire, whence, according to the custom of his time, he was usually known as Richard of Conisborough. The only record extant of his father's visiting the castle is a charter dated thence,

September 11th, 1376. (*Rot. Pat.* 50 E. III., Part 2.) This is probably therefore about the time of Richard's birth. He was left in England with his sister during the eighteen months (May, 1381, to October, 1382) which his parents spent in Portugal. His mother, dying in 1393, bequeathed him to the care of King Richard II., who had been his godfather, though the King was only nine years older than his godson and namesake; and she constituted his Majesty her residuary legatee in trust for her son, desiring that he would allow him 500 marks annually for life. This sum would be equivalent now to about £6,500 per annum. So long as King Richard was in power, the money was paid faithfully, £100 from the issues of the County of York, and £233 6s. 8d. from the Exchequer. (Lansd. *MS.* 860, A, fol. 274; Nicolas' *Test. Vet.*, i. 134; *Rot. Pat.* 16 R. II., Part 3.) During the sanguinary struggles between King Richard and his cousin Henry IV., nothing is seen of Richard of Conisborough. He was not with the King in Ireland nor at Conway, neither does he appear in Henry's suite. He probably kept himself very quiet. When his brother and sister were imprisoned in 1405 for the attempted rescue of the Mortimers, no suspicion fell on Richard. Whether he was really concerned in the plot can only be guessed. In 1406 he was chosen to escort the Princess Philippa to Denmark, and on account of his poverty a grant was made to cover his expenses. The poverty was no great wonder, for though a show of confirming his royal godfather's grant had been made, yet practically poor Richard's income was reduced to £40 per annum. (*Rot. Pat.* 1 H. IV., Part 3; *Rot. Ex., Pasc.*, 3 H. V.) He was probably created, or allowed to assume the title of, Earl of Cambridge, which really appertained to his brother, only a short time before his death; for up to December 5th, 1414, he is styled in the state papers Richard of York. The accusations brought against him, by which he was done to death, were so absurdly improbable as to be incredible. It was asserted that Charles VI. of France had sent over "a hundred thousand in gold," (which probably means crowns) to Richard Earl of Cambridge, Henry Lord Scrope of Upsal, and Sir Thomas Grey de Wark, urging them to betray Henry V. into his hands, or murder him before he should arrive in Normandy; that thereupon the trio conspired to lead March into Wales (a simple repetition of Constance's defeated attempt), and to proclaim him King, if King Richard were dead—which Henry V. perfectly well knew he was, and so did the accused trio; that they carried into Wales the banner and crown of Spain, for the purpose of crowning March, the said articles being pawned to the Earl of Cambridge which crown had in reality been bequeathed by the Infanta Isabel to her son Edward, and in default of his issue to Richard, and had never been in possession of the House of Lancaster at all; that they had sent to Scotland for two personators of King Richard, Trumpington and another (probably John Maudeleyn) whom they intended to pass off to the people as King Richard which is in itself a contradiction to the charge of setting up March as King. Cambridge and Scrope pleaded their peerage. A commission was issued, August 5th, 1415, by which their judges were appointed Thomas Duke of Clarence, Humphrey Duke of Gloucester (brothers of the King) Thomas Earl of Dorset (the King's half brother), who sat as proxy of Edward Duke of York; Edmund Earl of March, the very man whom they were accused of making King; and fourteen other peers. Neither Cambridge nor Scrope was allowed to speak in his own defence. Sentence was passed at once, and they were beheaded the day following on Southampton Green. There is no evidence that Richard had conspired for any purpose; the whole affair was apparently a mere pretext to be rid of him. In character, Richard seems to have been noble and honourable, with a slight taint of his father's indecision : there is no portrait of him known. The traces of Lollardism are very slight, but I think they may be fairly considered "proven;" and if this be the case, it fully accounts for the acrimony with which he was hunted to death. His age when he died was about 39. Richard of Conisborough was twice married; his wives were—1. Anne, eldest child of Roger Mortimer, fifth Earl of March, and his wife Alianora de Holand; born about 1390; very likely imprisoned in Windsor Castle with her brothers on the usurpation of Henry IV., 1400; released, if so, with her sister Alianora, and both provided for by the King (being described as "*omnibus suis parentibus et amicis destitutis*"), and all fiefs of their mother granted to them, May 13th, 1406 (*Rot. Pat.* 7 H. IV., Part 2); married, probably, 1408; most likely died in childbed, September 1410–11, aged about 20 years. 2. Maude, only daughter of Thomas, Lord Clifford of Cumberland (one of the two most uncompromisingly Lollard houses in the kingdom) and his wife Elizabeth de Ros of Hamlake; born probably about 1390, married, 1412 15; married, secondly, John Neville, sixth and last Lord Latimer of Danby; died without issue, August 26, 1446 (*Inq. Post Mort.* 25 H. VI., 21), aged about 56. The children of Richard of Conisborough (both by Anne Mortimer) were :—1. Isabel, born about 1409, married (1) to Thomas Grey de Wark (son of the man condemned with her father), before February 18, 1412 (*Rot. Pat.* 13 H. IV., Part 2); (2) her second cousin, Henry Bourchier, Earl of Essex and Count of Eu; died (leaving issue by second marriage) October 2nd, 1484, aged about 75. (*Inq. Post Mort.* 2 R. III., 53.) 2. Richard, Duke of York and Albemarle, Earl of Cambridge, Lord of Teviotdale and Hol derness: born September 21st, 1410 or 1411 (more likely the earlier year. (*Inq. Post Mort.* 11 H. VI., 39, *Annæ Comitissæ Marchiæ;* 3 H. VI., 32, *Edmundi Comitis Marchiæ;* 3 H. V., 45, *Edmundi Ducis Ebor;* 12 H. VI., 43, *Johannæ Ducissæ Ebor.*) He afterwards set up his claims against the House of Lancaster, which were brought to a successful issue by his sons, though he himself never was King. Married about 1438,

Cicely Neville, daughter of Ralph, first Earl of Westmoreland and his wife Joan Beaufort; called the Rose of Raby. Beheaded after the battle of Wakefield, December 30th, 1460 (*Inq. Post Mort.* 18 E. IV., 60), aged 50; buried at Pomfret, 1466; Fotheringay, 1476.

DESPENSER, CONSTANCE PLANTAGENET, LADY LE, COUNTESS OF GLOUCESTER,

Only daughter of Edmund Duke of York and his wife Isabel of Castilla; most likely born at Langley, in or about 1374. On the 16th of April, 1378, the marriage of Edward, son and heir of Edward late Lord Le Despenser, was granted to her father for her benefit. (*Rot. Pat.* 1 R. II., Part 5.) But the infant bridegroom was dead on the 30th of May following, and his brother Thomas was evidently substituted in his stead. (*Rot. Pat.* 1 R. II., Part 6.) Thomas and Constance were married before the 7th of November, 1379, as on that day her uncle, John of Gaunt, paid £22 os. 4d. for his wedding present to the bride, a silver gilt cup and ewer on a stand, and he speaks of the marriage as then past. (*Register of John Duke of Lancaster*, II., fol. 19, *b.*) Constance remained in England during the absence of her parents in Portugal, 1381 2. Eighty marks per annum were granted to her from the Despenser lands, January 14th, 1384. When she took up her residence at Cardiff with her husband is uncertain; but there is every probability that it was not till after the death of her mother, in February, 1393, and very likely not till after her father's second marriage, about the following October. The approximate date may be given as 1394-5. Two pardons are recorded of persons accused of murder, June 22nd, 1395, and April 27th, 1396, "at the request of our beloved kinswoman the Countess of Gloucester." There was no Countess of Gloucester at the time, for Constance had not yet attained that title. The words *may* be slips of the scribe's pen for the

Duchess of Gloucester. It was not until September 29th, 1397, that Thomas Le Despenser was created Earl of Gloucester. There is no evidence to show the presence of Constance in London during the stormy period of her cousin Henry's usurpation; she seems to have remained at Cardiff. On the 22nd of February, 1400, about six weeks after her husband's murder, a grant of £60 per annum was made to the King's son, John Duke of Bedford, out of the issues of her lands (*Rot. Pat.* 1 H. IV., Part 8); but on the 3rd of March, the custody of her son Richard was granted to her, and £30 worth of gold and silver of her late husband's goods in the hands of the Mayor of Bristol. (*Ib.*, Part 6.) Moreover, on the 19th of February, a concession was made to her of eleven manors, two towns, two castles, two lordships, and other lands (*Ib.*, Part 5); followed by a grant of "the price of certain vessels of silver, brooches, jewels, and other goods" which had belonged to her husband. (*Rot. Ex., Pasc*, 1 H. IV.) In 1404 she was "restored to her dower" by Act of Parliament. (*Inq. Post. Mort.* 4 H. V. 52.) When and where she met with her second husband can only be guessed; for that Edmund Earl of Kent was really her second husband I think there is the strongest reason to believe. His sisters afterwards chose to deny the marriage; it was their interest to do so, for had the legitimacy of his child been established, they would have been obliged to resign to her her father's estates, which, as his presumptive heirs, they had inherited. Their excessive anxiety to prove her illegitimate, the persecution which Constance subsequently underwent, the resolute determination of Henry IV. that Kent should marry Lucia, and the remarkable coincidence of time between Constance's imprisonment and Lucia's marriage, go far to show that the marriage (though perhaps clandestine) was genuine, as alleged by Alianora; and I cannot avoid a strong conviction that a great deal of this hate and persecution were due to the fact that Constance was actually or suspectedly a Lollard. The denials of Kent's sisters may be attributed to their wish to retain his estates; while as for his nephews and nieces, who nominally joined in the petition, they could only know what they were told; for Joyce Lady Tibetot, the eldest of the group, was only three years old at the death of Kent. But to what cause can be attributed the violent determination of Henry IV.? If it be supposed that he wished to benefit and advance Kent, how did he do it by preventing his acknowledged marriage with a well dowered Princess of England?—or if to lower him, how was this done by purchasing for him, at the cost of 70,000 florins, the hand of a foreign Princess? Beside this, Henry showed throughout that while he had no mercy for Constance, he was on the best possible terms with Kent. Modern writers are altogether at fault on the subject, most of them alleging that Constance's daughter Alianora was born before her marriage with Thomas Le Despenser; whereas it is shown by the Register that when Le Despenser and Constance were married, the latter was only four or five years old, while Kent was not even born. The rescue of the Mortimers comes in to complicate matters; but what shall be said, from the point of view of some writers, who submit that the whole was a mere pretext to imprison Constance and her brother, that the Mortimers were never stolen away at all, or that the real agents remained undiscovered, and that Constance's alleged confession is a pure fiction from beginning to end? One thing is plain: there was evidently *some* reason in the mind of the King why Kent must not openly marry Constance : and knowing Henry's character, and Kent's character as well, I can see none that suits all the facts of the case, unless Constance were one of the hated and proscribed Lollards. The marriage of Constance and Kent, if it really occurred, of which I cannot feel the least doubt, must have taken place between 1401 and 1404 inclusive. It was about February, 1405, that (if this part of the story be true) she broke into Windsor Castle and carried off the young Mortimers, by means of false keys; and she and they had nearly reached Wales when they were recaptured. She was tried before Parliament. Henry IV.'s records (but he was an atrocious falsifier of state papers) tell us that she confessed that her brother Edward had been her instigator; and that he had attempted, the Christmas before, to scale the walls of Eltham Palace, and assassinate or at least imprison King Henry. This may or may not be true. What is undoubtedly true is that Edward and Constance were arrested and imprisoned; the latter in Kenilworth Castle, whither she was taken at a cost of £10, in charge of Elmingo Leget (*Rot. Ex., Michs.*, 6 H. IV.); and that all the estates, goods, and chattels of both were seized by the Crown. (*Ib.*) But Kent remained in favour. The length of time which must necessarily have elapsed shows that no sooner was Constance safely shut up than Henry began negociating with his old friend, Galeazzo Visconti, for the hand of his beautiful cousin Lucia as the bride of Kent. When all was arranged, but not sooner, in November he presented himself at Kenilworth. (*Rot. Pat.*, 7 H. IV., Part 1.) What means were taken to torture his unhappy cousin into compliance with his iron will can only be conjectured. She did at last consent to disown her marriage, unless the facts alleged in the petition of Kent's sisters are fictions. On January 19th, 1406, "all the goods that belonged to the said Constance, in the custody of the Treasurer of our Household, and were lately seised in our hands for certain causes," were munificently granted to her "of our gift." (*Ib.*) On the 24th of the same month, Kent and Lucia were married, and if his sisters may be believed —Constance was present. (*Rot. Parl.*, iv. 375.) And on the 18th of June following, all the lands and tenements of Thomas Le Despenser were restored to his widow. (*Rot. Pat.*, 7 H. IV., Part 2.) In May, 1412, she had again offended; for her son was taken from her, and his custody and marriage were granted to trustees, one of whom was his uncle, Edward Duke of York. (*Ib.*, 13 H. IV., Part 2.)   No more is heard of her until the accession of Henry V., when the immediate favour shown to her confirms the suspicion that her offence was in some way connected with political, if not religious, Lollardism.   On the 18th of July, 1413, the young King confirmed *all* his father's grants to Constance (*Ib.*, 1 H. V., Part 3), which concession restored her boy to her custody.   But when Henry V. turned against Lollardism, he turned against his cousin with it. All the Despenser lands were granted to her brother Edward for life, April 16th, 1414, in compensation for the loss which he had sustained by Richard Le Despenser's death (*Ib.*, 2 H. V., Part 1); the truth being that the grant to him in 1412 had been cancelled by the subsequent concession to his sister, so that he had sustained no loss at all.   Troubles came thickly upon Constance now.   The sudden and violent deaths of her brothers, within three months of each other, must have been no slight shock to her; and shortly after that she was again under royal displeasure.   The nature of her offence is matter for conjecture.   We only know with certainty that she died on the 28th of November, 1416, aged about 42 (*Inq. Post Mort.*, 4 H. V. 52); and that she died under a dark cloud of royal wrath, which was manifested by the withholding of permission for honourable burial for four years.   Constance was interred in Reading Abbey, in 1420. No portrait of her is known.   Her character appears to have been as I have represented it— warm hearted, impulsive, and eager, but wayward and obstinate. Her children were four in number; three by her first marriage, who were: 1. Richard, born at Cardiff, November 30th, 1396.   On the 23rd of May, 1412, he was removed from his mother's keeping, and his custody and marriage were granted, "at the request of Edward Duke of York," to ten trustees: Archbishop Arundel, Thomas Bishop of Durham, Edward

Duke of York, Sir John Pelham, Robert Tirwhit, Robert Wyntryngham, clerk, John Bokeland, clerk, Thomas Walwayn, Henry Bracy, and John Adam. They were charged with the custody of "all lands whatsoever now inherited by the said Richard, and in our hands, or any lands that may or can descend to him; and all that since the death of Thomas his father, for whatsoever cause or pretext, has been seized by us." More comprehensive terms could scarcely be used. Richard's marriage took place immediately under this grant. The bride chosen by the trustees was Alianora, second daughter of Ralph Neville, first Earl of Westmoreland, by his second wife Joan Beaufort, half sister of King Henry. On the accession of Henry V., March 20th, 1413, this grant was revoked, and Richard restored to his mother. He survived his return home only six months, dying at Merton Abbey, Surrey—to all appearance unexpectedly—October 6th, 1413, aged nearly 17. How he came to be at Merton is an unsolved question; for it looks as if he were in Arundel's keeping still, and as if the concession to Constance had remained ineffectual. His child widow re-married Henry Percy, second Earl of Northumberland, and became the mother of a large family.—2. Elizabeth, born and died at Cardiff, probably in 1398. 3. Isabel, born at Cardiff, "on the feast of the Seven Holy Sleepers," July 10th, 1400; baptized in the Church of St. Mary in that town, the same day, by Thomas Bishop of Llandaff (*Prob. æt. dictæ Isabellæ,* 2 H. V. 23); married (1) July 10th, 1411, Richard Beauchamp, Earl of Worcester (2) 1422 4, his cousin, Richard Neville, Earl of Warwick; died December 26th, 1439, aged 39 (*Inq. Post. Mort.* 18 H. VI. 3), leaving issue by both marriages; buried in Tewkesbury Abbey. (*Harl. MS.* 154, fol. 31.)—The fourth and last was the unfortunate, disinherited Alianora, born between 1402 and 1405, both inclusive, and most likely, at Kenilworth, in 1405; married (date unknown) James Touchet, Lord Audley of Heleigh; date of death, portrait, and character unknown : left issue.　In 1430 she claimed the coronet and estates of her father, alleging herself to be the legitimate daughter of Edmund Earl of Kent and Constance his wife. A counter-petition was presented by Joan Duchess of York, Constance's step mother ; Margaret Duchess of Clarence, her sister (and contrary to all mediæval usage, the younger sister is named first); and five nephews and nieces, all of whom were unborn or in the cradle when the events referred to took place. The sisters of Kent pleaded that "never any espousals were had ne solemnised in deed betwixt the said Edmund and Custance ; but that the said Edmund, *by the ordinance, will, and agreement of the full noble Lord late King Henry the IV.,* that God rest, after great, notable, and *long* ambassad' had and sent unto the Duke of Melane for marriage to be had betwixt the said Edmund and Luce, sister to the said Duke of Milan, took to wife and openly and solemnly wedded the said Luce at London, living and then and there present the said Custance, not claiming the said Edmund unto her husband, ne any dower of his lands after his decease.　The said espousals so had and solemnised betwixt the said Edmund and Luce continued withouten any interruption of the said Custance, or any oyer during the life of the said Edmund."　These ladies were very wrathful against the " subtlety, imagined process, privy labour and coloured means " whereby certain persons had been so wicked as to depose that the said Alianora was born "in espousals had and solemnised between Edmund and Custance," particularly considering that "the said suppliants" were "none of them warned" of her intention to appear and make her claim. (*Rot. Parl.* IV. 375–6.)　The passage in Italics, when viewed with the surrounding circumstances, told as much, if not more, in Alianora's favour, as against her.　And it did not please the Duchess Joan to mention a few other little circumstances, which it was more convenient than just to leave out of the account.　The fact that it was not the first time that Henry had applied to Galeazzo for assistance in what is expressively termed "dirty work" (Froissart, book iv. chap. 94); that Constance, however willing to protest against the projected marriage of Edmund and Lucia, had been physically unable, being a prisoner in Kenilworth Castle; that she had been set free just in time to appear at the wedding (if she did appear); and that the bundle of grants to her, dated about the same time, suspiciously point to a purchase of her consent:—such facts as these, it was more convenient to leave in the background. The petitions were received by Humphrey Duke of Gloucester, a Gallio who cared for none of these things, whose cruel treatment of his own hapless wife shows that no chivalrous feeling could actuate him, and no desire to right a wronged woman influence his acts; but who probably was not desirous to blacken the memory of his father, and had no wish to disturb his brother's wife in the enjoyment of Kent's estates. So the answer returned to Joan's petition was—"*Soit fait comme il est desiré*,"—an answer fatal to the hopes, the claim, and the birthright, of the unfortunate Alianora.

DESPENSER, ELIZABETH LE, BARONESS OF CARDIFF,

Only daughter and heir of Bartholomew, fourth Baron Burghersh, by his first wife Cicely de Weyland; and Baroness Burghersh in her own right. She was born probably about 1340, and brought up under the care of her step mother Margaret de Badlesmere. About 1360 or earlier, she married Edward Lord Le Despenser, who left her a widow November 11th, 1375. Her family numbered eight, of whom Edward, Hugh, and Cicely, died infants; Elizabeth married John de Arundel and William third Lord de La Zouche; Anne married Hugh Hastings and Thomas fourth Lord Morley; Margaret married Robert, fifth Lord Ferrers of Chartley; Philippa apparently died unmarried; for Thomas, the youngest, see the next article. Elizabeth stood sponsor in 1382 to Richard Neville, afterwards the second husband of her grand daughter Isabel. (*Prob. æt. dicti Ricardi*, 4 H. IV. 44.) The custody of her son Thomas was granted to her during his minority (*Rot. Pat.* 11 R. II., Part 2.) She died "on the feast of St. Anne," July 26th, 1411, aged probably about 70. (*Inq. Post Mort.* 4 H. V. 52, *Constanciæ Le Despenser.*) The inferences are slight which tend to show her Lollardism. The terms of her last will are decidedly Lollard; she was joined in the baptism of Richard Neville by Alice, widow of Sir Richard Stury; and she was niece of Joan, Lady Mohun of Dunster—two of the most prominent Lollards of the period. Le Despenser was a Lollard house by tradition and inheritance. No portrait known; character imaginary.

DESPENSER, THOMAS LE, BARON OF CARDIFF, GLAMORGAN, AND MORGAN.

Youngest of the eight children of Edward fourth Lord Le Despenser (a name sometimes mistakenly abbreviated to Spencer, for it is *le dépenseur*, "the spender,") and Elizabeth Baroness Burghersh. Born September 21st or 22nd, 1373 (*Inq. Post Mort.* 49 E. III. ii. 46, *Edwardi Le Despenser*), and named after his father's younger brother. He was left fatherless when only two years old, November 11th, 1375. (*Ib.*) During his minority he was committed to the custody of his mother. (*Rot. Pat.* 11 R. II., Part 2.) In or about May, 1378, he became Lord Le Despenser by the death of his elder brother, Edward, and was also substituted for him as bridegroom of the Princess Constance of York, whom he married between May 30th, 1378, and November 7th, 1379. (*Ib.*, 1 R. II., Part 6; *Register of John of Gaunt*, II., *fol.* 19, *b.*) Shortly afterwards, February 16th, 1380, all the Despenser lands were granted to his father in law during his minority—an unusual step, for which there must have been some private reason in the mind of the Regent, Thomas Duke of Gloucester. We next hear of Le Despenser when a lad of fifteen as at sea in the King's service, in the suite of the Earl of Arundel, and his mother was formally exonerated from all responsibility concerning his custody until he should return. (*Rot. Pat.* 11 R. II., Part 2.) On the 20th of May, 1391, when eighteen, he received the royal licence to journey to Prussia—then a semi civilized and partly heathen country—with fifty persons, and the arms and goods necessary. (*Ib.* 14 R. II., Part 2.) He doubtless accompanied the King to Ireland in September, 1394, since letters of attorney were issued for him on the 10th of that month. (*Ib.*, 18 R. II., Part 1.) Two indentures show us that Le Despenser spent the autumn of 1395 at Cardiff. (*Ib.*, 1 H. IV., Parts 5, 8.) Certain manors which had belonged to the Duke of Gloucester and Earl of Warwick were granted to Le Despenser and Constance, September 28th, 1397. He is styled in this grant Earl of Gloucester, (*Ib.*, 21 R. II., Part 1), though it was not until the day following that his creation took place. The custody of the Castle of Gloucester was also granted to him for life; and the manors were conceded with a (then unusual) limitation to heirs male. The next day, September 29th, he was created Earl of Gloucester in Westminster Hall, "girded with sword, and a coronet set on his head by the King in manner and form accustomed." (*Harl. MS.* 298, fol. 85.) Letters of attorney were issued April 16th, 1399, for the persons who formed the King's suite in Ireland—Thomas Earl of Gloucester being named third. The King was his guest on the journey, reaching Cardiff about the 9th of May, and Morgan on the 11th. They embarked at Milford Haven about the 27th, and were at Waterford on the 31st. But on the fourth of July Henry of Bolingbroke and Archbishop Arundel landed at Ravenspur, and the King hurried back as soon as he heard of it, landing in Wales, and securing himself, as he hoped, first at Conway and then at Flint. According to Froissart, Aumerle and Le

Despenser had remained behind in Bristol, and when they heard that the King was taken, they retired to Heulle, a manor in Wales belonging to the latter. But Creton, an eye-witness, expressly tells us that "the brave Earl of Gloucester" was with King Richard in Wales, and his indenture mentioned on the Patent Roll shows that he was in London in October. (Froissart's *Chron.*, *book* iv., *chap.* 114; *Harl. MS.* 1319; *Rot. Pat.*, 1 H. IV., Part 6.) It was on the 19th of August that King Richard and his faithful few were seized in the gorge of Gwrych. (*Harl. MS.* 1319.) The route taken to London was by Chester, Nantwich, Newcastle, Stafford, Lichfield (where the King all but effected his escape), Coventry, Daventry, Northampton, Dunstable, St Albans, and Westminster, reaching the last place on the first of September. It is difficult to say whether Le Despenser was present, or what part he took, at the coronation of Henry IV. According to Creton's continuator, the canopy was held by four dukes—York, Aumerle, Surrey (who accepted his post very unwillingly), and Gloucester. There was no Duke of Gloucester at this time. It might be supposed that Le Despenser, Earl of Gloucester, was meant, were it not that the writer more than once intimates that there were four *dukes* concerned. The probability is that he mistook the name, and that the fourth duke was the only other whom it well could be, and who we know was present Exeter. Le Despenser was still in London on the 27th of October. On the fourth of January, 1400, the six loyal friends met at Kingston, as detailed in the text. The account there given is strictly accurate up to the point of Surrey's death and the escape of the survivors from Cirencester, with the simple exceptions that it is not stated who suggested firing the hotel, nor who executed it. From this point the main incidents are true: the parting of Le Despenser and Salisbury near Berkeley Castle, the flight of the former to Cardiff, his escape (we are not told how) from officers sent to apprehend him, his adventure with the traitorous bargeman, imprisonment in Bristol Castle, seizure by the mob, and beheading in the market place. All chroniclers who name the incident record that his death took place by no official sentence, but at the hands of the mob; and this is confirmed by his Inquisition, which states the day of death, not that of forfeiture—contrary to the custom with respect to any person judicially condemned. In fact, Le Despenser never was attainted. He died January 13th, 1400 (*Inq. Post Mort.* 1 H. IV., i. 2, *Tho. Le Despenser*), aged 27. The particulars of his burial are given in the text.

HENRY IV., KING OF ENGLAND,

Fourth and youngest son of John of Gaunt, Duke of Lancaster, and his first wife Blanche of Lancaster; born at Bolingbroke Castle (not, as usually stated, in 1366, but) April 3rd, 1367, the day of the battle of Navareta, in which his father was engaged. (*Compotus Hugonis de Waterton,* Duchy of Lancaster Documents, *fol.* 4.) In 1377 he was attached to the suite of the young Prince of Wales, afterwards Richard II. (*Comp. Will'i de Bughbrigg, Ib.*) His tutors were Thomas de Burton and William Montendre. (*Ib.*) In 1380 he was married to Mary de Bohun, youngest daughter and co-heir of Humphrey, last Earl of Hereford, and his wife Joan de Arundel. The ages of bride and bridegroom were ten and thirteen. A gold ring with a ruby was bought for the bridal, at a cost of eight marks; and for the making of this and another ring with a diamond, 28s. 8d. was paid. The offering at mass was 13s. 4d., and 40s. were put on the book, to be appropriated by the little bride at the words, "With all my worldly goods I thee endow." (*Register of John of Gaunt,* II., *fol.* 48, *b.*) The allowance made to Henry by his father was 250 marks per annum—equivalent in modern times to about £850. He was not yet twenty when he became one of the five "Lords Appellants,"

who renounced their homage at Huntingdon, December 10th,
1386. Having succeeded in compelling King Richard to swear
that for twelve months he would not oppose them, towards
the end of that time they assumed an openly hostile attitude.
At the head of 40,000 men, they reached Hornsey Park,
November 11th, 1387; but it was not till the 14th that Henry
and his friend Nottingham joined the rest. On the 20th of
December was the encounter between the Dukes of Gloucester and Ireland at Radcote Bridge. The Lords Appellants
appeared before the City on the 26th, and encamped at
Clerkenwell on the 27th. They next granted themselves
£20,000. (*Rot. Parl,* iii. 248; *Issue Roll, Michs.,* 14 R. II.)
After the King had recovered his power, May 3rd, 1389,
Henry retired to Kenilworth. (*Rot. Pat.* 22 R. II., *Pt.* 3.)
It was probably about 1390 that he committed the atrocity of
drawing his sword on the King in the Queen's presence, for
which he was sent into honourable banishment. His first
journey abroad was to Barbary; but during 1391 we find him
at home, at Bolingbroke and Peterborough. In 1392 he
visited Prussia and the Holy Land. A safe conduct had to be
obtained from the King of France, in May. Two immense
sums of money were lent him by his father—first £666 13s.
4d., and afterwards £1,333 6s. 8d. Sir Thomas Erpyngham
was his fellow-traveller. He was at Venice on December 4th
(*Comp. Rob'ti de Whitteby,* 15–16 R. II., Duchy Documents,
ff. 18, 19), and there or at Milan, in this journey, he probably
made the acquaintance of Galeazzo of Milan. His wife died
July 4th, 1394, at Peterborough. On November 25th, 1395,
a treaty was signed between the Dukes of Lancaster and Bretagne, by the provisions of which Henry was to marry Marie
of Bretagne, who afterwards became his step-daughter. The
treaty was not carried into effect; and Marie married Jean
Duke of Alençon, June 26th, 1396. The five noble conspirators met again, to renew their guilty attempts, at Arundel, July

28th, 1397. Henry slipped out of discovery and penalty as is recorded in the story; and was created Duke of Hereford, with remainder only to heirs male, September 29th, 1397. A full pardon was granted to him, January 25th, 1398 (*Rot. Pat.* 21 R. II., Part 2.) His petition impeaching his former friend Norfolk was presented January 30th. The two appeared at Windsor, April 28th, and were commanded the next day to settle their quarrel by wager of battle. In the interim Henry visited his father at Pomfret. The combatants met on Gosford Green, September 16th, and were separated by the King. Henry was allowed licence to travel October 3rd, for which sentence of banishment was substituted on the 13th. (*Rot. Pat.* 22 R. II., Part 1.) He took leave of the King at Eltham. The armour in which the duel was to be fought had been sent by Galeazzo of Milan, " out of his abundant love for the Earl," at Henry's request. (Froissart, *book* iv., *chap.* 94.) Henry meant to have gone to Hainault; but by his father's advice, he settled in Paris. (*Ib., chaps.* 96, 97.) Here he fell in love— such love as was in him—with the beautiful Marie of Berri, whom he would have married had not the King interfered and prevented it. Henry never forgave Richard for this step. On the 3rd of February, 1399, John of Gaunt died, and Henry became Duke of Lancaster. He landed at Ravenspur with Archbishop Arundel, July 4th, marching at once in open defiance of the Crown, though his own son was in the royal suite. Had Richard II. been the weak and unscrupulous tyrant which modern writers represent him, that father and son would never have met again. On the 7th of July Henry reached St. Albans, where, if not earlier, his uncle of York met him and went over to his side. Thence he marched to Oxford, where his brother of Dorset probably joined him. His march Londonward is given in the last article. From the 3rd of September all the royal decrees bear the significant words, "with the assent of our dearest cousin Henry Duke of Lancaster." He commenced his reign on the 29th of September in reality, when he forced Richard to abdicate; but officially, on the 1st of October, 1399. His first regnal act was to grant to himself all the "honours of descent" derived from his father; in other words, to revoke his own attainder. He was crowned on the 13th of October. A year later, November 25th, 1400, Archbishop Arundel received him into the fraternity of Christ Church, Canterbury, which must have been an order instituted for those who remained "in the world," since a large proportion of its brethren were married men. From this point there is no need to pursue Henry's history, further than with respect to such items of it as bear upon the narrative. In 1404 he refused the request of the Commons that the superfluous revenues of the priesthood might be confiscated, and the money applied to military affairs. At this time, it is said, one third of all the estates in England was in the hands of the clergy. For the part that he took with regard to the marriage of his cousin Constance with Kent, see the article under the former name. He died of leprosy, at Westminster, March 20th, 1413, aged 46. His second wife, by whom he had no issue, was Jeanne, daughter of Charles II. King of Navarre, and Jeanne of France; she survived him twenty-four years. The children of Henry IV., several of whom are mentioned in the story, were: 1. Henry V., born at Monmouth Castle, August 9th, 1387; married, at Troyes, Katherine, daughter of Charles VI. King of France, and Isabeau of Bavaria, June 3rd, 1420; died at Vincennes, August 31st, 1422, aged 35.—2. Thomas Duke of Clarence, born in London, 1388 (probably in May); a "brother" of Canterbury; married, 1412, Margaret de Holand, sister of Edmund Earl of Kent, and widow of John Marquis of Dorset; killed in the battle of Baugi, March 29th, 1421, aged 33.—3. John Duke of Bedford, born 1389; married (1) Anne, daughter of Jean Sans Peur, Duke of Burgundy, at Troyes, April 17th,

1423; (2) Jaquette, daughter of a Count of St. Pol, at Thérouenne, April, 1433; he died September 14th, 1435, aged 46.—4. Humphrey, Duke of Gloucester, born 1390, admitted a "brother" of Canterbury 1408; married (1) Jaqueline, Duchess of Holland and Hainault, 1422, and repudiating her without any formal divorce, married (2) Alianora, daughter of Reginald Lord Cobham of Sterborough, about 1428; mur dered at St. Edmund's Bury, by his uncle Cardinal Beaufort, February 23rd, 1447, aged 57. 5. Blanche, born at Peterborough, 1392; married, at Cologne, July, 1402, Ludwig of the Pfalz; died at Neüstadt, May 22nd, 1409, aged 17.—6. Philippa, born at Peterborough, July, 1394; married, at Lund, October 26th, 1406, Eric King of Denmark; died at Wadstena, January 5th, 1430, aged 36.

KENT, EDMUND DE HOLAND, 7TH AND LAST EARL,

Probably *youngest* son of Thomas De Holand, fifth Earl, and his wife Alesia de Arundel; born at Brokenhurst, January 6th, 1382 (*Prob. æt. dicti. Edmundi*, 5 H IV. 38); baptized in St. Thomas's Church, January 8th. (*Ib.*) In 1403 he guarded the King to Shrewsbury; in 1404 he joined in the Duke of Clarence's expedition to Sluys; and Henry IV. made him Lord High Admiral. He was received into the fraternity at Canterbury, May 8th, 1405, about two months after the imprisonment of Constance. About New Year's Day, 1406, "when he assumed his arms," he made a grand tournament in Smithfield; the Earl of Moray challenged him to single combat, and was triumphantly vanquished by Kent. He appears to have lent himself with the most easy indifference to Henry IV.'s scheme for getting rid of Constance. The probability is that he was tired of her, and was deeply in love with Lucia. He was wounded in the head at the siege of Briac Castle, September 10th, 1408, and died after lingering five days. His body was brought over to England, and buried in Bourne Abbey, Lincolnshire.

KENT, LUCIA VISCONTI, COUNTESS,

Youngest child of Barnabò Visconti and Beatrice Scaligero
(surnamed Regina for her pride), and cousin, not sister, of
Galeazzo II., Duke of Milan. She was probably born about
1383, and was most likely still in her cradle when in 1384 she
was contracted with great pomp and ceremony to Louis Duke
of Anjou, afterwards King of Sicily. The Visconti ladies
were renowned for beauty, and Lucia's cousin Valentina,
Duchess of Orleans, was one of the most renowned beauties
of her day. Lucia was still in infancy when her father was
deposed and imprisoned by his nephew Gian Galeazzo,
May 6th, 1385; and she lost her mother about the same
time. Louis of Anjou did not fulfil his contract, and Galeazzo sold Lucia for 70,000 florins, as stated in the text.
She was married to Earl Edmund at the Church of St. Mary
Overy, Southwark, January 24th, 1406. After her husband's
death Henry IV. tried to induce her to marry Thomas Beaufort, Earl of Dorset, his own half brother. It is commonly
said that Lucia refused Dorset, and she certainly does not
describe herself as Countess of Dorset, but only as Countess
of Kent, in her will (printed in *Test. Vet.* i. 205). But she is
twice styled by Henry "our dear sister Lucia" (March 16th
and 28th, 1409—*Rot. Pat.* 10 H. IV.), which looks as if she
did marry Dorset. Stow says that she married Sir Henry de
Mortimer, and had a daughter Anne. However this may be,
in 1421 she was petitioning the Crown for aid on account of
deep poverty, caused by the overwhelming mass of debts left
behind by Edmund, who died intestate. (*Rot. Parl.*, iv. 143 5.)
Nothing more is known of her except the date of her death,
April 14th, 1424, when aged about 40. (*Inq. Post. Mort.*
2 H. VI. 35, *Luciæ Comitissæ Kanc'.*) She was buried in the
Church of the Augustine Friars, London. (*Harl. M.S.* 544,
fol. 78.) The English mistook Lucia for Galeazzo's sister.

MARCH, EDMUND MORTIMER, SIXTH AND LAST EARL,

Eldest son of Roger, fifth Earl, and his wife Alianora de Holand; born November 4th, 1391; imprisoned in Windsor Castle, about Christmas, 1399; stolen away by Constance Le Despenser, about February 14th, 1405; recaptured and again consigned to prison; bound with four others as surety for 70,000 florins, to be paid to Duke of Milan, January, 1406; marriage granted to Queen Jeanne of Navarre, February 24th, 1408 (*Rot. Pat.* 9 H. IV., Part 1), and afterwards sold by her to the Prince of Wales for £200 (*Rot. Ex., Michs.*, 1 H. V.); apparently released on accession of Henry V., 1413; married, 1414–16, Anne, daughter of Edmund Earl of Stafford, and his wife Princess Anne of Gloucester; sat as judge on his brother in-law's trial—with regard to whose crime, if the indictment were true, March must have been himself chief witness,—August 5th, 1415; received pardon for all offences, August 7th. The next mention of him is that he was living in Ireland, July 10th, 1424; and it was in Ireland, at Trim Castle, that he died, January 19th, 1425, aged 33. He was buried at Stoke Clare. He left no issue, and his widow re-married John de Holand, Earl of Huntingdon. The last mention of his brother Roger as living occurs on the Rolls, August 26th, 1404; but we are told that he was one of the boys stolen by Constance in February, 1405. After that nothing is heard of him but that he died young; probably before his brother's release, as his age would then have been at least fifteen. His sister Alianora married Edward Courtenay, and died issueless.

YORK, EDMUND PLANTAGENET, FIRST DUKE.

Sixth son (but fourth who reached manhood) of Edward III. and Philippa of Hainault. Born at Langley, June 5th, 1341; baptized by Nicholas Abbot of St. Albans; and committed to the care of Joan de Oxenford, Agnes de La Marche, and Margery de Wyght. He was brought up in the nursery palace at Chilterne, or Children's Langley, Herts. On the 8th of February, 1362, ambassadors were appointed to contract marriage between Edmund and Margaret Duchess of Burgundy. The marriage was appointed to take place at Bruges, February 4th, 1365; but Pope Urban refused to grant a dispensation (urged by the King of France, who wanted the Princess for his son), and the negociations came to nothing. Edmund was created Earl of Cambridge and Lord of Teviotdale, November 14th, 1362. In 1366 his name appears in the marriage treaty of his brother Lionel with Violante Visconti of Milan, which provided that Edmund should be substituted for Lionel if his brother died before the marriage. From 1369 to 1371 the Earl was on the Continent with his brothers, the Black Prince and the Duke of Lancaster. It was at Rochefort, near Bordeaux, about November, 1369, that Edmund first saw his future wife, the Infanta Isabel of Castilla; but he did not marry her until 1372. In 1374 he was Governor of Bretagne; Constable of Dover and Warden of the Cinque Ports, July 12th, 1376. At the coronation of Richard II., July 16th, 1377, Edmund was second of the homagers, and walked next but one after the King. In May, 1381, he sailed for Portugal, accompanied by his wife and eldest son. Little was done in respect of the errand on which he had gone the furtherance of the Infanta's claims to Castilla; and he came back, disappointed, in October, 1382. He was created Duke of York, at Hoselow Lodge, August 6th, 1385, "by cincture of sword and imposition of gold coronet on his head." (*Harl. MS.* 298, *fol.* 84, *b.*) A grant of £1000 per annum was made to him on the 15th of November following. During the long struggle between the various members of the Royal Family, York always sided with Gloucester, except when Lancaster was present. In 1388 he was co surety (with Gloucester, Derby, and others) for £5000 borrowed from the Londoners for Gloucester's purposes. (*Rot. Pat.* 11 R. II., *Part* 2.) The King visited him at Langley, April 18th, 1389. About September, 1391, he and his brother of Lancaster concluded a truce with France. His first wife died, and he married the second, in 1393. (See subsequent articles.) He was created Regent of England, for the first time, September 29th, 1394, during the King's first voyage to Ireland. King Richard relieved him of this charge by returning home about May 11th, 1395. His second regency was from August 6th, 1396, to about November 14th following It was by the advice of Lancaster and York but the latter was really the mere echo of the former, that Gloucester was arrested, August, 1397. Some of his brother Gloucester's lands were granted to York. After this, both York and Lancaster retired from Court to their own country homes. In 1399, on the death of Lancaster, York was created Steward of England *pro tem.*, "until Henry Earl of Derby shall sue for the same." (*Rot. Pat.* 22 R. II., *Part* 2.) In May, 1399, he was created Regent for the third and last time. About the 7th of July he met, and at once went over to, his rebellious and banished nephew, Henry of Lancaster. He was present at Henry IV.'s coronation, and remained a guest at Court for the rest of that year, where we find him several times during 1400. On November 25th, 1400, he made his will; and in 1401 he was received into the fraternity at Canterbury. His last recorded visit to Court was on the opening of Parliament, January 20th, 1402; and on the following first of August he died at Langley, aged 61. He was buried in the Church of the Friars Predicants, Langley. Edmund was unquestionably a weak man, both in character and abilities : indeed, Froissart goes so far as to hint that he was deficient in intellect. (*Book* iv. *chap.* 73.) His being made Regent by no means disproves this ; for the post was chiefly honorary, and his brother Lionel had filled it when only seven years old. For his wives see the later articles.

Eldest son of Edmund Duke of York and Isabel of Castilla; born probably about New Year's Day, 1373. He accompanied his parents to Portugal in May, 1382, and was formally affianced to the Infanta Beatriz; but her father subsequently broke off the engagement, by dispensation from the Pope, and married her to the rival King of Castilla. King Richard was deeply attached to him, or perhaps rather to the ideal being whom he believed him to be. He granted him the stewardship of Bury, January 22nd, 1390; created him Earl of Rutland, May 2nd, in the same year; gave him the reversion of the Constableship of the Tower, January 27th, 1392; employed him in embassy to France, February 26th, 1394, and again, July 1395; created him Constable of England, July 12th, 1397, and Duke of Aumerle, September 29th, 1397. A grant was made to him from the lands of Archbishop Arundel, September 27th; and his patent as Constable of the Tower was renewed, October 30th. In May, 1399, he went with the King to Ireland. When Lancaster's rebellion broke out, Aumerle merely waited to make sure which was the winning side, and then went over to his cousin Henry without a thought of the Sovereign who had styled him "brother," and had been the author of all his prosperity. In the midst of the tumult his patent as Constable of the Tower was once more renewed, August 31st. At the coronation of Henry IV., Aumerle was one of the peers who held the canopy. He is named as one of those who requested the usurper to put the King to death. How he betrayed his friends at Maidenhead Bridge is recounted in the text. Henry IV. trusted Aumerle as he trusted few others, in a manner incomprehensible to any one acquainted with the character of either. On March 10th, 1400, he pardoned Aumerle's debts; then he made him Lord Lieutenant of Ireland; and then Governor of Aquitaine. Edward became Duke of York by his father's death, August 1st, 1402. The next escapade of this singular individual was to address to Queen Jeanne a series of verses, painfully laboured, of which the first is the least uncouth, and even that halts in the rhyme.

> " Excellent Sovereign seemly to see,
> Proved prudence peerless of price,
> Bright blossom of benignity,
> Of figure fairest, and freshest of days !"

It is evident that Nature never intended Edward for a poet. His next adventure was a futile endeavour to scale the wall of Eltham Palace, and seize the King ; and the third was his share in Constance's theft of the Mortimers. He and his sister were both arrested, and all his lands, goods, and chattels confiscated. He was sent to Pevensey Castle, and there placed in keeping of Sir John Stanley ; but his imprisonment was not long, for on the fourth of November he was free and in London. Perhaps his experience was useful in curbing his plotting temper, for he kept very quiet after this, and we hear of him next engaged in a pious and orthodox manner, founding Fotheringay College. York did not sit on the bench at his brother's trial ; he had the grace to prefer a proxy in the person of Dorset. He made his will August 22nd, 1415, wherein he styled himself "of all sinners the most wicked ;" desired to be buried at Fotheringay, and ordered that the expenses of his funeral should not exceed £100. His death took place at Agincourt, October 25th, 1415, in the manner described in the text ; and his obsequies were celebrated at London on the 1st of December. He married Philippa, daughter and coheir of John Lord Mohun of Dunster, and his wife Joan Burghersh, one of the most eminent Lollards of her day. Philippa was married (1) before March 6th, 1382 (*Reg. Joh'is Ducis Lanc., fol.* 60, *b.*), to Walter, Lord Fitzwalter ; (2) between 1386 and 1393, to Sir John Golafre ; (3) after 1397, to Edward Duke of York ; and according to some authors (4) after 1415, to John Vescy. She died

July 17th, 1431. (*Inq. Post Mort.* 10 H. VI., 45; *Ph'æ Ducissæ Ebor.*)

YORK, ISABEL OF CASTILLA, DUCHESS,

Third and youngest daughter of Don Pedro I., surnamed The Cruel, and Maria Padilla, whose marriage is usually considered a fiction by modern writers, though Pedro himself solemnly affirmed it, and their daughters were treated as Princesses through life. Isabel was born at Morales or Tordesillas, in 1355. In 1365, when Don Pedro fled before his rebel brother, he was accompanied by his third wife, Juana, and his three daughters, Beatriz, Constança, and Isabel. They fled from Sevilla to Bayonne, and did not return to Sevilla till 1368, after the victory of Navareta. After the loss of the battle of Montièl and the murder of their father, in 1369, the Princesses were hastily taken again by their guardians to Bayonne. Constança was married to John of Gaunt, Duke of Lancaster, at Rochefort, near Bordeaux, about November, 1369. Isabel remained with her sister, and accompanied her to England in 1371. In 1372—between January 1st and April 30th—she married Edmund Earl of Cambridge, the brother of her sister's husband. It was at Hertford, March 1st, 1372, that John of Gaunt and Constança assumed the titles of King and Queen of Leon and Castilla; and as sixteen months had then elapsed since their own marriage, the probability seems to be that this date marks the marriage of Isabel, and the consent of her bridegroom to the exclusive assumption of queenship by the elder sister. (The other and really eldest sister, Beatriz, had become a nun.) Isabel is alluded to as Edmund's wife on April 30th, 1372. In May, 1381, she accompanied her husband to Portugal, on an expedition undertaken with the object of securing the recognition of herself and her sister as the true heirs of Castilla. The expedition failed; and Isabel returned to England with her husband in October, 1382.

Several pardons appear on the rolls, granted at the instance of Isabel. Doña Juana Fernandez, who appears in the story, was at first one of her damsels, but in 1377 became Mistress of the Household. Isabel became Duchess of York, August 6th, 1385. Her will was made December 6th, 1389. A grant of £100 was given to her, October 3rd, 1390, to pay her debts; but notwithstanding this and further grants of money, she was still obliged to borrow £400 from her brother in law of Lancaster, January 25th, 1393. This was her last recorded act, for on the third of February she was dead. (*Rot. Ex., Michs.,* 14 R. II.; *Compotus Roberti de Whitteby,* 1392-3, *fol.* 19; *Rot. Pat.* 16 R. II., Part 3.)—Much misconception exists as to the terms of her will. She is represented by some writers as having been driven to provide for her son Richard by the purchase of the King's favour, having bequeathed all her goods to his Majesty on a species of compulsion. The fact is that she bequeathed to him her son and her goods together, requesting him to provide for the one from the proceeds of the other. She made the King simply trustee for her boy, his own godson. And how much King Richard gained or lost by the transaction is set down in plain figures: for the jewels, &c., bequeathed by Isabel sold for £666 13s. 4d.—just two years' income of the annuity paid for seven years (the rest of his reign) to Richard. (*Rot. Ex., Michs.,* 17 R. II.) The monastic chroniclers speak of Isabel in terms of unqualified contempt—particularly Walsingham, who invariably vilifies a Lollard. And that she was a Lollard few can doubt who read her will with attention. Possibly the entire accusation brought against her in early life is a calumny; possibly it is a fact. Many women that *were* sinners have washed Christ's feet with tears; and perhaps they will not be found the lowest in the kingdom of Heaven.

YORK, JOAN DE HOLAND, DUCHESS,

Second daughter of Thomas Earl of Kent and his wife Alesia de Arundel; sister of Thomas Duke of Surrey, Edmund Earl of Kent, and Alianora Countess of March; born 1383, married (1) before November 4th, 1393, Edmund Duke of York; (2) William, Lord Willoughby de Eresby, pardon for unlicensed marriage May 14th, 1409, but named as husband and wife, March 26th, 1406; (3) before December 9th, 1410, Henry Lord Scrope of Upsal; (4) Henry de Vescy, Lord Bromflete —pardon for unlicensed marriage, August 14th, 1416. She died April 12th, 1434, aged 51 -during the absence of her husband at the Council of Basel—leaving no issue by any of her marriages. Her character is shown in several small matters, but above all in the rancour of her petition against Alianora de Audley, and the deceit which prompted the putting forward of her younger sister Margaret in her place. The indication in the story that the device for annulling Constance's marriage proceeded from Joan is suppositious, but by no means improbable.

CHILDREN'S ANNUALS.

OUR DARLINGS.

With beautiful Coloured Frontispiece, Twelve Coloured and Tinted Plates, More than Two Hundred Large Illustrations, and Attractive Stories for the Darlings of various ages.

In brilliantly-executed Coloured Boards, price 3/-;
and Cloth extra, gilt edges, price 5/-.

LITTLE FROLIC.

An Annual for the Little Ones.

In Large Type, profusely Illustrated, full of Interest from cover to cover.
In most attractive Boards, 2/-

SUNDAY SUNSHINE.

A Sunday Annual for Children of all Ages.

Edited by CATHARINE SHAW, author of "Something for Sunday." &c.
In very attractive boards, 1/6.

BY SEA AND LAND.

Stories of Adventure, Travel, and Conflict.

In most attractive Boards, full of Illustrations.   Price 1/-

B

Tales of English Life in the Olden Time.
BY EMILY S. HOLT.

ALL'S WELL ; or, Alice's Victory.
With Illustrations Large Crown 8vo. 3/6.

THE WHITE LADY OF HAZELWOOD. Large Crown 8vo. 3/6.
"An entertaining book of the instructive type, which we always take a special pleasure in commending." *The Christian.*

BEHIND THE VEIL. A Story of the Norman Conquest. 3/6.
"Interesting from first to last." *British Weekly.*

THE KING'S DAUGHTERS; or, How Two Girls kept the Faith.
Large Crown 8vo. Illustrated. 3/6.
"We never met with a book more suited to read aloud to young people on a Sunday afternoon." *Record.*

YE OLDEN TIME. English Customs in the Middle Ages. 3/6.
"We have seldom met with a more useful book." *Notes and Queries.*

MISTRESS MARGERY. A Tale of the Lollards. Crown 8vo, 2/6.
"A page in history which our young men and maidens will do well to saturate with holy tears."—*Sword and Trowel.*

JOHN DE WYCLIFFE. The First of the Reformers.
And What He Did for England. Crown 8vo, cloth extra, 3/6.
"An admirable exposition of the opinions of a remarkable man.'
Notes and Queries.

A FORGOTTEN HERO ; or, Not for Him.
The Story of Edmund Earl, of Cornwall. Crown 8vo, 3/6.
"We trust many will become acquainted with Miss Holt's 'Forgotten Hero.'
The Christian.

THE MAIDEN'S LODGE ; or, None of Self, and all of Thee.
A Tale of the Reign of Queen Anne. Crown 8vo, cloth extra, 2/6.

AT YE GRENE GRIFFIN. A Tale of the Fifteenth Century.
Small 8vo, cloth extra, 2/6.

THE WELL IN THE DESERT.
An Old Legend. Small 8vo, cloth extra, 2/-

FOR THE MASTER'S SAKE. Small 8vo, cloth extra, 2/-
"We heartily recommend this well-written tale." *Churchman.*

OUR LITTLE LADY ; or, Six Hundred Years Ago. 2/-
"A charming chronicle of the olden time." *The Christian.*

THE WAY OF THE CROSS. A Tale of the Early Church. 1/6.

THE SLAVE GIRL OF POMPEII. With Illustrations. Cloth extra, 1/6.

ALL FOR THE BEST ; or, Bernard Gilpin's Motto. 1/-

LONDON : JOHN F. SHAW & CO., 48, PATERNOSTER ROW, E.C.

STORIES BY BRENDA.

UNCLE STEVE'S LOCKER.   Large Crown 8vo, with Illustrations, 5/-
"Brenda has never drawn two more charming pen and ink sketches.' *Spectator*
"An attractive story of one of the bravest and sweetest of girl heroines.'
Saturday Review

THE SHEPHERD'S DARLING.   Large Cr. 8vo, with Illustrations, 3/6.
"A pretty pastoral with an attractive heroine, whose chequered life story is told with the grace and delicacy that harmonize with the author's original conception of the child Bonnie; and a story that is well told and well devised must needs be good."—*Saturday Review.*

THE PILOT'S HOUSE; or, Five Little Partridges.
With Illustrations by M. IRWIN.   Large Crown 8vo, cloth extra, 2/6.
"One of those admirable sketches of child life which this writer can so well portray." *Bookseller.*

FROGGY'S LITTLE BROTHER.   A Story of the East End.
New Illustrated Edition.   Square cloth extra, 3/6.
"Very pathetic and yet comical reading "—*Guardian.*

A SATURDAY'S BAIRN.
With Illustrations.   Large Crown 8vo, cloth extra, 5/-.
"A pleasing story, skilfully written, and in an excellent spirit.' *Record.*

LITTLE COUSINS; or, Georgie's Visit to Lotty.
With Illustrations by T. PYM.   Square, cloth extra, 3/6.
"Sure to satisfy any little girl to whom it may be given." *Athenæum.*
"Little girls who read it will long dream of the delights of the shops and the Zoo.' *Guardian.*

VICTORIA BESS; or, The Ups and Downs of a Doll's Life.
With Illustrations by T. PYM.   Square, cloth extra, 3/6.
"A charming book for little girls." *Literary World.*
"Told with Brenda's usual brightness and good aim as to teaching."—*Aunt Judy*

LOTTY'S VISIT TO GRANDMAMA.
A Story for the Little Ones.   With Fifty Illustrations.   Square, cloth extra, 3/6.
"An admirable book for little people."—*Literary World.*
"A capital children's story.' *Record.*
"Would form a nice birthday present." *Aunt Judy.*

NOTHING TO NOBODY.
With Illustrations.   Crown 8vo, cloth extra, 2/-
"A very pretty story." *Athenæum.*

THE MERCHANT AND THE MOUNTEBANK.
With Illustrations by H. PETHERICK.   Cloth, 1/6.
"One of Brenda's delightful tales." *British Weekly.*
"A sparkling little sketch, very prettily got up." *The Record*

STORIES BY LOUISE MARSTON.

MISS MOLLIE AND HER BOYS; or, His Great Love.
Large Crown 8vo, cloth, 3/6.
"The love of God is charmingly illustrated by a recital of the loving devotion of a young woman who bestowed affectionate care upon some poor lonely lads."
The Christian

TWO LITTLE BOYS; or, I'd Like to Please Him.
Crown 8vo, cloth, Illustrated, 2/6.
' A wonderfully pathetic story. It will be read with deep feeling, especially by chi dren, to whom the strikingly illustrated cover will prove an additional attraction." *The Record.*

MR. BARTHOLOMEW'S LITTLE GIRL.
Crown 8vo, cloth, Illustrated, 2/6.
"A story that should turn the hearts of many to the Saviour. It is well written, and the teaching is pure and true."—*The Christian.*

CRIPPLE JESS. The Hop Picker's Daughter.
Crown 8vo, cloth, Illustrated, 2/6.
"Fully as engrossing as anything from the pen of Hesba Stretton."
The Christian.
"A sketch well drawn of a sweet flower blooming in a very humble place."
Woman's Work.

ROB AND MAG. A Little Light in a Dark Corner.
Crown 8vo, cloth, 1/6.
"A beautiful sketch." *Churchman's Magazine.*
"We believe this little volume will be found the means of leading many to Jesus." *The Christian.*

BLIND NETTIE; or, Seeking Her Fortune. 1/-

JITANA'S STORY; or, Light in the Darkness. 1/-

BENNIE, THE KING'S LITTLE SERVANT. 1/-

STORIES BY JENNIE CHAPPELL.

BERNE'S BARGAIN.
Large Crown 8vo, cloth, with Illustrations, 3/6.
"A delightful story. Boys cannot fail to like it. It is full of incident and adventure. The illustrations are excellent.' *Manchester Examiner.*

FOR ELSIE'S SAKE; or, A Seaside Friendship.
Crown 8vo, cloth, Illustrated, 1/6.

LITTLE RADIANCE. A Year in a Child's Life.
Crown 8vo, cloth, Illustrated, 1/6.
"A charming book for children." *Footsteps of Truth.*

HAND IN HAND; or, Radiance at Beechdale.
Crown 8vo, cloth, Illustrated, 1/6.

LEFT BEHIND; or, A Summer in Exile. Cloth, 1/-

OUGHTS AND CROSSES. A Story for Boy. 1/-

STORIES BY EMMA MARSHALL.

BLUEBELL. A Story of Child Life Now-a-days.
Large Crown 8vo, with Illustrations, 3/6.

LITTLE QUEENIE. A Story of Child Life Sixty Years Ago.
Large Crown 8vo, cloth, with Illustrations, 3/6.
"A pretty story of child life." *Guardian.*
"'Little Queenie' is particularly pleasing."—*Saturday Review.*

EVENTIDE-LIGHT. The Story of Dame Margaret Hoby.
Large Crown 8vo, cloth, with Illustrations, 5/
"A charming gift book, especially to girls in their teens; it deserves, and will no doubt command, a wide circulation." *The Record.*

THE END CROWNS ALL. A Story of Life.
Large Crown 8vo, cloth, 5/-
"A most exciting story of modern life, pervaded as Mrs. Marshall's tales always are by a thoroughly wholesome tone.'—*Record.*

BISHOP'S CRANWORTH; or, Rosamund's Lamp.
Large Crown 8vo, cloth, Illustrated, 5/
"This is a delightful story, with a considerable flavour of romance. The elder girls of our families will give it a special welcome." *Baptist.*

LITTLE MISS JOY. Crown 8vo, cloth, Illustrated, 2/6.
"A pretty picture of childish influence."—*Brighton Gazette.*

HURLY-BURLY; or, After a Storm comes a Calm.
Crown 8vo, cloth, with Illustrations, 2/
"Simply and touchingly told.' *Aberdeen Journal.*

CURLEY'S CRYSTAL; or, A Light Heart Lives Long.
Cloth, 1/6.
"A readable narrative, forming the vehicle of good thought as to life and its duties." *The Christian.*

ROBERT'S RACE; or, More Haste Less Speed.
Crown 8vo, cloth, Illustrated, 1/6.
"Written in the author s well known and attractive style, and is both cheap and good." *Teachers Aid.*

STORIES BY M. E. WINCHESTER,

Author of "A Nest of Sparrows," etc

CITY SNOWDROPS; or, The House of Flowers.
Large Crown 8vo, cloth, Illustrated, 5/-
"We have read very few stories of such pathos and interest." *British Weekly.*

GRANNY'S CABIN; or, All He Does is Love.
Crown 8vo, cloth Illustrated, 2/6.
"Will do any one s heart good to read." *Spectator.*

LOST MAGGIE; or, A Basket of Roses.
Cloth, Illustrated, 1/-
"A pathetic and interesting story."—*Record.*

STORIES BY E. EVERETT-GREEN.

SHADOWLAND ; or, What Lindis Accomplished.
Crown 8vo, with Illustrations, 1/6.
"A charming story for children, very prettily got up." *Record.*

HER HUSBAND'S HOME ; or, The Durleys of Linley Castle.
Large Crown 8vo, cloth extra, with Illustrations, 3/6.
"Some of the scenes are particularly effective."—*Spectator.*

MARJORIE AND MURIEL ; or, Two London Homes.
Small 8vo, cloth extra, with Illustrations, 2/6.
"A capital story, very prettily got up." *Record.*

HIS MOTHER'S BOOK. Crown 8vo, cloth extra, 2/-
"Little Bill is so lovable, and meets with such interesting friends, that everybody may read about him with pleasure." -*Spectator.*

LITTLE FREDDIE ; or, Friends in Need. Crown 8vo, cloth extra, 2/-
"There is real pathos in this story, tel ing how a poor little waif is protected from evil by the recollection of a lost mother s teaching "—*Liverpool Courier.*

BERTIE CLIFTON ; or, Paul's Little Schoolfellow.
Crown 8vo, cloth, 2/-
"Seldom have we perused a tale of the length of this with so much pleasure."
The Schoolmaster.

LITTLE RUTH'S LADY. Crown 8vo, with Illustrations, 2/-
"A delightful study of children, their joys and sorrows." *Athenæum.*
"One of those children's stories that charm grown people as well as little folk."
Guardian.

OUR WINNIE ; or, When the Swallows Go.
Crown 8vo, cloth, Illustrated, 1/6.
"The beautiful life of little Winnie is one which all children will do well to take as an example." *Banner.*

STORIES BY J. M. CONKLIN.

JUST AS IT OUGHT TO BE ; or, The Story of Miss Prudence.
Large Crown 8vo, cloth extra, 5/
"Very original, interesting, with many good and suggestive thoughts '
"A capital book for girls." *Baptist.* *English Churchman.*

BEK'S FIRST CORNER, AND HOW SHE TURNED IT.
Large Crown 8vo, cloth, 3/6.
"Bek Westerley is a very charming person."—*Standard.*

OUT IN GOD'S WORLD ; or, Electa's Story. Large Crown 8vo, 3/6.
"One of the best girls' stories we have read.' *The Congregationalist.*

LONDON : JOHN F. SHAW & Co., 48, PATERNOSTER ROW, E.C.

STORIES BY L. T. MEADE.

Author of "Scamp and I," &c

GREAT ST. BENEDICT'S; or, Dorothy's Story.
New and Cheaper Edition. Crown 8vo, cloth extra, with Illustrations, 3/6.
"The description of Dorothy's life is excellent." *Spectator.*
"At once a noble book, and a most interesting story." *Court Circular.*

A KNIGHT OF TO-DAY. A Tale.
New and Cheaper Edition. With Illustrations. Crown 8vo, cloth extra, 3/6.
"A finely-imagined story of a good man. It is a book well worth reading."
The Guardian.

BEL-MARJORY. A Tale. Crown 8vo, cloth extra, 6/-
"Most interesting; we give it our hearty commendation.' *English Independent.*

SCAMP AND I. A Story of City Byeways.
Crown 8vo, cloth extra, with Illustrations, 2/6.
"All as true to life and as touchingly set forth as any heart could desire.'
Athenæum.

THE CHILDREN'S KINGDOM;
Or, The Story of a Great Endeavour. Crown 8vo, cloth extra, with Illustrations, 3/6.
"A really well-written story, with many touching passages. Boys and girls
will read it with eagerness and profit."— *The Churchman.*

WATER GIPSIES. A Tale.
Crown 8vo, cloth extra, with Illustrations, 2/6.
"It is full of incident from beginning to end, and we do not know the person
who will not be interested in it." *Christian World.*

DAVID'S LITTLE LAD.
Crown 8vo, cloth extra, with Illustrations 2/6.
"A finely imagined story, bringing out in grand relief the contrast between quiet,
steady self sacrifice, and brilliant, flashy qualities.' —*Guardian.*

DOT AND HER TREASURES.
With Illustrations. Small 8vo, cloth extra, 2/-
"One of the tales of poor children in London. of which we have had many
examples; but none finer, more pathetic, or more original than this."
Nonconformist.

OUTCAST ROBIN; or, Your Brother and Mine.
Illustrated. Small 8vo, cloth extra, 2/-.

WHITE LILIES, AND OTHER TALES.
With Illustrations. Small 8vo, cloth extra, 1/6.
"Stories of a singularly touching and beautiful character."—*Rock.*

LETTIE'S LAST HOME. Small 8vo, cloth extra, 1/6.
"Very touchingly told." *Aunt Judy's Magazine.*

THOSE BOYS. A Story for all Little Fellows. Small 8vo, 1/-

LITTLE TROUBLE THE HOUSE. Small 8vo, 1/-

STORIES BY CATHARINE SHAW.

Price Three Shillings and Sixpence each.

THE STRANGE HOUSE; or, A Moment's Mistake.
"A charming story. It is characterised by simplicity of treatment, but the interest is cleverly sustained, and the characters are well drawn.'
Manchester Examiner.

LILIAN'S HOPE. Large Crown 8vo, cloth extra. With Illustrations.
"One of the best gift books for girls we have seen. The story throbs with the power and pathos of real home life." *In His Name.*

DICKIE'S SECRET. Large Crown 8vo. Illustrated.
"We heartily welcome 'Dickie's Secret.' It is a delightful story.'—*Record.*

DICKIE'S ATTIC. Large Crown 8vo.
"The prettiest story Mrs. Shaw has yet written."—*Standard.*
"A naturally pathetic subject treated with much skill as well as taste.'
Spectator.

ON THE CLIFF; or, Alick's Neighbours. Large Crown 8vo.
"It is refreshing to come upon such a book as this, written with a clear, modest aim of revealing the beauty and happy privileges of the Christian life."
Church Sunday School Magazine.

FATHOMS DEEP; or, Courtenay's Choice. Large Crown 8vo.
"Not 'Fathoms Deep,' but on the surface, our Authoress has placed the life giving Gospel. This is a capital book, and is cheap." *Sword and Trowel.*

ALICK'S HERO. Large Crown 8vo, cloth. Illustrated.
"Mrs. Shaw has added to our delight in noble boyhood, as well as to her own reputation, in this most charming of her works."—*The Christian.*

HILDA; or, Seeketh Not Her Own. Crown 8vo, cloth extra.
"A charming story, illustrative of the blessedness of self-sacrifice."
Literary World.

Price Two Shillings and Sixpence each.

ONLY A COUSIN. Crown 8vo, cloth extra.
"In our excavations among heaps of tales we have not come upon a brighter jewel than this.' Rev. C. H. Spurgeon in *Sword and Trowel.*

THE GABLED FARM; or, Young Workers for the King.
Crown 8vo, cloth extra.
"A charming story, wherein the children are described naturally."
Evangelical Magazine.

IN THE SUNLIGHT AND OUT OF IT.
A Year of my Life story. Crown 8vo, cloth extra
"One of the pleasantest books that a girl could take into her hand, either for Sunday or week-day reading." *Daily Review.*

NELLIE ARUNDEL. A Tale of Home Life.
Crown 8vo, cloth extra, Illustrated.
"We need scarcely say that Mrs. Shaw holds out the light of life to all her readers, and we know of few better books than those which bear her name.
Record.

JACK FORESTER'S FATE. Crown 8vo, with Illustrations, 2/-

POPULAR HOME STORIES.

By EMILY BRODIE.

OLD CHRISTIE'S CABIN. Crown 8vo, 2/6. Illustrated.
"A capital book for young people, depicting the loveliness of a ministering life on the part of some happy children." *The Christian.*

COUSIN DORA; or, Serving the King. Large Crown 8vo, 2/6.
"An admirable tale for elder girls.' *Nonconformist.*

HIS GUARDIAN ANGEL. Large Crown 8vo, 3/6.
"Should find its way into school libraries as well as into homes."
Sunday School Chronicle.

FIVE MINUTES TOO LATE; or, Leslie Harcourt's Resolve.
Large Crown 8vo, cloth extra, 3/6.

NORMAN AND ELSIE; or, Two Little Prisoners.
Large Crown 8vo, extra cloth, 3/6.
"So true and delightful a picture that we can hardly believe we have only read about it; it all seems so real, and has done us so much good." *The Christian.*

NORA CLINTON; or, Did I Do Right? Crown 8vo, 3/6.
"Will be read with pleasure and profit.' —*Christian Age.*

LONELY JACK and His Friends at Sunnyside. Crown 8vo, 3/6.
"Its chapters will be eagerly devoured by the reader." *Christian World.*

THE HAMILTONS; or, Dora's Choice. Crown 8vo, 3/6.
"Miss Brodie's stories have that savour of religious influence and teaching which makes them valuable as companions of the home."—*Congregationalist.*

UNCLE FRED'S SHILLING : Its Travels and Adventures.
Crown 8vo, cloth extra, 3/6.
"Children will follow it with as eager interest as the little people who listened to it in the book itself." *Christian World.*

ELSIE GORDON; or, Through Thorny Paths.
Crown 8vo, cloth extra, 2/6.
"The characters have been well thought out. We are sure the volume will be welcome at many a fireside."—*Daily Express.*

JEAN LINDSAY, the Vicar's Daughter. Crown 8vo, 2/6.
"The tale is admirably told, and some capital engravings interpret its principal incidents.' *Bookseller*

ROUGH THE TERRIER. His Life and Adventures.
Illustrated by T. Pym. Square, cloth extra, 2/6; or boards, 1/6.
"A clever autobiography, cleverly illustrated.'—*The Christian.*

SYBIL'S MESSAGE. Small 8vo, cloth extra, 1/6.

EAST AND WEST; or, The Strolling Artist. 1/6.

THE SEA GULL'S NEST; or, Charlie's Revenge. 1/6.

RUTH'S RESCUE; or, The Light of Ned's Home. 1/

BOOKS FOR BOYS.
BY M. L. R DLEY.

Price Two Shillings and Sixpence each, with Illustrations.

SENT TO COVENTRY; or, The Boys of Highbeech.
Illustrated. Large Crown 8vo, cloth extra.
"A really good story of boys' school life."—*Pall Mall Gazette.*
"Eminently interesting from start to finish." *Pictorial World.*

KING'S SCHOLARS; or, Work and Play at Easthaven.
Illustrated. Large Crown 8vo, cloth extra.
"Full of all those stirring incidents which go to make up the approved life of schoolboys. Both adventure and sentiment find a place in it." *Pall Mall Gazette.*
"A schoolboy tale of very good tone and spirit."—*Guardian.*

OUR CAPTAIN. The Heroes of Barton School.
With Illustrations. Crown 8vo, cloth extra.
"A first-class book for boys."—*Daily Review.*
"A regular boy's book." *Christian World.*

THE THREE CHUMS. A Story of School Life.
With Illustrations. Crown 8vo, cloth extra.
"A book after a boy's heart. How can we better commend it than by saying it is both manly and godly?" Rev. C. H. SPURGEON in *Sword and Trowel.*
"Ingeniously worked out and spiritedly told.'—*Guardian.*

HILLSIDE FARM; or, Marjorie's Magic.
Crown 8vo. Illustrated.
"A very well-written story which all girls will thoroughly enjoy." *Guardian.*

Price Three Shillings and Sixpence each, with Illustrations.

GOLDENGATES; or, Rex Mortimer's Friend. Large Crown 8vo.
"An excellent story of boyish love." *Sunday School Chronicle.*
"A first rate story for boys. The hero is a fine specimen of a manly young Christian."—*Congregational Review.*

OUR SOLDIER HERO. The Story of My Brothers.
Large Crown 8vo, cloth extra. With Illustrations.
"Contains the healthiest of matter presented in the most entertaining of ways."
Schoolmaster.
"An autobiography very simply and pleasantly written." *Times.*

WALTER ALISON: His Friends and Foes.
Crown 8vo, cloth extra. With Illustrations.
"Schoolboys are sure to like it." *Churchman.*
"A book boys will be sure to read if they get the chance."—*Sword and Trowel.*

STORIES BY GRACE STEBBING.

A REAL HERO. A Story of the Conquest of Mexico.
With Illustrations   Crown 8vo, cloth extra, 3/6.
"We can cordially recommend this to all youthful lovers of adventure and enterprise." *Academy.*

IN ALL OR DOINGS. A Story for Boys. Large Crown 8vo, 3/6.
"A story for boys, in which the lessons of the daily Collects are brightly brought home to them."—*Times.*

GRAHAM McCALL'S VICTORY. A Tale of the Covenanters.
Large Crown 8vo. Illustrated. Cloth extra, 5/-
"Stirring, and ably written."—*Guardian.*
"We heartily commend it to English boys and girls."—*Sunday School Chronicle.*

WINNING AN EMPIRE ; or, The Story of Clive.
Crown 8vo. Illustrated. Cloth extra, 3/6.
"Miss Stebbing is one of the few ladies that can write really good boys' stories. She has caught, not only the phraseology, but the spirit of boys." *Standard.*

ONLY A TRAMP.
Crown 8vo. Illustrated. Cloth extra, 3/6.
"Miss Stebbing holds the attention and extorts the admiration of the reader from first to last. Many a weighty lesson may be learnt from her pages."
The Christian

FUN AND FAIRIES.
Fully Illustrated by T. Pym. 4to, cloth extra, 3/6.
"With its dear little pictures, is quite charming." *Athenæum.*

SILVERDALE RECTORY ; or, The Golden Links.
With Illustrations. Crown 8vo, 2/6.
"We can heartily recommend this story."
Church of England Sunday School Magazine.

BRAVE GEORDIE. The Story of an English Boy.
With Illustrations. Crown 8vo, cloth, 2/6.
"It is refreshing to meet with such a spirited and thoroughly good story."
The Christian.

IN WYCLIFFE'S DAYS ; or, A Safe Hiding Place.
Small 8vo. With Illustrations. Cloth extra, 2/6.
"A delightful invigorating story." *Daily Review.*

LOST HER SHOE AND OTHER THREADS.
Small 8vo. Illustrated. Cloth extra, 1/6.
"Five short stories sure to be devoured by young people."—*Sword and Trowel.*

London : JOHN F. SHAW & Co., 48, Paternoster Row, E.C.

SPLENDID STORIES
FOR BOYS.

By DR. GORDON STABLES, R.N.

HEARTS OF OAK. A Story of Nelson and the Navy.
Large Crown 8vo, with Illustrations, 5/-

TWO SAILOR LADS.
A Story of Stirring Adventures on Sea and Land. Large Crown 8vo, cloth, with Illustrations, price 5/-

"A sea story, big with wonders.'—*Saturday Review.*

"A capital story in Dr. Stables' best style."—*Spectator.*

FOR ENGLAND, HOME, AND BEAUTY.
A Tale of Battle and the Breeze. Large Crown 8vo, cloth, with Illustrations, price 5/-

"Dr. Stables has almost surpassed himself in this book. Certainly we have read nothing of his which has pleased us more perhaps we might say, as much."
The Spectator.

EXILES OF FORTUNE.
The Story of a Far North Land. Large Crown 8vo, cloth extra, with Illustrations. price 5/-

"A capital book; written with this popular writer's accustomed spirit, and sure to be enjoyed."—*Scotsman.*

"Boys of all growths will relish this story." *Manchester Examiner.*

FROM SQUIRE TO SQUATTER.
A Tale of the Old Land and the New. Large Crown 8vo, Illustrated, price 5/-

'Just the sort of book that boys delight in, as the story is crowded with exciting incidents."—*Schoolmaster.*

"The story is naturally and brightly wr tten, and shows a marked advance over former productions by the same author.' *Standard.*

IN THE DASHING DAYS OF OLD; or, The World-wide Adventures of Willie Grant. Large Crown 8vo, Illustrated, price 5/-

"We can commend this book as the best story for boys which we have read for many a day." *English Churchman.*

"Can be safely recommended as one of the very best books that could possibly be placed in a boy's hand."—*Schoolmaster.*

By LADY FLORENCE DIXIE.

THE YOUNG CASTAWAYS; or The Child Hunters of Patagonia.
Large Crown 8vo, cloth, with Illustrations price 5/-

"A lively story of adventure, drawn a good deal from personal experience."
The Guardian.
